Printed by CreateSpace, An Amazon.com Company
Published by Farquhar Publishing
Copyright © 2016 Loulou Farquhar. All rights reserved, including the right to reproduce, distribute, or transmit in any form, or by any means. For information regarding subsidiary rights, please contact the Publisher.

Website: farquharpublishing.com
Email: linton@farquharpublishing.com

ISBN 978-0-9935525-0-2

I0678921

Although this book is in no way affiliated with or endorsed by Facebook, my thanks go to the Facebook team, and all its users for being the inspiration for this book.

ALL CHARACTERS AND
EVENTS IN THIS BOOK...
EVEN THOSE BASED ON REAL
PEOPLE... ARE ENTIRELY FICTIONAL.
ALL CELEBRITY VOICES ARE
IMPERSONATED... IN YOUR HEAD. THE
FOLLOWING PAGES CONTAIN
COARSE LANGUAGE AND DUE TO
THEIR CONTENT THEY SHOULD NOT BE
READ BY ANYONE ♥

Table of Contents

Facebook Blues
by Trixie Bloom

FACEBOOK BLUES

It was one moment, one bored and idle moment that turned my world upside-down. One click of the mouse, and my life changed forever.

I was sitting, suicidal and sleepless, in the same room, on the same chair, at the same computer screen I'd been staring at weeks ago. It seemed as if nothing had changed. Nobody here had noticed the difference in me.

How could so much have happened in so short a time? Turning into a sneaky slut, making a whole village hate me, and the worst crime of all, falling in love. It didn't seem real, yet here I was in front of the damn computer that started all of this... but really, who was I fooling? It was *Me* that started it ALL.

I'd looked up many friends before on Facebook. I loved getting in virtual contact with old mates, and during lunchtimes and quiet moments, I was always generally chatting away online. My job is nothing exciting after all; I'm a secretary in an office. I hate it. I'm forty-three years old, divorced and bored shitless. Six weeks ago, it was no different in that respect...

I remember being ultra-bored that day and in a bad mood. It was a usual rainy, shitty grey day in London. A normal ride on the tube, all of us stuffed in like the rubbish in my bin at home.

That day, I couldn't wait for lunchtime to get my Facebook fix. I was online the moment 1pm came, but that day the usual chitchat was bringing me no pleasure.

I clicked the mouse in the search box that said '*find friends*'. I'd thought of doing this many, many times, but whatever reasoning had stopped me before did not this time.

Don't do it, Lauren..., my brain was saying, but my fingers typed the name '*David Palmer*' and I clicked the search button.

David had been 'The One' in my past. My first big Love. He could make my stomach flip just by looking at me. When I was fifteen years old, David was my God. If he'd asked me to run across a packed motorway, I would have. I was his faithful beagle for four whole years. He was my Zeus, Achilles, Romeo, and Lucifer. Intense and life changing, he was the devil in an angel's skin. When I was nineteen we parted messily. I was angry, lost and confused, and we were both still in love.

The last contact we had was when I was twenty-nine, and I never saw or heard from him again. He met a girl not long after we'd split up; *Angela*, whom he'd ended up marrying. They had a child, who I remember they named *Nicholas*. Of course, Angela had hated me, and the fact that we all lived in the same area. I'm sure she had prayed nightly that I would die violently, and soon. Also, could the good Lord see fit that I would be buried, so that she could come and literally dance on my grave.

The screen in front of me told me there were no matches found, so I went a step further. Backspacing, I typed *Angela Palmer*, and there she was. Top result. I clicked on it and before me on her Facebook page was her entire life. They had moved to Devon, and there was the village, and the name of her house. David had not been lazy, producing a family of four kids; three boys and one girl. I saw a photo album called '*Wedding*' and clicked on it. My breath still caught in my throat, as there he was before me, just as I remembered him. Beautiful David, with his flop of chestnut hair. Baby-blue eyes, twinkling and sparkling with life.

My heart felt heavy. I knew a long time ago, I was no longer in love with David, but I'd always carried a tiny torch for him. It was nice to know he was still married, and I hoped happily.

I came out of that album and clicked on a recent one of David and Angela. He had aged well. His hair was slightly thinner, and the flop was a bit tired and limp, but his eyes looked the same. Angela had put weight on, which pleased me in an infantile way, as my very petite five foot two frame could still pass for a twenty year old's.

I would like to point out that this is not good luck, or fantastic genes, but due to an utter dedication to exercise that doesn't come naturally. I never awake with the lark, raring to perform my daily routine; in fact, it is the complete opposite. My rectum always seems to pucker at the mere thought of exercise, followed by a twitching of the eye. I've used every excuse in the book to avoid working out; lazy eye, foot fungus, swollen everything, too hot, too cold, and my number one favourite - getting my period. Though I naturally have the apathy of a 101-year-old woman when it comes to exercise, sheer vanity and the feel good factor are enough to make me dedicate myself completely.

I stared and stared at the photo, jumping when my boss, Mr. Forrester, came over and tapped his fingers on the desk.
"Just here to have fun, or here to work?" he asked, looking at my screen.
I could feel myself blushing as I minimized the page and got on with my teeth-grinding, tedious work.
Over the course of the next few days, I became obsessed with Angela's Facebook page. I also looked at Nicholas's page, their eldest son, now twenty-three years old. I had seen him once when he was two, with David. With the same devastating good looks his father had had when he was young, except Nicholas was even more beautiful. Short choppy dark hair, gray-blue eyes, and a smile that would melt anyone. I had looked at Josh's page, the second eldest, but his page, like his younger brothers, was secured, and I couldn't look. But they didn't interest me as much as Angela's. They lived in a small village called Elderton, and with the help of the internet, I knew exactly where they lived.
I started to wonder how David was. *Does he enjoy being a Father? How is Devon?...*, and more besides.
I printed out route maps to their very front door, and kept them in my desk at work.

My mind started to conspire with my self, telling me how much I could do with a holiday. How nice it would be to get away from my shitty job, and at that time, my boring life, just for a while.
"Lauren, don't be so stupid," I heard myself saying out loud, more than once.

3

Nevertheless, the days that followed found me possessed. I looked at holiday homes to rent near to where they lived. I found a cottage that was a bit dilapidated, 4 miles from the village and near the sea. Every day I gazed at the picture of the cottage, and on a day of insanity I rang, booked the cottage for 1 month, and told my very pissed off boss that I was going away.

Armed with all my information, maps, and my run-down 20-year-old Ford Escort, Maisie, I headed down to Devon.

MADNESS

As I bounced and rattled along in Maisie, I realised I had no idea why I was doing this. Did I really want to see David after all these years? Would he want to see me? I kept on convincing myself I really *did* need a holiday, and besides, I might not even see him. I told myself sternly I was not to go stalking him, or actively looking for him. However, if we should meet by chance, then surely it was meant to be? Of course, if I were thinking rationally, I would have thought that if we bumped into each other in London, then yes - it was meant to be. The fact I was almost camping in their back garden meant chance had nothing to do with it. I kept imagining how our chance encounter would happen; a stroll along the beach; the roof needs fixing and he's the local handyman; a problem with my car and he's the mechanic... These schoolgirl fantasies made me giggle, and I actually felt excited about my adventure.

After six long hours I was nearing my rendezvous point with Mr. Warbling, who apart from having a very funny name, was the owner of Warbling Cottage, which was to be my home for the next month. The pub in which I was to meet him was called 'The Dry Thrush' and as any woman would agree, it's not a name you'd have to write down. I was also starting to get nervous, as the pub was located in the village that David lived in, Elderton.

Maisie spluttered like a tired old dog as we pulled into the village. I followed the directions Mr. Warbling had given me. Even at night, I could see what a quaint place it was. As I drove in there was an old water mill on the right, then almost immediately, I was in the village square. To the left, on a corner stood a big ancient two-storey pub, with hanging baskets outside filled with colourful flowers. The sign with a picture of a bird bore the words 'The Dry Thrush'. To the right, also on a corner was a smaller pub called 'The Thirsty Nun'.

Must be Devon humour...

In the centre of the square was a monument, which looked like a statue of a fisherman to me. Bakers, grocers, hardware, and butcher's shop dotted the rest of the square. There were only two roads, one in, and one out. I parked Maisie, and walked over to the pub.

For one moment as I walked in through the door, I thought I might have forgotten to put my clothes on. Perhaps on the way from the car my breasts had somehow become free, or unbeknownst to me, a wild dog had ripped off my skirt and knickers, running off into the night.

I looked down quickly to make sure none of these things had happened, but all appeared well, so why had the whole place gone quiet? Why was everyone in there looking at me? I stared at all the knitted Aran jumpers and tired faces before me.

"Mr. Warbling?" I croaked.

A table of old men began to laugh, and a man stood up, and speaking in the local dialect, said

"You're far too pretty to be Mr. Warbling," and they all laughed again.

Give me London any day..., I thought.

Smiling my sweetest smile, I tried again. "I'm looking for Mr. Warbling?"

The man took my arm and led me gently to the table of men, which was next to a huge roaring fire.

"I am Mr. Warbling my flower. I've been waiting for you. Now take a seat - Miss Bower wasn't it?"

"Oh sorry, yes that's right. Lucy... Lucy Bower," I said, hurriedly.

Lucy was the first name that popped into my head. I proffered a handshake, and he whisked it up to a mouth that looked like it had smoked from birth, kissing the back of my hand gracefully.

"Lovely, lovely, my flower. I'm Stanley Warbling, but most people call me Stan."

"Amongst other things," One of the wrinklies said, whom I found out later was Angus.

"That's enough, not in front of my lovely tenant" Stan said, and patted the seat.

I was not really in the mood for socializing after my long drive, but the heat of the fire was welcoming, and if I did refuse they would all think I was just another stuck up city girl, so I sat. A succession of '*How-do-you-do*'s' followed while Stan got the white wine I'd asked for from the bar. Angus, who had already spoken, was followed by Seth, Bumble, and Thomas.

"So, what brings a maid like you down 'ere?" Angus beamed broadly at me.

"I just fancied a holiday away from it all," I replied.

"A maid like you would normally go in for one of them holidays with sun, and all them grockles," Seth said, in between puffs on his pipe.

"Now you lot, let the maid in peace. She couldn't have chosen a lovelier place to come and stay, and it's not like we don't get the sun 'ere."

I looked up at Stan and smiled a thankful smile that said - '*Yes, that's enough questioning for one night...*'

For the next half hour, the five of them talked, and I listened. Each one had their own opinion of what I should see and do whilst there. I half listened, but really, I was too excited and nervous. What if He, David, should come into the pub there and then? I wasn't ready yet for such a chance meeting. I didn't look my best after the drive. I was tired and wanted to go to the cottage, but I was excited.

What if he does come in?...

I would recognise him immediately, but I was undercover. On the other hand, maybe he would recognise me straight away. I had changed a lot over the years, but with the love we had had for each other, surely he couldn't forget my face, even with age? Aroused suddenly from my twilight thoughts, I was aware of someone standing talking to me; it was Stan.

"Roit maid?"

"Yes, er, sorry Stan, I think I'm a bit tired," I mumbled. *I must remember my name is Lucy now....*

"Of course you are my lovely, so you follow me in your car to the cottage. I've got a Bedford van parked in the square, I'll meet you outside."

"Thank you Stan," I said, bidding goodnight to the aran knit wrinklies, saying I was sure I would see them again.

I got Maisie and followed Stan to the cottage. The first couple of miles were thin, bendy lanes, which would just about let a rabbit past coming the other way. I saw no turn off, and eventually the road turned into a sandy gravel track which went on for another mile or so, until there at the end was *Warbling Cottage*.

It was very dark, but with Maisie's headlights, I could see some of it. My first impression was that it looked like an old pensioner that had given up on life long ago, but kept receiving new parts to keep them going. The whole left side of the cottage seemed shorter, as though it were sinking. The roof, in places, had bits of old plastic held down with stones. Nearly every window had tape covering the cracks, as if someone had forgotten to tell the old girl the war was over. The gate was hanging askew, as was the wall to which it was half attached.

I sighed. *What have I done?...*

Stan was already opening the front door, and as I got out of the car, I saw a light go on inside the house. The cold wind nearly cut me in half, but the strong smell of salt and sea being blown around me was comforting, along with the sound of waves hitting the shore. Peering beyond the house into the darkness, I saw nothing. I got my case, walked up the path into the cottage, and shut the door behind me.

I was standing in the kitchen, and I could see Stan moving about in the front room. I wondered how old the house was. Shivering deeply I went through the kitchen and into a small but cosy looking front room.

"Come in, my flower. I'm just lighting a fire for you. I would have done it sooner, but I just wanted to make sure you were coming," Stan said.

The centrepiece of the room was a big warm open fireplace. I

8

watched Stan as he set about creating heat. Never in my life had I made a fire. I watched him intently for almost two minutes before I let my attention wander, being the most impatient person in the world.

Thinking - *I'm sure there will be no problem getting the hang of it...,* my eyes scanned the snug room.

A moth-eaten sofa was pushed up against the wall in front of me, a big bay window above. There was a small table in the middle of the room, and two worn-out armchairs, which didn't match. To the right, next to the kitchen was a small alcove that held a table, with four completely different chairs.

As I started to feel the heat, the room grew more inviting.

Stan stood. "There you go, the fire is the heart of the house, my flower."

As I looked at his big, round, ruddy-cheeked face, and his kind eyes, I felt I'd be happy here for my short stay.

"Now I'll show you round, but mind now, with the fire there's enough wood out the front for two days. There's someone in the village who delivers wood, an' I'll ask them to come on Wednesday, in two day's time. Now I'm sorry but you'll have to buy the wood, but it's a fair price, and hopefully you won't need any more while you're here. Being June, it should soon brighten up."

He didn't sound too convinced on that last point, but right then I could couldn't have cared less about the weather. I was more concerned about what I was going to sleep on. Maybe a bed of straw, or a mattress as thin as a slice of bread because so many dead bodies had lain on it?

There's always the floor...

"Now my flower, this is the parlour, that's where you eat, and here - is the spare bedroom," Stan said.

I followed him and he opened a door through which cold air howled. I poked my head in and saw a single bed and a wardrobe. That was it. I surmised that Stan was a man of simple taste.

"This is the bathroom, with a bath." Stan informed me. "All mod cons - flushing toilet..."

He demonstrated the flush. Maybe he thought all us Londoners were still squatting in bushes, so I had to point out that I also had one at home. He just looked at me and winked, as if I had just gone up a level in his estimation.

Back into the parlour, and over in the corner was a small door which looked like a cupboard. Stan opened it, and ducked through. I heard his footsteps going up stairs, and followed. A small winding wooden staircase took us up to a large square room with a window seat on the left, and big scatter cushions to the right. I loved it.

"Mmm - yes, they were Mrs. Warbling's idea. Very bohemian of her," Stan explained.

"I love them, Stan. And what's through this door?" I asked, pointing ahead of us.

"Oh, that's the main... hmm.. bedroom."

I turned the knob, opening the door to a Broderie Anglaise nightmare. Everything was covered with intricate fine cream lace. Dressing table, bedside tables. I was relieved to see a double bed and a chair (covered). I looked at Stan. He had turned bright red.

"Mrs. Warbling?" I enquired.

"Yes." He smiled.

He showed me how to do the hot water, and where I needed to bang the cooker to make it work, and left me to discover everything else. I went straight up to the bedroom, got under the huge Broderie Anglaise quilt, and went straight into a sound sleep.

I was woken by strange loud noises. I tried to think what they might be, and somewhere from the depths of my childhood memories, I remembered these sounds as *Birds*. I stepped out of bed, fully clothed, and opened the curtains. I had not expected such a view, and it was enough to dissipate my oncoming blues. I hated early mornings normally but that morning my outlook was different. I thought the view was lovely.

There was a long garden, which looked like it went all the way round to the front. I could hear the sea, and on tiptoe, I could see a golden yellow streak. I assumed it was a beach. In contrast, the view from my front window in London was a plain street crammed with cars, and the back windows revealed a courtyard full of rubbish bins, invariably with at least four cats shagging.

I yawned and went downstairs to the kitchen.

Half asleep, I opened my case in the parlour, getting out a change of clothes. First, I needed a bath, then afterwards breakfast, which that day was cheese and onion crisps and a Mars bar. I needed to go shopping a.s.a.p. The one thing I had brought was my *emergency 'miserable cow'* pack. I pulled it from my case and took it to the kitchen, putting it all out. Real coffee, espresso kettle, sugar, powdered milk and even my own small milk pan to heat the milk. I like my coffee to be real, and I MUST have some as my first beverage of the day. So then, I tried to operate the cooker. I turned the knob, banged the side, struck the match and... Nothing. The match burnt my fingers.

Or was it bang first, then turn the knob?... I tried that, and still nothing.

Panic set in, and I tried banging another spot, doing the first and second methods. Frantically banging in different sequences, I must have looked like some demented one-man-band, until I started sobbing for the loss of my coffee.

I'll have to ask Stan again...

Now, my mood was not so full of birdsong, and I slunk miserably to the bathroom.

Okay - please work...

I turned the hot tap fully on, left it for a count of three, and then turned it halfway back. I waited for the hot water, and saying a silent prayer, I cautiously put my hand under the tap.

Cold. Once more...

This time I did a small anxiety dance, to bring forth the hot, but still it flowed cold. I screamed, then began to cry.

Why am I here? What have I done? I'm here on a whim....

I was the total cliché of curiosity killing the cat, and presently the cat was very pissed off. I would take Maisie, I decided, and go to the village for provisions, and maybe to contact Stan. I was too miserable even to look around me in the daylight as I left the cottage, and wearing the same clothes as I had slept in, I started Maisie and headed off.

Staring blankly at the road ahead, I thought of my lovely flat in London, and wondered again what had possessed me to come here. I ignored all the beautiful scenery around me.

"Damn computers!" I shouted at no one.

As I entered the square, it looked busy.

Monday morning...

I failed to find a space and went round three times before I decided to park in the car park behind The Dry Thrush. Sitting there, looking down at myself, a horrific realisation came over me.

What if I had put my whole life on hold, done the craziest thing ever, only to meet David now whilst looking like a wandering vagrant? In my misery, I had come out wearing the slippers I had put on in preparation for my lovely bath. Also bright pink knitted socks, jogging bottoms and a huge green jumper. My hair was stuck together in greasy clumps and I was without make-up. Had I really driven two hundred and thirty miles to bump into the man who had once idolized me, only to make him jump backwards and throw loose change at me? No, I had not.

I sat in Maisie and contemplated my options. Drive back to the cottage? No. I needed to make my coffee.

Coffee... My eye twitched at the thought. I would call Stan. He would have to meet me in my car. *Yes, that's the only way...*

I called him, pleading.

"I know it sounds odd Stan, but, er... you see I can't get out of the car, okay?"

Well he seemed to understand, I thought. I waited and waited. Half an hour went past and I began to grow anxious. Eventually Stan appeared and leant down to my window. I motioned for him to get in.

Opening the door, he asked - "Are you alright, moi flower?"

"Yes, yes, can you please get in the car?" I asked.

His worried face swam before me. "Now, don't you worry. Took a while for me to get the boys, but they're here now."

I was totally confused. "What boys, Stan?"

"The fire boys. I told them you were trapped in your car."

Dumbfounded I stared at him. "Whaat?... I still.. What, the fire brigade are here, Stan?"

"Don't be cakey," he smiled reassuringly.

I don't have any cake..., I pondered. I looked quizzically at Stan. "Why would I want cake now, Stan?"

He raised his eyebrows to the heavens. "Daft or silly it means." He was smiling again. "Haven't got the 'ole brigade, but two of the village men are here."

Oh my god!... This will be it.. He, David, will be one of the men. Here to rescue a hysterical city girl, who could simply open the door and step out. 'Who is this unkempt fool?,' he will think...

"Please Stan... I'm fine. I'm not trapped, I just don't want to get out. Please say I'm very sorry, but really, nothing is wrong."

His look said he thought something was very wrong with me, mentally.

"Okay, flower. I'll tell them, then I'll be back."

I heard him telling them, but couldn't make out the words. Probably; 'Sorry boys, these grockles don't understand. Seems like a nice maid, but of course she's proper cakey,'

He got back into my car.

"I'm sorry Stan. Please can we go to the cottage?" I asked.

"Of course, my flower," he replied.

On the way, I told him about my problems in the cottage. He said he would help, but I knew I had gone down a few levels in his estimation. Of course I didn't mention *not* wanting to see David, looking like I did right then. Instead, I told Stan that I felt it was important what people thought of me, and that I didn't want to give the wrong first impression. He nodded, smiled, and said nothing. Of course, by now I'd definitely made an impression.

When we arrived back at the cottage he showed me the cooker and hot water again, this time making me do it until I had the knack.

"I'm so sorry Stan. It must seem like I'm raving mad to you, but I just need to de-stress here. It's the city, you see... London. I really do need a holiday."

"I understand, no need to explain yourself to me, flower," he said. "Just wish it was going to be better weather for you - today and tomorrow is supposed to be cloudy and a bit chilly." and then he was gone.

I spent the rest of that day and the next hiding in the house. This was not quite how I had imagined it was going to be. I unpacked and resigned myself to surviving on coffee, having no appetite left. I spent the good part of a morning trying to light a fire, crying at my utter lack of basic skills, and totally failing. I retreated to bed that afternoon and slept. I slept, and slept, completely forgetting that the firewood was being delivered the next day.

Again, the dawn chorus woke me. I looked at the time. *8am.* I felt much better, though, after such a long sleep - ready to bash and turn knobs all day. That morning the cooker seemed to like me, and I sat on the couch with my coffee, looking out at the garden. An array of colour flooded through it. A small path ran down the centre, and three big trees stood further away. I had no clue as to what anything was. Not knowing the difference between a weed and a plant, I decided not to touch a thing. To just enjoy it instead.

Looking at the fire, I made the decision to try again. It wasn't so cold, but it would be nice after my bath. I put my coffee down, and put my chimney sweep head on. Crouching in the fireplace and peering up into the blackness, I assumed it must be blocked. Some light was coming in, but only a tiny chink.

No, it must be blocked..., I concluded.

Commandeering a broom from the kitchen, I began violently thrusting it up this unknown entity. First, I heard a BANG!, then a whooshing sound, after which I remembered nothing until...

Opening my eyes, I felt the pain on my head first.

Ouucch!...

I managed to raise my hand, and touched the spot the throbbing was coming from. There was a huge lump. I checked for blood, but found none. I realised I was laying halfway into the fireplace, and saw the offending item next to me. I must have hit a brick, or rather, it had hit me. Shakily, I got up and stared down, open mouthed and unbelieving. I could see the perfect silhouette of my entire body. I'd unwittingly stopped a ton of black soot from falling on the floor. I looked at the perfect white shape, exactly like a crime scene.

I think it was about this point that I wished I were dead. Lying in that spot. I gripped the mantelpiece, reeling, and thought I heard a knocking.

I'm having pseudo-hallucinations now....

Then louder – BANG! BANG!

No, it's not my head, maybe it's the door?... It must be Stan. Now he'll really think I've lost the plot....

I flung open the door. The boy jumped back as if the grim reaper himself had appeared. He froze. I froze. I could not speak; my jaw flapped about in the wind. Now I really did want to die. For it all to end, right there, right then, that second. I looked at the face before me. A face I had known so well, yet this face was younger. It was David's son, Nicholas.

Neither of us spoke. My mouth made gurning motions, suggesting the look of a dribbling, half-witted fool. Shaking and swaying from the bump to my head completed the picture. Apparently terrified, he didn't move, not even to blink.

"Lucy - I'm Lucy!..." I managed to shout, and promptly fainted.

NICK

I came to on the sofa, and heard noise coming from the kitchen. Without saying a word, I got up and went to the bathroom. Looking in the mirror, my eyes slowly took in everything. I was totally black from the soot. My blonde shoulder-length hair was now black, and had trapped within it on the left hand side what appeared to be the corpse of half a dead bird. My eyeballs, normally bright blue, but now devil-red with irritation, stuck out wildly against the contrast of my blackened face. All I saw was a kind of inappropriate racist fancy dress. The only thing missing was a bone through my nose to be totally taking the piss. I burst into tears.

Nick... its Nicholas...

I hadn't anticipated that. My only thoughts had been of David, no one else. Through my sobs, I heard my new name, and felt an arm on my shoulders.

"Lucy, you should sit down. Come back to the sofa with me." I let him, as if I were a defeated child.

As we sat, I looked at his kind, concerned, stunningly beautiful face, and I sobbed even harder.

"Please don't.. I'm making a tea, do you like tea?" he asked.

I just nodded, even though normally I never drank tea.

"I'm Nick, I was delivering your wood for you. You did give me a fright I must admit. I've called Stan, and Mrs. Warbling is on her way over."

I looked at him like a frightened fawn. "Please... no, I'm alright."

"I don't think you are," he said, looking over at the fireplace.

"I bumped my head. I don't really remember much... The fire... I couldn't light it."   He stood quickly. "Bumped your head? I'd better take a look." His careful hands parted my hair. Then sitting again, his face close to mine, he held my hand. "Don't worry, I can't see any brain, but you'll have a nasty headache, and a bump to match."

"I'm not worried - there's no brain in there to damage." I smiled, weakly.

His lips broadened. Perfect white teeth gleamed at me, and his eyes sparkled just like his fathers. I began to sob again.

"I'll make the tea, I think maybe you've got some concussion." He left me sobbing, made the tea, and returned quickly. There was another knock at the door.

"That'll be Doris," Nick said, and noticing my uncomprehending face, added, "Mrs. Warbling"

He went to the door and I strained to hear the conversation.

"She's very upset, Doris. Bumped her head. Probably concussed."

"You're a good boy, Nick. You put all the wood outside, and we'll sort out the cost when the poor maids feelin' better."

"Okay, Doris. By the way, she was trying to light a fire."

"Oooh... tis a licker right enough. Alright, you say hello to your mother and father for me."

"I will, Doris…"

I heard the shutting of the front door, then a small and very neat old lady entered, her grey hair tied tightly in a bun.

"Lovely boy, and his family... Now, my lovely. I'm Doris; Stan's wife. Oh dear, you do look like you've had a fright. Let me take a look at your head..." She tutted. "Oh dear... we shall have to get this cleaned, and apply iodine to do it proper."

Smiling warmly at me, she stood and busied herself, running me a bath, and fetching the dreaded iodine. On her return, she handed me a glass of water.

"Take these tablets, my lovely. It'll help with your headache."

I took them without complaint. It took two baths before I was clean, and the bird had to be partially cut out of my hair. Doris fussed about, bringing my nightshirt down and fixing me up. A roaring fire was thriving again in the grate.

"Lay down here my lovely, and here's a nice cup of tea," Doris said, leading me to the sofa. "You'll need to sleep. Stan will be along later."

I tried telling her I was fine, but she hushed me and told me to rest.

I don't remember falling asleep, but the room was getting dark when I awoke. The fire was still alight, and my silhouette in the fireplace was gone. Going into the kitchen, I noticed a cardboard box on the side, with a small note propped up against it;

Hope you feel better.
If you need anything, please let us know.
Here are some bits that might help. Love Doris x

The bits were; eggs, fresh bread, what looked like home-made jam, milk, butter and some smoked mackerel, which I love.

What lovely kind people...

I remembered what Doris had said about Nick's lovely family.

I have no right to be here, to intrude upon other people's lives...

Nicholas, or Nick, might have been thrown into my path, but with any luck, he would never want to meet me again. I would have to be careful, and stay out of people's way. Enjoy my time here at the cottage. Go for walks and runs, have a normal holiday, then just leave without a trace. I felt better after having made this good common sense decision, and fixed myself something to eat. Afterwards I made my way up to Lace Land, and went to sleep.

The next day I opened my curtains to a different world. The sky was a flawless blue and the sun was shining. I felt much better, and as I fixed myself breakfast, I decided I would finally explore the end of the garden. I changed into some short shorts, a bikini top, and an open shirt. I swept my hair up, clipping it with pins, and put some mascara on to make my eyelashes even more dramatic than they are naturally.

I'm very lucky. Most people think I wear mascara all the time, and with my bright blue eyes highlighting them, I am aware that my lashes are my most striking feature. A touch of lip-gloss, and I was out the kitchen door.

I was right, the garden did go all the way round the house. I took the path down to where I had seen the trees, and towards what I hoped was sand.

Breathing deeply, I smelt fragrant perfumes and wished I had a bit more botanical knowledge. I came upon the trees, which looked huge compared with my small self. Continuing, I came across an old wall made from stones just piled on top of each other. Jumping over, my feet crunched on small pebbles, and I could hear the sea.

As I ran forward, the pebbles turned into sand, and the sea revealed itself. Magnificent powerful waves crashed onto the shore. There was a low outcrop of rocks, getting engulfed with every wave. Seagulls cawed loudly above. I took another deep breath, and holding my sandals, I skirted the edge, letting the white foam cover my feet. I hadn't gone far before I heard a soft soothing accent calling my alias.

"Lucy...Wait, Lucy..."

I turned and saw a dark-haired boy running towards me. I only knew three people here, and I was sure it wasn't Mr. or Mrs. Warbling.

Nick...

He reached me quickly and stood dead in front of me. Once again, he was motionless.

Oh God, he's re-living it...

"Wooaahh. Wait a minute... can this be the same girl I saw yesterday?"

I blushed. I still enjoy it when people mistake me for a girl rather than a woman, despite my years. Once again, he smiled that big smile, whilst running a hand through his hair.

"Sorry, don't mean to stare, but you sure do brush up well. I didn't even know you were blonde."

"Well, after my recent behaviour, I'm surprised you didn't guess."

This time we both smiled. I continued walking, and Nick walked with me.

"I just came to see if you were alright. I didn't really know what to do yesterday. Don't think I've ever come across such a thing."

We looked at each other and burst out laughing.

18

"Sorry Nick, don't think I ever have either."

"Well, I also came to show you how to make a fire, if you like... not that you need it today," he said, looking up at the perfect sky.

I didn't know what to say. I didn't want to encourage him to come to the house, but I didn't want to be rude.

Shit! Why does he have to be such a lovely boy, inside as well as out?... David *had* done well.

"If you don't mind, but I don't want to be any trouble... I'm sure I'll get it eventually."

He started grinning again.

"What?" I demanded.

"Well, I didn't want to say anything yesterday, but a few bits of newspaper with a big log on top... well, that just won't do it."

"Okay, so I'm a city girl, I admit it. Born in London, always lived in London. I'm a Londoner through and through. I never took my girl-guide badge in fire-building."

"So I'll take that as a yes, then?" He was still smiling.

"Er... yes?"

As we walked back to the cottage Nick told me what some of the flowers were, and I tried to listen, but found it difficult. I was remembering the years I'd lived in the Home Counties. That was where I met David. I was still there when Nick was two, and now here he was again twenty-one years later. His cheekbones were perfect, and more defined than his father's was, and his nose was slender. His plump red lips were telling me that it was honeysuckle around the door, which is why it smelt so sweet.

Entering the house, I busied myself putting the espresso kettle on again.

"I'll clear the fire, and show you how to build it." He winked at me, and went through.

I felt myself blushing deeply. "Tea or coffee, Nick?"

"Well if you have it, I'd love a coffee."

God no, he drinks coffee, another brownie point to him. A lovely, good-looking, kind-hearted coffee-drinking man, who is David's eldest son...

I took the coffees through. Nick had finished preparing the fireplace.

"Now first, put your paper down. Doesn't have to be newspaper, you can use anything..." He ripped the paper into thin strips, laying them in the hearth. "Next, very small sticks on top, and then slightly bigger." Getting a small log, he placed it on top of his creation, then sat next to me and picked up his coffee. "So all you have to do now is light the paper, and you'll get a fire."

I smiled at him. "Thanks, Nick. You really have helped."

"No trouble. Who'd have thought that *you* were underneath all that yesterday..." Now he was staring at me. He broke the spell and sipped his coffee. "Fantastic looking, and you make fantastic coffee."

"I bet you say that to all the ladies."

"Yep." He laughed, and I couldn't help but join in.

We sat enjoying our brew, both of us looking out at the garden. A long, relaxed comfortable silence. Nick eventually looked at me.

"How long are you here for, Lucy?"

"A month..."

"Great. If you don't mind, could I show you round a bit? Trouble is, the trucks my dad's, and I can't always get the use of it."

Without thinking, I said - "Well I've got Maisie, she's my car."

"So I'll take that as a yes then." He stood up and put his coffee down. "Sorry Lucy, have to get my old man's transport back. I'm free tomorrow... I could come round, see if you had any problems with the fire, and show you the sights of Elderton."

What am I doing?... "Yes, Nick, that would be lovely, if you're sure you don't mind."

Turning and opening the door he said - "For you Lucy - anything. See you tomorrow." One more wink, and he was gone.

Lauren Bowman, you really have done it now...

CREAM TEASE

I awoke excited, and opened the curtains with gusto, to be greeted by a painter's palette sky. A blue background was smudged with red, orange, deep purple and crimson. Each colour was uniquely brushed.

Wow, now we don't get this in London...

It made me reminiscent of sunrises I had seen during my travels.

It must be a good omen. Such a beautiful day...

I readied myself, but today I took longer, paying special attention to my hair and make-up. I prefer the natural look, especially at my age. Luckily, Mother Nature has been very kind to me. No wrinkles, great skin tone, and breasts that have won against gravity.

Lauren, this is NOT a date..., my consciousness kept saying. *No, I know it's not, don't be silly....*

Still, I fussed around, not knowing what to do with myself until Nick arrived. He had said 'about eleven' and from ten-thirty onwards, I listened out keenly for the sound of a vehicle. Having time on my hands now, I began to doubt what I was wearing. A short, lilac, cotton summer dress. The neckline was low, and the whole thing clung defiantly to my size eight frame.

Maybe it's too tarty... lilac... Is that me today? Oh, I don't know....

As clothing panic set in, the knocking began.

Shit! - I didn't even hear him arrive....

I calmed myself, and smiling, I opened the door.

"Nick!... I didn't even hear an engine."

Grinning, he looked me up and down quickly. "Lucy, and how are you this fine morning?"

"I feel great... please, Nick, come in."

"Thanks..." He shut the door behind him and followed me into the parlour. "Anyway, you wouldn't have heard an engine, I cycled here. I like to keep in shape."

Looking at him, I could tell from his toned athletic body that it was working.

Eyes off now, Lauren.... "Mmm, yes, sorry would you like a drink?"

"No thanks. So any ideas on what you would like to do, Lucy?"

"Not really, I'm ashamed to say. I don't know anything about this area. I do need supplies for the house though, so maybe a shop bigger than a broom closet would be nice?"

"Oh, I don't know if we've got such a thing round here," he teased. "But, I've got some ideas, so I'll run them past you, and you can tell me what you fancy."

"Great. Sounds good."

"So there's the Pedwidge Caves, Blossoms Mount beauty spot, and the Blue Lagoons, which are on Southpoint beach. There are natural forest trails, you can take a boat around the bay, and there's... a Tescos supermarket."

I laughed at the latter suggestion, and thought about my choices. *Caves? No. Get lost in the pitch black, break my leg, and get rescued by emergency services after a week. Survive by drinking each other's urine, and eating our own hair. Not today. The beauty spot? No. Far too romantic, as were the blue lagoons. Forest walk? No. Again, get lost and half-eaten by something wild. Boat? Sea, drown, dead. No!...*

"Tescos." I said.

He laughed. "Okay, Tescos it is. They have fantastic scenery."

"I've got time to do the other things, honest. After the last few days, I could do with something harmless and normal. Oh. Yes, then I'd like a cream tea. Is that possible?"

"Now, that's more than possible. Glad to see you like food, you being so small, and with, well... such a good figure."

I put my head down slightly, so he couldn't see me blush. "Yes, I love food, especially sweet things. My motto is 'eat big, workout hard'."

"Great to see it working for you." He smiled. "Shall we go then?"

I reached for my bag, and happiness spread through me like a warm glow.

Nick opened the door, one arm extended. "Madam?"

Giggling I obliged, curtsying. "Sir..." and walked out.

As we both got into Maisie, I had a sly thought. "Do you have to be back by any particular time, Nick?"

"Not really. My dad's gonna swing past early evening. He needs the truck, there's some wood to be delivered."

I was jolted back to reality.

Here I am with David's Son, about to go out for the day. David is going to 'swing' past here, tonight....

Panic replaced the feelings I had just had. I sat in the driver's seat, staring at the steering wheel, while untold moments passed.

"Umm, I think you have to start the engine, Lucy, to get it to move."

"What? Oh yes, mmm... maybe we shouldn't go, not if your Fathers coming."

"Yes, but that's seven hours away. We're only going to Tescos, not Scotland."

Lauren, get yourself together...

I turned and looked at Nick, and knew I wanted to spend the day with him. Putting my fears about David to one side, I started Maisie up.

We bounced down country lanes, through rolling hills. I noticed how green it all was. Every shade was represented. Nick chatted easily about where we were, and what was nearby. The sun was high in the sky, and my tension eased.

Somehow, Nick sensed this and said; "So, feel more relaxed now?"

I flicked a quick glance at him. "I'm fine, why?"

"Well I don't think you've heard anything I've said. Up until now, you could have almost kissed the windscreen."

I thought about saying, I was fine again, and that I *did* listen to him, but that would have been a fib, and somehow I knew he had the ability to see through lies. Being observant meant he watched, and took things in quickly. I opted for the truth.

"Actually you're right. Sorry, didn't hear a word."

He smiled. "Well most of it is a load of shit, anyway. I tend to babble... when, well, I just do."

I took my eyes off the road to look at him. He looked shy as he ran his hand through his hair, and lowered his eyes.

I drew my attention back to the road. "Okay, so it's my turn to talk, I guess. Just don't forget to tell me where I'm going."

I only had time to tell him general information about myself - My Job, where in London I lived, my friends...

At Tescos, he pushed the trolley, casually leaning on it and guiding it effortlessly round the aisles. I gladly let him, as I didn't want him to see me rugby tackling the thing around. Like a threshing machine on amphetamines, I threw food in, moving forward as fast as I could. I *hate* shopping. Get in, get out. Do not look at anything beyond the big bold names on the packets.

I grabbed as many sweet things as possible, an occasional departure from my normal diet.

"Jesus. Do you always shop like this?" he asked.

I turned on him like a viper.

A whole two seconds taken off my best time...

"Whoah, okay. Friendly trolley dolly here," he said.

Immediately, I relaxed, and laughed. "Sorry, yes I do always shop like this. I can't stand it."

"Do you have a list?"

"No, no. That would be far too organised. Panic buying suits me fine."

Nick shrugged. "Go ahead. I'll try to keep up."

He started to run, and catching him up, I jumped in front like I was holding a train up. He skidded sideways. We bumped together, both of us laughing loudly, and carried on shopping like a happily married couple.

Maisie's back seat was full of goodies, and we set off.

"Cream tea now, Lucy?"

"Yep, my stomach's complaining."

He directed me to a picturesque thatched-roof cottage by the sea. To me it looked just like a postcard. Outside, a board informed us of all the treats within. Above the door, in old-fashioned writing it said - *Tuffle's Teas*.

Nick opened the door, framed by the roses that surrounded it and a small bell rang. If you would imagine the owner being just as quaint as the cottage, you'd be spot on. A plump, red-faced, beaming matron, she wore a white cap with lace edging and matching apron.

"Hello, Nick. What can I do for you my lovely?" she asked from behind the counter.

"Hi, Mrs. Tuffle. Could I have the table by the sea, please?"

My mind expanded. *Were we to make this poor elderly woman*

keep running to and from the cottage, while the sea lapped round our feet?...

"Of course, my lovely," she said, beaming at him.

I got the feeling she was eyeing me up and down as she took us to the table.

Don't be silly Lauren, of course she's looking - I'm a stranger here, with a boy she obviously knows...and she's the type of grandma every home needs...

We sat by a big bay window with a sea-view. The table was perfectly laid out. White china cups and tea service sat on a lace tablecloth. Doilies adorned two plates. I sat down and let Nick do all the talking.

"Two full cream teas please, Mrs. Tuffle."

"Right you are, Nick." She bustled off.

I stared intensely at him. "How did you know I wanted the full cream tea?..." It was the four scones each, double clotted cream, strawberry and blackcurrant jams and a full pot of tea option. He said nothing. "I mean, how can you know I'd crave the most sugary option?"

"Don't know. It's my favourite, so I just thought you'd want that one too. Don't forget, I did just go shopping with you, and I saw how much sugary stuff you bought..." He raised his eyebrow.

The evidence was conclusive. Placing his elbows on the table, he looked out to sea. Not wanting to spoil it, and enjoying the comfortable silence, I too looked out. The waves gently lapped against the shore, and foam sprays projected up as they hit the rocks. The sound was mesmerizing.

Mrs. Tuffle came and served tea. Of course, it was totally delicious.

"Thanks, Nick, for bringing me here. I love it, really."

"So do I, Lucy. I love being by the sea, it has a calming effect on me. Not sure why, but there's something, just something about it..."

"Lots of sharks, and nasty things."

"Yep, them too. The sea's a powerful force."

"So are Mrs. Tuffle's cream teas." I said, leaning back and rubbing my full stomach as he laughed. "There's no way I can eat all this. You'd have to carry me to the car. Could we get a doggy-bag for the rest?"

"Of course," he said, leaning forward. "For you, anything." He locked me into his gaze.

Mrs. Tuffle's discreet coughing broke the spell. Nick looked up.

"Will that be all, my lovely?"

"Yes, thank you, Mrs. Tuffle, and as always, a pure delight to eat your cooking."

She preened herself.

He could charm the birds from the trees...

When she brought the bill and began to clear the table, Nick insisted he pay. Mrs. Tuffle took the money on a small white plate.

"Please say hello to your mother and father for me will you, Nick?"

"Of course I will."

"Lovely people, lovely family," she said to me, and turned back to Nick. "And Jenny, you must say hello to beautiful Jenny."

Nick shifted at the mention of this name. He ran his hand through his hair. "If I see her, Mrs. Tuffle, I will, of course."

Our exit was far more rapid than our entrance had been. In the car, Nick only spoke to direct us back.

I knew not to ask, but, *Who was this Jenny?...*

It was the first time I had seen him looking serious.

Eventually, I had to say something. "Is everything okay? Did I do anything?"

He looked directly ahead. "No. I had a good time. We have to get back in time to meet my father."

Any thoughts I had of *Jenny* disappeared, replaced by fear.

David...

After the recent turn of events, and meeting Nicholas, now I didn't want to see David. Far too complicated. I would simply have my holiday. Stay away from the village. Stay away from David, but could I stay away from *Nick*?

As we approached the cottage, I lowered myself in the driver's seat, whilst looking around furtively.

Nick finally turned and looked at me. "Are you alright?"

"Yes... why?"

"Well, you seem to have shrunk."

"No, I have cramp."

He raised an eyebrow, and got out of the car. I had the front door key ready in my hand. Leaping from Maisie and slamming her door shut, I ran past Nick like an Olympic champion, slid the key straight in, opened the door, and promptly stood behind it. All this, because of my utter terror of seeing David.

Nick walked through. "You are definitely different, Lucy."

I pushed the door shut.

In the kitchen, I began the ritual of coffee making. Nick was on the phone, and I knew he was talking to David. When he was finished, he came into the kitchen looking more relaxed.

"So, shall we get all that shopping in?" he asked.

"No!..." I jumped round to face him. "It's fine, I'll do it later."

His stare told me he was having trouble trying to figure me out. "Okay."

I took my bag through to the parlour and Nick followed, sitting heavily on the couch. Five long minutes passed before we both heard the beeping of a horn. At the sound of it, I rose sharply and shrunk into a corner of the room.

Nick stood and turned to me. "Okay Lucy, I'm off."

I stayed right where I was. "Thanks, Nick. It really was a nice day..."

Without comprehending this strange creature hiding in the dark recesses, he turned away and left. I didn't move until I heard the truck pull away.

So, Lauren, You have dealt with it in your own style. There's no way I'll see Nick again now. Who would come back to see this ageing loony?...

I was so wrong.

GOSSIP

I was awoken by a loud banging noise. I crawled out of bed, not thinking about my night attire, a small slightly see-through t-shirt that barely covered my bottom. I drifted in half sleep down the stairs. Nick was at the kitchen door. I opened it, and he looked at me like a naughty boy who'd been caught stealing sweets. He sat in the parlour while I banged the cooker, preparing the essential coffee.

"Sorry I woke you," he called through.

"That's fine, but I must have my coffee… You fancy one?"

"Yeah, that'd be great."

He sat quietly while I made them. I was grateful for that, as I hate to be talked at until I'm completely awake. I took them through, put them on the table, and sat beside him.

"Wish all my drinks were brought to me by someone with that outfit on."

"What, even if a man was wearing it?" I teased. That made him smile. "To be honest, I'm surprised you're even here. You must have a soft spot for casualties," I said.

"I wanted to give you an explanation about yesterday."

"You don't have to explain anything to me, Nick. You're entitled to your own thoughts."

He ran his hand through his hair. I recognised this gesture already. He did it when he was nervous. I picked up my coffee, giving him time to say what he wanted. We sat, sipping, and looking out the window.

"It's because of Jenny. Mrs. Tuffle mentioning her yesterday, well it sort of put me in a mood."

"She must be someone special to make you feel that way?"

"She's my ex-girlfriend. We were together five years, and yes, she was someone special to me, but *Was* is the operative word there..." Gulping his coffee down, he continued. "She had it all mapped out for us, our future, what was going to happen, and well I... I just don't want that. We're close, but she's not The One. You know, my soul mate?..." I knew exactly what he meant. I nodded sympathetically as he continued to explain. "I don't want my life to be taken control of. Trouble is, everyone thinks we were meant to be together. My parents think she's great as well. The fact that I've finished with her is craziness in everyone else's eyes. And she won't accept it - she thinks I'm just panicking... Bit of a mess really."

"I must say, Nick, it is a rare thing for childhood sweethearts to stay together. And I agree with you - if she was your soul-mate, you *would* know."

David had thought *we* were soul mates, and that we would be together forever, me popping out children periodically. For me, in the end it had turned out to be totally different, so I felt for Nick, in a similar situation. Subconsciously, I placed my hand on his knee.

"So, I will no doubt be The Slut of Warbling's Cottage, if Mrs. Tuffle is the gossiping kind."

He laughed softly. "Well, she's not the quiet type."

Both of us started then, as we heard a banging on the front door. I looked at Nick, as if he could possibly know who it might be. He shrugged.

"Word must've got out, and help is here to save you from the slut." I said, pushing him playfully, and putting my coat on before opening the door.

Standing there was Doris; Mrs. Warbling, a small basket in her hand.

"Hello, my lovely. I thought I'd pop round to see how you were. I've brought some eggs with me. They're fresh, mind. From our very own chickens."

"Please come in Doris, thank-you. I really am feeling much better."

She entered the kitchen and placed her basket on the side. Nick was bringing the cups in.

"Oh my!..." She clutched her heart, as if it had stopped beating. "Nick... well, my my. I didn't expect to see you here."

"Hello, Doris. I just stopped past to see if Lucy was alright."

"Oh, you are a good boy. Always thinking of everyone else."

"Anyway I must go, things to do…" He shot me a glance. "Thanks for the coffee Lucy. I'll see you around."

I knew that this show was for the benefit of Doris, especially after what he had just told me.

"Thanks for calling round, Nick," I replied.

Just as he was about to shut the door, Doris called out, "Say hello to lovely Jenny for me."

Nick did not respond as he closed the door softly.

Poor Nick…

I spent the next half an hour chatting with Doris, who pumped me for information about my life, like a cunning old fox. I gave her what I thought were the appropriate responses, all the while thinking about Nick.

How many others would have come back?... I had obviously worried him. I admired him for sticking to his convictions, no matter how painful that was.

When Doris left, I changed into a bikini, grabbed a book and a towel, and went to spend the afternoon in the garden. I let the sun's warmth re-energise my soul. I wondered where Nick had gone, and about Jenny. I understood that *she* must have been feeling pretty shit losing her dreams like that.

She's bound to hear that Nick's been seen with me... As I contemplated that, I must have fallen asleep.

A subconscious feeling that something was crawling on me disturbed me.

Yes,… there's definitely something... I screamed, jumping up violently.

Nick howled with laughter. I was sucking in gasps of air, like a fish out of water, not believing what was before me. Nick held in one hand what appeared to be two live lobsters, and a bottle of plonk in the other.

He was still laughing. "I'm sorry, but it *was* funny."

Still in gasping mode, I stared, then Nick began to stare back.

"Okay, have a good look, yeah… Funny, funny." I stood

defiantly, hands on hips.

He turned as red as the lobsters he held. "Well... err, it's because the view is so nice."

My shock subsided, as did my confidence. Earlier I'd removed my top, and now my breasts stood out before me, bold and snappy as the lobsters.

"Ahhh..." I covered them with my arm.

"Please, don't on my account." Now it was my turn to go red. "I'm sorry, Lucy. I didn't mean to scare you... with our dinner."

"Are you serious, they're still alive? I don't do the cooking thing, and I have to get these chilly puppies indoors," I said, looking down.

I looked up, and we burst out laughing. As we walked to the house, Nick told me not to worry, he would cook everything.

He can cook too. This boy has far too many pluses. I'll wait, there must be something hideous about him, like, when he gets drunk his public trick is to drink his own urine straight from the source, one legged on a bar stool. A showstopper I grant you, but a definite minus...

While I took a bath and changed, I could hear Nick clanking and banging around in the kitchen.

How could his presence here feel so natural?... I'd only met him days ago.

As I came down the stairs into the parlour, delicious aromas engulfed me. The table in the alcove had been set, and the fire blazed away. I was wearing a small white cotton dress, and my hair was still wet. I leant against the door-frame, watching him in action. At first, he didn't notice I was there, and as he turned to take something from the cooker, he almost dropped it.

"Do you always have this effect on people?"

"What? Make them want to drop things and run?.. Yep, I sure do."

He smiled, continuing what he was doing. He was totally at ease in that environment; whisking, chopping, stirring, and tasting.

"Is it good, Mr. Chef?"

"I think so. It's hard to rate your own cooking, but it won't kill you. It'll be ready in about two minutes."

"Can I help?"

"No, you just take a seat... I'm the waiter as well."

"So many different talents. I don't know how many more I can handle." I went to the alcove and took a seat. A moment later, Nick entered, lit the candles and put fresh bread on the table.

He opened the wine. "Glass for Madame?"

"Oh, tonight I think I will... Thank you, waiter."

He poured, then returned to the kitchen. Watching the glow from the candles as I sipped wine, I allowed myself to absorb the romantic atmosphere. Shortly, gourmet food arrived before me, and Nick took his seat.

He raised his glass. "Here's to not poisoning us."

"Hear! Hear!" I said raucously.

His eyes looked straight into mine, and his gaze went down into my very soul. Those eyes saw my desires, my dreams, my fears... *Me*.

I took a big gulp. *He'll know if I'm fake...*

For once, I didn't want to be. I had always had a tendency, when meeting the opposite sex, to adapt myself. To become what I thought they wanted me to be. There had to be a strong sexual and physical attraction. For example, if they loved football, I would appear to love football, or make myself seem more intelligent than my normal dizzy self. Then one day they were left, feeling hurt and bewildered, when I, like a butterfly, fluttered on to my next flower.

When I got married, I gave it my all, well, for three years anyway. Like Nick, I had known he wasn't my soul mate. Being true to myself, and shit to my partners, I carried on flitting. Being with David had taught me from a tender age not to give everything, or else risk being hurt. In the end, it had been David who was really crushed.

"Lucy... hello, Lucy?"

Okay, I'm back in the room... "Yes?"

"Thought I'd lost you there, you were miles away."

"Sorry, Nick, yes I was… But I'm back now, to enjoy this lovely food."

I leant forward to dish up the lobster, putting it first on his plate, then mine. He handed the bread to me.

"I do have many, by the way, in answer to your earlier question..." I had no idea what he was talking about. "…My talents."

Oh, God.... please, I can only think about his pee-drinking skills. It could be a talent I suppose... I smiled weakly at him.

"You don't remember, do you?" he asked.

"No-o?"

"It was just about my many talents, and yes, I do think you can handle them..." He leaned further forward. "Of that I'm sure."

"Rice?" I asked, holding the bowl up.

"Yep, great."

The food *was* delicious. Nick had some minor complaint with every dish; could be more fluffy, could have stayed in the pot a few more minutes, bread not as soft as he would like.   Personally, I'd died and gone to food heaven. I simply smiled in reply to each self-criticism. Nick filled my glass twice, then I refused a third, feeling quite drunk. Lobster bisque was floating in my stomach, and I didn't want to thank him for the food by projectile vomiting across the table, recreating the famous exorcist scene.

We chatted idly as we ate. Nick had another glass of wine, then cleared the table.

"So, pudding?" He asked upon his return, swaying slightly.

"No, I simply couldn't eat another thing..." I stood, also swaying. "It was one of the best meals I've ever had, Nick. Thank-you so much."

I kissed him lightly on the cheek, and quickly ran to the couch. I jumped into the corner of the old, sad cushions, putting my knees under my chin and shielding myself from his charisma. I was feeling and acting like a girl. Nick grabbed the wine and glasses, and kicking off his shoes, he joined me at the other end of the sofa. His legs stretched towards me, and he clasped both hands behind his head. His muscles pressed against his t-shirt, and my heart beat faster.

Lauren, get a grip....

"Lucy?"

"Yes?"

"Why don't you relax? You're acting like you think *you're* the pudding."

Once again, he totally defused me with his easy truthful humour. Nick radiated calmness. I straightened my legs, and when the tips of our toes touched, I jumped as if I'd received an electric shock.

"Oh dear, did our toes touch? Shit! Maybe you'll get pregnant." Nick grinned.

"Very funny. Everyone knows it's through the belly button, stupid."

We both laughed. I let Nick talk me into more wine, determined not to drink it all.

Loose pissed lips sink ships, Lauren....

"Do you like London, Lucy?"

"Well... yes I love it. For the diversity and nightlife. As for the rest, including my boring job, I do not."

"What do you do?"

I'm just a secretary, that's it. Boring. I've got a small flat that

I pay a fortune in rent for, but I wouldn't want to live anywhere else in England."

"I've been a couple of times, but I'd like to spend more time there and get a real feel for it. It'd be great."

Now most people say London's unfriendly, a shithole, but not Nick. Open to new things, experiencing life, not afraid to take chances. Though I had travelled alone for many years around the world, I would have loved to have experienced it all with someone special. No one was ever willing to take that jump, they always lacked the requisite sense of adventure.

"Do you like it here, Nick? Would you ever leave here to travel?"

"Mmm... Okay, that's two questions in one, and I'm a bit drunk, Lucy. So, er, yes. I love it here. I only work with my dad doing the firewood, and a few odd jobs, but that's great too... As for travelling, I'd go tomorrow, as long as my family knew where I was. My mum would have a fit otherwise. She'd probably never forgive me if I did that to her, or she'd be very pissed off for a long while..." He paused, contemplating. "My dad wouldn't be so dramatic."

Entering the world of David made me move my knees uncomfortably under my chin. How could he know, that when he spoke of his mother as if she was a stranger to me, in actual fact she wasn't. I did know her, but only as Angela, David's wife. With flame-red hair, and a temper to match. I did not know Angela the Mother, whether her grip had tightened, or whether she had totally released her jealousy, and irrational fears. I wanted to change the subject.

"I think I've got room for pudding now, Nick."

"Mmm, great, me too." He sauntered to the kitchen, then wobbled back with chocolate cake and cream.

"Ooh... that looks lovely, Nick."

As he took up his previous position, he said my name slowly, like he was going to ask me something.

"Luucyy?"

"Yeeaas?" I responded, in the same way.

"Can I crash here tonight please? I don't feel like cycling. It's Saturday night and I'm a bit drunk."

I couldn't help but giggle. "Yes, you've told me that, Nick."

"So it's okay?"

I didn't know what to say, but I didn't see the harm. How wrong can you be about something. "You can crash here on the couch, I

34

guess."

"Thanks, Lucy, you're great. Though it would have been nice to have double cream with this cake," he mumbled, a spoonful in his mouth.

I laughed out loud. It was the last thing I clearly remember...

Awakening, I was aware of a massive pain in my neck. My cheek felt like it had been dragged across a very cheap carpet. Heaving my eyelids open, I saw Nick opposite me. A blanket covered him below his waist, his top half bare. As I moved my head, the crick in my neck belched pain forth. Slowly I lifted the blanket that was also covering most of me. Only my underwear was on.

Please, God, let Nick have something on. Surely, I wasn't so drunk that something happened?...

I had just fallen asleep, I hoped. I started to move, unable to lift my head from my shoulder. I looked in the mirror by the side of the fireplace. The movie, *Death becomes her* sprang to mind. My neck was totally bent, as if it had been snapped off and put back on at a right angle. Or should that be wrong angle? My head must have been on the arm of the sofa, gently falling to a complete wrong angle as I'd passed out. I rubbed my cheek, by now bright red and woolly looking. One side of my hair stood on end. I looked like a car crash survivor in Ann summers lingerie. This is how I opened the door, which someone had been banging on while I was trying to wake up. There before me stood a girl. She flinched for only a split-second.

"Good morning. You must be Lucy. I'm Jenny. Jenny Setterton..."

JENNY PERFECT

She thrust her hand at me, shaking vigorously. My mind, soaked in alcohol, tried to remember if her name should mean anything to me.

Jenny? Jenny Setterton?... No, I couldn't place it, though in the deep bog of my brain, a tiny bell rang.

"May I?" She asked, indicating beyond the door.

"Umm...yes?" I replied.

Jenny stood in the middle of the kitchen, a set smile on her face, as she surveyed world war three from the night before. Every single space was full of dirty cooking equipment. She turned and gave me a look as if I were a small creature, about to be slaughtered.

"I was talking to Mrs. Warbling, and she told me how you hurt yourself here in an accident, and that my Nick, had been here to help? He always helps everyone, that's the way he is. I'm also like that, and I'm here to help *you*, Lucy." She smiled a tight, false smile.

I hadn't said a word. I stared at Jenny Setterton. A nice, good, wholesome country girl, she had flushed red cheeks and very neat brown, shoulder-length hair. Her outstanding breasts had grown wonderfully in the country air. She stood, completely composed in her sensible clothes.

I had picked up on two things, now that I was thinking more clearly; *'My Nick'*, and her name - *Jenny*.

Oh, shit. Her possibly totally naked ex is slumped on the sofa in the next room....

Quick action was needed. So, looking the way I did, I talked as loudly as I could.

"JENNY! JENNY! HOW LOVELY TO MEET YOU, JENNY!..."

She took a step back, looking at me as if I'd just performed oral sex on myself.

I shouted again. "WOULD YOU LIKE A CUP OF TEA, JENNY?"

She looked like she was weighing up the situation. "Are you alright, Lucy? You seem to be speaking quite loudly."

"AM I JENNY? SORRY, JENNY!"

Where others would have left very quickly, Jenny did not. Jenny was not a giver-upper. She was always the girl picked first for the team. Others would hear of the courageous struggle with this clearly unhinged, lunatic, city girl. I could almost hear Mrs. Tuffle saying, *'Oh you know Jenny, so kind she would try to help the village idiot. Such a lovely girl...'* I bet Jenny bathed in that kind of adoration. I bet Angela loved her.

"I think we should go through to the parlour... then I'll make some tea," Jenny said, advancing towards the door.

A small scream escaped from me, and she stopped and turned. Her big, brown eyes looked at me piteously, as she went like a flash into the next room. I breathed hard, without moving, and waited for a scream, shouting – anything... I heard nothing.

I walked into the parlour as if there were broken glass on the floor. Jenny was sitting on one of the armchairs, with her knees together, and her hands clasped primly on top of them. Eventually I got to the sofa, and sat down as if I were about to take an interview. *Jenny* thought the evidence was clear. Sleeping on the sofa, wine on the table, my satanic appearance, and my shouting outbursts. The strange catlike motions I'd adopted in place of walking. The kitchen fit only for pigs. Clearly, I was an alcoholic, she had concluded, and *She, Jenny,* had caught me off guard on a Sunday morning.

Triumphant at first, her look gradually changed to one of pity, and for the rest of her visit she adopted a tone, as if she were speaking to a fifteen year old.

She stood and placed a hand on my knee. "Lucy, would you like a cup of tea? ...Do you like tea? Tea..."

Oh, God, I wish Jenny, fucking perfect, Setterton would go....

While she was in the kitchen, I looked around a little for Nick. Under the table, behind a chair, there were not so many places to hide in such a small room. I was back on the sofa as Jenny came in with the tea. I drunk it as quickly as I could, blowing on it wildly to bring down the temperature.

Hopefully she'll go quickly once it's finished...

She talked about Nick, and how in love they were. She also talked about, oh yes, Nick. Did she tell me, by the way, about Nick? I was zoning out, all this talk of Nick, was making me daydream about him. Attractive, carefree, easy to be with, Nick. Natural charm oozed from him. Honest, fun, David's son, Nick. Now I wished he *had* stood on a barstool and drunk his own urine the night before.

I'd no idea how long Jenny rabbited on for, but finally she left. As she departed, she seemed to be gloating, no doubt clutching her prize of mis-information, to be shared with Nick, next time they met. *'That woman, Lucy, in the cottage is a raving mad, alcoholic. I saw it with my own eyes.'*

I remained motionless, waiting to see if anything else would happen. Minutes passed.

Softly, I called out; "Nick.... Nick, are you here?"

...nothing.

I went to the bathroom, wet my face, and calmed down my erect hair. I went to the loo, brushed my teeth, and headed upstairs. As I entered the bedroom, I saw where Nick had hidden. He was still in the house, tucked up in bed, asleep. I couldn't help but smile as I gently pulled the covers back, slid in next to him, and fell asleep as well.

Air blowing gently on my face roused me. I opened my eyes, and saw Nick, lying on his side, his face just a few inches away from mine. I inhaled sharply, and pushed myself away. He thought *he'd* made me jump, and placed his hand on my cheek to reassure me.

"Sorry Lucy, I didn't mean to scare you."

I let his hand linger on my face longer than I should have. I sat up quickly and changed the subject.

"Anyway, I can't believe it, all the time Jenny Perfect was downstairs, you were up here, asleep." I pretended to sound angry, but I think he knew I wasn't.

Smiling, he asked, "Is that what you call her then? - Jenny Perfect?"

"Umm... yes. Sorry, I know she's your ex-girlfriend. I didn't purposely think that up, but I'm guessing she's the type of girl who will have a go at most things, and be good at them, right?"

"Well... she is like that, as long as they're fairly safe things. Cooking's safe. Horse riding's just about acceptable. Clay-pigeon shooting, tug of war, they're acceptable. Motorbikes, skydiving, sex with attractive strangers, or flying to Las Vegas for the weekend - *not* so acceptable." He sat up.

What a great body he has... Lauren, - control!...

"Okay, I get it... and it's the *un*safe type you want?"

"Yes, Lucy, that's the type I want. Someone who's not afraid, to live their life..." He leant towards me, cocking his head slightly. "By the way, did I tell you how amazing you look in black lacy underwear?"

"Don't think so," I muttered, my resolve crumbling. "Nick, are you wearing anything?"

"Of course," he beamed. "Got the old CK's on." He jumped out of bed and did a twirl for me in his Calvin's, only making matters worse.

"Yes, nice, nice. Now I think it's time we dressed. Doesn't it bother you that Jenny was here?"

He stopped dressing, one leg in his jeans. "I'm sorry she came here, but while I'm alone with you, it doesn't bother me. Later, it will, but now... no."

For a moment, I couldn't say a thing. He really had meant what he'd said. Flattery tied my tongue. Nick was still standing with one leg in his jeans, his eyes looking into me again.

"You're nice company, Nick."

On that note, I got dressed quickly, and went downstairs to clean the kitchen. Not long after I'd begun, he joined me.

He took my hand. "Lucy, do you want me to go?"

The truth was that I didn't. "No Nick, I don't, but I don't feel like going out. People will have enough to say, I'm sure."

"They always will, but it's harmless in the end."

"Thanks... well, just for being you. We'll get this cleaning done, then go out to the garden, what about that?..."

"Sounds good, Lucy. We can go down by the trees."

By the time we eventually got to them, it was 4:30pm. Nick laid out the blanket he had brought from the house onto the ground. We both lay on our backs looking up at the blue sky through the leaves and branches. We both somehow knew that neither person wanted, or needed to say much. Every now and then one of us would point out a cloud that looked particularly like something. One of mine was an elephant, and another an odd shaped penis. Nick pointed out a flying saucer, and a top hat. We thought the penis shaped one was the funniest.

Together, at peace, we watched the once ripe sun, sink slowly down, taking the day's light and warmth with it. Neither of us knew what time it was, but I was getting cold.

"We should really get going," Nick said.

We walked back to the cottage, using the orange afterglow of dusk to guide us back. He got his cycle from the side of the cottage, and brought it round to the front. Our parting was awkward, neither of us wanting to part from the other.

"Thanks, Nick, for a lovely meal, and a great weekend." I kissed him quickly on the cheek, turned and went straight into the house.

My evening was filled with ghosts and torment. It was insane to miss him so much. The responsible thing would be to go, but I wasn't, and I couldn't. This was far worse than seeing David after all these years. This was Danger with a capital D. For God's sake, Nick was Angela and David's son. If I wanted to unleash the full force of her Irish temper, I was definitely on the right track. Not only had her husband been deeply in love with me, but now – Pop! - Here I was to finish the job, this time with her eldest son. David would be a different matter.

God, Lauren. This time you really have done it...

A fitful sleep deprived me of any relief, after which I decided I would stay away from Nick. I would definitely not see him, not open the door to him. Hide. Whatever it took, I knew I must be strong. Before dawn broke, I had made a promise to myself that I would absolutely stay away from Nick.

We spent the next three wonderful days together.

OUTINGS

Monday, at 10am, I was ready. The cottage was fresh and clean, and I was scrubbed and fed, with hair that was trying very hard to shine. I wore just a hint of make-up, and purple dungarees that I'd cut the legs off, turning them into dungarshorts. Frantic knocking at the door made me slightly nervous, without knowing for sure who it could be.

"Hello?" I called through the closed door.

"Lucy?... it's Nick."

I smoothed down my hair, any resolutions I had made the night before abandoning ship. I put on my big smile and pulled the door open enthusiastically.

"Beautiful day, needs a beautiful girl to be in it." He was carrying a picnic basket.

My heart began to melt. I could hardly be called a girl at forty-three, but I didn't want to spoil it.

"So... where to?"

"The blue lagoons. It's a perfect day for it. The water can be a bit chilly though. You just need swimming stuff, a towel, and your car keys."

"How far away are they?"

"Twenty-seven miles, but they're worth it."

"Yup, okay I think I'll need to bring Maisie. I don't fancy a backie on your bike that far."

He ran his hand through his hair, and I knew this had bothered him for some reason.

"Don't worry, Nick, I don't mind driving at all. It gives me a chance to see round these paarts." I hammed up the Devonshire twang.

"You've not quite got the accent, but thanks, Lucy. I wish I could drive you, but my dad's got the truck today, he's using it for work."

"Well if we need the truck for anything, I'll let you know. We'll go in Maisie."

He looked over at her. "Yep, sexy little car."

How did he do that?... When I bought her, one of the first things I thought was; Sexy little car...

"Well it's nice chatting, but my arm's kinda aching holding this basket."

"Why don't you just put it down?"

"Errr... because I didn't realise it would take so long... and now it's even longer because you asked me a question."

"But now you've made it much longer, because your reply was even longer than my question."

"Now it's even longer, Lucy." He just dropped the basket, and we howled with laughter.

"Wait there, I won't be long." I said, and I gathered what I needed.

I felt like I was fifteen years old, with full parental approval; a feeling of being utterly free.

We jumped into Maisie, once again the intrepid explorers setting off on an adventure. It was another glorious day. The Devon countryside was one giant tapestry, weaved to perfection.

"I'm curious Nick... can you pick and choose when you work? I don't mean to be nosey, only... only I've been spending a lot of time with you."

"Yes, that's exactly what I was thinking. I don't know how you do your magic, but soon I'll slap on a surcharge for entrance to my brain." He continued smiling, as always.

"That would be worth every penny," I said, and felt myself blush. A few moments went by.

"I always help my dad when we have an order for wood, chopping, and delivering. My brother sometimes helps."

Must be Josh...

"My parents have a bed and breakfast, mostly run by my mum, but we all help out. I suppose my dad's like an odd-job man, he keeps the house and garden looking good. My little sister takes up a good part of my mum's time, she's only five. I work hard, so they don't mind if I slack off for a few days sometimes. Also, to be honest, you're a good excuse for getting out the house. My mum keeps going on about Jenny. It's easier to be busy, or out. There's no arguing with my mother."

Yes, I would agree with that...

Crossing swords with Angela was a thrill I never wanted to repeat. It was the first time Nick had talked about his family. I could hear a range of emotions in his voice as he spoke.

I broke through my thicket of thoughts.

"So, just a good excuse am I, then?" I enquired teasingly, stealing a glance at him before he turned to me.

"The best excuse I've ever had."

In my mind, he was now the knight on the huge shining black horse. Lance at the ready, coming to save me. As I drove, I kept quiet. Nick talking about his family had made me feel like a giant Shit. A spy, holding all the secret information, my presence here totally based on lies. Fuck! Even my name wasn't real.

Nick directed, while I drove silently. The sneaky fraud that I was, I was relieved when we passed a sign that said; **Blue Lagoon - 2 miles**.

We can stay a while, and then I'll tell Nick I don't feel well and need to go home. This is not what I wanted at all...

The trouble was, I wanted everything I was forbidden to have. Nick felt my mood change, and left me to my thoughts. I was sure if he knew what they were I would see a different side to him, but which side would it be? I didn't want to see him upset or angry when at that time, there was only happiness in him. I forced myself to smile, not wanting him to think anything was wrong.

"Nearly there... there's a bit of gravelly land we can park on," Nick said, as we rounded the bend and left the country lane.

Straight away, I spotted the car park, pulling Maisie into a very tight space of fresh air, as there were no other vehicles there. We collected our stuff and walked to where the edge of the cliffs overhung.

"Follow me, Lucy."

Gravel turned to larger stones as we walked round the outcrops. I saw the cove in front of me. It had no sand, only big, flat, smooth rocks. I imagined the moon, or mars to look like this. It was as if a giant had stood knee deep in the sea playing skim the pebble against the shore.

We walked over to the lowest one, as the sea gently lapped against the bottom of it.

Nick looked up. "We have to get to the top stones, but the rocks are very slippery. We'll have to hold hands to help each other up."

I raised my eyebrows. "I think I can manage to climb a few stones, Nick."

"Look, if I wanted to hold your hand I would just take it. I'm not into silly mind games, Lucy. Bullshit takes too long."

Indignant, I stuck my chin out and placed a foot in a niche. I held the edge of the stone above and pulled myself up. Immediately my foot slipped out from under me, and the stone crashed into my proud, foolish, stuck-out chin. Pain tore through my tongue as my teeth bit down on it. I landed in a heap, with not a shred of dignity intact. Nick acted like it was one of the funniest things he'd ever seen. My pride was hurting a lot more than my injuries. He was clutching his stomach, tears rolling down his face.

"Oh... oh, I'm... I'm sorry...shit!... It's so funny, though...shit!"

Pain screamed in my chin and mouth. Inwardly I was running around as if my vagina was on fire, but I'd be damned to hell before I would let it show to Nick. I held my hand in front of me, and tried to say; "No, no, I'm fine, please don't help, I can manage," but something else came out.

Nick stopped laughing, and craned his head slightly forward, looking intently at me.

"What?..." he asked.

I could only shake my head. My tongue was swollen, and with the pain, no way could I manage to repeat that.

"Something... no time?... help slam-age?" he suggested.

Even with my pain and my shame, I had to smile. He came to me, and I let him help. His strong arm went round my back and lifted me to my feet with ease. It was a moment. One single moment. Our eyes interlocked, and nothing else existed as we breathed deeply.

"Lucy," he said, tenderly.

I stepped back. "HEEK!" It sounded nothing like *Nick*, which was what I was trying to say. I pointed to my tongue. "Eat ma onge.."

"Are you trying to say you've bitten your tongue?"

I nodded.

He was smiling again. "So, now you've got no choice, you have to do as I say. Could be fun for me…"

I poked him in the ribs and made him jump.

"Hey, you have to be nice to me."

I held out my hand with a gesture that showed I was willing to co-operate.

Nick got our stuff, and took my hand, helping me up the staircase of giant discs. When we got to the top, my mouth fell open, and not because of the pain… Three natural sea pools were placed in each of the flat rocks.

"Ooww," I said.

"Did you mean 'Wow'?"

I nodded. He took my hand again, although now there was no need. The uppermost rocks were perfectly smooth and level. I couldn't fight the naturalness of this setting. He took me over to the first pool, where the water was a beautiful turquoise colour. I looked at him, smiled, and made a thumbs-up sign.

"Yep, cool. We'll plot ourselves up here. It could get busy later, though," Nick said, smiling.

We got everything out, apart from the food Nick had brought. I made him turn away while I changed into my bikini. I made myself turn away while he put his beach shorts on. I lay on my back, and absorbed the sun, and the atmosphere. Slowly my tongue went down, and after about an hour, I was able to make myself understandable. Rolling onto my front, I faced all three pools. Sunshine shone directly onto them, and the sparkles of light hypnotised me. They seemed like fairy conventions being wiped out by a gangsta sun.

"It's beautiful here, Nick, in a different way."

"I knew you'd like it."

It was so hot, the fairies were calling me to join them in the water. I stood, stretched, and wandered over to the pool nearest to us. Now, I think there are two styles of water entry. The slow, easy, bit by bit, splashing yourself with water, style. Or the jump, dive, run in fast, style. Mine is the latter. One big, swift jump, and I was under.

'Cold' is a word one can bandy about. It doesn't really cover the different levels of cold. For example; your feet are cold because the heating is off… On a snowy day, your face is… cold. A million frozen pins puncturing your skin simultaneously… That's Cold. Before this moment, I'd never had freezing cold seawater shot up my vagina, but I can assure you it will never be repeated. Although it does give a temporary youthful glow.

Like the victim in a Jaws movie, I swam to the surface. My head emerged, and I gasped as if it were my last breath. As soon as I realized it wasn't, I screamed.

Nick jumped up from his towel. "Lucy, Lucy..." he shouted.

I was gasping harder and faster, the fictitious shark now clamping down on my legs. Nick came to the edge of the pool.

"What's wrong, Lucy?"

"F-frreeezing c-cold water."

I placed my hands on the edge and pulled myself up and out, before I lost all feeling.

I ran to get my towel and wrapped it round myself, shivering like a Chihuahua.

Nick came over, chuckling. "Yeah, I told you it was a bit chilly. I jumped in like that one time, but I'd never do it again. Shit, no!..." He sat down beside me and enveloped me in his arms. "...I'll help keep you warm, but I must admit, it is nice." I lay my wet head on his shoulder, waiting for the shivering to stop. "You are funny, Lucy," he said.

"Glad I can be of some amusement for you..."

Nick, and the sun, soon warmed me. I sat and stared at the scrummy picnic he'd brought, while he told me why the pools were here. My tongue was still too sore to cope with food.

Apparently, in spring and winter there were high tides that came over the stones. In summer, the algae in the pools came alive and made them the colours they were. We had to leave by sunset, as the tide came in and could make the route back impassable.

"Better keep an eye on the time then," I said nervously, not wanting to camp the night there.

"Don't worry – I am. I've been here so many times."

"Did you come here with Jenny?" It popped out of my mouth before I could think.

"Yes. A few times, but she didn't really like it here." He continued eating.

"Thanks for bringing me here, Nick."

"Welcome," he said, with his mouth full.

After watching Nick eat his lunch, I repositioned my towel to face the sun and lay on my back again. Even though my eyes were closed, I felt him put his towel down next to mine. We were laying closely, my arms at my side, and Nick's fingertips touched mine. He didn't move them away, and neither did I. Small, tiny electrical charges pulsed between us. His hand held mine gently and electric currents charged up my arm. I'd never felt like this. I was Eve, looking at the forbidden fruit.

Damn it, let the tide come in. Trap us here, so we can never leave. No one will ever find us... No one will see what's growing inside me - my feelings for Nick...

I lay there letting foolish fantasies take me, as I listened to the sea. They felt like waves crashing through me. Some time elapsed.

"Lucy, we should get ready to go soon. Sun's going down."

He rolled onto his side, head in his hand, looking down at me. His other hand was still holding mine.

Quickly, I rolled out of the way, flustered. "Mmm, well, we'd better go then. I just want to look at the water once more."

I turned and ran over to the pool. I'd only been looking for a minute, when I heard Nick shout a warning.

"Lucy, look out!"

A wave came crashing over my head, and water pushed under my feet. As the wave retreated both feet slipped out from under me. I went down hard, banging my head on the rock. Then I remember nothing, except through the blackness, I heard a name being called.

"Lucy, Lucy, please!..."

Who the hell is Lucy?...

Again; "Lucy?..."

As I opened my eyes, reeling from head pain, I said -

"Lauren…"

ICE CREAMED

Nick drove Maisie back. I was dizzy and felt sick. Blood clotted in my hair, and I could taste more in my mouth. As I came round properly, horror struck me.

Lauren... I'd told him my real name.

Nick hadn't mentioned it yet. He just appeared to be sick with worry, and wanted to take me to the hospital. I refused, asked if he would please just drive me back to the cottage, and he did.

"Sorry, Nick. I think I must have booked the 'how many times can you knock yourself out?' holiday."

"So this isn't normal for you?"

"Well... yes I suppose it is, but I don't normally get so many knocks to the head."

When we got back to the cottage, Nick made me lay on the sofa. He made a fire, and poured me a shot of whisky. It made me cough, but it felt good and warming.

He sat on the edge with me. "Lucy?"

"Yes?"

"Earlier, when you hit your head, I was calling your name, and you said, 'Lauren'."

"Did I?"

"Yes."

I tried to think quickly. "I must have been concussed. My cousins called Lauren. I must have thought you were her."

"Oh yes, you must have been... since when did I look like a girl?"

Whew. I got away with my disgusting lies...

"Maybe you should go to bed, Lucy."

"I think I will, Nick."

"I'll come up and check on you in a bit."

"Why, what are you doing now?"

"I'm staying here on the couch. I'm not leaving you. No way, you're my patient now."

"Nick…" I started to say, but I was too tired to argue with him.

He came up as I started to fall asleep.

"I have to go early in the morning, but I'll be back later." He kissed me on the forehead and I slipped into sleep.

When I awoke and went downstairs, he'd gone. My head was agony, so I took some painkillers with my coffee. The cottage seemed quiet and empty without Nick filling it full of his positive energy. I wandered through the house like a pup trying to find its mother, and ended up right back where I'd begun, in bed. I tried to read a book. Every ten minutes I looked at the time. Followed by every two minutes thinking of Nick, followed by eight minutes of berating myself for thinking of him. *Twelve O'clock. One O'clock. Two O'clock.* This was torture. I still didn't feel like moving around much. My head was still aching and dizzy. All I had were my wicked, sinful, self-loathing thoughts. I wished the bang to my head had knocked some sense into me.

No sense in there, Lauren. You gave that up the day you clicked on 'find friends' in Facebook...

However, I still had feeling, my head and my heart proved that. I thought maybe I should just tell him the truth, but I knew I was too much of a coward for that. Honour, would cost me Nick. Just a few more days, and I would disappear. How naïve I was to delude myself that it would be that easy.

The honking of a horn outside interrupted my thoughts. I went to the window, and there was the truck, with Nick leaning out and waving up at me. *Please let it be just Nick...* He cut the engine and jumped out.

"Hey there, Lucy," he called up to me.

I went downstairs and opened the door. He opened the back of the truck, leaned in, and pulled out...

What... what is that?...

"The twenty-first century comes to you," Nick said.

I just stared. First, he brought in a big flat screen TV, and took it upstairs. Next, a DVD player with a selection of discs, and lastly, a large cool-box, which he put on the side in the kitchen. He flung his keys down next to it.

"Right, madam, up to bed you go."

I was so intrigued I did as he said. In bed again, I watched him set up our viewing equipment. He was making me giggle, swearing when he got things wrong.

"Shit!.. no, not that one..." he'd say to himself.

I was happy. Happy he was back filling in the colour of my black and white life.

"Right...," he said, jumping on the bed next to me, holding a stack of DVD's.

Personally, I think someone's movie choices say a lot about him or her. For instance if Nick's stack had contained such titles as; STOCK CAR RACING HIGHLIGHTS, ANAL LOVERS II, THE BEST OF HANDGUNS, FARMYARD FRIENDS III and SCARFACE. That would conjure up quite an image. Now, all would be revealed.

"I figure we should choose maybe two films each, and after that, if we want more, you choose one. Sound fair?"

"Yeah, that sounds fair enough. Nick, you've gone to so much trouble again... thanks."

"Can't have people saying I'm a shit doctor. Anyway, today's cloudy, and I've got the truck till tomorrow, so it's a perfect recovery day."

"Okay - hit me with what you've got."

Thankfully, he had a good selection, and we settled on AIRPLANE, an old comedy from the eighties, which Nick said was one of his favourites. I chose the first; TWILIGHT, which I still find impossibly romantic. Between us, we chose the first three ALIEN films, both of us in total agreement at the wickedness of them. Sci-fi at its best.

"So, which one first?" he asked.

"Umm... the aliens first."

"Right on the button, I was thinking the same thing… you have a knack for knowing what I want, or what I'm thinking."

"First, I have to pop downstairs. So please make yourself comfy, for your viewing pleasure." He exited mischievously, and I could hear noises coming from the kitchen, as I made myself comfy.

When he returned he kicked open the door, holding a tray. He placed the tray next to me. *Ice cream. Three different types, by the look of it...*

"Real, Devon, ice-cream. Made with double cream. This one's vanilla," he said, pointing to a thick, yellow mound. "...and toffee and strawberry, made from real strawberries."

My mouth watered, and I put my hand on his.

"Nick, I think you're an angel..."

He blushed. "It's only ice-cream."

Nick put in the disc, got under the covers with me, and pressed play. For nearly six hours, we watched the Alien films. We ate ice cream constantly for the first hour. I never knew it could taste like that. It was so nice, I would have made the drive from London for that alone.

We could hear the rain on the window, driving us both deeper under the covers. We watched Airplane. Nick was right, it was funny. I had some recollection of watching it once in the past. Now I watched with a new appreciation. We took a break for more ice cream. Nick had brought a lot, and like me, he had a very sweet tooth. For the next film, Nick turned off the light; Twilight. The couple that were not meant to be. Just like Nick and I, only in real life, *I* was the vampire. The romanticism of the film was infectious. We held hands tightly, and I laid my head on his shoulder.

When I opened my eyes, it was dark. The TV was off, and Nick was asleep next to me. Even in the dark, I could see his peaceful, beautiful face. Every part of me wanted to kiss him.

For God's, sake, Lauren. The boys asleep....

The need for it was too great. Carefully, not wanting to disturb him, and feeling slightly like a pervert, I lowered my lips onto his. My lips tingled madly, and the sensation remained, even when I took them away. I felt like I'd just got away with a small crime. I lay and enjoyed the feeling, for as long as it lasted.

The sun came up, and woke me. I carried the tray downstairs, determined to do something nice for Nick. I attempted to make coffee, toast, boiled eggs, and smoked salmon. Precariously balancing it all on the tray, I carried it upstairs, and woke him gently.

"Morning, room service... Did you order breakfast, Sir?"

He yawned, stretched, and smiled. "No... I ordered the maid that brought it."

I placed the tray on his lap. "I don't think your payment covers that, Sir." I opened the curtains and joined him on the bed. "What time do you have to go?"

"I need to get the truck back by ten-thirty. What time is it now?"

"About nine." *So I only have another hour and a half left with him...*

"Is it okay if I take a shower?"

"Sure."

After breakfast we took the tray down to the kitchen, and as I ran some water into the sink, his arms went round my waist, his lips millimetres from my ear.

"Thanks for that, Lucy. It means a lot to me."

He kissed me gently on the neck, and I froze. Releasing his grip, he made his way to the bathroom, whistling. When the door closed, I exhaled and leant heavily on the sink, hanging my head.

I'll lose him again soon...

The sunshine of my soul stood whistling under running water, without a care in the world. I would tell him nothing - keep it all to myself. I would be utterly selfish. So far, I'd managed to stay away from David.

Wednesday... that leaves a week and a half... I can do it. Then I could just spend time with Nick, with it naturally ending when my holiday ends. When I have to go back to London...

I didn't want to hurt Nick. I never wanted to hurt Nick.

"So, no big towels then?"

I hadn't heard him come in the kitchen. Turning from the sink to answer, I knew I was gaping, but I was unable to stop myself.

His perfect torso rippled in front of me. Droplets of water slid down his body, over his chiselled abs, and down his neck, along strong shoulders down to perfect biceps. In his right hand, he gripped the corners of a very small hand towel, like a micro-skirt, around athletic thighs.

A dream-scape had hold of me. I watched the water run slowly down his inner thigh, as I gulped drily. I was imagining I was one of those droplets, slithering down that sensational physique.   I came back to reality as Nick clicked his fingers.

"Hello?... Lucy?... Come in, over."

"What?... Sorry, what did you say?"

"Towels, big?"

"Don't think I have any." I giggled.

"Funny. Okay then." He turned and ran upstairs.

I stayed where I was. An almost naked, Nick, was upstairs in the bedroom. My desire levels were going through the roof.

Lauren, for God's sake, try not to make this worse....

I started to attack the washing-up. Halfway through, Nick came down.

"Gotta go, honey..." He picked his keys up. "I'll be gone most of the day." I sighed. "Would you mind if I came back later?"

I turned to look at him. "I'd like that."

He beamed. "And then I'll tell you my secret," he said, and tapped his nose.

Shit, we both have them... "What kind of secret?"

"Don't worry, you'll find out…"

"Yeah, but -"

"I'm only teasing you Lucy. I hate secrets, unless they're nice surprises. Lies eat you away from the inside."

I should tell him... "Nick…"

"No, really, Okay, I'll tell you now. I wasn't asleep last night. There."

Winking, he went outside and got into the truck.

Wasn't asleep last night? Funny thing to say... Oh no!... I suddenly remembered my kiss. *OH NO!...* He had been awake. *Foolish, foolish...*

What was I going to do without Nick, for the whole day?

Jesus, Lauren, you seemed to manage okay without him two weeks ago...

But that was pre-Nick. Now there was a need in me. The feeling of his absence was almost physical. I needed to get out the house and do something. Therefore, knowing Nick was with his father all day, I decided to be brave and walk to the village.

I can't get in any trouble there...

It never occurred to me that Angela might be there.

ANGELA

I changed into my tight-fitting jogging bottoms, a white long-sleeved cotton shirt, and a Nike jacket, just in case. There was no rain, but clouds jostled with the sun for domination. As I walked along it felt good to be outside, getting some much-needed exercise. Not exercising always makes me cranky.

Why does country air smell so good?...

It took longer than I realised it would to get to the village, and I built up quite a sweat. With no particular goal in mind, and needing a drink, I decided to go into The Dry Thrush.

There were only a couple of people inside. I made my way to the bar and noticed Angus, sitting in the same spot by the fire. I ordered an orange juice and went over to the familiar table.

"Hello, do you mind if I join you?"

He looked up from his paper. "Why - hello there... Lucy, isn't it?"

"Yes. I'm staying at Stan's cottage."

He smiled coyly. "Yes. Yes, I know."

Angus folded his paper and pointed to a stool. I sat, and stuck for anything to say, I looked round the pub, then back at Angus. My face must have said - '*I'm sorry, I have no idea why I'm here.*'

"Bit of a loose end?"

"Umm... not really. Well, a bit..." I shrugged. "Sorry Angus. Don't really know why I came to the village." Then I thought about what I was saying. "OH! That sounds terrible... it's beautiful here, it's just me. My head's all over the place."

"Country air. ...Does it every time for you city folk."

That made me smile. "Yes, maybe that's it."

Even though Angus had wiry ginger hair that had never heard of a brush, let alone felt one, and the tip of his wild beard touched his chest, his face seemed kind and wise, nevertheless. I wanted to unburden myself on him. Tell him all my dirty lies.

"Do you know Nick, Angus?" I tried to ask casually, leaning forward and squinting.

"Oi do."

I waited for more information, while I fiddled with my drink and avoided his gaze.

"Well, it's just that he's been very kind to me."

"Nice boy, Nick, not many like that one."

I totally agree with that...

"Listen, Lucy. You seem like a lovely maid. I'm not prone to gossip, but it's going round the village that he's been at the cottage a lot. What two single people get up to is their affair..." He paused, now that he had my full attention. "As I said, I'm not prone to gossip."

"I don't want to cause any problems, Angus. He's just a nice boy."

"No need to justify yourself to me, my lovely."

No, I was justifying it to myself... I wanted to lighten the mood. "So, Angus, Nick tells me you have a fishing boat?"

"Yep."

"Maybe one day I could come on it? See it all from the sea?"

"You just say when, my love. If I'm not fishing, I'd like that. Not many maids look like you want to go out to sea with an old scrote like me." A big broad smile spread across his face, plumping up his coarse, bright-red cheeks.

I relaxed and laughed. "Thanks, Angus. You're a lovely old scrote."

"Just tell Nick when you want to go."

He winked. A wise old scrote, I liked him very much. As I finished my drink, I bent and kissed Angus on the cheek. His entire face and neck went redder than his hair.

"Take care, my lovely."

I left the pub feeling much better than when I'd gone in.

Wise old country sage, that Angus... I'll go to the butchers, then back to the cottage. I'll cook Nick some nice steaks up for when he comes home... Lauren, it's not even your home. It's his fucking home. I'm the self-invited guest. Still, I'll go to the butchers, then I'll slither back like the snake that I am...

Quietly, I opened the butcher's door. An old-fashioned bench sat along the window. There was a lady customer in front of the counter, but no one behind it. A girl of about four or five spiralled round, holding the edge of her dress. She was humming lightly, perfectly happy. As I sat down, she looked over at me. She was a very pretty girl with big dark-green eyes, and a constant smile. Her hair was hanging in chestnut-red curls. She was captivating, but I returned my gaze to the woman at the counter, who had long, flame-red hair.

"Charlie!" she shouted.

There was no mistaking the strong Northern-Irish accent. My stomach contracted, and I tried to hold down the sick.

"Be with you in a minute, Mrs. Palmer...," a man's voice shouted.

Bile was slowly creeping up my throat. A man stepped through the plastic curtains, wiping his fat sausage fingers on the slaughterer's apron. "Sorry about that, Mrs. Palmer. I've just cut all the meat, an' I 'ad to get it in the freezer."

"Don't worry, Charlie. I'm in no rush today. All the boys are out with their father. It's just me and Maggie."

Charlie leant over the counter. "Mornin', Maggie, my lovely."

She stopped spinning and looked up at the jolly butcher.

"Maggie..," her mother chided.

"Good mornin'," Maggie said, then continued her twirling.

He tipped his hat to me, finally acknowledging my existence.

"Here's the list, Charlie. Need a lot this week, we've a lot of bookings."

"That's dandy, Mrs. Palmer. I'll get this order ready for you."

I had mentally shrunk myself to the size of an ant. I squeezed myself into the corner of the bench, breathing softly.

Maybe she won't even turn round... the power of invisibility would be very handy at this moment. Why of all people does it have to be her in front of me? I'd prefer anyone else. Peter Sutcliffe would be better than HER. Angela...

The butcher was making idle chitchat.

"How are those two love-birds doin' then? Patched things up yet?"

Angela sighed. "Nicks just going through a stage. All men do. Love and responsibility makes them panic."

"Ah, yes. Maybe you're right there."

"My Nick's a clever boy. Deep down he knows, him and Jenny are meant to be together."

"Ahhh... they are indeed. The 'ole village would agree."

"I'm just giving him some time out. Nick can be stubborn. Takes after his father…"

While this chitchat was commencing, the child, now bored, turned her attention to me. She joined me on the bench, swinging her legs back and forth.

"Hello," she said.

I said '*hello*' back at a low pitch, as if I was in a library.

"Been hearin' some distressin' stories, about some grockle maid stayin' at the Warbling's," the butcher said.

Angela made a scoffing sound. "Totally on the booze… She opened the door practically naked to poor Jenny." My eyes widened. "Came down here to dry out, but she doesn't even leave the house. Probably can't walk."

I wanted to protest, but didn't dare.

"Are you a new lady here?" the little girl asked.

My eyes quickly flicked to Angela.

"*Yes*," I whispered.

Maggie moved up the bench, nearer to me.

"All I know is, that drunken slut had better stay away from my Nick," Angela almost shouted.

"Nick!..." Maggie said loudly, smiling and clapping at the mention of his name.

Angela turned around. She saw her child sitting next to me.
"Maggie, come over here. Stop bothering the lady."
I said nothing. Bags of meat crammed the counter.
"So, that's all. I'll send the bill round," the butcher said.
"Thanks, Charlie."

Jenny appeared in the doorway. I wanted time to stop, so I could just slip back out onto the street and run away.
"I've brought the car, Angela. It's outside." She turned towards me, and her smile was replaced with a look of mild shock. "Hello, Lucy."
Angela spun round.
"Maggie, come here now," she commanded. Maggie did as she was told, knowing that tone meant business. "Jenny, could you take Maggie to the car please?" Her eyes never left me. Jenny Perfect did as was told. "And Charlie, could you put the bags in the car for me please?" Charlie looked at me, then Angela, then likewise, did as he was told. She strode over to me. "I'll only tell you this once. Stay away from my son. See that girl out there? That's his fiancée. They're going to be together. If you don't stay away from him, you'll wish you'd never fecking been born. Crawl back into your bottle, then feck off to wherever you came from."

Her Irish eyes flamed with fire and murder. She turned indignantly, and was gone. Tears stung my eyes as Charlie got back behind his counter. I timidly asked him for what I wanted, and he handed me the paper bag like it was filled with dog shit, taking the money without a word.

Bitch....
I cried myself back to the cottage, feeling very sorry for myself, and reassuring myself that it was better for her to be angry about the fact that I was a vodka-guzzling whore, than to know who I really was. That cheered me slightly.

I made myself a coffee and sat in the parlour, not even wanting to light a fire.
What a mess, a big bloody mess...

About an hour later, there was a knock on the front door.
"FRIEND OR FOE?" I shouted.
"Definitely friend," came Nick's voice in reply.

I opened the door feeling utterly dejected, even though it was Nick.

His smile drooped. "Oh, Lucy. What's happened?"

"Nothing." I let him in, and jumped back onto the sofa.

He sat next to me. "No... Something's wrong."

"I met your mother today, Nick."

"Oh.... Okay, what happened?"

I told him what happened, trying not to be brutal.

"...So, the whole village thinks I'm an alcoholic, slut stealing, man grabber."

He put his arm round me. "I'm sorry. I love my mum, but she's got a very strong personality. She only wants what's best for me, and she'll accept it in the end that Jenny is definitely not best for me."

"Please, Nick, just don't say anything. I'm fine. She's your mother, she's just worried."

"Sometimes she worries too much. I'm not a kid.... I'll decide what I do, and who I see. Ignore the gossip. It's a village, there's always gossip."

He gently kissed my forehead and then got up and started to build a fire.

"I was there buying steaks. I was going to cook them for us," I said.

"Sounds great, if you still feel like it?"

"For you, I'll make the effort. Cooking and I just don't get on. So I never normally feel like it."

I went through to the kitchen while Nick weaved his magic, making me feel calm and protected. I gathered everything I would need for this meal. This time he didn't ask, but I could hear the water running in the shower. He'd come straight from work, without even getting changed. This had to be a sign. He obviously wanted to be near me as much as he could.

I cooked with gusto, putting my all into a feast, of steak, duchess potatoes, and peas. Nick laid the table, each of us left to our own thoughts. The mash was not turning out as creamy as I would have liked. '*Make the potatoes soft and fluffy in order to squeeze through the piping bag,*' said the instructions in the cookbook.

Mine looked grey, lumpy, and tasteless. I added more salt, and half a pint of milk, and mashed away. It seemed very runny, and too thin to put in the piping bag. I decided to just put it on the plate. I was cooking the steaks the way I like them - well done. I left them to sizzle away while I concentrated on the peas. By the time I'd turned back, the steaks had turned black. Yelping, I removed them from the heat.

"Everything okay in there?" Nick called through.

"Yes, fine... in fact it's nearly ready, so do take a seat."

I dished up my gourmet delight and took it to the table, placing Nick's in front of him.

It looks like I'm serving him two tiny black smoker's lungs, with a pale phlegm sauce... Only the peas actually looked like peas. He looked down and said nothing until I'd sat down.

"Thanks, Lucy... it looks, er, interesting."

He managed to cut some steak, and trawled it through what was supposed to be potatoes, before popping it into his mouth. I did the same. Nick's chewing got progressively slower, and a strange expression came over him. He gulped hugely, trying to get it down.

"That's a different sauce... what is it?" he said, finally.

"It's mashed potato."

"Oh…"

He cut some more '*steak*' off and put it in his mouth, with a look of trepidation. He attempted the mercy eating again. To me, the entire meal tasted like an old tramps shoe.

"Do you like it, Nick? Please be honest."

He put down his cutlery. "Really... I don't want to be rude, but I don't think I can eat it."

"Of course not - it's foul."

I put down my knife and fork as well. I felt utterly dejected after this, yet another in a long line of culinary disasters. He was looking up, trying not to laugh.

"Well go on then, let it out," I growled.

And he did. He apologised through his laughter.

"I'm sorry, Lucy, sorry... It's bad."

Then I started to laugh as well. "I told you. I did tell you."

"Look, it's not all bad. Those were the best peas I've ever had."

We carried on laughing as we cleaned the kitchen together, coming to perfect compromises. He liked to wash up, I like to dry. Then I followed him through to the sofa, and we lay down. His arms wrapped round me, and we were intertwined in each other, listening to the fire's noises.

Nick blurted out; "Do you believe in fate, Lucy? ...Destiny?"

"Err... yes, I think I do."

"I'm a firm believer in it. Fate has sent you to me. You could have come anywhere on holiday. Anywhere in the entire world, but you

60

came here." I shifted warily. "Destiny has brought us together."

*I wish it had...,*I thought. *Facebook and erratic planning actually brought us together...* Instead, I said; "Maybe, maybe, but Nick... we're just good friends. Fate brought two good friends together." I sounded totally fake, as if I were rehearsing the lines for a play.

"Friends, mmm... Is that what we really are? I like you, Lucy, a lot. I know there's a problem with Jenny, still, but she'll get the message soon."

He knew I liked him too, but I was resisting it. He assumed it was because of Jenny. How much fight did I have left in me? Each day was becoming harder. My strength was evaporating, my feelings were mounting up. I was glad I was not a man, carrying round my elephantiasis stricken, and desire-laden balls.

"I do like you, Nick, but this is all a bit unexpected... Please, just give me some time."

"Of course... I know there's something holding you back, I can feel it. You'll let me know when you're ready. All I care about, is that for now, I'm here with you."

His arms wrapped even more tightly around me and I sunk into him like a hit of heroin.

I'll never be ready...

DREADED ENCOUNTER

We talked late into the night, sharing dreams and desires. I told Nick about my ex-husband, that we had been married for just a short time, and that I was still searching for something I'd not yet found.

"Well, Lucy. That's *my* good fortune, and I'm glad you're single. That's what I meant about destiny. I could have so easily still have been with Jenny. We were meant to meet. I feel different when I'm with you, like anything is possible. The whole world's opening up. You're an intoxicating drug..."

Wow... nobody has ever said these kind of things to me...

Trouble was, I felt exactly the same. I was a rocket, zooming through space, headed straight for Planet Nick.

I jumped up. "I'll make us a drink."

He smiled. "Do I make you nervous?..." I stuck my tongue out at him, avoiding the question, and skipped to the kitchen. "Lucy, it's late, do you mind if I crash here?" he called through, and then as an afterthought, "On the sofa, of course."

I couldn't have had him in my bed many more times, me being only human, and his magnificent body only millimetres from mine.

Soft, silky flesh, encasing a perfect man. Just too much…

I returned with cocoa. "Yes, Nick, of course you can stay… on the couch."

"Great, I have to get up early. I'm only working the morning with my dad."

"I don't want to be a party pooper, but won't staying here again just make things worse?"

"Like, how?"

"With Jenny, and your mother."

"Lucy, please. I decide what I do. I am twenty-three years old, I'm not a boy. I won't give this up just because other people don't like it."

I admired him even more, if that were possible. He was prepared to fight for his cause, Me, I felt ashamed that his winning prize was totally unworthy of his defence.

"Okay, but really, Nick, I'm not worth all this."

He turned and looked at me incredulously. "How can you say that, Lucy? I know you are." He kissed me gently on the cheek.

"Nick…," was all I could say.

I was falling for him. My bones ached for him. My soul cried out to him. He kissed me again, this time on the mouth. A tender, life-altering kiss, to which I responded.

I'm going to hell…

"I really must go to bed now," I said, pulling away from him, afraid things would go further. "You need to sleep if you've got to get up early… what time is it now?"

He looked at his watch. "Shit. Its 3:30am. Maybe I should."

I slipped over to the little staircase door, saying, "Beddings in the spare bedroom. I like you, Nick, very much. Goodnight."

I went upstairs quickly, like an excited teenager. I jumped into bed and pulled the covers up around my shoulders, protecting myself from desire and love, and rapidly willing myself asleep.

Swinging my legs from the bed and stretching out, I felt good and ready to embrace the day. The few hours I'd slept had been heavy and dreamless. Without opening the curtains, and having no idea of the time, I padded downstairs wearing my usual night-attire - a small, clingy, hardly-worth-bothering-with tee shirt. I sat on the toilet, thinking how much I needed a coffee to shake off the remains of my drowsiness.

Opening the kitchen door, yawning and stretching, I focused properly and saw someone leaning against the kitchen units, arms folded. Nick was making coffee. Now fully awake, I screamed, jumped back, and ran upstairs. I shut the bedroom door, panting as if some madman was making his way slowly up the stairs with an axe.

David. David's here... right downstairs... I was pacing, pacing. *David's here... shit.... No, no, this is not good...* Someone was knocking lightly on the door. *Oh my God, I think I'm going to faint again...*

"Lucy?" It was Nick. My mouth had dried completely and my power of speech had gone. "Lucy, I'm coming in…" He opened the door. I pounced on the bed, trying to control my shaking. Nick sat next to me and put an arm round me. "Lucy... What's wrong?"

"I, I thought no one was here," I lied, squeakily.

"Oh, darling, sorry…" He kissed the side of my head.

Always concerned...

"I overslept. My dad came to pick me up, and I've kinda gotten into your coffee habit. I can't leave home without one now."

"It's just that it scared me, sorry."

"No, it's my fault. Now, why don't you come downstairs, and I'll make you a coffee?"

I looked at him, scared and unable to hide my emotions. "Your *dad* is downstairs, maybe I should meet him some other time, Nick."

"Look, don't worry, he's not like my mother. You'll like him, he's great."

Yeah, I will like him. I've always liked him, and a long time ago, I was desperately in love with him... "I need to get changed, but I'll be down soon," I said.

"Great, see you in a minute." He stood and kissed my head before he left.

Well, Lauren, you have no choice…

I put on clothes, unaware what they were. My brain was in turmoil. I grabbed a brush, back-combed my hair, and mounted it into a huge mass, covering my face with a long fringe.

I'll have to act as if it's the first time I've ever met him... Please let me be able to pull this off... I was breathing deeply as I descended the stairs.

It was one giant step for mankind into the kitchen, and one big trip for me. I caught one foot on top of the other, propelling myself forward. Arms flailing, I fell straight into David. He caught me and helped me steady myself.

"Sorry, oh no...Very sorry. How embarrassing," I mumbled, as Nick chuckled.

"So, Dad... This is Lucy."

David smiled his big warm smile I knew so well. His smiles had broken my heart many times. They'd been full of lies, lurking behind them.

he offered me his hand. "Hi, I'm David, Nick's Father."

"Hello, David. I'm Lucy." I shook hard and firm like a man.

Nick put the coffees on the table.

"So, Lucy, Nick tells me he's been showing you around?"

"Yes, he's been very kind..."

I didn't want to talk. Can you forget a voice? Maybe over time a face becomes faded, but a voice? To me it was as if I'd only heard David's yesterday.

"He's okay," he said, playfully.

"I'd better be more than that if I'm helping you for the day, old man."

Both Father and Son laughed. Their relationship seemed easy, unstrained, and friendly.

"So, Lucy, you like our village then?" David asked.

"Yes, it's very pretty." I was talking as softly as I could.

"Our Lucy's not a great talker when she wakes," Nick announced.

His father looked first at him, then at me.

"Sorry David, it's true. Mornings aren't my best time." I drank my coffee.

"No problem... so you both had a late night then?" His tone was slightly more inquisitive.

"We were just chatting. Sorry I woke up late, Dad."

"Don't worry. Just don't let your mother know I came here and got you. My life won't be worth living."

"Mum's the word." Nick laughed. "...She'll soon chill."

David didn't look so sure. "Anyway, Nick. We'd better go. It'll take a while to get there. We'll probably be gone most of the day."

"Okay, I'll just pop to the bathroom, won't be a sec," Nick said.

I wanted to scream *'NO!, Don't leave us alone!,'* and I started to feel nauseous again. David stared intently at me, as if he was trying to work something out. Alternatively, maybe I was just being totally paranoid? I stood fiddling with my hands, not wanting to meet his gaze.

"So, Lucy, where are you from?"

"Kent…" It was the first place I could think of. "But now I live in London."

"I lived in Surrey. Do you know it?"

Of course I do, that's where we met. Lots of memories from Surrey…

"Umm, no, not really."

Nick came back in, saving me from David's stare. "Okay, lets rock."

David turned to me as he opened the door. "Nice to meet you, Lucy."

"You too, David."

"Nick, I'll see you in the truck," David said, and he was gone.

Nick came over to me. "We won't be back 'till late."

"You need to spend some time at home, Nick." My tone was empty.

"I don't want to, but if you'd rather I did, then I will." He made an unhappy face.

"Yes, Nick, I do."

Seeing David had brought everything crashing down. The only way I could deal with it was to be cold, hard, and horrible.

"Okay," he said, clearly hurt and confused.

"You'd better go, your father's waiting. I need to go to the toilet."

I was pulling further away. He didn't understand. How could he? He closed the door as he left, saying nothing further. Immediately I burst into tears. I cried and cried. It was all so unfair.

Why did Nick have to be David's son? God, I wish I'd never come here…

Sun was streaming in the windows and it was promising to be a glorious day, but my world was dark, full of demons and torment.

I retreated to bed again, pulling the covers over my pain. I looked at the big TV that Nick had made so much effort to bring here, and started crying again, curling up into a safe fetal position. Thankfully, all that crying drained my energy, and I fell into a fitful sleep.

By the time I woke, night had replaced day. My eyes felt sore and puffy, and my mouth was dry. I got some water from the kitchen, and noticed it was ten-thirty.

Shit, I'll never sleep now... Now I really should go...

Meeting David had scared me. Before, I'd wanted to ask him so much. Now, nothing. Meeting Nick had changed everything. How could I just go, and leave him thinking it was his fault.

If I stay, and he finds out, it will destroy so much...

Even in the short time I had just spent with David, I could see what a strong bond he had with his eldest son.

Maybe I am a witch, and should be burned at the stake in the village square?... If all this comes out, Lauren, you probably will be...

Even in my utter despair, I missed Nick. I knew he was now a part of me. Resistance was futile, no matter how much I tried to convince myself otherwise.

I flinched at the sound of knocking. Without asking who it was, I opened the door. Nick stood there, with a big bunch of wild flowers in his hand.

"Sorry... I know it's late, but I was just going to leave these by the door. I saw the light on, and well, I couldn't help but knock."

I was flabbergasted. "I... I..." I was stumbling to find words.

Shunning him the way I had that morning, the last thing I expected was flowers. He held them out in front of him, as if seeking forgiveness for a crime he hadn't committed.

"Nick..." I took the bouquet from him. "They're beautiful." I couldn't be cruel any longer, just to hide my own atrocities. "I'm sorry for the way I was with you. It was unfair."

"I thought you were angry that I scared you."

Angry with him? Not possible...

I leant forward and kissed him on the cheek. "Not enough sleep makes me all Jekyll and Hyde."

I'm glad I'm the potion that keeps you awake." He smiled.

"How come you're always so nice to me, Nick?"

"Dunno... I don't even have to try."

"I still don't get it."

You will, Lucy, you will."

I clutched his gift and our eyes met, locking, searching, holding, wanting.

He ran his hand through his hair. "Anyway, I have to get the truck back. Tomorrow I've got a surprise..." I raised my eyebrows. "No - you'll like it.... I'll pick you up at eleven. I'm driving."

"Okay, I accept. I can't refuse you... Thanks again, Nick, for the flowers."

He walked to the truck, turning halfway.

"You're worth so much more than flowers. Let me give you THE WORLD!"

You already are my world...
I watched him drive away.

PICKNICK

I was determined to be in good spirits when Nick arrived, and started the day by putting all thoughts of David from my mind. I knew he'd been in my dreams, judging by my lack of sleep. The curtains opened to reveal another glorious day.

The calls of the birds against the backdrop of waves lifted me, and I dealt with my morning routine easily. I tried to decide what to wear, as I became excited about seeing Nick, and his surprise. I chose a white halter-neck dress with small daisies printed on it. It ended halfway down my thighs, clinging to all the right bits, and showing a healthy cleavage. I very carefully applied subtle make-up, and I was ready at nearly eleven, timed perfectly so that I had no time to start stressing about everything again.

In the kitchen, I looked at the flowers that I'd arranged in the vase the night before.

Oh, Nick. What have you done to me?...

When I heard the truck, emotion exploded in my stomach, matching the backfiring exhaust. He only managed one knock before I opened the door.

"Wow.... You look as... as…"

"As… as…" I repeated.

"As sexy as hell," he managed to say.

We blushed simultaneously.

"So, all ready?"

"I think so, seeing as I don't know where we're going."

"Well, looking at you, I think you must have been tuning into me again - you couldn't be more perfectly dressed for the occasion." He was constantly charming. "Madam... Your carriage awaits," he said, motioning towards the truck.

Giggling, I went over and climbed in. It was nice being the passenger for a change, able to take in the landscape. The day was already hot and I opened a window to let some breeze in.

"I think today's gonna be a scorcher. Couldn't be more perfect."

"So, mystery man, do I get any clues?"

"No."

"What, not even one?" Our banter was playful.

"Okay, there's water nearby."

"Mmm, you know what happened last time I was near water."

"This is different, trust me."

"I do, but remember, caves also have water in them."

"Of course, you've guessed. Oh no, you've spoilt it now."

I was smiling happily. "Yep, I've busted you."

We sat contentedly, saying nothing for a few moments.

"You're just so easy to be with, Lucy. Most people feel like they have to fill the silences because they feel awkward so they jabber a load of useless shit. With you, it's different. You leave me to my thoughts, without asking me what's wrong every two minutes, or making me feel guilty for not talking. It's refreshing, in fact it's a new sensation for me."

He didn't have to ask if I felt the same.

"Nick, I know exactly what you mean, but sorry to say, I'm usually that silence-filler, babbling on about the weather and the price of knickers and such."

He grinned. "Err... knickers?"

"Yeah, I know that's random."

"So, how much is the price of knickers?"

"Haven't a clue."

We laughed.

"Nearly there now," Nick said, and seconds later pulled into a tiny country lane.

We pulled up by a metal gate, behind which was a beautiful meadow.

Nick cut the engine. "We have to walk from here."

"I'd love to, especially if it's through that meadow."

"Yep, it's all the way across," he said. I sighed as if I'd just eaten a contented meal. "Just need to get some stuff out the back…"

As I got out, the heat of the day struck my body. I looked at the meadow and it seemed utterly still. Not a whisper of wind disturbed the heat. To me, all the grass and flowers looked as if they were asleep, drooping slightly.

Nick spoke from behind me. "Ready? Just need to open the gate."

I turned and saw a huge hamper, which took both his hands to hold.

"Picnic?" I enquired.

"Yes. Good guess."

"You're a cheeky one aren't you?… It's a very big one by the look of it."

"Well, thanks. Maybe it looks bigger 'cause I'm leaning back, but I've had no complaints."

I felt my face redden. "I'm talking about the picnic."

"Yes, of course. Anyway Missy, I'd love to chat more about what a fantastic manhood I have, but my arms are aching, and I need you to open the gate."

I loved his sense of humour. With his helpful instructions, the latch opened with ease. I let him through, and closed it behind us. We left a threshed trail of flattened grass behind us as we walked. The heat was insatiable and beads of sweat ambled down my skin. Nick didn't complain once as he quietly carried the giant wicker box.

We neared the far edge of the meadow, and I realised we were going into the trees. I felt a little less guilty about Nick carrying everything, knowing what a blessed relief the shade of trees can be. The big oaks stood proudly, spreading their UV protecting branches. As we walked, we became cooler. I could smell the forest all around me. A huge green grassy carpet was soft under my tread. I followed Nick, wondering if I should leave a trail of bread. I was looking out for a cottage made of sweets.

71

We came into a small clearing. My eyes opened wide and my jaw dropped. A stunning picturesque scene lay before me. The grass was as green as grass could be. There was one, solitary heavily bowed oak tree. It was plump and succulent, and some of the branches were so heavy they almost touched the floor. To one side a lazy river wound through. It was like Disney. In my mind, I saw bunnies hopping round the tree, and Bambi drinking from the water's edge. Bluebirds were flying round our heads.

Nick put down his heavy load. "So... what do you think?"

I looked at him like a child on Christmas morning. "It's the sort of place that makes you glad to be alive."

He smiled. "I knew you'd like it."

"I don't like it…" I began to run. "I LOVE IT!"

I was running fast, then I span round with my arms out wide, just as Nick's little sister, Maggie, had done that day in the butchers. Nick carried the hamper over to the tree, and I ran up to him, laughing youthfully. He scooped me up and swung me round, making us both dizzy.

"Stop, stop!..." I shouted. He released his hold, and we both wobbled about. "This is more than great, Nick. It's straight out of an Enid Blyton book."

He opened the hamper, pulled a big thick red blanket from the top, and with one deft flick laid it perfectly on the ground.

"Very slick," I said.

"Why, thank-you, I took classes." He grinned.

"Glad I'm in professional hands."

"Please, be seated," Nick said, gesturing towards the blanket.

I sat and kicked off my sandals, and then I lay back and wiggled my toes, looking at a perfect sky through the branches.

Happiness can be fleeting or long lasting. I wanted the latter, wanted that feeling to go on and on. Flocks of birds threaded the sky, swooping and gliding as effortlessly as my heart seemed to be. I could hear Nick unpacking.

"May I look? Or is that a surprise as well?"

"Yes, Madam, you may look."

I rolled on my side, and head in hand watched the banquet unfurl. There was water, a bottle of white wine and orange juice; Baguettes of fresh bread, and a big round cheese that looked like the sun; Another kind of cheese with holes in, like cartoon cheese; Tuna and sweetcorn mayonnaise and salad; Grapes, strawberries and mangoes;

Double cream and natural yogurt. It was a Roman feast, laid out before me.

Finally, Nick closed the hamper, holding a radio. "I think that's everything…"

"Are we staying a week?"

"Very funny."

"No really, Nick, this is amazing. The place, the picnic, and you. It's all totally perfect."

"Then that's all that matters."

He pulled off his top, his body as perfect as this romantic, idyllic setting. I lay down, wishing I'd brought a bikini on this boiling hot day. I tried not to think of my tingling erogenous zones.

"So, you want to eat, have some wine, or just chill for a bit?"

"Chill sounds good, is that okay for you?"

"That's just what I was thinking, but then, being a wicked witch, you would know that."

I sprang bolt upright. *Witch? Burn me for being a witch…* Hadn't I only thought that yesterday?

"Wooohh… so you really are a witch." he said, putting both hands up.

"I did think of that word yesterday." I felt compelled to explain.

He clicked his fingers triumphantly. "I told you, we're interconnected. You can't deny cosmic forces, Lucy."

I lay back down. "Okay, but that *is* a bit creepy."

He lay down next to me and we held hands, as we had done that day by the blue lagoon. My senses were highly charged and I was taking in all the sounds of the forest. Birds called to each other. Water ran, cheerfully thankful the summer had not evaporated it. Small insects buzzed lazily through the hot, thick air, laden down with summer goodness. Nick was breathing deep, deep breaths. I could feel his blood pulsing through his hand. Naturally, my breathing became in time with his. To me it began to feel as if each breath was dense with sexual tension. My heart was going like a champion racehorse.

I sat up. "So… food then?"

"Why, do I make you that nervous?"

"Why do you just come out with what you're thinking? …and I'm not nervous."

"First off, you can't answer a question with a question. Second, I always think it's better to just come right out with it. I hate mind games. It's much better without them. Thirdly, yes you are nervous.

...and fourthly, yep I'd love to eat." He sat up, grinning.

Of course, he was right. The way he thought was always right, no malice, or judgements, only truth.

"Well, I am a bit nervous, but not in a bad way, I just don't know what's going to happen next."

"Don't be nervous about that, Lucy. Be excited. Wine?..." He held up the bottle.

"Only a small one, please. Wine goes straight to my head, especially in the heat."

"Good, it does that to me as well."

Filling the glasses moderately, we drank.

I tried eating something of everything, and couldn't move afterwards.

Rolling on my back, I felt like a beached whale.

"I think if I blink, I'll be sick. Oh, God. That was sooo good."

"It sure is," said Nick, in between mouthfuls.

"Oh no, but really, is it possible to eat so much your stomach splits?" I joked.

"Yeah, but what a way to go…"

Laughing only made it worse.

"Nick, no, stop, really.... I won't be able to move until its dark."

"I'll have to roll you up to the car."

I had to stand, and walk slowly round. "Will you stop making me laugh?"

I was so full of food I didn't know what to do with myself.

Nick was howling with laughter. "You look like you need to lay an egg."

I joined in, taking it a step further by imitating the chicken. He was hitting the ground with his hands, tears rolling down his cheeks.

"No, I have to sit," I said.

"No, you have to lay!"

He joined me in a fit of giggles that proceeded for about fifteen minutes. The food was slowly moving past my stomach. He was so natural, so easy to be with. I didn't have to try in any way. I just had to be myself.

"You're right Nick, about the things you said earlier. I can be myself with you. I don't have to worry.... It's liberating."

"It's freedom," he said.

He held my hand and I closed my eyes, drifting into light

sleep. The sound of music roused me. Nice, soft Balearic house. Lifting myself onto my forearms, I could see all the food had been cleared away. Nick sat cross-legged on the blanket, moving his upper body with the beat. His hands tapped his legs in time with the drums. My movement disturbed him, and he looked at me.

"Sorry, did the music wake you?"

"I wasn't totally asleep. No problem, I love music. Not everything, but I love this."

"Me too... My faves have to be drum and bass, house, techno and Frank Sinatra."

I had to smile. "So, you're not such a country bumpkin... I like all that too. Can you dance?"

"Maybe the bumpkin can."

"I'd love to see that."

"Well, if I dance, then you have to as well."

My food hadn't yet reached its final destination. "Okay, deal."

I felt supremely confident, as the one thing I *can* do is dance. He turned the music up and stood waiting... and waiting.

"Okay, and?..." I demanded.

"Well, I feel a bit silly. I mean it's a bit random... just getting my beats down..."

No one can tell me that having a bad dancer for a boyfriend doesn't bother them. I'm talking about the chicken-slaughtering moonshine dance kind of bad. I hoped that Nick was not that kind of dancer as he began to move, and held my breath, before I slowly released it, mesmerized at what was before me.

Man, this boy can dance...

Bogling, bouncing, hip shaking, stokin'. It was totally infectious, and not wanting to wait my turn, I joined him. I came in close to his body, and we shook together, each anticipating the other's moves. We were both flowing into one another. The music took us and lifted us, until we were embracing the sheer deliciousness of it all. We danced for maybe three or four songs before we sat, both of us out of breath. At exactly the same nanosecond we turned to each other, saying word for word in unison;

"Wow, you can dance!"

Our eyes widened, his were glittering blue. There was no need for any words. I childishly wished we could stay like that forever.

"So, are you hot enough for a dip in the stream? It gets deeper a bit further along," he said, without removing his gaze.

"Well, I don't have a costume, and if I'm a tad hesitant, you couldn't blame me after what happened last time," I mused.

"The water's warmer here. It's not that deep, and on a day like today it'll heat up nicely."

"And my costume?"

"Just take your dress off. It's not like I haven't seen them before." I recalled the day in the garden with the lobsters.

"Oh yes, the day you were perving on me. I remember."

"Okay, if you're not game then. I thought you were more adventurous than that," he said.

Strike to Nick. How could he already know me so well, to know which button to press? I undid the knot on my halter-neck, and it dropped, revealing my breasts. I pulled the rest of the dress down and stepped out of it. This left me in just my Minnie mouse cotton briefs. His gaze luxuriated over me.

"Very nice Minnie you have there," he quipped, releasing me from my embarrassment.

"Thought you'd like her…"

He undid his jeans and took them down, slowly. The Diet Coke advert music – *I just want to make love to you*, came into my head…

He took my hand, and we walked to the refreshing water. To prove to me that it was warm enough, Nick walked straight in, only stopping when it reached his shoulders.

"Look, Lucy, this is as deep as it gets. I can touch the bottom."

Cautiously, I entered the stream. Nick was right, it was pleasantly warm. Now I wanted to go in further.

"Yes, once again you're right… it is nice," I admitted.

The water on my bare flesh felt exotic and tantalizing as it covered my breasts, but still I hadn't reached him.

"Come on," he said, and splashed me.

I splashed him back. The splashes became bigger and more frenzied, signifying our built-up sexual tension.

Why is it that all over the world, splashing is so sexual? I have no idea. If a random stranger splashed you, you'd be pissed off, but between two people who are attracted to each other, the fun of splashing takes on a whole new significance. There were whoops, high-pitched screams, and comments like 'wait 'till I get you!' Soon we had splashed ourselves into each other, and Nick's naked torso was pressed into mine. Playfulness slowed, and serious desire overtook us. Strong arms went round me and my face tilted up to his. His hand slid up my neck, fingers running through my hair. Our lips came together, at first tenderly, then harder as our denied passion overflowed. I pulled away from him. If I didn't stop now, I would just let it ALL happen. I felt as if I'd been sniffing poppers, amyl nitrate. Every wanton vessel open, my blood was glowing.

"Race you back to the tree," I said, splashing him one last time, and heading out of the water as fast as I could.

"Oi, not fair!" He started after me.

I got there before him easily. My normally healthy exercise routine had some advantages. Nick crashed down onto the blanket, only seconds behind me. He caught his breath before speaking.

"So, you can run."

"Faster than you, it would seem."

He tickled me, taking me to the floor. Then he lay on his side, his hand on my stomach.

"Have you ever been in love, Lucy?"

His question was totally unexpected. I decided to play the truth card. "Yes, once."

"Your husband?"

"No, when I was young."

"Have you been in love since?"

"Er... No." All this love talk was making me feel uncomfortable.

"Is that why you're searching for love?" Nick's probing was getting way too sharp.

"Well, it was me that finally finished it. I gave love, and it was misused and painfully under-valued. So I withdrew it. I'm not searching for an old love full of hurtful secrets, but it did teach me how I think love *should* be. I've never found it. I don't want to waste it on false suitors - that takes too much from me."

"How do you think love should be, Lucy?"

"Unconditional, sexy, fun... best friends, happy..."

Nick bent forward and kissed me on the lips. "I think you're a genius of love. Couldn't have put it better myself."

"Were you in love with Jenny?"

"I thought I was. You judge love on what's around you, but for me it needs to be real, not just acted out. I'm glad I worked it out in time, before it went too far."

"What's your definition of love then, Nick?"

"That's easy... Someone that values another's spiritual growth, truly loves them."

I thought about it. "Good way to put it. No-one ever valued me like that."

"Then maybe it wasn't love."

"Anyway, young love rarely lasts, even though it lurks in your heart forever."

"My parents have been together for quite a long time."

I flinched inside. I didn't want to hear about them, and spoil all this, but my curiosity got the better of me.

"Do you think they are in love?"

He tilted his head, deep in thought. "In general, I think they are. My dad's easy-going. I suppose it's because my mum's got such a strong personality. Sometimes though, I think my dad... oh, I don't know. Anyway let's not talk about them."

Thank heavens he can feel what I'm thinking...

The sun had begun its daily descent, and a light breeze cooled my skin.

"I think I'll put my dress on, I'm getting a bit chilly."

"Shame... actually it is a bit cold now."

I threw his jeans at him. "You too, Country boy."

He caught them. "Technically, I'm a man."

My voice grew tender. "But with the face of a beautiful boy."

He ran his hand through his hair and got dressed.

"Do you have to get the truck back?"

"No, not till tomorrow. I have ta help me ma." It was the first time he'd used an Irish accent. "Well, it does help to ham it up, especially if I want to soften her up..." He shifted guiltily. "Can we stay and watch the sunset then?"

We sat on the blanket, and enveloped ourselves within it. Nick's arm was round me, his head on my shoulder. Together we were peacefully, silently, saying goodbye to a day we wanted to keep. We stayed quiet on the journey back, catching snatched glances at each other. A day like this, our first kiss... I knew what would normally happen next. A dense smog of heightened sexual tension encased me.

We arrived at the cottage and started going through the motions to make us comfy. Nick lit the fire, while I made hot chocolate. He was sitting languidly on the sofa when I brought them in. I sat down by his feet, his strong right hand massaging the back of my neck as I stared at the fire. Still, neither of us dared say anything. I sipped my chocolate until I was unable to stand it any longer.

"Are you staying tonight?"

"If you want me to…"

I took a big gulp. "I suppose the main question is, where are you going to sleep?"

"Where would you like me to sleep?"

"No, no, you can't answer a question with a question. You just broke your own rule."

"Okay you're right. I'd like to stay with you."

I looked at him. "I would like that, but Jim-jams are mandatory."

"Don't have any."

"Well, it'll have to be jeans then."

"Not very comfy, but I accept."

I turned back to the fire. "How can it be so cold tonight when the day was so hot?"

"Probably a storm coming."

I scoffed at him. "Yeah, of course."

"How would you know, City girl?"

"We'll see."

"So, do you feel like crashing yet?" he asked.

"Yeah… I'd better find some decent PJ's though."

"I like your usual nightwear."

"You would." I stood and took his hand. "Let's go."

In a short while, Nick was in my bed. I chose a long shirt, turned the light off, and got in. He coiled round me.

"Nick?"

"Yes, Lucy?"

"Today meant a lot to me. You made it special."

He kissed my neck gently. The wanting was tangible.

"Goodnight," I said, shutting my eyes, knowing I'd have to make myself go to sleep.

"Goodnight. Sweet dreams."

They are if you're in them…

If only I'd known that the next day was to be a living nightmare.

INTO THE LION'S DEN

I could feel he was no longer beside me, before I even opened my eyes. It seemed I hadn't had to force myself to sleep after all. The country air was a natural valium, sending me deep into unconsciousness. I wished it could be bottled. I padded downstairs to find Nick, cooking and making coffee in the kitchen.

"Ahh, your Ladyship, you're up then?" He winked at me, frying pan in hand. Bacon and eggs sizzled away. "Take a seat at the table then, it's nearly done."

Nodding and plodding, I did as I was told. The table was all set out with jams, marmalade, toast, and oranges. Nick brought the plates out, then the coffee.

"There, that's it," he said, as he sat.

I sipped coffee, and revived my humanity. "You'd be a gay man's dream, Nick."

"Always glad to serve the community."

I smiled at his wryness. He let me be while we breakfasted. He knew I needed to slide into the day, not be pushed into it. On my second cup of coffee, he approached me.

"Lucy?"

"Mmm?" I replied, my mouth full of toast.

"Well, I was thinking about something…"

"Mmmm?"

"I need to go home for about twenty minutes."

"Mmmm."

"Well, I'd love you to come with me."

I choked on the toast, as it lodged in my throat.

"You could follow me in Maisie. I have to give the truck back."

I finished my coughing fit. "Sorry, Nick. I think that's a bit much. I'm the scarlet woman. I'll just wait here."

He looked disappointed. "Well, it's only my mum. My brothers will be there, and Maggie, who you briefly met in the butchers. I really would like you to meet them. Everyone has to get used to the fact that Jenny and I are no longer together."

"And you want to put me through that, just so you can prove a point?" My voice was sharp.

He looked hurt. "I wouldn't be so cruel, just to prove something…" And then as an afterthought; "Anyway, I'm proud to be seen with you, not ashamed."

Any other family or parents, of course I wouldn't have minded, but for me, this was like going to dinner at the Manson's house.

"Nick, I'm a little old to be going round to meet parents."

We hadn't yet talked about my age. Of course, he knew I was older, but not twenty odd years. He hadn't asked, and I certainly wasn't going to volunteer that information.

"I don't care how old you are. You're not coming to meet my parents, just to meet my family and to have a small look into my world," he said.

I looked at him, and he looked so dejected because of my fears. It tore at me.

"Well… if you're sure it'll be quick…"

"Great." He smiled as he got up, came over to me, and kissed me on the head. "Don't worry, you're with me, I'll protect you."

But who will protect me from myself?…

Following Nick in Maisie, my knuckles turned white as I gripped the steering wheel.

Why are you doing this, Lauren?…

Once again, insanity had overtaken me. I knew that Nick would probably have done anything for me, which is why I was doing this. Last time it had been a nice quick encounter with David. I was increasing my chances of being recognised a million fold by going to Nick's house. I was hitting the steering wheel, talking out loud. "Shit! Shit! Shit!..." My foot joined in, stamping on the floor. "Shit! Shit! Shit!..." The rest of the way was spent shitting, of course only in a metaphorical sense.

We pulled into a gravel courtyard. It was very well kept, with pot plants and flowerbeds all carefully attended to. Garden steps led up to a patio on which sat tables and chairs with red and white parasols, closed tightly in preparation for the dark clouds that gathered. The big white Victorian doorway was garnished with a hanging basket either side. Red roses grew down the side of the house. It was a picture of calm and tranquillity

Nick took the truck to the side of the house, and I followed. We both cut our engines. I took deep breaths, emitted a couple more '*Shit!*'s, and managed to replace my smile, just as Nick got to my door. I opened it and got out as if the air itself might kill me.

"Lucy, really, It's safe… We always go in our house at the back…"

I must have looked uncomprehending.

"Well, the front part is the bed and breakfast."

We walked round the corner and up to a little white porch. Nick pushed the door, sighing when it didn't open.

They are making him knock...

That morning's breakfast began to grumble in my gullet. As the door flew open to reveal Angela, the grumble became a rumble.

"Nick…" Her green serpent's eyes narrowed into slits upon spotting me. She spoke directly to Nick. "Yuv some tars on yer bringin her ere."

"Ma, please. Lucy's my friend, be nice."

Angela focused fully on me, looking at me as if I actually *had* been shitting all the way there. She opened her door further to let the giant shit pass, and I went through, fighting down nausea. We entered a big kitchen, the complete opposite to the serene facade at the front entrance. A large table, which could seat eight, took pride of place in the centre of the room. Sitting in one of the chairs was a teenage boy with short, wiry rust-red hair, staring down at something he was reading. Maggie was singing and running round the table. Mrs. Tuffle from the cream teas shop appeared to be making cakes. An adolescent boy was searching the fridge, his back to me. The radio was playing. Nick threw the truck keys on the table. Angela was silent and staring, boiling. Maggie stopped at the sound of the keys.

"Nick! It's Nick!" she cried, running gleefully to him.

The boy at the fridge turned, and seeing me, raised his eyebrows. Nick held Maggie in his arms. Children obviously loved him, just like I was beginning to.

"Lucy, this is Josh, my brother."

Josh closed the fridge with his elbow, his arms full of food.

He smiled clumsily. "Hi, I would shake, but…" He looked down. "kinda full."

All I could do was nod as he made his way to the table past Angela, and Mrs. Tuffle. Both women were now eyeing me grittily. As Josh sat down, he seemed tense, spilling his cargo and blowing his fringe. My chest and throat were burning.

"That's Kieran." Nick said, motioning towards the reading boy.

Without taking his eyes from the page, Kieran made a peace V-sign in acknowledgement.

David came into the kitchen, and I started to gag involuntarily. I pushed it back down, and then reached again. It sounded like a very old duck trying his mating call for one last time. David stopped for a moment.

"Hi, Lucy," he said, on his way to the fridge.

All the while, my duck sounds continued. All eyes were now upon me, apart from David's.

The last duck call was unsuccessful, and the sick won, travelling up into, and out of, my mouth. Unable to run to a bathroom I had never been to, I frantically put my hands over my mouth. Spotting the sink, I ran over to it as my hands filled with vomit, which sprayed through my fingers and dripped a trail on the floor. I released the rest into the sink, where it splattered up the sides, while I screamed like a braying donkey at the plughole, amid big gut-wrenching heaves.

Still, I was conscious of what was being said behind me.

"That'll be the alcohol." *(Angela)*
A lot of tutting.
Nick chastised his mum. "Ma, will you leave it?"
"The nerve of her…" *More tutting. (Mrs. Tuffle)*
"Maggie, come here." *(Josh)*

I felt an arm around my shoulder.

"Are you alright, Lucy?"

"Yes, sorry, I'll be alright in a minute."

"Why is the lady sick?" Maggie enquired.

"Because she's a -"

"Ma, that's enough..." interjected Nick. "Lucy's sick, Maggie, because she had too many buns for breakfast."

"I like buns, and fairies."

Nick turned the tap, and I cleaned my mouth and sipped some water.

"I'm not feckin' cleanin' that up," Angela announced.

"I'll do it Ma, then we'll go and fix that roof, eh, Dad?" Nick took me over to the table, and sat me opposite his father. I kept my head down. "Dad?..."

"Sorry. What, son?"

"Do the roof, for Mum, now."

"Oh yes, fine. Shouldn't take too long."

"Gonna be a storm, an' it needs doin'," joined in Mrs. Tuffle.

"Yep, best get it done." David stood.

Nick bent down. "I won't be long. You okay?"

I tilted my head slightly, so I could see him through my hair. "Yeah, honestly, I'm fine."

Angela left the room with the men, and Kieran looked up at me.

"That was phat." He returned to his reading.

It was the first glimpse I'd got of his face. He had kind eyes, unlike his mother's, and a fuller face, with freckles tumbling across it. A totally cheeky look.

"Maggie, come over here and help us make cakes." Mrs. Tuffle held out her arms.

Maggie climbed off Josh's lap, narrowly avoiding the trail of sick. Nick was back swiftly, with a mop and bucket, and I sat, ashamed, as he cleaned, and then kissed me on the cheek before darting out again.

Josh leant across the table, his voice a whisper. "So, you and Nick, eh?"

I half looked at him. "Well…"

He leant further forward. "It's okay…" He eyed Mrs. Tuffle. "I didn't like Jenny anyway. Not right for Nick."

He sat back again. Josh's eyes were the palest blue, with flecks of grey. Caramel hair flopped over his eyes.

Kieran got up lazily, and went out of a different door.

"He's only sixteen, he only really cares about his Xbox games," Josh informed me.

Maggie giggled under Mrs. Tuffle's care, and time inched its way forward. No one else spoke. Loud groans came from my empty stomach, and echoed round the room. I kept my head down, hiding, feeling like a naughty five year old. Maybe in my fucked up psyche, this was some kind of self-imposed penance. I figured I probably deserved to feel like this.

Oh, Nick, please hurry up...

A door opened, which caused me to look up and wish I hadn't.

Jenny! Great, does it get any better than this? Yes, this is my karma...

I was the first thing she saw. Once more, she was totally composed. I'm sure that even if she'd walked in to find a naked man playing a flute through his penis, she wouldn't have flinched outwardly.

Perfect Jenny...

Josh was the first to say hello to her, before shooting me a sympathetic look that said '*Sorry, good luck, and bon voyage.*' I was officially in Hell.

"Hello, Lucy," she said tightly.

"Hello, Jenny." I was glad I had no more vomit in me, or I would have brought it back up.

Mrs. Tuffle swung round, greeting her like a long lost friend. "Jenny, my lovely. What a nice surprise. Let me make you a cup of tea." She wiped her hands on her apron as she went to the stove.

Jenny sat down primly.

Maggie turned to her. "Jenny, I make cakes."

Jenny beamed overly at the child. "Well done, Maggie."

Maggie turned her attention back to her cakes, balancing on a chair to reach the work surfaces. Mrs. Tuffle was making tea for Jenny. I'd not even been offered a cup of spit.

A door opened, and in came Nick, Angela, and David. Angela was enthralled to see Jenny, and went over to her, offering hugs and kisses.

Nick straightened. "Hello, Jenny."

"Nick," she replied, gushily.

Nick turned to his father. "So we'll do some more, another day?"

"Yep. Best see what damage the storm does as well."

"Cup of tea, Nick?" asked Mrs. Tuffle.

"No thanks, we're going now."

Maggie stopped and turned, speaking to no one in particular; "The lady was sick, she had too many buns."

"We know, Maggie." David said.

"Nick kissed her better."

BANG! Down came the hammer. Death penalty for this one, milord. All eyes were now burning into my flesh, except Josh, who'd now assumed my previous head-down pose. I was at an axe murderer's convention, and I'd forgotten my axe. If I'd remembered it, the child would have been the first to get it. I was heating the room with the red I'd turned.

"Maggie, it was a friendly kiss..." Nick replied. "Anyway, we're off now."

I stood quickly, knocking my chair over.

"Oh!..." I spun on the ball of my foot, and slipping on the still-wet floor, both legs went under the table.

Nick got to me a split second too late, as my throat smacked on a strut. Pain exploded in my windpipe, and guttural pig noises came from my mouth.

Nick helped me up, and I squealed "Goodbye..." as he guided me outside to the porch.

The pain of embarrassment racked me. I'd made a sensational entrance, and exit, one I was sure they wouldn't forget in a hurry.

Lauren, the travelling clown...

We went to the car, and Nick put his arm round me, kissing the side of my head.

"Oh, baby, I'm so sorry I put you through that..." It wasn't his fault, but I shrugged him off, angry at myself. "Lucy, okay, you were right. It was a bad idea to come here." He stood before me holding my shoulders. "Can you forgive me? Could I be your willing servant?"

Oh, Nick. You're going to break my heart... I could only grunt in response, the pain in my throat was still too much.

"I hope that grunt means you forgive me."

86

His normally relaxed face was ridden with lines. I nodded.

He was breathing heavily. "Good. Do you want me to drive?"

I did, and handed over the keys, no words or nodding necessary. I tried speech, but the pain made me give up.

"Well, I think that went really well." Nick said confidently, as we set off.

I turned to him incredulously, before I noticed his huge smile. Nick began to laugh. My laugh started as small wheezes, and built up to a crescendo of hound-dog barks. I put my hand across my throat, hoping it would offer some relief.

As we neared the cottage, Nick looked at the sky, concernedly. "Good job we're nearly there, it's black as bog up there."

It was. The day was very angry, the Gods badly bruised. As soon as I got out the car the cold bit at me. The trees creaked in the wind as both of us ran into the cottage. The temperature had dropped dramatically, especially as the day before had been continental.

"I'll light a fire - it's freezing," Nick said.

I cavewoman-ugged at him, meaning - "Yes." Big thick jumpers were upstairs, and I wanted to get them. Pointing up, I 'ugged' again at Nick.

He looked up. "You want to go upstairs?"

I nodded, pointed at him, then myself, and pulled at my top.

"Ahh, you want us to go upstairs and take our clothes off?"

I hit him playfully on the arm.

"Hadn't I better wait for your throat to be better first?" he joked, clearly bemused.

I made a face at him as I went.

Upstairs, I sat on the bed and gaped out at the sky. It was as black as the blood that ran through my veins. For, if I'd been decent, moral, and admirable, I would have ended it all then.

However, I am none of the above. Lauren is faulty, imperfect, and downright dangerous. Storms rage and love is made...

Sexy thunder rumbled in time with the throbbing in my throat. *Oh well, sucking cock's off the menu...*

I was trapped in the cottage with Nick, listening to a voluptuous, arousing storm. Rain pelted the windows, assisted by a strong, healthy wind. It sounded to me like small stones were being thrown at the glass.

What a day.... Shit, not even a day, just a morning...

Most of the day was still left.

Did David know it was me or not?...

When Maggie had announced that Nick had kissed me, David had turned rapidly to look.

However, this puking queen was in no fit state to analyse it correctly.

The rain was by now torrential.

"Lucy...Lucy?" Nick called up to me.

Still unable to evoke the power of speech, I stood and went downstairs. It was going to be a long day.

THE STORM

An hour later, sitting by the fire gargling salt-water, my throat started to feel better. My father was always a firm believer that salt-water cures any ailment, and on this particular occasion, it did.

Nick made us a coffee, but I was still unable to swallow properly. We both sat on the couch and observed the storm. A real fire holds many comforts, and being there in the cottage with Nick diminished my foreboding. Lightning snaked through the sky, momentarily lighting up the garden like a black and white postcard.

"It's awesome," Nick awed.

"Agee."

"Is that 'agreed'?"

I nodded.

"Good job I can interpret 'Lucy language'. I've had to do it a few times now."

"Orry."

"Sorry?"

I nodded again, and we both smiled.

"Still, I could have some fun, with you not being able to talk."

I shook my head and my finger.

"Unh, unh, unh…" I pointed to his balls, and my fingers imitated scissors.

"Whoa there!" He covered them protectively with both hands. "Are you angry at me for this morning?"

'NO,' I shook.

"Not at all?"

'No.'

Smiling, he looked back out the window. On a day like that one, there was a drink that called out to me.

Whisky…

The devil's spunk, my grandma called it. I got up and hunted in the kitchen cupboard, found the treasure, and two glasses, and put it all down on the coffee table. I turned the bottle so the label faced Nick.

"Glen Fiddich whisky, eh? Perfect day for it. Best of gear, too," he said.

I felt we were perfectly tuned, thinking as one. I handed him a glass and poured us both a healthy portion.

He raised his. "To Storms."

I couldn't have said it better, in fact, I couldn't have said it at all, but that was beside the point. Sipping the devil's jizz felt real good. It was the equivalent of dropping a lit match into a pool of petrol. *Whisky - BOOM!* Both of us coughed, like a satisfied cigar-smoker would, and our eyes were back on the storm. Alcohol coated my throat, soothing my pain, and numbing my aching brain.

Nick shuffled up the sofa on his knees next to me, and drinks in hand, we viewed an opera of angry weather, as my loins tingled.

I finally regained my voice enough to talk. "I don't suppose you can go home in this weather. You haven't even got your bike."

"Well, unless I can fly on a broomstick, I think I might have to stay. Can we upgrade to underpants, though? Jeans aren't the most comfortable thing to sleep in."

I managed a real giggle. *You're flirting again, Lauren...*

We finished our drinks, and I poured us both another.

"Well, Lucy, on a day like today, there's only one thing to do."

Fuck?..., was my first thought. I quashed it down. "What's that?"

"Watch movies."

Whew! Yes, of course… I nodded in agreement.

We took our drinks upstairs, chose some thrillers, kicked off our shoes, and got under the duvet. Two movies later, I had an empty glass and a fluffy head. The wind was shrieking and the old windows were rattling in their frames. Lastly, we watched Fatal Attraction. I'd already explained to Nick that it was an old film, about a man who cheats on his wife.

"It all goes tits-up for him, and somewhere along the way, a bunny gets boiled. Classic viewing…"

When the movie ended, Nick got out of the bed, stretching as he went over to the telly.

"Do you think Jenny is a bunny boiler?" I asked.

Slightly drunk, he giggled girlishly. "Yeah, but she's a lot subtler than that."

"Will she ever let you go, Nick?"

"She's got no choice, but let's not get a bunny just in case."

My laughter sounded coarse, but I was glad to have my speech back.

"I like your new voice, Lucy. Deep, and very sexy."

"It's easy to obtain, just pole-vault with your throat on a hard chair."

I sounded like I was a ninety year old who had smoked fifty a day, their whole life.

Tears rolled down his cheeks. "God, stop... you can always make me laugh, Lucy, always."

For a second a wave of seriousness ran through me.

I hope so Nick...

I only wanted to make him happy.

"So, more films, whisky, or... or?.." He ran his hand through his hair.

"Whisky - yes. More films - no. Let's have a break."

"Maybe it would be nice to go down by the fire?" Nick suggested.

"Good idea."

On the way out of the bedroom, he turned to me. "I hope no bunnies ever get boiled on my account."

If only he'd known that his own father had been responsible for a few hot bunnies. Back when David had actually finally realized I meant what I had said - We were over. He didn't react well on the countless occasions we'd broken up. I always relented when he wanted me back, while people around me mocked my devotion to him. After four years, I'd had enough. He sent cards, flowers and gifts, but it was all too late. I'd locked myself away, only leaving my parent's house to go to work and back.

It was an early lesson in massive self-discipline. Over all those years, of all the drugs I'd taken, David had been the hardest to give up. A huge hypodermic shot, straight into my vein. Then I went cold turkey.

About four months after David, I met a really cute guy, whose name I will never remember, and said yes to a drink with him.

My parent's house was a small cottage, the last one in a row. The boy picked me up, and I'd been vaguely of headlights flaring as we set off. I chatted, while he drove.

After a while, the boy said, "Someone's following us."

"What?.. No, out here?" I said.

He was insistent.

Turning, I saw David's car behind. "Shit! It's my ex."

The boy stopped his car. "Right, I'm not 'avin this."

Looking back again, I saw David exit the car, a baseball bat in his hand.

"Please, just get back in the car…" I appealed to the boy, who was halfway out his door.

The boy took one look, and thought; *Shit, it's not worth all this...*

He got back in and drove like a nutter, losing David, and after that night, I never saw the boy again.

However, the problem of David stalking me had persisted. Now he wanted what he couldn't have. He realised all too late that he was truly in love with me. It eventually became such a problem, the police had to get involved.

Looking at him now, how he'd been here in Devon, It was hard to imagine him ever being like that. David had definitely been *my* bunny boiler. I shivered. I didn't want to think of him. I went downstairs to join Nick.

"Been in another wibbly wobbly world of your own?" he asked, full length on the sofa, one hand behind his head.

Shit. He really is stunning...

"Want more whisky?"

At that point, I should have said no. Instead, I said - "Yes, but not too much…"

Loose lips sink ships, and open up your vagina. The whole house moaned and groaned, complaining about the weather. Nick poured more whisky, then added more wood to the fire, making it roar. Then he wobbled over to where I'd sat down.

"Do you think I'd like London, Lucy?"

"Mmm. I don't know. Mmm, yes, as it's you, I think you would. Why?"

"I was just curious. It'd be a good way to get away from Jenny."

92

"Yes, but would you have to go all that way?"

"No, but... well it would help me if I knew someone that lived there," he angled, but the penny wasn't dropping.

Alcohol clouded my perception. "Yes, you're right, it would."

He jumped on me. "Are you doing this deliberately?"

"What?"

"Exactly *that*."

"What's *that*?"

He fell back laughing, then sat up, more serious. "Lucy?"

"Yes?"

"You're so beautiful."

My breath caught in my damaged throat at the way he said it. He sounded sensitive, truthful, and loving. I kissed him on the lips.

"Touché...," I whispered. *Quick, make yourself busy, Lauren...* I sprung up. "So... food?"

"Mm, I'm hungry."

"Good. What for?"

"You!..."

He pounced on me and I offered up a small squeal of resistance. Like a cat catching a mouse, he pinned me down on the sofa. A gleam in his eye meant that he would play with his prey before eating it. I kicked my legs, at least attempting to play the indignant card. His hungry lips crushed down onto mine. Denied fruits taste so much sweeter when finally allowed. Soft lips met probing tongues as our bodies ground together. This alone was sheer ecstasy.

Welcome to the snail trail express..., my knickers thought.

Our chests heaved with passion as I pushed him away, panting.

"I think I need food."

"Food, now?"

"Yes."

"You're definitely unpredictable, Lucy. I know something's up. I can feel you want me, but if food is the excuse, then okay, food it is."

I didn't really want food, Cock au vin was what I wanted.

But I'll make things so much worse if I sleep with him. If I didn't know who he was, it would have already happened. Nevertheless, I do...

I felt like Demi Moore, would you sleep with the son of the love of your life, for free?

Yes, but she's also in love.- I'm not in love..., I told myself sternly and silently.

Nick was already in the kitchen. "So, what does the queen desire?"

"Toast?" It was the first thing that came into my head.

"That's not so difficult."

"I just need something to soak up the alcohol."

In his whisky-ridden state, he burnt the toast, spreading on mayonnaise instead of butter.

"Sorry, I'm not that good on alcohol," he explained.

We burst out laughing, and ate the toast anyway. When you've had a drink it seems any food is worthy of eating. Scabby old dead cat's bum?... Lovely, make mine well done.

"What's the time?" I enquired.

"Seven-thirty."

"I think I'll take a bath."

"Alone?"

"Yes, alone!"

I ran a hot bath to clear my senses. It filled the bathroom with steam, and I lowered myself into the hot water.

Ooh, that's good...

I lay there listening to the sea crashing, and thunder bombing the sky. The wind sounded like a thousand screaming banshees. The hot water soaked my body. It was definitely doing something to my senses. My erotic ones. The water became like Nick's tongue moving over my skin. Strong imaginary hands gripped my inner thighs, and pushed down on my pelvis. My eyes were closed, my hands on my breasts, and my fingers teased my nipples before heading down my flat stomach. My hand stopped on my clit, and I gasped, as I thought of Nick. For a split second, my eyes opened with pleasure, and there He was, standing next to the bath with a drink in his hand. My throat didn't allow me to scream, instead I could only cry like a tired old cockerel. My arms splashed down, spraying water. He didn't move.

"Nick, I, I... what are you doing in here?"

"Watching you get it on, apparently..."

I was indignant, having been caught. "Well, you could have knocked."

"Knocked one out, maybe!" He roared out laughing at his own joke.

I scooped up a great handful of water, and soaked him. Now, I was laughing.

"That should help." He placed his glass down, and started taking off his jeans.

"What are you doing?"

"Well, I'm wet now."

Wearing only his Calvin's, he jumped into the bath. I squealed, knowing my powers of abstinence would hold no longer. He lay back, and his abdominals rippled as he retrieved his drink. He offered it to me first, and I accepted it, bravado taking over. Draped against the taps, he surveyed me as if I were his last meal.

"I don't know how old you are, but no-one has a body like that when they're old," he said.

"I'm sixty, but I eat a lot of vegetables."

I was carefree and elated, soaring through a galaxy of delight. Our toes were touching. Nick wiggled his, and I reciprocated.

"Bring it on, Granny."

He gulped down some whisky and handed it back to me. I downed it in one. Nothing like the good excuse of alcohol. The words '*I was pissed*' cover almost every conceivable eventuality. '*I can't believe I sucked off that donkey, but I was so drunk...*'. A naked man in the park with a gun, shoots and kills four ducks. He is believed to be legless. A woman sits on the pavement in a busy high street, vomiting onto her exposed vagina. Ahh, bless, well she *was* pissed.

So sorry to everyone, but I *was* pissed.

I placed the glass on the floor and stretched my legs, sliding my feet up his torso and resting them on his chest. "Don't mind, do you?"

"Why would I?" Nick replied.

His hands ran along the top of my toes, down the sides of my feet, and slowly up the back of my calves. Even underwater, my skin ignited. I slid my right foot down gently over the front of his Calvin's with whisky courage. Nick's eyes closed, momentarily.

"One of us is over-dressed," I cooed.

He torpedoed himself up, grabbing his pants, and pulling them down and off in a single movement.

Magnificent... Not the feat, but the treat that swings before me... Perfect. Totally, perfectly, prizewinning. If I were Jenny, I would fight 'till the bitter end for him...

He slipped back under the water, throwing his lucky underpants to the floor.

"Like what you see, do you?"

"Yes, it's not often you see something so wonderful." *God, I want him...*

I placed my feet back on his chest, Nick leaned forward, and his hands ran up the front of my thighs. We were staring into each other's eyes, with a hungering thirst.

"Lucy, I've never wanted anything more than you."

I gulped. "The water's getting cold. Let's go and dry off by the fire."

We took a towel each, made our way to the warmth, and stood holding the towels round ourselves. My blood vessels swelled, and my nerve endings fizzed. Mini explosions erupted throughout my body. Outside, a huge bolt of lightning cracked down, symbolically. As if it were a sign, we pounced like panthers onto each other as our towels dropped to the floor, greedily discovering each other. Nick kissed down my neck and ran his hands gently over my breasts, making my nipples stand to attention. His fantastic penis was pressed against my stomach. We were falling in a sexual heap before the fire. Our bodies morphed together, transference of souls bonded together forever. Nick was on top of me, and a tiny voice somewhere inside, was calling to me – *Lauren! Lauren!...*

Mustering every sinew of strength, I stopped him from entering me. He didn't complain, or try to coerce me.

"When you're ready...," he whispered.

For hours, our desire raged, along with the storm. We explored each other, and indulged our cravings. Everything felt different with Nick. He was lavish, transporting me to a place I'd never been before.

I had no idea how we ended up in bed, exhausted, completely fulfilled and at peace. I awoke first. Everything seemed quiet outside, and it was still dark. I sat up and looked down at Nick. There was no point denying it. No point running, hiding, or pretending. I was irrevocably, devastatingly and sensationally in love with him. Something inside me had changed. I didn't know what it was, or how to describe it, but I knew I was looking down at my future. One I couldn't have.

We could run at first light, where no one can spoil this by finding us...

He turned in his sleep onto his side, and put his arm round me. I lay back down, and let the feeling of love caress me back to sleep.

I opened my eyes, and felt as good as Snow White. Now, Nick was looking down at me.

"I'd be a happy man waking up to that face every day," he said.

"Flatterer."

He kissed me. I knew I loved him.

"Storms gone. It's a nice bright day outside. I've had a look round. The old girl's lost a few tiles, but other than that, it's all fine."

My hero... I kissed him back, and flung myself down, delirious with happiness.

"Lucy?" His tone had changed.

"Yes?"

"Lucy, I…"

"Yes?"

"Oh, nothing…"

I raised myself up on my elbows. "Nick, what? Is everything okay?"

"More than okay. I made breakfast. I hope you like chocolate pancakes."

"Mmm, scrummy. They can soak up the whisky."

"You stay here, it's breakfast in bed."

He sprang up like a newborn lamb, and was out the door in a flash.

The Gods can certainly be cruel and unkind, throwing me love, like that. There you go, this will make things more fun...

I was a gladiator in an emotional arena.

When I heard his footsteps, I sat up. He kicked open the door, bearing a tray, and dressed only in his Calvin's. He came over to the bed, his crotch level with me, and it was too delicious not to touch. I stroked his cock, slowly.

He moaned; "That's unfair, I'm holding the tray."

I continued, applying slightly more pressure. "I know."

"Bad girl."

"Maybe I need to be spanked?"

"You will be when…" He was breathing heavily. "…when I put this tray down."

Reluctantly, I stopped. He placed the tray across my legs, ensuring there'd be no more shenanigans from me. We had our coffee, and chocolate pancakes.

"So, I was pretty drunk last night. Nick, did anything happen?"

"Yes. Are you sure you don't remember? It was awful."

I stopped chewing for a moment. Then panic turned to amusement as I realized he was joking, and we continued eating amiably.

"Nick?"

"Yep?"

"You know the plant pot outside the kitchen door?... Well, I'm going to put the key under it. That way there'll be no more knocking, or surprise visitor panics. You can just let yourself in."

"That's a great idea."

We tried to finish breakfast but Lust got in the way. Crockery smashed, and pancakes flew. Nick heard the door. "Someone's knocking…"

"Umm?"

"Lucy, someone's at the door."

Oh, crap. Why does this have to be spoiled?... "I'd better get it. How would it look if you answered the door?"

"Not as good as you."

Light-footed, I went to the door. David stood in front of me. His voice was tight.

"Is Nick here, Lucy?"

I had the sensation I was wetting myself. My mind was unable to form a cohesive sentence.

"Well, is he?"

Panic, panic, lie, run, stab him!... "Yes, he is."

I opened the door to let him in, on automatic pilot. I followed him to the kitchen, and stood, quietly and guiltily, not knowing what to do or say. We both heard Nick's footsteps running down the stairs, and David raised an eyebrow as Nick appeared in the doorway, still only in his underwear, looking like the epitome of radiance.

"Oh. Hi, Dad. Everything okay?..."

David looked from his beaming son to me, then back to Nick. "Not really. We had some bad storm damage. It's at the front of the house, so it's got to be done quick. I've a job on this morning, Nick, so I'll take you home to help your brothers."

"Of course. Give me a few minutes to get dressed. I'll be with you in a bit. I'm sure Lucy will look after you."

I sneaked a glance at David. Noises came from above as Nick

dressed clumsily.

"Bad was it, here?" David asked.

"What?"

"The storm."

"Oh yes... yes, terrible..."

"Bad business."

I had the feeling David wasn't talking about the storm now.

Nick bounced back in. "Okay, ready."

David opened the door to go, and Nick came over to me.

"Don't forget the key," he whispered, and kissed me.

After the truck had pulled away, I put the key under the plant pot. David's surprise visit had made me feel dirty. I wanted another bath. Although, sitting in it, nothing could wash off the sensation of Love. I was reeling from Its power and magnitude.

So this is what it feels like when souls collide...

As I dried myself, there was another knock on the door.

Silly. He's forgotten about the key already...

Towel wrapped round me, I skipped to the door and flung it open.

"Have you..." I stopped in mid-sentence.

It wasn't Nick. David stood before me once more.

DAVID

"Must get dressed," I called over my shoulder, as I bolted breathlessly up the stairs.

Panic gripped me as I threw on some clothes. I had an uneasy feeling about this. When I returned he was still waiting at the door.

"May I come in?" He spoke officiously.

Nodding, I let him pass. In the kitchen, I immediately started banging the cooker much harder than necessary. I busied myself getting cups for drinks.

"Did you forget something?" I asked.

I tried to make myself sound calm, but I knew my voice was giving away my nerves.

"Funnily enough, that's an ironic question," he replied.

I kept my back to him. My hands were shaking as I held the cups.

"Sorry, David, I don't understand."

"I did try to forget. But some things can't be completely forgotten." His voice was soft and reminiscent. "From the first time we met the other day, I've been having a strong sense I've met you before, that I've known you before. I started to think I'd gone mad, I had to chastise myself - '*Not this again, David...*' But, there never was anyone as clumsy as you. The cherry on top, so to speak..." He stopped. I had made myself busy the whole time he'd been speaking. I'd taken the kettle off the boil twice. "...Lauren, please, will you stop that, and turn around?"

As I did, I thought - *Any last requests? Yes please, tell Nick I love him... Maybe not an appropriate thing to share with his father...*

David was in front of me, but I couldn't look him in the eye.

"So, it's real. Not my imagination. It's really you?" he asked. I said nothing. His voice grew harder. "Answer me, Lauren."

I faced the music, and raised my head. "Yes, David. It's me."

Even though he'd known, the confirmation temporarily struck him dumb. All the blood drained from his face, and my heart slowed to a very dull thud.

"I want to sit down." His words came out slowly.

He went through, and sat with his head in his hands. Right then, I wasn't sure of anything. The air around us seemed to have taken on a surreal quality. Slowly, I sat on one of the armchairs. He slapped his hands hard on his legs, making me jump, and his eyes made direct contact with mine.

"I have so many questions, but there are a couple of prominent ones... What the fuck are you doing here? With my Son? This is like a mad fucking dream." He stood violently, making me shrink to the back of my chair, and began to pace. "So many years, Lauren. So many years, without you in my life. Then, out of the fucking blue, you're staying near our village. My Son's here all the time, running round the house in his pants. I've fantasised about meeting you again so many times, but like this? You've got to be fucking joking..." By now, he was almost ranting, like he'd forgotten I was even in the room. He spun, half-demented, staring at me, then composed himself, and sat back down. "What are you doing here, Lauren?"

"I'm here on holiday."

"How did you meet Nick?"

"By accident. He delivered the wood."

David thought for a moment. "Well, you can understand if I'm a little freaked out here."

"Yes, David."

He wrung his hands, once again, his eyes locked intently onto mine, and brimmed with tears, as his whole demeanour changed, and softened.

"You look good. Actually, amazing. Yep, amazing. Still head-turningly beautiful."

"David..."

"I can't really take all this in. A part of me is elated to see you, and another part is devastated that it's really you..." He stood again. "Shit, Lauren, what's going on with you and Nick?"

"We're just friends," I utterly lied.

"This is... oh shit, I don't know. This is so fucked..." More pacing. "You have no idea how long it took me to stop thinking about you, Lauren, and then, Bang! You're right here. Shit..." He threw himself back down. "This is so mythical, so unbelievably random." I shifted uncomfortably. "I put you out of my life. I'm not proud of how I did it, and believe me, it was the hardest thing I've ever had to do. You must have wondered what happened to me?"

I had wondered, for a long time. I remembered that David had been like a magician back then. No matter where I moved, he always found out where I was. He would call, and nearly every time arrange to meet for a drink. We both still got on extremely well, reminiscing fondly and talking about our lives. It's vain to say, but I'd known David was still in love with me. Our rendezvous were fraught with danger with him married to Angela. To him it seemed worth taking the risk. Sometimes we would meet by sheer chance, and if we had the time on those occasions, we would steal a moment for a swift half of lager. These encounters became less and less frequent. It was not fair on David. In addition, the thought of Angela decapitating me and riding through the streets on a horse, holding my head high, did not encourage me.

Two years later, out of the blue David had called. He'd sounded elated, and for me it was nice to hear his voice. We arranged to meet. I turned up at the agreed location, and David did not. It was so unlike him, he'd never stood me up on our previous meets. I sat waiting for nearly two hours, worrying in case he'd had an accident. I had no phone number to call as he shared a phone with Angela, so I couldn't call him. Eventually, realising he wasn't coming, I'd left. That was fourteen years ago. He was right, we hadn't seen each other for sixteen years.

"Lauren... Hello?" He brought me back from my memories.

"Yes, yes I suppose I did wonder what happened to you... I suppose that's why I'm here."

His forehead bunched into heavy thought lines. "Wait, um... that's why you're here? That sounds like you were meant to be here, as if you knew you were coming here?"

"Well..."

"Well what, Lauren?"

"I kind of knew I was coming, but I did need a holiday."

"Mmm, that's a bit vague. I think I'm entitled to a little more than that."

"I tried to find you on the internet. Only to see if you were well, and... stuff."

"And it would appear you succeeded. So let me get this right. You came here to find me, to ask me face to face how I am, and why I didn't turn up in a pub fourteen years ago?"

"Yes." I concurred weakly.

He was angry now, no longer kind, amiable David.

"Let me think, how am I?... well I'm a fucking mess now. Why didn't I meet you that night? Because I didn't want to put myself through more torture. So I cut you out of my life."

Once again he was standing. This information shocked me. Ultimately, I'd always assumed that Angela had found out.

"I always thought it was because of Angela."

"She would have cut my balls off if she'd found out, but don't be so omnipotent, Lauren. It was all me. I was possessed with an obsession about you. I programmed myself to stay away, and put you to the back of my mind. Instead of forever taking prime position at the front. It was my idea to move here, not Angela's. Distance is a good thing, but now, ironically, it's you that has sought me out."

"David, please sit down, you're making me nervous."

"Good. You should feel very nervous, Lauren. You.... You've opened Pandora's box."

Now I felt like I was thirteen again. About to get my period any moment, and break out in spots. Hoping a friend will ring the doorbell, and take me away from it all.

No one is going to save you, Lauren. Suck it up, deal with it...

"So, when in your grand plan were you going to talk face to face with me?... Possibly when my wife found out, or maybe after my eldest son has started to fall in love with you?..." I began to offer some objection, but he raised his hand in a stop sign. "I know my own son very well, thanks, Lauren, and I can see when he's falling in love. Fucking hell, serial love with the same woman. You can't even begin to know what that feels like..." Seeing him like that racked me with guilt. A guilt that came too late. "How did you find me? I'm careful to hide myself from the web."

"I didn't find you, I found Angela on Facebook. Everything's there, photos, house on the map, everything."

He sighed and shook his head.

"You're the only one not on there. I just assumed Angela, being a tincey bit jealous, wouldn't let you," I said.

Wouldn't let me? I'm not a child, Lauren. I know my wife has a strong character, but I'm not led round by my balls."

"Sorry David, I didn't think…"

He didn't allow me to finish my sentence.

"NO. You fucking didn't. Coming here on a fancy. This is my life, Lauren, you can't just fucking pop by, say hi, have a chat… If Angela was to find out who you really are…" He raised his hands and looked at the ceiling, mock-laughing. "…It's not worth fucking thinking about. She might even think we planned it together. Luckily, blind hate for you has clouded her memory."

He sat on the floor, hugging his knees as if he were young again, placing his heavy, burdened head on them. My heart lurched for him. I felt compelled to go to him. Crouched next to him, I placed an arm round his back without thinking. He let me do this only for a comforting moment, then he pulled away, looking confused, his voice barely above a whisper.

"I can't do this, Lauren. It was so hard getting over you. You cannot be in my life at all."

I looked down at him, utterly regretful.

"Sorry is so inadequate, David, but I am. You're right. I didn't think. I got my questions answered really, on Facebook. Your photos looked happy. Still with Angela, more children."

Thinking about this, I'd got a lot of questions answered, but that hadn't been enough.

His face shot up from his hands. "All the info… my children. So you knew Nick was my son?"

"I… I…"

"- knew what he looked like?…" My silence spoke volumes. He rose up further. "Is this a fucking sick joke? Some kind of revenge? …Let me guess, you're the Reaper, and you've come to collect my soul?" He laughed satanically. "Well, this is not how I imagined it would be. Do you know what I'm thinking, Lauren? DO YOU?" he shouted. I shook my head. "Now I've only got one burning question…" He paused. "Have you fucked Nick?… Can you comprehend how fucking sick it makes me feel to ask that question?"

Creeping back to my chair, I looked at my feet and mouse-like, replied; "no."

"No, you don't know how it makes me feel, or no, you haven't fucked Nick?"

It sounded so coarse, dirty and demeaning the way he said it. Nick and I had made love without any actual intercourse taking place at all. To me, it was the most meaningful thing in my life.

"No, I haven't fucked him." I barked.

That made him sit up. "I take it of course, that he doesn't really know who you are?"

"No."

"I want it to remain that way, Lauren. I don't want him coming here anymore."

"How can I stop him?"

"Stop encouraging him...." he shouted. "I saw the way you were dressed when I first came round. You were flirting with him. For God's sake look at you, a Rembrandt of desirability. Your dizziness is intoxicating, Jesus, I should fucking know..." I could not defend the undefendable. "I'll keep him busy with work. How long are you here for?"

"Thirteen more days."

"Shit. ...you'll just have to go early."

My shackles rose. I don't like being told what to do.

"I'll go when I'm ready," I told him curtly.

"I never asked you to come, you're not a guest."

I raised my voice. "I'm not sleeping in your house, David."

He shouted back. "You might as well be. You're fully sleeping in my life though. Stay away from Nick. Keep your mouth shut, or go. If this gets out, my life will be over. It's not a price I want to pay. Please, Lauren, if you've any empathy for me, go."

He stood and walked out, shutting the front door behind him. I heard the truck start, and he was gone.

Wallowing in self-pity after that joyous reunion, I downed two glasses of whisky. Not even able to go upstairs, I fell onto the sofa. Of course, everything David had said was true, and this thought only made me feel worse. Crying into more whisky barely gave a tendril of relief.

I continued with this theme for a couple of hours, exhausted myself, and fell asleep. The rattling of a key in the door awoke me. I hazily remembered leaving it there for Nick.

He bounced in, and straddled me on the sofa.

"Lucy, Lucy, are you awake?"

"Sort of," I croaked.

"Lucy, I tried to tell you something earlier, but I couldn't say it. I love you. I'm in love with you. The words are inadequate to describe how I feel. I want to be with you for infinity, experience my life with you. Spend every breath with you, here on this planet..." He kissed me on the lips. "I Love you."

It was a cruel, sick play. Oh yes, the Gods were really having fun with me now. Tears stung my eyes. David was right, I had to go. There was only one defence I knew of; Cruelty.

"Go home, Nick." I responded coldly.

He sat upright. "What?"

"Go home."

"Ere, hang on a minute, I'm confused dot com. I confess my love to you, and you want me to go home. Well, that's one response I hadn't thought of."

Hating myself, I continued. "Well, just because you tell me you love me... I don't love you, in fact today I've been thinking you shouldn't come over so much."

Sitting stiffly upright, he looked as though he were being lacerated.

"I... I don't get it. You were fine when I left. Now you've been drinking, and by the look of your eyes, crying too."

"Don't analyse me. I don't want your love, I never asked for it."

At that point, he jumped off me as if I had struck him. For the first time I heard anger in his voice.

"No, you didn't ask for it. Is teasing me like fuck also a part of your sick plan?..."

I acted distant, but inside my soul began to wither.

"I don't know what fucking skeletons you've got in your closet, but if you haven't got the balls to tell me... especially as I've told you I love you, which means you can trust me. Maybe I was wrong. You're not worth that kind of love."

He slammed the door on his way out, as huge great sobs of pain poured from my mouth.

I cried until sunrise. Sleep eluded me, prolonging my agony. Not today. I couldn't go today. I'd drunk way too much, and my concentration was about as good as a goldfish in a very small bowl. Time - *Six-thirty*. I wanted to, needed to get out. Without coffee, without changing my clothes and without hope, I slammed the front door behind me.

FISHING WITH ANGUS

Everything was only just waking up. The walk brought me to the village. Birds had just started their morning chatter. A new heat was birthed and projected from the early sun. To me, all the sounds were in monotone, and all the colour was black and white.

On autopilot, I took the second lane behind the Dry Thrush. The lane turned into a beach, scattered with fishing boats. It was totally different here. A hive of activity. Drawn towards it, I continued walking, and wove my way through them, to lots of 'Morn', 'Mornin', and one 'G'day'. I nodded politely, feeling under-dressed without a thick knitted aran sweater on.

A bright green boat caught my eye. I could see the name *'Lovely Maid'* in red, painted on the side. A man was crouching down, brushing stuff from underneath. He turned, as if he had felt someone watching him. Smiling broadly, his red beard was even redder in the bright sun.

Angus... I smiled faintly.

He motioned for me to go over. His little boat seemed very well taken care of.

"Morn' Lucy. This is my beauty."

"Lovely, Angus."

"So, what you doin up so early? Wanderin' roun' the beach as if a spirit was callin' to you."

"I just couldn't sleep. Are you going out fishing?"

"Yep."

"Can I come with you?"

He pushed up his flat cap and scratched his head. "What, just you and me?"

"Yes."

"Dressed like that?"

"Yes."

"Well... I don't normally take anyone with, less its Thomas, or Seth."

I sighed and kicked at the sand. "Oh... that's okay."

He sensed I was a bit lost. "Well... alright, but just don't scare the fish."

How could I?..., I thought, but didn't remark on it.

Ten minutes out to sea, I began to wonder what I had been thinking. Boats and I had a chequered background. I'd had no coffee, sleep, or food, and I had the wrong clothing on. Angus held the rudder that was attached to the small engine, as we bounced uncomfortably over the waves. His nets were at my feet, along with a small anchor. A bucket of bait sat near Angus. He constantly looked round, every now and then chancing a glance at me, checking I was alright. His fisherman's intuition told him where to drop anchor, and he cast his net. Then we just sat and waited. Not even ten minutes passed, before I was wishing I wasn't there.

"I don't know why I'm here, Angus."

"Umm."

"You see, I've got myself in a bit of a pickle."

"Mmm."

"It's Nick."

"Nice boy, Nick," he said, raising an eyebrow.

"I know. Oh, I know, that's the trouble Angus, I love him. I'm totally, emphatically in love. This has never happened to me before, not like this... never like this."

"Where's the pickle then?" He watched the water while he spoke, looking for signs of life.

"The pickle is huge. Why am I telling you all this?..." Not waiting for a response, I carried on, about to unburden myself on this old man, surrounded by a listing expanse of sea. "Well, it's Nick's father, David. I know him very well. That's why I'm here. Not in this boat, I mean here in the village..." I was babbling now. "He was my, well, my first ever love. Over thirty years ago. I first met him when I was fourteen. For me, it was love at first sight. It ended badly, but afterwards we did eventually salvage a good friendship... but now I've met Nick. All I wanted to know was if David was happy. It's all gone horribly, horribly wrong."

Angus spat in the bucket. "Best not go lookin, you might not like what you find."

"I know," I wailed loudly.

"Shh, you'll scare the fish."

"Sorry Angus, I'm forty-three, and I feel like puberty is attacking me."

He looked right at me. "You? You're that age? Well, I'll be. City life must agree with you. I had you pegged for about thirty."

"Thank-you, you're most gracious."

"Well, I'll be..." He seemed more shocked about my age than anything else I'd told him. "But yes, it is a bit of a pickle. Shouldn't you be telling all this to Nick?"

"Yes, but David's told me not to. If Angela finds out, he'll lose his family. He was horrible to me. Angry. I'm going to go, its best all round."

"Best for Nick?"

"No!..." I started crying again.

"Shush now, you'll scare the fish." He came and sat next to me, making the boat wobble. "There now my lovely, these things happen." He patted my knee.

"Not best for me, either. I can't bear to think of being apart from him. Oh, Nick!..."

My crying took on a harder intensity than before. Angus periodically patted my knee, checked the nets, and wished he hadn't brought me. The movement caught his eye before mine. Nets moved and fish flapped. Grabbing one side, he began to pull. I thought I'd help. I stood and leaned forward to take the net. The boat began to wobble and I leant forward instinctively, panicking. It wobbled more and I grabbed the net.

"No. don't do...," I heard, but too late, I was over the side.

I used the panic swim technique, getting caught in the net

along with the fish. It tangled round my arms and legs, and under I went. As I stuck my head above the water and gasped a breath of air, I heard Angus shouting, but I couldn't hear the words. Under I went again.

Then I remember nothing for a while, although somewhere in my subconscious I was aware of being in a car. I heard heated, anxious voices as reality crept back, and realised I had no idea where I was. Nick was talking to another man, all I could see was an old faded ceiling. I sat up, and Nick came to me.

"Lucy! Thank God, Lucy."

"Wha...what happened?"

"You had an accident. This is Doctor Bunty," he replied, indicating towards an oversized man with a slight stoop in his shoulders, who lumbered over and shone a light into each eye.

"She appears to be fine, but I would advise you to stay with her, and call me if there's any change." He winked at me mischievously.

"I will, Doctor, I will." Nick shook his hand vigorously.

"Remember, she must rest."

"Don't worry, I'll make sure she does."

Nick escorted me out, his arm protectively round me. Outside, I saw a car that looked just like Maisie. Nick helped me to it, jingling the keys in his spare hand.

"I don't..."

"Shhh... don't worry, it's all under control. I'll explain when you're back safe at the cottage."

He hugged me, and kissed my forehead.

Perhaps David coming over was a bad dream?...

Nick seemed concerned, but happy, as if nothing at all had happened last night. He drove me back, occasionally asking if I was alright. My head hurt again. I couldn't even be bothered to lift my hand to feel it. A thick fog swam in my brain, and my mouth tasted very salty.

Fishing... I remembered that much, but no more, my head was too cloudy.

Once in the cottage, Nick insisted I went to bed, and I obeyed. He helped me get undressed, and tucked me in.

"Right, you rest. I'm going to make tea."

Nick..." My hand touched his.

"Don't worry, we'll talk later. Now you rest." He opened the door. "Maybe I understand a bit more now. Angus told me everything."

It was a good job I was already laid down. Listening to him whistle as he made the tea, I concluded that Angus had not told him everything. *Alternatively,* he had, and Nick was over the moon to be keeping it in the family and all that. I concluded it was the former.

He did his, by now customary, *Bruce Lee* kick on the door, and it flew open to reveal him standing there, holding the tray. I was beginning to get deja-vous. He placed the cups on the bedside table and put the tray on the floor. Then he handed me my tea.

"You must be getting sick of taking care of me."

"Nope. It's called looking after your elders."

I was enjoying sipping the hot sweet tea. "Excuse me? Your elders?"

He picked up his cup and blew on the surface. "Well, Angus told me how old you are."

"Oh."

"He seemed to think that's one of the things that are worrying you. Is it?"

"It is twenty years difference, that's a lot."

"Lucy, I had no idea how old you are, because I don't care. You act like a teenager, and your mind, your body, your face... They give nothing away. No need to fret at all about our age difference. Angus said something else." I could feel my pupils dilating.

"What?"

"That you love me. Head over heels," he said, grinning.

I finished my tea and put the cup down.

"Angus is old, and doesn't know what he's talking about." I buried myself under the covers.

Nick put the cups on the tray. "You have to rest. I'll be here. All I know is that you love me, and everything else can be worked out."

He kissed me softly on the lips. They responded.

"But don't you have to work?"

"No. My dad knows I'm here. I was with him when Angus called me..." I worried about David. He would be angry about this. That thought made my head pound. "Now you rest. I'll tell you more later." I'd wounded Nick deeply the day before, and yet here he was making sure I was alright. He stood up to go.

"Nick?"

"Yes?"

"Angus was right... I do love you. I'm sorry I was such a bitch, it's just that..."

"Shhh, I don't care about that. I love you too. I'll check on you soon."

Quietly the door closed, along with my eyes, and heavy sleep followed.

The first thing I felt when I woke was my head. Dull pain oozed through it. I turned it slowly to look around, and saw Nick standing by the window, looking out onto the garden. My movement alerted him and made him turn. I noticed a glass of water and two painkillers on the bedside table.

It's true, real angels do exist...

"How do you feel?" he asked as I reached for the tablets.

"My head... Please don't tell me it happened again?"

He sat on the bed, smiling.

"Yes, it happened again. Poor Angus got the fright of his life."

"Oh no, Angus.... Is he alright?"

"He'll live. Put his back out hauling you in. He might not sleep so well for a while."

I was baffled.

"Hauling me?"

"You fell overboard and got tangled in the nets. You must have gone under the boat and hit your head, which knocked you out. Angus had to pull you in. Said you were the biggest thing he'd ever caught..." I offered a wry smile. "...When he got back to shore, you mumbled my name, so he called me. My dad dropped me at the cottage. I looked under the pot, but the key wasn't there, so I, I..." He ran his hand through his thick sun-kissed golden hair.

"What did you do?"

"I kicked the back door in, got the keys for Maisie, and came for you."

"You kicked the door in?" I exclaimed.

"Don't worry, I'll tell Stan, and I'll fix it."

"Was... was your dad angry?" I asked timidly.

"Angry? Why would he be?"

"Well, because you were working."

"We were, but actually it's the total opposite, he seemed really concerned."

I bet he is..., I thought. *...concerned I'm going to pump his Son...*

"So then I took you to the doctor. A bad bang to the back of the neck. Luckily you didn't swallow too much water."

Oh yes, lucky, that's exactly how I feel..., I thought, sarcastically. *I wish the bang had made me think I was Kylie Minogue or someone, then none of this would matter. I would go off singing my heart out...*

"Thank-you, Nick, for doing this."

"To be honest Lucy, it's beyond me how you've got through life so far unscathed."

"I carry it all on the inside."

He tilted his head. "Yes. You do."

I wanted to tell him, reveal all, and release the lies. I was totally torn between betraying David, or Nick.

Shit. More punishment...

Now, because of this I would have to stay longer, with the doctor's firm instructions for Nick to stay and look after me. Me, who was here in bed, naked. Oh, now the Gods were in full ecstasy, cocaine-sniffing heaven, roaring their asses off laughing at me. I could feel myself pouting.

"Don't do that."

"What?"

"That thing with your lips."

"What - this?" It was more animated the second time.

"You're not supposed to be so sexy when you're ill."

He leaned towards me, and I could feel his breath.

"Well then, it's all your fault," I teased.

"I assume responsibility for everything," he said, before pressing his lips onto mine, relieving my headache.

My hand ran through his hair and down his neck, my fingers dragged down his spine.

If I'm going to hell, I may as well go with a bang...

Once more, the passion ignited between us. We were laying down again, his body crushed down onto mine, grinding against me. My pelvis was pushed up to meet his. Nick kissed down my throat and lightly over the skin running down to my breasts. I arched my back, wanton with Lust. Young but experienced hands roamed over me and in me. I was loving the touch of his superior manhood.

Both of us heard the loud knocking at the door though. Nick was panting hard.

"Shit. Who's that?..." He pulled up his jeans as he hopped over to the window. "It's my dad."

Instantly my headache returned. Nick looked for his white tee shirt as the banging continued. "Great timing," he mumbled, as he found it and pulled it over his beautiful torso. He went to open the door, and I heard a muffled conversation taking place, and then footsteps approaching. Nick came back in.

"Everything okay?" my voice squeaked.

"Yeah, fine. My dad's come round to see how you are. He said is it okay if he just says hi, to wish you better?" I said nothing. "Is that too much? Him coming up here? Personally, I think it's a good thing. He really does look worried, it must mean he likes you." His face had hope in it.

"Well... okay, just for a minute."

"Great, I'll make a drink." He ran back down.

I didn't hear David on the stairs. He quietly entered the room. He did look troubled, and I felt it.

"Lauren?"

"Yes?"

"Sorry for the way I was. It scared me when Nick got that call. If something had happened to you, I, well..." He looked down. "Well, thank God it didn't."

"Sorry David, about Nick being here."

"There's not much I can do about that, not today. Someone has to be with you, but I did mean what I said."

"I know you did."

There was a kick, and the door flew open.

"Drinks..."

How contrived it was with all three of us there in the bedroom. It was all too much for me.

"I'm sorry David, I hope you don't think I'm being rude, but I feel very tired..." I looked to Nick. "Do you mind?"

He did look a little disappointed, but he said, "Okay, you need to rest. I'll leave your drink here."

"Thank-you David, for stopping by."

"You're welcome La...Lucy."

Father and son left me to my own thoughts. I could hear their voices, at first quiet, then they rose. Nick shouted, then David. More stifled conversation, then a door slammed and the truck drove away.

What was that about? A tiny tear in the bond between them?...

When I heard Nick's footsteps outside the bedroom, I closed my eyes and pretended to be asleep. The light in the room was fading. Once I heard the door close, I opened my eyes again. Somewhere in my subconscious, I knew that the argument had involved me. I'd probably introduced rivalry now, into this comic tale. My curiosity took pride of place over my pain.

I got dressed, with a need to go downstairs and find out what had just occurred. I startled Nick, as I opened the door. He was in the process of throwing the logs into the fireplace that lay around like skittles.

His minds not on the fire...

He stood quickly. "What's wrong?"

I tried to smile warmly at him to dispel any anxiety.

"Nothing... I just wanted to see if you were okay."

I went to him and put my arms around his waist.

"Did you hear us?" he asked, shuffling nervously.

"Not the details, but it sounded heated."

"Sit down Lucy, and I'll finish the fire. I thought you were asleep."

I sat down.

"Sorry, I was just pretending, but then I needed to see if you were alright." *Let's be honest now, Lauren, if you want to find out what was said...*

He began to build the fire again. "I hate it when me and my dad argue. It's so rare. He's the easy one, going along with most things type of guy..." I could sense his agitation. "He never presses me like that normally. I told him, you need looking after, tonight and tomorrow. He was actually pissed off, so I'm sorry Lucy, but it turns out I'm working for a couple of hour's tomorrow morning." He turned his eyes to me.

"Nick, you can't stop your life because of me. Also I don't want to be responsible for you both arguing."

"Fuck him, Lucy, I've got two brothers that can help him..." He was angry now. "One minute he's genuinely worried about you, the next he's telling me we have three days full work to do..." He shook his head, bemused. "I told him I'd only do a couple of hours tomorrow. He didn't like it..." Thoughtfully, he added, "It's just so unlike him."

I remembered back to a fiery, hot-tempered David, the one Nick had never met.

"Truly, I don't want to be a pain."

He softened, and looked intently at me.

"Truly, it would be a pain if you weren't with me."

I felt myself blush at the compliment. I felt torment in my heart at having to leave him soon. Obviously, cruelty was a card I could not play.

I decided I would leave that Thursday, in two days time. I left myself a day to pack, give the key back to Stan, and think of how it must end. Willing myself not to cry, I went to him and embraced him with all my power. Nick sank into me. The emotions within me were worse than all the bangs to the head in the world.

One more day with him. Not even that, half a day...

As much as I needed him, wanted him, I didn't want to make love with him until it was totally pure. No filthy secrets. Maybe it was selfish, but I needed it to be free and unabated, on equal terms.

We sat intertwined, the warm rug underneath, and a roaring fire before us. We were both lost in our own thoughts for some time.

"Nick?"

"Mmm?"

"You were right when you said about me having skeletons in the cupboard..." I paused dramatically, but he said nothing, giving me the time to formulate what I needed to say. "It's nothing like, I murdered all my ex'es, or... I used to be a man, but it's complicated... This is very much a cliché, a classic line, but I need time to think, to air my cupboard so to speak."

"Well, I'm glad about the always being female bit, but when you say time, what are we talking here? A few days? A few weeks?..." He paused. "Or more than that?"

"I honestly don't know..." I was at least being honest about *that*. "It's hard to think straight when you're around, you devolve me of my senses. I was toying with the idea of going home, to London, and cutting short my stay."

His whole body tensed, and his tone matched. "Well, I'll be honest, I would hate that. But if it helps you to resolve your issues quicker so we can be together, then it would be worth it. Maybe you should think about this tomorrow. You've had a big day."

"Yes... maybe you're right..." His body relaxed again. "Nick, I do love the way you're always so patient. Saying the right things. Allowing events to take their own path."

"It's only you who thinks that. Jenny thought my head was in the clouds, that I lacked ambition. She doesn't think love is an ambition, but to me it's the only one. Everything else will fall into place after that."

My heart swelled to the same size my head felt.

"You're right, true unconditional love is ambitious."

He squeezed me tightly.

"I don't want to lose you Lucy, not now I've found you."

You won't lose me, because I'm running away, like the coward I am... Suddenly I felt very sleepy. "Nick, would you mind if I, or we, go to sleep?"

I didn't want to say 'go to bed', it sounded too sexual. The passion within me had died down. I was swirling round in a giant witch's cauldron of sentiment.

"Course not," he said.

We settled down in the comfy bed, body heat radiating between us. As my body drifted off to sleep, my mind bombarded me. Nick had saved my soul from the everlasting pit of non-believers in love. Unshackled me from my un-trusting bravado. He loved me, but he was unarmed with the truth.

Would he still love me if he knew?... Questions like this ravaged me until a guttural sleep overtook.

When I awoke, he was gone. A small folded sheet of paper lay on his pillow. It simply said;

I won't be gone too long,
Love you,
Nick*

It made me smile that he'd signed his name. How many men did he think I'd had in this bed?. I got up and prepared myself, packing while Nick was out. I needed to call Stan.

Jesus, I haven't used my mobile since the day I got here...

I wasn't even sure where I'd put it.

First, coffee...

While it came to the boil, I used the time to phone-hunt, just finding it as the kettle made its '*I'm ready!*' strangled whistle. My phone was as dead as an old horse on Grand National day. So, I just needed the charger. I decided to search for it after my coffee. It took me one whole frustrated, pissed off hour to find it. It was in a shoe, how logical was that? But then again, I'd looked in the oven twice...

I put it on to charge while I dolefully packed, and switched it on after a few minutes. It was so lucky I did...

CALL TO NORA

I put in the pin-code and left it to its own devices in the kitchen, while I went to the bathroom. The message tone yelled at me, then again, and again. It continued until I managed to get to the phone. Twenty-eight messages and fifteen missed calls. My eyes widened. One message was from my mother, the rest were from *Nora*. They started enquiring and ended up hysterical. Skimming through the drama queen chat, I felt guilty.

Nora was my best friend. He was twenty-eight years old and Cuban. He was christened Noel, but everybody affectionately called him Nora. If you were to look up the definition of a screaming, gay, hysterical queen in a reverse dictionary, it would say - *Nora (formerly known as Noel)*. He was the epitome of a straight man's nightmare. We met out clubbing. He'd stood out in his bright red rubber chaps, a pink cowboy hat with a matching feather boa and red glitter all over his nipples. Nora was dancing on one podium and I on the other. By a sheer coincidence, I also had a dark green cowboy hat on.

As I said before, I can shake my booty anytime, anywhere. Together, for that magical night, we held the crowd. We have been best friends ever since, and as Nora says, every straight girl needs a gay man in their life. I hadn't told Nora I was going away. I'd been so wrapped up in myself, and my fantasies.

He will not be pleased...

I dialled his number, I was missing him and needed to talk. I held the phone away from my ear while Nora screamed, took some gulps of air, then continued screaming.

"Nora!... Nora, calm down."

"Lauren! Donde va? Joder! Lauren..." Nora always spoke Spanglish, mixing English with South American Spanish. Some words I knew, and others not a clue. "Oh my God! Darlink, where are you? Have you been hurt? Has anything happened to your anus? ...Oh, if so you's a lucky girl."

"Nora, Nora," I said firmly. "Yes, I'm alright, well, physically I am, but emotionally, No. Well, that's not true, I've had a lot of accidents since I've been here."

"Darlink, you making no sense. Who is blackmailing you?"

"What?"

"Well something is wrong. You wouldn't just vamos without telling me."

I sighed. "Sorry Nora, I did."

He screamed in a shocked and hurt way.

"It's a long story, but basically I'm okay. I'll be back in London tomorrow, and my bottom is fine, I assure you."

"Shame," he crooned.

"Yes, actually it is."

"Oh!..." There was shock in Nora's voice.

"I've fallen in love, Nora."

I could imagine him clasping his perfectly manicured hands to his chest, excited by the mystery of it all.

More screams. "Darlink, I have to sit down... Is he guapo? What his culo look like?"

"If you mean stunningly, film star handsome. Yes, he is. His butt's my business, and not being you, I'm not obsessed with arses."

"Girl, you need to get with the program." He giggled at his own piquant wit.

"Nora, I don't have time to discuss the merits of bottoms. I've got to get ready to go. I thought as you left so many messages, I'd better call."

"Well you know the police did ask me to keep trying." Now he was sounding mysterious.

"Nora..."

"Well, you *were* missing. I went to the police."

"You what?"

"Darlink," he purred.

"Well I only hope they didn't take you seriously."

"No, they didn't."

"Well thank God for that."

"Not at first, but Nora is persistent."

"How persistent?"

"Darlink, for you, very. I had to go five times to see those gorgeous policemen."

Queens... They probably did something in the end just to get rid of Nora...

He got off on displaying his gayness.

"So what's happening now?"

"There is a missing persons out for you."

"But Nora, I'm not missing. I know exactly where I am."

"Si, but no-one else does, not even your boss."

"My boss? ...Great, and how is he involved?"

"The police went to your work, and questioned people."

"Oh that's great, what a warm welcome I'll get. So then the police must know I'm on holiday?"

"They don't know. You tell your boss you're going on holiday out of the blue, next day, nada, gone. You can't be called on your mobile... You say nothing to me, no to anyone."

"That's because I'm on fucking holiday," I barked.

"Que pasa chica? Is suspicious, no?"

"No, it's not, Nora, and you have to go the police and tell them I'm fine."

He tutted. "Puta madre..."

"Nora?"

"Okay, okay I will."

"Thanks for caring about me, even if it is a drama."

He sniffed. "Cariño."

"I'll call you tomorrow to make sure you've been to the police."

"Of course, darlink. Just make sure you get some pictures of your new love."

Taking pictures had been the last thing on my mind, but now that Nora had said it, I realised I did need something - a reminder of Nick.

"Mmm... I'll try."

"Kisses, darlink, on all your brown bits."

"Yours too, darleeng." I tried to mimic his accent.

Sniffing once more, he hung up.

So, for the moment I'm officially missing. Missing brain cells in my head...

Psychologically, I was lost.

Next, I called Stan. He told me to meet him in The Thirsty Nun at five, as he was in their darts team, and that was their practice time. I tried to protest, as that was the last thing I wanted.

"Best face to face," said Stan.

I could do nothing more but relent. Packing came next, done with the ardour of a young ripe girl being packed off to a convent. I checked the time - *One-thirty*. I wondered when Nick would be back. I didn't know how I was going to explain going to the pub. Nick would want to come. The stress was panicking me, and I hoped The Thirsty Nun wasn't going to be busy. A quick in and out, as the actress said to the bishop. Another great line from my grandma, along with 'Sluts go where whores fear to tread'.

Oh no! I think I'm the slut in that one...

I grumpily took my case to the car, and put it safely in Maisie's boot. I turned and looked at the cottage, which was transformed in the sunlight, its imperfections no longer noticed. Others here may not have liked me, but the cottage remained unbiased. It held our secret of love admirably.

Silent tears fell down my cheeks. I had no one else to blame but myself. I had chased the past, and the present had come right up and bitten me on the arse. This self-chastising didn't stop the tears. I was creeping away. No champagne, no partying, and no Loving.

I walked back into the cottage and spent the next hour wandering from room to room as if I had turned into a dog looking for its owner. I checked the time - *Three O'clock*.

Where is Nick?...

He didn't know this was our last afternoon together.

My method of communicating this dastardly departure will be a note. Yes, a crappy, short, cop-out note. My reason for breathing will read; Sorry, blah blah, needing to go, will be in touch. The stuff of Shakespeare. Avoidance is shit...

I flounced round the garden for a while, that took up an hour. The door had not shut properly since Nick had kung-fu-ed it in. Four O'clock, and still no Nick.

My phone rang. It was Nora.

"Darlink, guapa..."

"What's wrong now?"

"Nada. Why there always got to be something wrong?"

"Okay, so what is it?"

"There is a small problemo."

"Isn't that the same as something wrong?"

"No, darlink. I went to see the loverly policemen today. Why their badges are sooo shiny? On their beautiful, clean shirts. Big strong chest muscles under that lucky shirt. I say to him, 'How you make it shine like that? Is it your strong man juice?'"

"Nora!"

"Well, it could be... I try to clean my mirror tonight with some. Jus a small mirror." He tittered.

"Nora, please, I don't need to picture you cleaning everything with your sperm."

He screamed. "Ahhh, shiny!"

"Nora!" I snapped.

"Que pasa?"

"What happened at the police station?"

"Oh, well, you have to go there when you get back, but I come with you. Aaargh!..." He did his loud fiesta cry. "Oh darlink, Nora *will* come."

I sighed. Sometimes I despaired. "Okay. But why?"

"They jus' have to see you in flesh, sí?"

"Alright Nora, Okay. I have to go now."

"Don't forget picture." He blew a shower of kisses and hung up.

Nearly twenty past four, and the waiting was torture. I decided to walk to the village one last time. I left the key under the plant pot, with a note telling Nick where I was, and that I wouldn't be long.

I set off wearing only my red cotton mid-length dress, free from the restrictions of underwear. I thought I would just be quick. How wrong can you be?...

CUBAN WAVE GOODBYE

Opening the door to The Thirsty Nun, I was amazed at how busy it was. Inwardly I groaned, scanning the room for Stan, while all eyes scanned me. Folk music played from somewhere, and everyone in there was in jovial spirits. All it needed was a juggling monkey on an organ, and the picture would have been complete.

There was too many people to see where Stan was, so I made my way to the bar. A brassy, fifty-something, blonde barmaid asked me what I'd like to drink. I heard that Devil's spunk calling to me.

"Whisky, straight please."

No harm in having a quick one...

Round the corner, I could hear whoops and jeering. Two tables of variously aged men sat playing cards, shaking their heads, stroking their beards and mumbling under their breath. Another table next to them vexed me. Two of the women I'd never seen before, but there was Doris; Mrs. Warbling. Her smile was tight, but she nodded politely. Her friend Mrs. Tuffle did not even have the decency to pretend to smile. Instead, she gave me her most scornful look, as if I had personally affronted her. Mrs. Tuffle's companion, a man, was tiny in comparison, a toothpick of a man with tiny round spectacles, who sat twitching. Probably Mr. Tuffle. Previously been beaten within an inch of his life by the same hands that made those yummy, tasty cream teas.

Near to the fireplace, much newer than the one in The Dry Thrush, stood a semi-circle of jumpered men, every single one sporting a pipe and the mandatory aran sweater. Their chat mostly comprised of nodding, and puffing on their pipes.

God, is the whole village in here?...

Luckily, I couldn't see Jenny or Angela.

"That'll be three pounds fifty, love," The barmaid chirped at me.

"Arll get that, Shirley," A voice behind me said.

I turned to see Stan. His kind, smiling face relaxed me.

"Thank-you, Stan." I downed it in one.

Stan nodded admiringly. He went to pay, adding, "Same again for me, and another of whatever the young maid had... Cheers Shirley."

My cheeks were flushed by the whisky already.

"Oh, Stan I..."

"No, no my flower, it's no trouble."

I suppose one more won't hurt, especially looking at the menacing faces at Mrs. Tuffle's table...

"Don't mind that lot, let's take our drinks round the corner, to the darts."

As we joined the men, a big cheer went up. Seth had just thrown a bullseye. Lots of backslapping commenced, interspersed with '*Ooo-aar*'s. Spotting Angus amongst them, I gave him a big smile. He held his hand up, pulling a face of pain.

Oh no, his poor back.... I felt terrible.

"Now then, my lovely, what's the problem?" Stan enquired.

He must have heard everything about me, and yet he acted perfectly gentlemanly towards me.

"I have to cut short my holiday, I'm afraid." I tossed back my whisky.

"Oh, that is a shame."

"I don't want any money back Stan, but what should I do with the key? I'm going tomorrow..."

He sipped his pint and thought about it.

"Just leave it under the mat, I'll collect it. Tomorrow you say?"

"Yes, but please, I don't want anyone to know. Is that alright Stan?"

"Up to you how you come and go..." Another cheer exploded, the whole darts team were elated. "We'll win for sure this year." Stan commented.

Then he beamed at someone behind me, and raised his glass. I turned round to see Nick approaching. He looked irritable, his smile pinched.

"Hello there, young Nick." Stan greeted him.

"Hello Stan. I'm sorry, could I talk to Lucy a moment?"

Instantly I knew something was wrong by his voice.

Where has he been? What has been said?...

I wanted another drink. Nick led me by my elbow back to the bar. Shirley slouched over to take our order.

"Whisky, double please, and..." He looked at me. "Same?" He obviously thought I might need it. He didn't say another word until he'd downed his drink. "Same again?" he asked.

"No, no."

He shrugged and downed his second. This was a new side to Nick I hadn't previously seen. Not knowing what was going on, I mentally prepared myself. He exhaled a great breath.

"That's better... Shit, I needed that."

He leaned forward and kissed my forehead, and for one split-second, everyone stopped, looked, and then carried on what they'd been doing. However, this single action of affection let me know that nothing had been discovered.

"What's wrong?" I whispered. "Where have you been?"

"Working," he hissed. "with my fucked up father..." My heart took a few more beats. "He's been a complete wanker all day. He knew I wanted to get back. We drove fucking miles to a job that didn't even happen. He took a detour to look at another one as well... Shit! We've had a big row. All day he's been snappy with me, edging on anger. I haven't done anything wrong..." Perplexed, he put his hand on top of mine. "So when I saw your note, I thought - *Perfect, I want to get drunk...*"

Drunk? This was not how I wanted Nick on our last night. By now, I was also swaying slightly. Poor Nick was caught in the middle without even knowing it. He was better off without me in his life.

He may think he loves me, but in a few weeks, his life will go back to normal. Mine will never be the same again...

"I think... a pint of cider next," he said.

I couldn't stop him, he obviously needed to do this, so for me the only natural conclusion was to join him.

"Why not?" I said.

He smiled. "That's why I love you."

Two golden, bubbly, refreshing pints of cider were served to us by Shirley, who herself was none of those things. Nick drank half quickly, while I sipped on mine.

"Want to sit at a table? ...or I'll grab some barstools?" Nick asked. I felt safer here at the bar with life-stained Shirley.

"Barstools please."

He popped round the darts corner, and returned with the stools. We propped ourselves up on them and continued our pints. Nick resumed his tale of his day of woe.

"I know him and Mum haven't had a row. My mum was in a good mood when I went home, but even when they do argue, he just goes quiet for a few days. Honestly, Lucy, *everything* I did was wrong today. Each time I mentioned your name, he actually told me to shut-up, and stop talking about you. Shit!..."

How can I comfort him, when I am the cause? And in such a public place...

He finished his pint and ordered another. I hadn't even drunk half of mine, but I was glad I was sitting down.

"We've never had such a big row..." He looked into my eyes for the answer, and the travesty was, I had it. He shook his head. "...Sorry Lucy, I haven't even asked how you are today."

"Me? ...Oh, fine, my day wasn't as bad as yours." *Fucking David...*

He was being unfair to Nick now, and I was sure his anger was really meant for me. I couldn't tell David I was going, just because there was no way to do so. Then at least he could have shouted at me, happy that I'd be out of his life the next day.

A tiny man came to the bar, as nervous as a sparrow, and stood purposely at Nick's side. I could see him, but Nick's back was to him, and he didn't see him at first. The tiny man's hands nervously played a piano that wasn't there, while he looked directly ahead. I was sure that if I blew hard enough he would fall over. Nick became aware of the presence behind him and turned.

"Hello Godfrey." He leaned back on his stool further than was safe.

Godfrey twitched and glanced at Nick, nervously replying - "Oh, yes... Hello, Nick. Yes..."

He turned away rapidly, fumbling for change in his pocket. As it clinked onto the bar, I finished my pint.

"Been told not to talk to us, Godfrey?"

As Nick asked him that, I looked over at the table with the four women, now set in stone and glaring at poor Godfrey, who was by this time as red as my dress. He seemed very ill at ease as he clutched the

126

tray of drinks.

"Not at all Nick, it's um...please excuse me."

He scuttled back to the nest of vipers. Nick had been outspoken, the drinks inside him working their charm. He looked at me with bravado.

"Let's have another drink."

"Do you want more?" I exclaimed.

"Yes I do Lucy, why?... Don't disappoint me, and tell me I've had enough already."

"No, I'm not your mother," I replied, though in truth it had flickered through my mind that he was drinking too much.

"Good. Then this time I'll have a Bacardi. And for Miss?"

This was now the time for me to say 'Oh, I'll have a mineral water,' but instead I thought;

When in Rome..., and being totally crap at abstaining I said; "No, I'll have another whisky."

He smacked the bar. "That's a girl."

He called over our order just in time before the bar filled with darts players. Some were coming straight for refreshment, and others were spilling over to the tables or groups. A good feeling radiated from these men, and filled the acrid air, changing the atmosphere. I was glad they were there. Nick swivelled round and some of the men greeted him. I swallowed my whisky down in one, once again. My bladder was complaining, I needed the loo. I put my hand on Nick's arm.

"Where's the toilet?" I asked quietly.

He pointed to where the darts had just been. Jumping off the stool made me dizzy, and I had to grab Nick's shoulder.

Uh-oh, I'm drunk...

As he turned to me, our faces were only a few millimetres apart. Then for a moment, as we kissed, everything around us was stillness, like we were the only ones there.

Our lips unlocked, and the horror of the reality hit us.

Everyone around us was completely still. I looked at Nick, and without knowing why, we both began to giggle.

"Absolutely disgusting," Mrs. Tuffle commented, breaking the spell, and everybody returned to what they were doing.

When I began to walk, it became apparent that the alcohol had removed my balance. This was the last place I wanted to fall over, so to

127

avoid looking stupid, I decided to try and stand bolt upright and take very small, slow steps. On reflection, I think falling over would have been better.

To someone observing, it looked like a woman had entered the 'clutch the pencil between your buttocks' race. Across a busy pub. I stepped inaccurately to one side to let someone pass, still clutching the imaginary pencil between my cheeks and leaning forward, sticking my bum out to avoid toppling over. I knew that people's attention was being drawn to me.

After successfully performing this dance all the way to the toilet, I decided to assume the same walk on my return, and managed to get all the way back to Nick at the bar. He was talking to Stan.

Oh, shit....

"Arrr she is." Stan beamed as he spoke.

So did Nick, who was also very drunk. He put his arm around me. "Love of my life, Stan."

Stan shifted visibly. "Oh I'm sure, I'm sure."

It took me two go's to get back on the stool.

"I was just telling Stan about the back door."

Whew....

"Not a problem, it was an emergency," Stan reassured me.

Three more fresh drinks sat before us.

Think I'd better leave that one....

"Oh yes, was there any damage to the cottage other than the door?" Stan asked Nick.

"A few bits, but nothing to worry over, Stan."

"Oh good. I did pop by the day after, 'bout midday, but I saw the truck there, and I knew you'd be helping."

Nick took a gulp of his Bacardi. "Yes, I was there, then my dad came as well, but that was earlier, Stan. Surely you mean earlier?"

I reached for my drink, and sipped it in an angst-ridden state.

"No, no, it was definitely midday. Mrs. Middrie comes to collect the eggs at eleven forty-five every day on the dot. I went to the cottage after she left..." Stan lifted his hand to someone, an acknowledgement, and picked his drink up. "Any-ways, no harm, just going to have a quick chat with Angus."

I had about two seconds to decide, truth or dare? Nick was looking at me quizzically.

"Your dad came round." I had decided to go with truth, but as usual not totally.

"You didn't tell me."

Flamboyantly, I acted. "Oh, I had completely forgotten.... He was only there for a moment, he thought he'd left something." I finished with one of my sweetest smiles.

"And had he?"

"No, no."

He shrugged his shoulders, which meant I had got away with it.

Maybe I should take up acting as a professional career... I could begin my debut as the stage's largest Shit. Now that role would get me a Grammy award...

I finished my drink, now absolutely drunk.

"Nick, can we go soon?"

"Let's have one more, and then I'll ask Stan if he can give us a lift."

Oh, yes...

I remembered we had both walked there. There was no way I could walk back to the cottage. Maybe I could make it to the first bush, and then sleep in it. People talking sounded distant, and the whole place had gained a slight wobble now. Nick ordered our last two drinks and turned to me, raising his glass. I reciprocated.

"A toast - Being in love," Nick whispered.

"Hear, hear," I added, and our glasses clinked. If this was the way we were going to spend our last night together, then so be it. Maybe it was Fate, because if I had been with Nick all day at the cottage, then my firm resolve would probably have left me. He leaned in close to me.

"Lucy?"

I swam in those outstanding eyes.

"Yes?" I answered dreamily.

"What would you say if I asked you if I could come to London with you?"

His question snapped me out of my reverie.

"What?"

"Well... after you've had time to sort your skeletons out, then maybe."

Yes!... My head and heart both screamed. *Go now!... We both go, now...*

"Maybe," was all I could answer.

He kissed me on the lips. This time I didn't care, with the courage of Johnny Walker running through my veins.

"I'll ask Stan then..." Nick looked round, spotting him. "Stan! Stan!" he shouted across the packed bar.

Stan, who had been talking to Angus, made his way over.

Angus followed slowly, probably fearful of being in my vicinity.

"Yes, Nick?" Stan asked as they approached.

"Hi Angus," I said. "I haven't had a chance to say how sorry I am for what happened."

Nick was chatting to Stan.

"Oh, well. Twas an accident," Angus said, politely.

"Yes, but your poor back. Are you in much pain?"

"Only a bit, my lovely." Now he drew in close to me. He'd also been drinking whisky. He kept his voice down and acted slyly. "Well to be honest, it was all worth it, for that view of your bottom." He leant back, smiling as he winked.

My already hot skin burned. *It was probably one of my no-knickers days, like today...*

"Yep, that's fine, Lucy," Nick was saying.

"Uhh?..." I was getting confused, forgetting what we'd been talking about earlier. "Well of course that's fine. If I don't want to wear underwear, I won't."

Nick started laughing. "What are you talking about?"

"Mmm... I'm not sure." I began to giggle. "What's fine?"

"The lift home... from Stan."

"Oh!..." I was laughing now. Stan and Angus looked at us both, like they didn't get the joke. "Nick, we're drunk!"

"Yes, we are. It's fun."

At that point it kinda was. I was too pissed to care about much. Raucous laughter was building in both of us. I leant back, trying to lift my bum cheeks, which had stuck to my dress. Lifting, leaning, laughing, I started to feel myself falling backwards.

"Arrggh!..."

As I went, the natural thing was to grab hold of something to stop me. Unfortunately, the only thing there was Angus's beard. I grabbed and yanked on it, bending him over, his head and beard travelling with me to the floor. There was an audible CRACK! as my back hit the floor. My legs were up in the air, balanced on the side of the stool. Angus roared in pain, causing everyone to stop and look.

Some people quickly came over, and a small circle formed. Nick screamed with the stupidity of it all, and because my dress was now high around my waist, totally exposing my neat and trim ladies parts. In shock, I let go of Angus's beard and joined in with Nick's laughter.

Laughing insanely, while my beaver was there for the entire pub to see, I heard a male voice say -

"Ere, is that one of them Cubans?"

Someone was trying to help me up, but my lunatic laughter was making it difficult, and one of my legs fell off the stool to the floor.

"Ahhh...." went the crowd.

Now let's all look into the beaver's cave...

Nick was trying to help me.

Another voice; "Oo said she's got a Cuban cigar?"

"What, down there?" replied another.

"I think you'll find that cut is a Brazilian." Someone joined the debate.

Nick managed to close my legs and Stan pulled me upright. Slowly my dress came down, closing the show.

An old, old man perked up; "She's got a cut Brazilian cigar down there."

"Best thing that ever happened 'ere," some younger man commented.

One of the pipe-smoking circle joined in; "Is she going to light it now?"

There were murmurs and tuts all round.

"Come on you two," Stan said. "I think it's best to go now."

All the way back to the cottage, Nick and I sat in the back of Stan's van giggling. When he opened the back door to let us out, we staggered and swayed before him.

"You two, you're like a couple of young-uns..." I kissed him on one cheek, Nick the other. "Now, now, that's plenty," Stan said.

"Thanks Stan," Nick said loudly, and we giggled up the path as Stan drove away. Eventually, between the two of us we managed to open the door. After that, everything became a blur. We made out with each other in that sloppy drunk way, and ended up in bed where we fell into a spinning spiral sleep.

OVERHEARD TRUTHS

My eyelids creaked open. My mouth felt like the bottom of a blocked toilet. Nick was sound asleep next to me. The room held some light; to me it felt early. I got out of bed.

Ouch. My head...

Every footstep was like walking through glue.

Water. I must have some...

I went slowly down to the kitchen. Even the sound of running water hurt. As usual with alcohol; The night before - All fun and games. The next day - Grim normal reality. I started to groan. The whole pub, indeed the whole village had seen my front bottom. Discussed it even. Probably by now the story was; She got on a bar stool, opened her legs, put a Cuban cigar into her Brazilian, and smoked it. My parting gift to everyone.

As I sipped the water slowly, and made my way back upstairs, I felt utterly embarrassed.

Fucking hell.... Perfect Jenny and Nick's whole family will find out about this, and I'm about to dump the lot on him...

I slid back into bed, laying down my fragile head. I turned gingerly so I could look at Nick.

Will he find it all so funny when he wakes?...

I gazed at him until I fell back to sleep.

I knew he wasn't there, even before I opened my eyes. The space where he'd been was still warm, he hadn't been gone long. My descent from the bed was slightly less painful this time, though my head was still as heavy. I went to get more water from the kitchen.

"NICK!..." I called, but he didn't seem to be around. *He probably had to work, poor Nick...*

Coffee, strong and black was called for. I started hitting the cooker, and the same banging tinny noise was echoed in my head. I stared at the pot, deep in thought. Would I see him before I left, or was that it? A fumbled, crude, pissed romp.

Oh, shit.... I hope it wasn't more than that though...

I bent my head and lifted my sleeping shirt, trying to sniff for evidence. I lifted my leg to the side, and took deep sniffs, looking for that unique, pungent sex smell, of fishy cheese. Not very lady-like, I grant you, but a successful method, nevertheless.

The coffee cried out its readiness. My detective's conclusion was that all seemed to be natural woman down there. I went through the motions, trying not to cry. I heard an engine outside.

My heart leapt. *Nick...*

Even before the door could be knocked, I opened it. My big smile evaporated as David came up the path.

"Can I come in?" he asked, looking round nervously.

"Yes?" I said, standing aside to let him pass. *This is just what I wanted, David here, and me with a great big hangover...* "What's wrong now, David?" I asked softly.

"Is Nick here?"

"No, I thought he was with you." I gulped my hot coffee too quickly, burning my throat. David paced the kitchen.

"We had a big row yesterday."

"I know, he told me. David, please stop pacing."

He shot me a look of pure evil. "Well, I bet he did, Lauren. Came running straight here, into the arms of the woman I used to love."

"David...." I implored. "This is getting us nowhere, now have a coffee, and calm down. It's... it's..." I gulped and looked at the floor.

"It's what, Lauren?"

"It's... I'm going today... back to London."

Instantly he changed his stance from aggressive to passive. "You are?"

"Yes," I snapped. "Isn't that what you want?... You should be happy."

His blue eyes twinkled a little less, holding sadness.

"Happy? Ha!" he mocked. "Happy you turned up, and now I can't stop thinking about you? Happy my son has fallen in love with you? Or happy to be reminded how deliriously happy I'd once been in my life?... Happy is not the word I would pick to describe how I'm feeling, Lauren."

With my banging head keeping time, I made more coffee. I couldn't think straight, but I looked him straight in the eye.

"David... I'm truly sorry. It wasn't my intention to hurt anyone. I'm ashamed to say, as you know, how selfish I can be. Nick doesn't know anything, and when I'm gone, you can tell him what an utter bitch I am."

"That's not my style, Lauren. I've already caused enough trouble between me and my son... over you," he added.

I handed him a coffee with milk and two sugars. He sipped it, looking surprised.

"You still drink it like that I assume?"

Despite himself, he smiled. He put his coffee down and pulled himself up to sit on the kitchen side. I mirrored him on the other side of the room.

"Do you remember a lot about me, Lauren?"

"I remember you hate overcooked steak, and runny eggs."

He laughed lightly. "I still hate those things..." We both paused, with the old familiar ease that had once existed between us. "I wish this had been different, Lauren. That I could have spent some time with you. That's why I was angry yesterday."

"Yes, but you're angry at me, you shouldn't take it out on Nick."

"Don't you think I know that?" He was raising his voice. "I'm angry at myself, not at you... well, maybe a bit, for coming here and looking so good, but I'm jealous, Lauren. Jealous of my own child. Jealous that you're with him instead of me, and he's finding out everything about your life. Jealous he can be near you. You have no fucking idea how sick and angry it all makes me feel. I often wondered what you'd look like... you've aged better than I could ever have imagined. I'm jealous my son has fallen in love with you. A love that I once had..." He held up his hand. "I know, a love that I destroyed. I'll have to pay for that for the rest of my life, Lauren."

I took my coffee, jumped down, and sat next to him on the work-surface as if we were teenagers again. He turned to look at me.

"I took it out on Nick as if he was my rival. For God's sake, he's my son. I'm in such a mess, and Angela knows something's wrong."

"It's a good thing I'm going, then."

"It won't remove you from my mind now you're back in it. I even think of you when I'm asleep. Nick's grieving will be open, mine will be trapped inside. I'm even jealous that he'll be able to do that... vent his emotions. He will be able to say he loves you. I don't have that privilege." He looked down at the floor.

My voice was barely a whisper. "I thought you didn't love me anymore."

He looked back at me. "We can all lie, Lauren..." I didn't know what to say. "If I didn't love you all this would be much easier. I should hate you for letting Nick fall in love with you, but... but I can't. The fucking ludicrousness of it is, I totally understand why he has."

"David, I don't know if this helps, but a part of me will always love you."

He moved closer to me, his legs were now pressing into mine.

"I think that's always made it worse. It was easier way back, when you hated me."

"You know I never really hated you."

"I can run away from my old life, but I can't run away from my mind. Today you're gone again, and that makes me feel scared when I think how long it will take to push your memory back again. Now Nick will be an everyday reminder of you."

His eyes filled with tears, and mine followed suit.

"David...," was all I could manage. We let our foreheads rest together, two old flames lost in a moment of forgiveness.

Both of us jumped at the sound of slow clapping.
"Well, isn't this touching?"
Nick's acid tone cut through the air. I gasped, turned and froze.

David jumped down to the floor.

"Nick, now Nick, this isn't what it looks like."

Nick moved very slowly, looking from one of us to the other. His face said he thought he was witnessing something very bad happening before him.

"Why? What is it then?" he snarled.

"I just came to see if you were here, and, and..."

"Come on, Dad, let's hear that fucking bullshit. You've both been fucking fantastic actors up till now..." His tone was utter venom. He turned on me. "So, what's your bullshit story on this one, Lucy?... but that's not even your fucking name, is it, Lauren?" He punched the side of the oven, and David went towards him. "That's not a good idea at the moment, Dad." David stopped. "LAUREN!..." Nick shouted, and the name didn't sound right in his angry voice. I looked at him. "This? ...This was your fucking skeleton?" Nick asked, still shouting.

"Yes."

"And if I hadn't gone to the village to get a new lock for the back door, and if I hadn't gone round the back to fix the fucking door, and if I hadn't heard every single word between you, then you would never have told me?"

Again, I said nothing. He turned to David.

"Dad, can you go? I want to talk to Luc... Lauren."

"I don't think that's a good idea, not the mood you're in."

"You have no fucking idea what mood I'm in. Don't panic, I won't hurt your precious love." He threw his head back and laughed like a lunatic. David took a step towards him. "Don't, Dad, really. I've never felt this fucking angry or dangerous, but I want you to go. I need to talk to *Her*..." He motioned towards me, unable to call me by my real name. "Before she goes, which won't be long now."

"Maybe I should wait in the truck, Nick."

"I WANT YOU TO GO!..."

David hesitated, in turmoil over the right thing to do. He sighed. "Okay, I'm going, but I don't like it."

"Well... well fucking neither do I."

As David reached the door, he turned.

"You're my Son, Nick. We'll talk later, but don't hurt her."

"Hurt her? Hurt her? No, Father. I will not hurt her," Nick cackled.

David closed the door. Now it was just Nick and Me.

CONFRONTATION

I jumped down from the kitchen side, watching him. He swayed like a cobra before me. I took one step towards him and he recoiled away from me.

"As you can imagine, I'm a little confused, Lucy... Fuck it, Lauren..." He looked wild-eyed. "It's not even your real name. I don't know if anything you've told me is true."

I cut in pathetically, trying to diffuse the situation. "Yes, it was all true, apart from..."

"Apart from you and my dad once being in love," he spat. "Was it some fucking joke with me?"

"No, Nick..." I implored. "I just wanted..."

"Wanted? WANTED?" he shouted. "What you wanted was an upgrade, a younger model. Just like the one you were so fond of. That's what's so attractive, a new and improved version."

"It's nothing like that. Yes, of course you're like him, but you're not a replacement."

"I'm so glad we didn't fuck..." He said it now as if the idea was filthy. "Then you would have been able to compare cock size and performance." I began crying softly. "Oh, feeling sorry for yourself now are you?"

"Maybe I should go now," I said, moving nearer to the door.

So I'd wanted to see if there was another side to Nick, and here it was. I was experiencing it all now.

"No, you won't get out of it that quickly... You can't run away, like you were going to, without even telling me. You were going to let me think it was something I'd done forever."

"I was going to write a note..." I mumbled, slightly afraid of him now.

He threw his hands in the air. "Oh, a note. I'm worth a scrap of paper with a few lines scribbled on it. You take my heart, then stamp on it, leaving a fucking note.... You are priceless."

I looked down at the floor again, which in the last half hour had become very interesting.

"Nick, this is hard for me too... I've fallen in love with you."

"Don't talk to the floor, hello?... I'm here. Truth and Honesty - *That's* love. All the times we've been together. I even told you I knew something was wrong. YOU..." He pointed at me. "...should have told me. How do you know how I would have reacted? You judged me not worthy of the truth. Love should be worth taking that risk. You didn't take it, so I now judge that you're not really in love with me."

I started to sob gently again.

David told me not to tell you as well," I appealed.

He stepped towards me and raised his fist. For one moment, I thought punches would rain down on me. There was a loud BANG! and a cracking sound, as I covered my head with my arms. Peeking from under them, I could see Nick had hit a cupboard door to the side of me, completely splitting the wood.

"Maybe you're right about going... I've never felt like this before." he said, as he moved back to the other side of the room.

"Nick, please, you can't blame your dad for any of this. I came looking for him. He had no idea..." I trailed off, realising that no defence of any kind would help. He just looked at me, and even from where I was standing, I could see tears threatening to leave his eyes.

"Why you?..." he demanded, his voice now aloof. "Why have I fallen in love with you?... I'd like you to go now."

"Nick..."

"Please, the pain is too much."

Now I was crying harder, and as I opened the door, I turned to look at him one last time, but he'd gone from the room.

I left the key under the plant pot for Stan, and walked to Maisie. There was a piece of paper under her wipers. I snatched it without reading it and threw it on the back seat.

I'd only just driven past the village when I had to pull over. Great heaving, soul-wrenching sobs poured from my body. I wanted to turn back time. I wanted the pain to stop. I wanted Him. After twenty minutes of agonizing sobbing, I was able to drive. Now I just needed to increase the distance between us, to get away from everything here. I blubbered all the way home, even when I had to stop to fill up with fuel. I was plagued with questions.

What will Nick do? Have a showdown with David? Tell his mother? Get back with Perfect Jenny? Maybe all three?...

Knowing I might never know made it even worse. I couldn't bear to think about never seeing Nick again.

Driving back into London offered no solace as it usually did. It was so well known to me, yet seemed so alien. Even pulling into my street gave me no comfort. I parked and sat in Maisie, dispirited. I didn't want to get out, even though I'd just spent six hours in her.

"Come on, Lauren," I said to myself out loud.

I got my case, dragged it up to my flat, and opened the front door to nothingness. Before, I'd always loved the sensation of entering my private cocoon, and shutting out the outside world. Now it just seemed lonely, and void of life. I imagined Nick coming out of the lounge, greeting me. Kissing my stresses away. Telling me he'd been cooking, and the delicious smells emanating through the rooms. The weight of '*What if?*' crushed down on me.

Leaving my case in the hall, I threw my keys down on the coffee table and lay on the sofa. I didn't want to go to my own bed, so big, so empty without Nick. I fell asleep in my clothes, exhausted by the whole thing. I had dreams of Nick, which turned into nightmares. Subconsciously I heard my phone ring twice.

A bell ringing frantically alerted me from sleep. It took me a moment to remember where I was. No more banging at the door.

The doorbell became manic. With that kind of ferocity, it could only be Nora. Deciding it would be easier to answer it, I shuffled to the front door. Nora screamed when he saw me. As always, he was a picture of camp glamour. His beautiful chiselled bone structure was free from even a wisp of hair. His deep, playful brown eyes were alive with life. He was wearing green snakeskin trousers, with a matching waistcoat over a black silk shirt, and black Cuban-heeled boots.

I greeted him with lacklustre.

"Hi Nora."

Then I went back to the sofa and lay down again. Nora went into the kitchen, and I could hear him gasping and talking to himself. He came into the lounge.

"Girl, Nora making you coffee. Why you lay aroun' like a dead fish? ...I know, believe, love hurt in the culo!" He tittered at his own joke.

Of course, I knew he meant a pain in the arse. He made the coffee and brought it in, then shooed me up the sofa, waving his hands and clapping.

"Come, come, vamos! You sit, darlink. Sit, sit!"

I did as I was told, and sipped my coffee.

"I've ruined my life, Nora," I lamented.

"Okay, so sit aroun' getting stinky, looking like old tramp then..." I could always count on Nora to give me some helpful advice. "Chica, you look like you walk back."

"Okay. Thanks, Nora, I get the picture. I feel like shit, and I look like shit too."

"Nora will run you a nice hot bath."

"I don't want to. Who do I have to look good for? ...I'll sit here and rot."

He gasped and tutted. "Es no bien... We must go see the police today."

I groaned, having totally forgotten.

"Must we? It's the last thing I feel like doing."

Nora stood. "Sí, sí, I run you bath."

As Nora filled the tub, he sang. At least the flat felt like it was starting to breathe. Following his commands, I readied myself. I thanked the Gods I didn't have to go back to work for another ten days. I sat on the bed and let Nora pick my clothes out and mother me. I had to say no to many of his choices, or I would have looked like a cheap hooker.

"Nora. We're going to the police, not out clubbing."

"Still need to look good, Lauren..." Nora gave a small gasp with matching clap. He was holding a shortish, green army looking dress. "This one, then we are the same colour, mismo, si?"

I relented, and complied.

"Nora?"

"Sí?"

"I really need to get stoned."

He threw his hands up.

"Of course, sí, I want as well. We ask nice policemen for some?" He laughed.

"Not today then, but tomorrow?"

"Of course, we will have fun."

I didn't want to dull my senses with alcohol any more, only to feel totally maudlin the next day. As I shut the front door behind us, Nora took my hand, and we set off to the police station.

SERGEANT COLE

Nora wanted to walk, and so did I. He linked his arm with mine in a gesture of comradeship.

"So, you tell me, are you going loco?"

I smiled loosely. "I do feel like I'm going crazy, but it's nice being with you, Nora."

He squeezed my arm. "Cariño."

At least he will take my mind off of things..., I thought, and I was right.

Nora chatted gaily all the way there, about his latest shags, and who he was thinking of shagging. For Nora, life was one long Tescos shopping trip for cocks. At least that way life was less demanding or complicated.

In the end, there was always something that turned Nora off; They snored. They ate their food badly. They farted, they walked funny, or they listened to country and western. It could be anything. Once he was seeing somebody for a whole month - *Jeff*. However, Nora hated the breed of dog that poor Jeff happened to own, and that was that. Or even if their house was decorated in brown. Nora hated that colour and thought it highly unfashionable, cars and clothes included, of course. That was a massive no-no. He loved green and red, and his whole house was decorated in accordance. Nora's parents had bought him a house in London because they thought it would help him become less Gay. He told them that this is where he wanted to be, and led them to believe it would help. As they were hotel owners in Cuba making a very good living, with Nora as their only child, he wanted for nothing. He had no need to work, receiving a monthly cash injection from his kind parents. That gave him more time for cock-searching.

When we arrived at the police station, Nora flung open the doors like he was entering a Wild West saloon.

"Darlinks!..." he said dramatically to the two officers behind the desk. Both seemed transfixed by the Broadway musical before them. He glided to the counter with me trailing behind. "Buenas dias, my beauties. We are here to inspect your truncheons. Ahhh!..." He released a small cry.

The bigger of the two policemen spoke. "Can we help you, sir?"

Nora put his hand on his own chest. "Oh, yes, you could help, mucho..."

"Nora," I cut in, stepping to the counter.

"Look at his badge, so shiny."

"Nora!"

"Okay, okay."

I directed my conversation at the officer who had spoken.

"I'm Lauren Bowman, and my concerned friend here..." I motioned towards Nora. "informed you I was missing. I'm here to say I'm not."

"One moment please..." He punched some keys on his computer. "Yes, I have it here. Wait there one moment, please."

"Maybe they'll have to arrest me, and spank me for wasting police time," Nora whispered, and then squealed.

The younger cop pretended to be busy looking at something, not wanting the problem of this screaming queen. A good-looking man came out of the inner office. Nora sighed.

"Would you like to come through?" he asked, in an inviting and pleasant tone.

Nora pushed me to one side. "I would love to."

Both of us sat in his small but warm office. Nora crossed his legs provocatively and placed his hands on the top knee. I just wanted to go home, and I was wondering why we were even in there.

The man sat down, smiling. His short, dark chestnut hair had started to go grey at the sides, giving him a distinguished look.

"Sorry about this, it won't take long. I'm Sergeant Cole. I deal with the missing persons..." His green eyes flashed at me. "So if I could have your name again?"

"Lauren Bowman."

He punched it into his computer.

"Address and phone number please?"

"Forty-three, Beauchamp Road, Holborn." I recited my mobile number. More tapping on his keyboard.

"You need anything from me?" Nora crooned.

"I will in just one moment..." He replied, smiling. That made Nora sigh again. Sergeant Cole turned his eyes intently back to me. "I'll also need to see some form of identification..." His warm smile persisted. I opened my bag and got out my driving licence. handing it over to him. he glanced at it, then handed it back. "So, just to clarify. Nothing untoward has happened, and you're safe and unharmed?"

I might be safe, but I'm totally harmed... "Yes, Sergeant Cole, I only took a holiday... admittedly it was very sudden, but really, I'm fine."

"Please, call me Laurence. Well, I'm glad everything's okay, but may I suggest in future, just to save any worry, that you tell someone?"

"That's what I said," Nora cut in. "I tell her this, does she listen to Nora? - No, she no escucha."

Laurence Cole raised an eyebrow. "So I presume you're the one who informed us that Lauren was missing?"

"I was." Nora preened.

"So, please can I have your full name?"

"Noel Emilio Rodriguez Sanchez," Nora said, while Laurence Cole typed dutifully. "and my phone number is..."

"That won't be necessary Mr. Sanchez."

"Por favor, call me Nora."

Laurence smiled. "Thank-you, Nora. I have enough information."

"Shame," Nora flirted.

"So, if that's all?" I asked as I stood up, only wanting to be shut up in my flat. I stood up, Laurence stood up, and Nora didn't move, blatantly gazing at Mr. Cole's policeman's package.

Lawrence shook my hand and I made my way to the door. "Nora!" I called, raising my voice.

"Please Lauren, if there's anything I can help with in the future, don't hesitate."

I squeezed the door handle. "Thank-you. Next time I'm missing, I'll give you a call."

Nora stood. "Gracias, bonito."

"You're welcome Nora, likewise, if I can ever help with anything."

"Oh, can you tell me where I can buy good marijuana?" he asked, giggling.

I was so mortified I pulled the door as hard as I could, and it smacked me hard in the face, making my nose explode.

"OWWW!..."

I staggered back and felt Laurence catch me.

Nora screamed. "I only joke... Oh no, sangre!..."

Laurence led me to a chair. Blood was dripping down over my lips, and dropping off my chin. I tilted my head back, tasting the oh-so-familiar taste of my own blood, while Nora jumped about in an animated panic.

Laurence, policeman calm, went and got a first aid kit, placing a swab gently against my throbbing nose. His six-foot plus frame loomed over me. Nick was five foot eight, perfect, just right for me to look slightly up to meet his perfect lips. I began to cry, less for the pain of my nose, than for what I had lost.

Maybe I can post a missing persons for him...

I imagined the police dragging him, kicking and screaming to me. My weeping concerned Laurence, and stepped up Nora's performance.

"Please Lauren, hold the swab..." Laurence replaced his hand with mine. He buzzed an intercom. "Can I get some water and two paracetamol's in here?"

A moment later, the door opened revealing the young officer bearing the requested items. Laurence took them and came back over to me.

"Okay, drink some water, and take these."

He held the tablets out in his large palm. I drank my blood down, and followed it with tablets.

Laurence knelt in front of me. "I'm sorry that happened. How do you feel now?"

I looked down at this kind man. "Embarrassed, with a big nose."

"It doesn't spoil you," he said, and looking embarrassed himself, he stood up.

I stood too. "Please, I'd just like to go home now."

"Of course."

"Oh darlink, your nose look like you take too much cocaíne."

"Nora..." Now it sounded like I had a bad cold when I spoke.

"I joke, I joke!"

Mr. Cole fetched me a card from his desk. "Here's my number, just in case. Are you sure you're alright to leave?"

"Thank-you, it's fine. You've been very kind," I whined nasally at him.

He held the door open for Nora and I, walked us out, and held the outer door open for us as well.

"I hope you feel better soon, Lauren."

"Thank-you, Lawrence."

The door closed behind us as we walked down the steps. No sooner had we left when Nora began -

"Oh my God, did you see that man? Oh, I'm in love. Great big strong body, big hands... I bet he have a great big..."

"Nora! That's enough."

"...truncheon." He giggled again, and linked his arm through mine. "What I could do with a man like that, aiiee!... Anyway, he seem to like you."

I stopped walking and looked at him. "Nora, the last thing, and I mean the very last thing I want, is a man. My heart is shattered." *Just like my nose feels...*

He patted my hand, and we continued walking.

"Okay, okay, when you ready, you tell Nora. What you gonna do today? Go back to slumping and feeling sorry?"

"Yes, Nora. That's exactly what I'm going to do."

He patted my hand again. "Okay, okay, you so secretive. Sit in your flat holding your little secret, Nora will dream of her Sergeant."

We reached the flat and I kissed Nora goodbye, and entered my lonely space, immediately closing the curtains. I needed it to be dark, because that's how I felt inside. I got changed into slumpy, feeling-sorry-for-myself clothes, and armed with coffee, I sat for the whole day watching shit television. At least the drudgery I was looking at took my mind off Nick, partially. I didn't eat anything all day. I was thinking of how food reminded me of Nick. Now I had to return to my servings of vomit, apart from when Nora cooked, but then the whole thing was such a drama it was mercifully rare.

At 7pm, Nora called, telling me we were all set for tomorrow night. He said he would come round about six-ish, and it was my job to supply cakes and sweets. I told him he had to, as I was not going out. "You buy! You buy!" he cackled, and hung up.

I spent the night in a zombie-like state, with just the TV for company, telling me what I should buy, what's good for me, what's not. I saw soap operas that made chewing my own foot off seem more pleasurable. One whole day and night without Nick felt like a week. I berated myself constantly for all the things I should, or could have done. *If I'd told him the truth, maybe I would still have him now...*

I lay down with the coffee buzzing through me. I knew sleep would not come. I wanted to watch a film, one that would haunt me, but ease me at the same time. One that Nick and I had watched together. I scraped myself up, and found it easily in my vast collection - *Twilight*. The story of forbidden love. I cried quietly from beginning to end. I imagined he was next to me, our toes touching again, hands locked together. When it ended, I fell into sleep and dreamed, of course, about Nick.

SATURDAY STONED

I woke with a stiff neck from sleeping crookedly on the couch. The routine of the day commenced where it had left off the day before; Coffee, darkness and television in the same clothes on the couch. There were two small differences however. First, my mother called and reprimanded me for a full twenty-five minutes. I let her do all the talking, as it was impossible to interrupt anyway. How could I have just gone off, not answering my phone, or calling?... The police had been round to ask them questions.

> "A very lovely man, a Sergeant Cole."
> "I know, Mother. I met him yesterday."
> "Ooh, I wonder if he's married?"
> *Not this again....*

My mother's opinion was that if I had a good man, then I wouldn't live my life like a teenager any more. She couldn't accept this young-at-heart, hippy crap. She had never met anyone I'd been seeing, and this irritated her, and became reason enough for her to deem them 'drug-taking hoodies'. Probably because my preference was always for younger, rather than older, bitter with life men.

Younger guys are full of life, ready to try out new things. A divorced man with three kids and huge financial responsibilities, is far less likely to just jump on a plane and swim naked round Hawaii on a whim. I am always open to new experiences, and in that respect, I will never change.

My dating choices reflected this, although thinking about it, a lot of them *had* been drug-taking hoodies. There's a lot of them out there in the world of clubbing, but unlike the stereotype the general public are led to believe, not all of them are going to rape your grandma and kick the hamster to death, as my mother wholeheartedly believed. She constantly remarked on what a shame it was that Noel, as she insisted upon calling him, 'preferred men's back bottoms.' She loved his cleanness and gaiety, as luckily, the one person Nora toned it down for was my mother. Hoping to take her mind off Sergeant Cole, I told her Nora was coming over later.

"Ooh, darling, please say hello to that delightful Noel."

"I will, Mother. Now I really must go, someone's at the door," I said, even though there wasn't.

She gave me one last little telling off, and she was gone. I loved my mother, but in some ways, she could be even more exhausting than Nora. My father was the strong silent type, probably due to the many years that he had never been able to get a word in edgeways.

More coffee, more tears, and more TV. At about 4pm, the doorbell really did ring.

Nora early?...

Impossible. He was never early. He spent all day waxing his body and choosing outfits. I opened the door a crack, as if a foul deed was taking place behind me. A man with a huge bunch of flowers stood on the step.

"Yes?..." I asked, through the small gap.

"Are you Lauren Bowman?"

"Yes."

"Well if you open your door enough, I can deliver these flowers."

For one delirious moment, I thought they were from Nick, but then I realised he didn't even know my real name, let alone where I lived. I opened the door enough to admit the flowers, and thanked the deliveryman.

As I carried them into the flat, I noticed the note tucked within the beautiful arrangement of summer flowers. They were mostly pinks and purples with sweet scents. I took them into the kitchen, found a vase, and lay them down while I read the note.

Dear Lauren,
I do hope you are feeling better.
Kind regards,
Laurence Cole.

Now, that I hadn't expected. I thought it was a kind gesture, but I wouldn't be thanking him. I put them on the coffee table in the lounge and thought no more about Sergeant Cole.

Three hours later, one hour later than arranged, Nora turned up. He gasped when he saw the flowers, and screamed when I told him who they were from.

"See darlink, I told you he like you. ...Ahhh, so romantic."

I looked at him scornfully.

"A bunch of flowers delivered by an unknown man is not romantic, Nora... Picnics, and movie days in bed are romantic," I recalled sadly.

"Okay then," Nora said, as he sat down and opened his small attaché bag, removing a small packet with Ganja, Rizla's and tobacco. "Nora's waited toooo long, mucho tiempo, waiting for *this* story."

Expertly, he rolled a perfect joint. Mine always came out like huge cigars that constantly went out. He looked perfect, sitting back in his salmon Gucci shirt and purple Don Lorenzo trousers, lighting up. He took the first toke, then passed it to me.

As I smoked, I felt my body un-tense. My neck was still stiff, but my muscles and brain heaved a collective sigh of relief. We passed it back and forth, both of us relaxing into the relaxation, a good feeling. I could put my brain on pause and think more logically than normal. Stoned was the only time Nora was not so hysterical. He smoked it mandatorily when he had to see his parents. If they saw how truly Gay he was, it would be Goodnight, Vienna.

I turned off the television, I'd overloaded on it by this time, and put some music on. Nora began to giggle.

"I think of that lovely Sergeant Cole, totally naked, whip cream all over his big cock."

"It would have been more fun if he'd delivered the flowers like that," I admitted, smiling.

"Ahhh! Yes, so naughty..."

I sat cross-legged on the floor and watched Nora roll another joint.

"So, you speak to your mother?"

"Yes... how did you know she called?"

"Darlink, she call Nora. She love me..." He smiled a big devilish smile and we burst out laughing. "She was worried when you gone..." He lit the joint and puffed long and hard on it. "I smoke my joints like I smoke my men. Aiieee!... So naughty."

Right at that moment, I could not have been with a better person in a better place. My flat started to feel like home again. I was relieved to have positive things to latch onto.

"So, Nora make you laugh, now you tell me, que paso?"

Yes, now I could rationally tell him my irrational story. I started at the beginning, how I'd looked up David on Facebook, and ended with the look on Nick's face as I'd left.

"...It will never leave me, Nora. Never."

Luckily, Nora was too stoned to provide his usual dramatic running commentary. The whole time he held his hand to his chest, mouth agape. When I'd finished, he pushed the weed over to me and opened his bag, getting his tissues out. He dabbed the corners of his eyes.

"Laauren... This is the stuff the movies are made of. So fantastical, so romantic. Amor del corazon..." He shooed his hands at me. "You roll, you roll, I cannot." I gave it my best shot as Nora threw his hands in the air. "Chica. The not knowing... es dramatico."

"It's my own fault Nora, but I'll love him forever. Nick is The One."

As I stared down at most of the contents of my joint on the table, the short fat blunt in my hand gave me some unknown pleasure. Some things never change.

"Ahhaha!" Nora gasped at the sight.

"You should be used to my joints by now, Nora.""

He tittered. "No, I was thinking that I throw men away with the cock like that..." We sniggered simultaneously. "No, I have a plan, darlink. I go there, and see what's happening."

"Oh no, Nora, you're far too excitable to keep things to yourself. That would be great, sending the world's gayest man to find out information in a tiny fishing village, population; 170 men and 20 women."

"I know, so horrible, but for you, darlink, I put myself through it." He screamed.

"I don't think it's a good plan, Nora," I said, but I was smiling. I could see the funny side, imagining Nora in Devon.

"Okay, spoil it. Nick, he sound creamy dreamy... You have pictures?"

I sighed and wished I had. "No."

"You so slack, chica." Nora took over the rolling again, after only getting six puffs between us on the one I'd wrapped up.

"It's not just the way he looks, although thinking about him does make my pussy a loaded gun. Everything, everything about him is right. Even when he was angry, I knew it was just because of his passion, too."

"Don't tell me, darlink, about angry sexy passion. I'm Cuban... Arriba!..." He rolled his R's loudly.

"Nora, I love passion, well, maybe not in all its forms, but you can't pick and choose between them. Nick was like that - accepting all that I am."

"You know, I look too, on Facebook, to my old love?" I was shocked to hear that Nora had ever been in love. "He was there, the big fat campesino. He got four muchachos now, boys. It's disgusting. Nora wouldn't even cross the street now..." He tutted with disdain.

I didn't question him further. If Nora had wanted to tell me, he would have. He liked the fact that I didn't pry into his life, and although he knew practically everything about me, he never judged. The combination worked very well between us.

"Only I'm fool enough to actually take things further," I said.

Nora got up, tutting. "Bastante, enough.... We gonna have poco fiesta!" He perused my music collection, gasped and clapped his hands. "This one is perfecto." I smiled at his joy, and wondered what his choice was. He put the CD in and clicked through the tracks, counting aloud. "Uno, dos, trés, cuatro, and cinco..." He spun round and pushed the sofa forward against the coffee table. "Okay, stand. Dance, Bailar..." He began to clap. "Quick, quick!" I came round the couch and joined Nora.

"Okay, what have you chosen?"

"Arrgh! You love it... Can only be Jimmy."

Jimmy? Jimmy who?...

Nora un-paused the pause button. First, a rhythmic eighties beat pumped out, followed by the lyrics -

Don't leave me this way,
I can't survive, I can't stay alive,
Without your love, so baby,
Don't leave me this way.

We began to move more and more, the tune was so familiar. We were waiting for the build-up... Here it came....

Aaaaaaaaaaaaaaaaaaaaaaaaah, baby!
My heart is full of love, and it's all for you...

We raised our arms in the air and tilted our heads back, singing along. Our feet were stamping fast, and we sprung up into the air on the -

Baby! So come on down and do what you got to do,
You've started a fire, down in my soul,
Now can't you see it's burning outta control,
So come on down and satisfy the need in me,
Cause only your good lovin' can set me free, set me free,
Aaaaaaaaaaaaaaaaaaaaaaaaah, baby!...

Both of us went berserk, jumping round until our faces went red, and the blood pumped through us. We were energised by weed, Alison Moyet and Jimmy Somerville.

By the time the song finished I felt good. Both of us had our hands on our knees, bending forward and laughing, in-between taking deep breaths. Eventually Nora stood straight, fanning himself with his hand.

"Darrlink, you've got to love that little man..." He replaced the CD with another. Then, going over to the flowers, he chose two pink varieties, and gave one to me. "Now, darlink, we in the mood to go Cuban, Aiiiee!..."

Nora pressed play, and Latino sounds filled the room. He put his flower in his mouth and held his hands high, clapping short, sharp claps. I copied the flower in the mouth, and began to rumba, luckily something I know how to do. We shook our hips, and danced and danced. We danced over the coffee table, over the sofa, and over Life. Nora shouted over the music -

"Where your phone, darlink? ...I take picture..." I pointed to it and he danced over to it. He pressed some keys, then looked and waved at me. "Darlink, it say is full. Can I delete?"

Full? I don't remember taking any photos...

I hadn't even switched it on until near the end of my stay in the cottage. Panting, I went over and turned the music down.

"Wait, Nora, I'll see what they are."

He handed me the phone and I browsed through the photos. The first one was so blurry I couldn't see the image. I scrolled on and gasped. The next picture was totally clear; Nick, lying on the bed in his Calvin's, poking his tongue out. My pulse was already racing from the dancing but it sped up some more. I scrolled on. A lot of them were out of focus, but the good ones made my heart ache. We must have taken them on the last night, when we were drunk.

"Que pasa?" Nora interrupted.

I looked at him in a daze. "They're... they're pictures of me and Nick."

Nora squealed like an excited pig, and rushed to my side.

He squinted his eyes at one of the not-so-good ones. "Darlink, all I see is pixels."

I also had a need in me to see them more clearly, to revisit every particle of him. Nora began to roll a joint instinctively. He jittered with excitement and anticipation. As I fetched my laptop, mixed feelings engulfed me. My hands shook as I set it up on the coffee table and pushed the sofa back into place. I made a folder on the desktop called '*Simply Nick*' and blue-toothed all the photos into it.

"Okay, they're ready."

I turned the laptop to face Nora, and sat closer next to him. He lit a joint, and we looked at each other, both of us with the same feeling, zapped back to being young, about to watch your first porn movie, discovered in some hiding-place. You want to press play so badly, but you're terrified of what you're about to see.

"Ahh, I can't stand it, open, open!" Nora commanded, shooing his hands at me.

I double-clicked. The first four were rubbish, and Nora was disappointed.

"Oh...Oh..." he went on each one, but the fifth one got him.
Oh gosh almighty, saints alive!...

Nick was standing there looking like a model in an advert. Nora gasped, then placed the knuckle of his index finger into his mouth and squealed. My skin sizzled. In Nick's drunk state, he'd obviously posed for the shot. He was standing in front of the fireplace, his jeans undone and his CK's exposed, with both thumbs wedged down into his waistband, as if about to pull them down. His head was cocked to one side, as if he was puzzling on something. Sexual confidence dripped from him, making the photo almost tangible.

Nora put his hand on my hand. "Darlink, this..." He gestured at the screen. "Is what you left behind?"

I reached over and took the joint from him. "Yes, Nora."

He gasped again. "Darlink, some things you can afford to leave behind... A bag with some old clothes in, cheap cosmetics, shoes that pinch or a full condom for example, but some things you do not leave.... Personally, darlink, I would drive sixteen hours if I'd forgotten my Louis Vuitton handbag. Never, never would I leave a perfect specimen like this..." He pointed at Nick. "For him, I walk to China barefoot." He sat back.

"He's not a bag, Nora. I can't just go back and say; 'Oh sorry, I forgot you,' pick him up, and bring him back home... He told me to go, what can I do?"

My head hung. Nora placed his finger under my chin and lifted my head gently.

"You must fight, Lauren. Fight for Nick."

I laid my head against his chest. "Nora, I can't. If I went to him, and he rejected me again, well, I couldn't bear it."

He stroked my hair. "Cariño...," he cooed.

I brought my eyes back to the screen. "Let's look at some more."

"If you want, chica."

I continued to scroll through. Most were too blurry, but there were some gems as well. One of Nick by the fire, one on the bed, and one of him standing in the kitchen doorway in only his Calvin's, both hands behind his head, stretching. Both Nora and I sighed deeply when we saw that one. There was only one of me that I liked, and Nick was in it with me. Both of us were laying down, our smiling, and happy faces side-by-side. The selfie was taken close, perfectly framing our head and necks.

"Ahhhh... I love this one. You look so cute together," Nora professed.

We did, he was right. It was worse than if he'd said '*OMG, darlink!... you look like Mother and Son... purleeese!...*'

I kept the primo ones and deleted the rest, setting the one of Nick by the fireplace as my screen-saver.

"Lauren, we need to go out, have fun..." Nora suggested, and though normally it would have been exactly what I needed, it wasn't this time.

"No, not yet Nora. Just give me a week or two."

He patted my head with mild understanding.

"Are you staying tonight? It is..." I looked at my watch. "Two-thirty in the A.M."

"Darlink, I would, but Nora go to the sauna." This meant he was going out to man-hunt. "Nora's hungry."

Giggling apologetically, he collected his things together and made sure his thick, dark hair was in shape. Then he sprayed some Paco Rabanne aftershave on, kissed me so many times on the face, and I was on my own once more. I lay back on the sofa and fell into a heavy, dreamless, weed-induced sleep.

POEM

For the next three days, I subtly managed to hide from the world. Nobody called, leaving me with only time to wallow in. I kept my laptop on constantly, so I could look at Nick whenever I wanted. After three days and nights in the same clothes, the coffee table still strewn with weed and tobacco from Saturday night, I looked like all I needed was a plastic cup and I could go and wander the streets. Action needed to be taken.

I'd already decided I wanted copies of the pictures blown up, so I could hang them in my bedroom.

Poor, sad, lovesick Lauren...

I decided to tackle myself first, and the flat later.

One hour later, feeling a bit more human, I copied the photos onto a usb stick, took a deep breath, and went out. The shops weren't far, but Maisie looked so neglected that I drove. I went the long way, past the police station where I'd been a few days before. The Gods of traffic were being kind to me, and my journey was swift.

I parked close to Posterprint, luckily, my destination. I handed the stick to the spotty, gum-chewing boy at the desk, and told him the size I wanted for each one. His face never changed, but his chewing increased in size and speed, allowing me to see into his mouth. I waited for a sign that he could form words, maybe even a coherent sentence.

Maybe he's a mute... I waved my hand at him. "Hello?" I pronounced slowly, in case he had enough brain-power to lip read.

So finally, at least this made him stop chewing.

"Whaa?"

I put both my hands on the counter. "Ahhh, it speaks."

This wonderful individual was reminding me why I hadn't wanted to leave my flat.

"You bein' funny?" he said.

"Apparently not."

My sarcasm was totally lost on him.

"We're not allowed to print porn," he informed me, as he eyed me suspiciously.

I bet... I thought. *They probably had to make that a rule, because of this spunk-drained lad wanking over them...*

I raised my eyebrows; this whole encounter was already draining my soul. "Look... did you understand what I wanted?"

"Course. I'm not an idiot."

Personally, I thought he could have won a prize for his impression of one.

"Well?"

What?"

Good God, I could have printed them myself by now....

I closed my eyes and willed myself not to bash him to death with an Olympus trip camera.

"So... is it possible?"

He started chewing again, and this seemed to bring him back to life slightly.

"Course it is."

"Now?" I asked sharply.

"Yeah, but there's no need to get angry, missus."

Please fucking help me to cope with this... I formed a tight smile. "Yes, please. Now."

"Well, you shoudda said."

He trailed off as he turned and headed towards a machine that I assumed a blind, arthritic monkey could operate. The whole operation took fifteen minutes, fourteen of which I spent staring at this Da Vinci's back. As he was performing his printing masterpieces, every few minutes he pressed a button, just to let me know he was still breathing. On completion, two were the wrong size, but I lacked the strength to say anything. I paid him and thanked him, glad to be leaving.

Outside, I opened Maisie's door and put the prints on the back seat, replacing the folded paper I had found the day I left Nick, which I threw onto the front passenger seat. As I drove straight home, I began to eye the note next to me. Doing the stereotypical woman-driving thing, I picked up the paper and attempted to multitask - driving and reading.

At the top it said -

Lauren, I have tried to put it into words,

Next thing I knew there was an almighty BANG!

I lurched forward, hitting my head on the steering wheel. I could faintly hear shouting.

Owww, that hurt...

I sat back and focused through the windscreen, and the sight hurt me even more.

Poor Maisie...

Her bonnet was wrapped round a pole, which held a sign that told people to be careful of the zebra crossing. The man who'd been shouting came up to the window dressed as a lollipop man.

"You 'oright Miss?... You just missed me, but you squashed me lollipop, Miss..." I started to laugh. At first, it was gentle mirth, but it progressed to mad, howling laughter. "Are you drunk, Miss?... I'm gonna have to call the police."

Through my madness, I could hear him talking. I'd probably written off my precious Maisie, and killed an innocent lollipop. I couldn't stop laughing, and the lollipop man moved away from the drunken ranting woman. As my laughter began to subside, I heard approaching sirens, and thought it best to stay put where I was, with my seatbelt on.

Safety first...

Two police officers got out of the car. One went over and talked to the lollipop man, who, devoid of his lollipop, was now just a man in a fluoro-jacket and a silly hat. The other came over to my driver's side, and opened my door.

"You alright, Miss?"

I turned to look at him. "I've had an accident, and killed two things."

His eyes flicked up to the blood on my forehead. "And what things would they be, Miss?"

"Mmmm, my car, and a lollipop."

A tiny hint of a smile danced in the corner of his mouth at the mention of the latter. "Do you think you're able to get out?"

Yes, but do I want to?... I clicked my seatbelt free. "Yes, I think so."

He held the door open while I got out. The lollipop man was still jabbering away, pointing in my direction.

"Okay, if you could just stand there..." The policeman motioned beside Maisie. "I noticed you've hit your head, would you like me to call for medical assistance?"

I felt and prodded the area in question. After the amount of bangs and knocks I'd had, this one was small.

"No, I'm fine, thank-you," I replied.

He looked in and around the car while he waited for the other cop to come over.

Why did I leave the safety of my flat?... Why did I drive?... Why did I try to read that - what was it?... a letter or something from Nick?...

I went round the car and started frantically to try to read it through my window.

"Stay where you were please, Miss..." I turned to see the other officer approaching. He took his colleague to one side for a brief chat, then sent him back over to me, nodding. "You'll have to come with us to the station. We'll need to check your documents and give you a breathalyser"

Again?... Back to the station?...Oh no... "Please, I have insurance, and..." I breathed hard, full into his face. "See? I've not been drinking."

His voice betrayed his loss of patience; "Miss, a breathalyser is a tube you blow into. We can't get an accurate reading by you simply blowing in my face. Now, please?" He gently took my arm.

"But my car?" I protested.

"It'll get picked up and taken to the police impound."

Oh no.... The photos, the letter...

"Please, please, kind Mr. Policeman, I have some very important things in the back. Not drugs, you can look, but please can I get them?..." I tried my best to implore him with my eyes and expression. He hesitated. "Please?" I pleaded.

"Who mentioned drugs, Miss?" he asked, before a quick motion of his head towards Maisie let me know it had worked.

However, he came with me and checked the back seat in case. I quickly put the note from Nick in with the bag of blown-up photos, and clutched them in the back of the police car, for the whole three-minute journey to the police station. The same station I'd driven past half an hour ago.

I stood at the same counter I'd stood at before, and gave my name and address again. I blew into the tube, and they marked it down as negative. Zero alcohol level. As I scattered my documents on the counter, one of the officers searched my handbag and inspected the stuff I'd retrieved from Maisie.

The larger faced, bald headed guy said; "We'll need to take a statement."

Oh good, what a fun way to spend the rest of my day...

Behind the counter, the door opened, and Laurence Cole emerged. He saw me immediately, and came round to my side of the counter.

"Lauren, what's wrong?"

The fat-faced cop seemed slightly taken aback. "You know this lady, Sergeant Cole?"

"Yes. Yes I do, Constable Hamby," he answered without taking his eyes from me. "What's happened here?"

"Well, the young lady's been involved in a traffic incident."

Laurence looked concernedly at me. "Have you hit your head?"

"Of course I have," I replied very matter-of-factly.

"I'm taking Miss Bowman into the office," Laurence told big face. "It's quite possible she has concussion."

"Yes, Sir."

Laurence led me through and sat me down in a comfy chair.

"Would you like a glass of water?"

"No, thank-you, I'm fine... apart from killing my car."

He looked bemused. "Well then Lauren, if you'll excuse me for a moment, we'll see if we can clear things up." Smiling and showing great teeth, he left the room.

I stayed put, my bag still held tightly against my chest, protecting its precious contents. It was a while before Laurence came back in.

"Lauren, how are you feeling now?"

"Pretty vacant..."

"Okay, well this is what's going to happen. You're clear on all counts. No charges are being brought. The only thing is, you'll have to pay for a replacement lollipop."

I looked into his emerald eyes. I could see he was trying to help me.

Sorry Mr. Cole, maybe, just maybe pre-Nick, I could have liked you, but now my world is only post-Nick... "Thank-you, Laurence. And for the flowers, too."

He blushed where he stood. "You're welcome..." He went over to a desk drawer, took some keys out, and placed them on the desk. "Now, you're without a car, and probably concussed, so I'm driving you home."

I stood. "No, no it's..."
He held his hand up. "You have no choice."

I followed him through the station and out the back to where the cop's private vehicles parked. As we got in, I began to tell him my address.

"No need, I remember," he cut in.

It took us less than ten minutes to get there. Both of us said nothing. I wished it were Nick who was taking care of my wounded head. We pulled up outside, and Laurence quickly got out and opened the door for me.

My mother would love this man. - An outstanding member of the community...

I went up the steps, rummaging in my over-full handbag. Twice I pulled out the same tampon and a lipstick, before I finally located my keys. As I opened the door, I turned round to face the smiling Mr. Cole.

"Well, thank-you, Laurence."

He took a step up. "I'm coming in Lauren. I want to make sure you're alright. You've had a car-crash."

Yes, but not in my flat... I suppose I could at least offer him a cup of tea...

I shrugged and went into my apartment, letting him shut the door. I put my bag down in the hall, and went through to the front room. Stopping dead still, my eyes bulged as I spotted the coffee table.

Shit! Shit!... why didn't I clean it up?...

"Lauren?"

He was standing right behind me, the firm hand of the Law, while Jamaica lay two feet away. Panic set in.

162

Great.... Survive the accident, only to be nicked for drugs and sent to a women's-only prison with my sex-starved cellmate who looks like Pat Butcher from EastEnders.. Trouble is, the kitchen is through the living room...

I turned to face him quickly. "Laurence, why don't we stay here, or should we have tea in the bedroom?" His eyes widened. *Why did I say that?....* "Sorry, I mean, let's have tea in the toilet?"

He took my hands. "I think you banged your head worse than you realize. Maybe you should lie down."

I stepped forward, out and away from the living room, and took another two steps up the hall.

"Yes, you're right," I agreed, as I lay down on the hallway floor. "Laurence, you're right, it is better."

He walked over to me, and stared down. "I meant somewhere more comfortable."

"No, no, it's fine here."

He sighed. "Well, okay, let me get you a drink. Hot tea maybe?"

He cannot go to the kitchen.... "Laurence, please, I'm fine. I don't drink tea, coffee, soft drinks, herbal tea, or milk. No water either."

He knelt down next to me. "Lauren, you may think you're fine, but if I were to examine the evidence, and I think I'm qualified to do so; You are laying in your hallway, and according to you, you never ever take any fluids other than alcohol?..." I nodded in the affirmative. "Yet at the station there was zero alcohol in your body?"

Shit, he's a cop!... "I haven't been thirsty." I said, quietly and ineptly.

"Look, it's obvious to me, you don't want me to go in the other room. But it's your house, and just maybe, you're always this kooky. You did also bang your head."

I raised myself onto my forearms. "Laurence, I do that a lot.... If I promise to look after myself, will you go?" I knew this didn't sound very nice, but I did want him to go.

His face softened. "I will if that's what you want, but be warned, I'll come to check up on you."

He made it sound like I'd committed a crime and he needed to keep an eye on me.

"Thank-you for bringing me home."

He turned to go. "All part of the service."

I watched him leave from my position on the floor. As the door clicked shut, I let out a long sigh and lay my head back down. Pre-Nick I could have dealt with this, but this was post-Nick, and I was laid out in my hallway for a long time.

If he were here, this would be different... He would stop whatever he was doing to come and lay next to me and offer solace, stroking my soul back to normality... Oh Nick, what are you doing now?... How are you feeling?...

Finally, I got up, leaving my bag in the hall. I went over to the coffee table and brushed all its contents into a pile. I stuck some papers together and made a joint, switched on the TV, kicked off my shoes, lay back on the sofa and lit up, shutting out the day. This led to a few hours of dozing. When I looked at the time, it was Ten past Ten at night. I rolled and lit the last joint, taking it with me as I retrieved my bag from the hallway. It was just the note I wanted. I pulled it out and put the bag to one side, shakily unfolding it. I'd read the first sentence already -

Lauren, I have tried to put it all in words...

Reading further, I could see it was a poem. I began to read -

I couldn't let this time go by without some words to tell you why,
I'm building up a love, something real, feeling true,
I breathe too deep when I think of you,
My heart explodes this is something new.
Driving me crazy, what am I to do?

A taste of thrill and captivation, sensuous gorgeous infatuation,
This lust could drive me insane.
Valentines spin in my brain.
Holding each other, close, desperate, so tight,
Can't help but notice it feels so right.
I know from now on I will never be the same,
Desire in my soul spills over again.

Real love in life is fleetingly grasped,
I will not let this moment pass.
As long as you're by my side,
You build up my foolish pride.
It's not something I can explain,
But without you, there is only pain.
Desire in my soul spills over again.
Nick *

Tears poured down my face, and my soul felt like it was the size of a cashew nut.

Nora was right, he is worth fighting for... I couldn't even drive there with my beloved Maisie gone. It's all so impossible... Go to Nick's house, 'Oh hi, it's me. Is Nick in?...Can he come out to play?'...

I thought maybe it would have been okay, if Maggie had opened the door and taken my messages word-for-word, but she was only five years old, and I knew I was clutching at straws. I lay down and faced the back of the sofa, staying that way for the rest of the night and most of the morning - the telly still on and my life on pause.

The doorbell rang normal polite rings, so I knew it wasn't Nora.

Maybe it's my mother? They'll go away...

But they didn't. Then there was a knocking at the window.

Okay, I get the message...

Dressed in the same clothes as the day before, I went to answer the door, opening it to reveal... Sergeant Cole.

I should have guessed. The police *are* very persistent.

"Lauren, you look like you really did stay in your hallway all night."

Wearing a dark green short-sleeved top that matched his eyes, and jeans with trainers, you would never have guessed he was a part of Her Majesty's Service.

"Laurence!" I tried to smile.

"I'm just checking to see if you're okay?"

I pushed back my hair and straightened my dress.

"Yes," I started to say to the trained police ear, who knew I wasn't okay.

"Please, would you mind if I came in today, perhaps further than the hallway?"

The coffee table was clean, and I was starting to think if I didn't let him in, he would start to think I had a meth lab in there, or dead tortured bodies... I opened the door wide, signalling entrance allowed, and he went through, waiting for me to lead the way. I took him through to the front room where Sergeant Cole looked round taking in all the details, including the flowers he'd sent me.

"May I?" he asked, pointing at the sofa.

"Err, yes... Would you like a cup of tea?"

He grinned. "So, today you drink tea?"

I tried to recall what I'd said the previous night. "Oh..." I decided to play the innocent. "Why wouldn't I have tea?"

I went into the kitchen, but the beauty of open plan living is still being able to carry on conversations from another room.

"Don't you remember what you said?" he asked.

Careful Lauren, he's police, he'll remember word-for-word. Just make tea and avoid eye contact... "I can't remember much from when I got home... must be concussion."

I busied myself even though he hadn't even said he wanted a drink. I was needing a coffee pretty badly, myself.

"Yeah... It must be that. And thanks, I'll have a tea with no sugar."

I felt totally fragmented as I prepared the drinks and he watched the crappy television. I brought his tea through first, then returned for my coffee, and sat in an armchair opposite the sofa. He sat with his arm draped casually along the back of the sofa.

"So... did you then?" he asked.

"Did I what?..." I countered dimly, looking guilty, being questioned.

"Sleep in the hall?"

I relaxed a bit. "Oh no, I went to bed," I lied.

"Lauren, does it make you nervous that I'm a cop?"

166

My mobile rang, saving me from having to reply; '*Yes, of course it fucking does!*'

I got up to answer it.

"Sorry Laurence, I'd better get that... Hello?" It was Nora. "Yes...no...No. Listen Nora, I kind of had a little accident yesterday, and Sergeant Cole is here." Nora cried out and hung up, and I carried on pretending to talk to him. "Really?...No....really?..." I left appropriate pauses.

Laurence was looking at me.

Maybe he knows I'm faking?... Could a good policeman detect if a woman was faking orgasm?... The thought made me smile. "Okay, thanks Nora. Bye."

I wound up my little charade and returned to my seat. "My friend Nora - he was at the station."

I noticed Laurence shift slightly. "Yes, I remember. He's not easy to forget."

I giggled. "No he's not, but Nora's got a heart of gold."

"I'm sure," he said, matter-of-factly.

I drank my coffee, then made a show of putting the cup back into the kitchen.

"Oh well, I really must get on with things. It was nice of you to stop by."

He brought his empty mug over and handed it to me.

"Okay, I can take a hint." He was very close to me. "But you shouldn't be afraid of me." Intensity flew from him.

"I'm not," I protested, as the mug fell from my grasp and I dropped it on the floor.

His look said; '*I rest my case,*' but he bent down to pick up the bits of broken cup for me. "If it helps, I *am* off-duty."

I went over to the bin and threw the fragmented crockery in, speaking with my back to him -

"It was just an accident. I'm not afraid of you."

"Well I am a nice guy. If you give me a chance, you'll find out."

I turned to face him. "I think you are nice, Laurence. I'll be honest, I've just had my heart broken. It sounds like a cliché, but it's only the second time in my life this has happened. I can't see beyond that at the moment." I stopped, unable to carry on.

He looked genuinely concerned. "Sorry. I know from personal experience how much that hurts. My wife left me, and took the kids."

Man with baggage... crossed my mind.

"But all I'm asking for is maybe just friendship." He fell silent.

Friendship with a copper?... I wasn't sure how I felt about that.

"Maybe," I said.

"So I'll see myself out then, oh, and about your car..."

"Yes?" I cut in enthusiastically.

"We don't need it anymore, so now you have to let the insurance company know, and they can assess it down at the vehicle compound."

"Thank-you, Lawrence."

He *was* kind. I held a small spark of hope, that Maisie could be saved.

As he left, I heard the door shut, and began to make another coffee. Not even five minutes went by before a frantic ringing on the doorbell announced the arrival of Nora, who was still panting when I opened the door.

He was wearing a dark green Paul Smith suit with a pale pink shirt, also by Paul Smith - Nora's favourite designer.

"Darlink!... I came as quick as I could."

I wondered if it was because I'd had an accident, or because Sergeant Cole had just been here.

"Come in then, Nora, but if you're here to see Mr. Cole, he's just left." The loud scream informed me that it was the latter. "But thank-you for your concern, and rushing over to see how I am," I said sarcastically, as I led Nora through.

"Darlink, of course, I come *rapido* for you."

I went through to the kitchen. "I'm making coffee, Nora."

"Please, darrrlink..." Nora also understood the difference between bean fresh ground coffee and a teaspoon of instant brown gravel impersonating coffee. He sat on the sofa. "But I cannot deny I am un porquito disappointed."

I brought the coffee through. "Well, you're welcome to have him."

"Ooh, so angry. ...So, tell Nora what happen?"

So, I did. He shrieked, gasped, screamed and stood up when I told him Maisie was probably dead, the fun we'd had in her mere memories. I told him up to the point when he just missed Mr. Cole.

"Why you get to have all the fun?"

"Funny, it didn't feel like that at the time, Nora," I answered sarcastically.

"Si, si. Okay, Maisie dying is not so fun. But, Cariño... now you in with the police. Lawrence Cole help you, so now you must suck his big police cock." He started giggling.

"Nora, I'm not '*in*' with anyone, especially the police. Jesus!

Look at how I live my life, I'm hardly a role model as a copper's girlfriend, or even friend. I can't worry about that too."

I stood up and flounced into the hall to fetch the photos.

"Okay, okay, Lauren. So, let me read the poem, por favor?"

I decided to let him see it, it was too good to keep a secret. I fetched that as well, handed it to him, and while I sorted the photos out, he read the lines in worrying silence. No drama or fuss.

He hates it...

He replaced it on the table and held his hand to his chest, breathing slowly. The suspense was killing me.

"Nora, say something." It was not a sentence I had to use often.

He looked in my eyes. "It's fantastico, bellissimo, sooo romantico!..." He stood up, shouting; "Aiieeee!... I love it, Lauren." He took my hands. "I have a friend, Leonard Goldstein, he make music. Please, I copy this and take it to him?"

What crazy idea is this now?... "Nora, I'm not sure,"

He cut me off; "Yes, you let me. Darlink, I must."

"Well, only if you copy it. You can't have the original."

He opened his bag and took out some Basildon Bond paper and a Parker pen. Everything to hand. He sat and copied over Nick's love to me.

I studied the photos, and decided to put the one of us together in the bedroom, the one of Nick poking his tongue out in the hall, and the other two in the lounge. I got a hammer and some tacks, and on the biggest wall, I put the one of Nick standing in front of the fire. On the smaller wall next to the window, I hung the one of him standing in the doorway.

"Finito!" Nora exclaimed, and put his writing gear back in his bag. He looked up at the pictures, big and bold on the wall, and sighed. "So preetty..."

Yes he is...

I wanted to curl up and stare at them all.

"So, darlink. I go to telephone Leonard..." He kissed me on both cheeks. "You need Nora, you call. Hasta luego."

I saw Nora out, and looked at the empty parking space where Maisie would normally be. It felt like I was pining for everything now.

Time to shut out the world again...

BACK TO WORK

For the next three days, I hid, counting down the days till, and dreading Work. That Sunday, I had no choice but to be sociable as my mother was coming over. This didn't happen often, but after a brief chat on the phone, during which I told her about Maisie, she'd insisted. That also meant I had to clean the place up on a Sunday morning. Either that, or open myself up to a barrage of criticism. Of course, it would never be good enough; up to her standard, but I'd given up trying to live up to that a long time ago. My mother also hated unpunctuality. One O'clock she said she would be there, and One O'clock on the dot the bell rang. I'd cleaned myself up, and was wearing appropriate '*Mother-friendly clothing*'. She would comment on how thin I looked, but that had been her mantra for years.

With a big fake smile, I opened the door.

"Hello, darling." She looked me up and down the same way Sergeant Cole did - inspecting me.

"Mother, do come in."

I kissed her cheek in the hallway, and hurried her through. She took her coat off and handed it to me, and I hung it properly in the hall. My mother didn't approve of clothing being flung on the backs of chairs, or furniture. Everything in its proper place. I returned to find her still standing, examining everything, as always. She looked as if she were planning to buy the property.

"You should open your curtains wider, darling. It will let more light in."

I closed my eyes as I turned to put the kettle on. My mother only drank tea.

"Tea?" I offered.

She was sitting on the sofa, and I could feel her looking at the photos of Nick.

"Yes please, but only one sugar, darling. I'm on a diet."

She was always on a diet, but never seemed to lose weight. '*I eat like a bird, darling,*' she would say, whilst eating a man-size portion of dinner, followed by an equally humongous pudding.

"Who is this?...On your wall? It's a bit large isn't it?"

"Oh... he's an up and coming model. A friend of Nora's. He gave them to me as a gift." *I must remember to tell Nora that little white lie...*

"Oh." She softened now she knew that Nora was involved. "He does have good taste. Such a good looking boy."

Tears welled in my eyes. "Yes, yes he is."

I carried the tea precariously in cups and saucers. My mother always said that mugs were for common people.

"Darling, are you eating properly? You look thin. Women of your age need some weight on them."

Here we go... "Yes, mother. I am eating."

Sitting opposite my mother, I could see the other picture of Nick, and it helped. I let my Mother do most of the talking as we drank tea, mostly about my father. The things he was neglecting, the fact he was always in his tool-shed. I couldn't blame him for that, it was at least nice and peaceful in there.

She told me that if I kept my mind on what I was doing more often, then I wouldn't have had an accident. Now it was my own fault I had no car. She shifted in her seat as she told me I needed cushions, and not the cheap ones that lose their plumpness quickly. Moreover, not blue, as it's such a cold colour.

I was nodding at the right moments, not letting my gaze leave Nick. I wondered if he could somehow feel me staring intently at him.

Lauren, you're losing it...

"Lauren!" My mother snapped, jerking me back into the room.

"Yes, Mother?"

"I do wish you'd look at me when I'm talking. It's very disconcerting when you're looking away."

"Sorry, Mother."

171

I was forty-three, but she always managed to make me feel young and silly.

"So, you're back to work tomorrow?"

"Yes," I groaned.

"Well, you've had enough time off now. Better than wasting yourself."

Work tomorrow, what a shit....

Back on the tube, back to my desk and my computer, where all this sadness had stemmed from.

My mother stayed for another twenty minutes to tell me passionately about my younger brother's latest successes. He was thirty-one, brainy, organised, accomplished, and good with money. My mother would never hear a bad word said about my baby brother, and she was right, he was all those things, but he wasn't the goody-two-shoes she thought he was. Jonathan travelled a lot as part of his job as a marine biologist. He was at that moment in the states, earning buckets of dosh, but occasionally he'd crash at mine, and we'd had some wild times. He'd sworn me to secrecy, so I took all the flak for being a dropout. I didn't mind, because we got on so well. It wasn't exactly his fault, that he was naturally good at most things he turned his hands or mind to. Most things I turn my hands or mind to end in disaster.

My mother was telling me she'd gotten a phone call from my brother at 3am, and how she didn't mind at all, as she understood the time difference. If I called her at that time of night, I'd have to be genuinely dying. Apparently, Jonathan was going to the Maldives for a month, and then maybe coming home for a few days. There was a time, way back, when I would have felt jealous, but all I wanted at that moment was Devon.

My mother air-kissed me as she left.

"You really should scrub your front step, Lauren. People will think you're common." She descended them as if they might contaminate her.

I changed into my slumping clothes as soon as she'd gone, and pulled the curtains shut. I tried not to think about work, and switched on the mind-numbing TV, watching it absently. The day ticked away, and for the first time since I'd got back, I contemplated the bed. I had to get up early, and that made sleep compulsory. It was hard enough waking up at some ungodly hour, but at least Nick's picture was in my bedroom.

172

At nine-thirty, I decided to get an early night and went to bed while sleep laughed at me. For hours, thoughts hounded my brain, as I looked repeatedly at the clock, thinking how tired I'd be if I didn't get any sleep. Around 5am, I finally dropped off, not long before my alarm clock screamed at me to get my lazy arse out of bed. I hit the snooze button five times, only delaying the inevitable. This left me with little time to spare, and cursing and rushing, I made it out the door within fifteen minutes.

The tube journey was as joy-filled as it had been a month ago. All of us had the same look on our faces, as if we were on the train of death. The carriages were devoid of children at this hour, who would at least have lent a smidgen of life to this giant metal cylinder we had trapped ourselves in. It seemed crazy that I coughed up One thousand five hundred pounds a year for my travel card, just so I could put myself through this delight, twice a day. It was particularly ludicrous that I actually lived in Holborn, Central London, and I paid to travel out to Woolwich every day.

My mother thought I was crazy, of course, but the job paid well, the staff force was smaller, and you could just sling casual clothes on, rather than have to flash it up in the city. This suited me fine; less demanding for me, and I could take holidays at the last minute. I tried to gauge how pleased my boss, Mr. Edward Forrester, would be about the police going there. I tried to concoct some kind of story, and by the time I'd arrived, I had one ready.

I worked on the third floor, and always took the stairs, but that day I sprinted up them as I was ten minutes late. I pushed open the double doors and entered the main office, clutching my alibi and fake positivity. The first person I saw was Gladys Tillman, and everything about the woman was tight. Her hair, her smile, her temperament, even her purse. Even her mid-fifties voice was tight and superior -

"Good morning Lauren. You're back then?"

No, I sent my double, I'm still on holiday..., I just managed to stop myself from saying. Without waiting for an answer anyway, she continued - "I think Mr. Forrester will want to talk to you," and walked off, tightly.

The other beauty of a smaller company, was the nice amount of distance between my desk and that of my co-workers, of which there were eight. Philip Shivers was my nearest neighbour. He was a bit of an Essex wanker, but he'd generally left me alone ever since I'd stapled him in the thigh for being such a letch. He was thirty-something with brown hair and brown eyes, and he drove a brown Toyota Celica, which he thought made him the dog's bollocks. Nora hated him, too much brown. Nora said if you drive around in a big shit, then you must be one. The feeling was mutual for Phil, as Nora took great delight in rubbing his gayness in Phil's face.

The only problem with the location of my desk really, was that it was the nearest to Mr. Forrester's office. I slunk past, thinking it had been a successful mission as I reached my desk, put my handbag on the back of my chair, and sat down.

"Lauren, could you come to my office please?" came Mr. Forrester's voice.

I took a deep breath, got back up and went into the lion's den.

Edward Forrester sat behind his desk, wearing his '*I mean business*,' look. On the whole he was a good boss, as long as you got all your work done, everything was fine. Disrupt the office, however, and you would incur his displeasure. At thirty-six, he still gelled his thinning, strawberry blonde hair in an effort to create volume. He had ultra-pure white skin that had never seen sun, having been in various offices for most of his young life, and watery grey tired eyes that gave nothing away and made him seem somehow soft and easy. However, if you pushed him too far, you'd find out that was not accurate at all.

I sat down facing him. "Good morning, Mr. Forrester." I folded my hands together.

"Good morning. Firstly I'd like to say you are ten minutes late on your first day back, after having a month off which I generously gave you at the last minute."

"I'm sorry, I..."

He held up his hand to stop me. Mr. Forrester had previously heard many different explanations for my lateness - I shut my nipple in a drawer as I closed it; Trains...; I fell in a rosebush and got pricked all over; I had my Period; I got bitten by a homeless person that I'd accidentally trod on, and I had to go and get a tetanus jab from the hospital; Trains, in combination with my period; Not being able to find my favourite shoes; Period again... All of which had been totally true, but I think Mr. Forrester's patience and belief had thinned, just like his hair, some time before.

"Are you aware that we had the Metropolitan police here?" He pulled his chair into his desk.

"Yes, Mr. Forrester."

"And are you aware that your..." He cleared his throat. "Cuban friend was also here on more than one occasion, disrupting work with his hysterics?"

"Yes, Mr. Forrester."

"Well Lauren, is there any explanation as to why the staff and myself were asked insinuating questions?"

I brought forth my innocent look.

"It's all been a terrible misunderstanding, Mr. Forrester. I'm sorry about Nora, I've told him never to come here..." I paused for effect. "I knew the police were here, as one of the Sergeants who came, Lawrence Cole, is a..." I was praying he'd attended. "shall we say, a good friend." I deliberately left this open to interpretation. "I foolishly told no-one where I was going, so my friend Sergeant Cole was a little over-zealous."

He squinted at me, then relaxed back in his chair. "I see. So, I hope you've learnt a valuable lesson. To tell people where you're going in future."

I nodded vigorously. "I have."

"I don't like the police coming here, but I must say Sergeant Cole was particularly pleasant."

Phew. He was here...

He stood. "I imagine there's plenty of work to do."

"Yes... Thank-you" I gushed, and I rose, and returned to my desk.

I started the computer, and clicked on the folder named; '*Tax returns May 2013*'.

"So, ball you out, did 'ee?"

I looked up to see Phil standing at my desk, grinning like a Cheshire cat and chewing gum.

"'bout the fuzz lookin for yer?"

"No," I replied, without taking my eyes from my screen.

"Crafty little minx int cha?"

Now I looked at him. "Go away, Phil."

"Course, babe."

He winked at me and sauntered back to his desk, next to Bernard Hew, an intense middle-aged man who rarely spoke, got on with his work and didn't like disruption. Mr. Forrester loved Bernard, with his big thick, black eyebrows, that joined in the middle to make one long giant eyebrow. My mother always said never to trust a man whose eyebrows meet in the middle, but could never offer an explanation as to why. Bernard's eyebrow raised as he fleetingly glanced over, then lowered down again to keep his eyelids warm.

The first thing I did was to put my USB stick in the slot on my machine, copy over all the pictures of Nick, and set them rotating as my desktop background. Barbara Cuthford came over, to say '*hello*' and to tell me she hoped I'd had a nice holiday, because '*it's good for our chakras to take a break*'. A bohemian child of nature, she was fifty-nine, but Babs, as she liked people to call her, must have had fantastic chakras, because she looked no older than me. She was a strict vegetarian, always positive thinking, and she loved everyone to get on. I thanked her graciously.

For the rest of the day I suffered few interruptions. After lunch, I noticed Davinder Patel, chatting and laughing with Phil. Dave, as he preferred to be called, was a London wise boy. Both his parents were from India, but they moved to London when he was one year old, and as a result, he spoke better cockney than most people born here. Dave had a black BMW 5 series, and shared Phil's interest in the ladies. They'd become mates since they started working together here. However, I did like Dave, his cheeky charm suited him, and I probably would have shagged him, had I not known that he would tell Phil everything, but of course that was all Pre-Nick.

They both looked over at me, giggling like a couple of young pricks, and I knew they were talking about me. I got my teeth into my work, and wished time would hurry. No-one else disturbed me and until the day finished, and all the way home that night, all I could think was;
Shit.... This is my life...

For the next three weeks, it *was* my life. Just work, and home. Sometimes, for part of my journey, Janice Croft, who worked in my office, would accompany me. She was thirty-one, painfully shy and mousey, but itching to burst out. Phil and Dave tormented her, but she seemed to enjoy the attention.

Nora called to say that he'd given Leonard the poem, that Leonard had loved it, and was going to put it to music. Nora also told me I was a party-pooper, and that I was neglecting my clubbing responsibilities.

I didn't feel like dancing or celebrating, in fact, I was becoming a reverse vampire, going out in the early morning and retreating at night. I'd been shutting the curtains on the long summer days, just going to work, but not Out-out.

Mr. Forrester remarked on my punctuality -

"Must be doing you some good, that friend of yours - Mr. Cole."

For the past three weeks, I'd heard nothing, however, from Sergeant Lawrence Cole. The only thing I'd done was ring the insurance company to find out how Maisie was, and I still had no idea. I'd had a couple of '*Sort your life out,*' phone calls from my mother, and a quick, time-delayed call from Jonathan, telling me he was in the Maldives, and asking how I was. Not wanting to say '*Totally shit*' I told him I was fine. He told me he was staying another month there, and then he'd be home for nine days. He'd told Mum it was only four days, leaving him five days to hide at my place, and have some fun. A woman's voice told me the time had run out, and his voice was gone.

The thought of hiding him did not appeal to me, but the thought of seeing him did. The last time had been thirteen months previously, and I missed him.

Other than these few brief interludes, my life became robotic. By the Thursday of my fourth week at work, I was unable to bear it any longer. Every moment, every half-second, every Nano-second, I thought of Nick, or tried to push thoughts of him away. I brought up Facebook to look at his profile page, but it had been locked down. **Only Nick's friends can view his profile.** I tried to look at Angela's, but that had been secured as well.

Panic set in as I wondered; *Has Angela found out?... Did David tell Nick how I'd found him?... Shitting shit! - the agony of not knowing...*

I was totally blocked from his life. I wished I could go home, as I tried not to cry at work for the sixteen-thousandth time. Amazing things, our tear ducts - they never run out. I didn't accomplish much in the next hours. By four-thirty, I was sitting there looking as if I'd taken half a packet of valium, and I didn't notice Lawrence Cole enter the office.

Mr. Forrester's voice filtered through to my sub-conscious -

"Lauren?... Lauren?..."

I stood quickly as Lawrence approached my desk, casually dressed. Mr. Forrester was standing in the doorway to his office.

"Is everything alright?..." I asked my visitor apprehensively.

Lawrence smiled. "Fine." Then he was serious. "Ahh, sorry. Did I scare you?"

177

"Well, you have come to my work."

"Yes, but I'm not in uniform."

I sat down, and looked around furtively to see if we were being observed. Everyone appeared to be busy.

"Sorry, Lawrence. Is there something I can do for you?" I asked, becoming all official and business-like.

"Well, I thought you might like to drive home today."

I was baffled, and I was becoming slightly annoyed.

"I don't know if that's '*police humour*' or something, but it's not funny."

He pulled some keys from his pocket, and put them on my desk. They were on a Metropolitan Police keyring. I looked from the keys to him.

"You're allowed to leave work now if you want. I've cleared it with your boss."

Perks of the job...

Softening now, I was curious, and I would have used any excuse to leave early. I switched off my computer, got my bag, and picked up the keys. He went over to the elevator, and I tutted at him.

"The stairs," I said, before swiftly navigating down them.

He tried to keep up, as I deliberately set my pace faster.

Nick would have easily been able to keep up...

I pushed the front doors open, ran out onto the pavement, and stopped dead. Parked out the front there, was Maisie.

My mouth fell open as Lawrence came through the doors behind me. I walked slowly round her. She was perfect.... No bangs or dents, paintwork restored. The second lap I skipped round her, then flung myself on her bonnet with my arms open wide. Mr. Cole walked up to me, smiling.

"She's alive," I exclaimed unbelievingly, as I stood up. "The insurance came through?"

"Well, sort of. I did lean a bit on the man who came to survey it. You had a surcharge of three hundred pounds, and he was going to write it off, so I persuaded him to save 'her' as you say."

"And what about the money?"

He shifted his weight. "Well... I paid it."

I started blinking rapidly. Lawrence Cole had just scored himself a massive brownie point. He'd saved my Maisie. I went to him and hugged him, quickly withdrawing.

"I, I don't know what to say, Lawrence, really. Thank-you, so much."

The colour came to his cheeks. "Well, there is one condition..."

Here it comes, first he's going to demand beans on toast, and then, BANG! - Anal sex... "Yes?"

"Well, I drove it here, so could you give me a ride home?"

I relaxed. "Yes, that's fine."

Delighted, I put the key in the door and got in.

"So, where to?" I asked, once Lawrence was sitting next to me.

"Twickenham, you know where that is?"

Of course I did, it was on the road to Surrey, where David and I were from. He directed me to his place. I was grabbing the happiness of having Maisie back.

"Oh, it's so good to have Maisie back, Lawrence."

He curled his bottom lip. "So, that's what you call your car. You seem to be fond of it."

I tried not to turn to look at him, knowing that kind of driving would elicit a police frown.

"I am. We've been everywhere together, and she's never broken down, or needed an expensive part. I'm totally dependent on her. She's been with me for years."

The area we were driving through looked very upmarket. Big independent houses sat in their own grounds, at the end of their long driveways.

"It's just up here on the left. The one with the maple trees either side..." He pointed to a beautiful gated entrance with a tree on either side. "Would you like to come in for a coffee?"

Gob-smacked, I accepted. He got out and opened the gates, closing them again after me and jumping back in. As I drove down the tree-lined gravel drive, I thought; *Well, divorce doesn't seem to have hurt Mr. Cole...*

We pulled up outside a huge white house, with cream marble steps leading up the front, and big stone lions either side. It was a disgusting display of wealth. I couldn't hide my amazement as we got out of Maisie. Lawrence looked slightly embarrassed.

"Well, there are some perks to being the only child of one of the country's top judges." He said, by way of explanation.

My mind raced as we went up the steps, and I scanned newspaper headlines in my head.

Oh my God! - Lord Montague Cole....

He was always on the very big cases, even serving at the European Court of Human Rights. He was a big fat cheese, and this was his heir.

My mother must never again meet Lawrence Cole...

Inside, the house was as immaculate as the outside. We went through a huge marble-lined hallway to the kitchen, also huge, like everything there. Giant bay windows overlooked a boat-shed, next to which a speedboat, moored to the jetty, bobbed about on a perfectly English waterway.

Weeping willow trees hung over into the water and ducks swam.

What a beautiful view to look at while you eat your breakfast...

Lawrence began to busy himself while I viewed.

"Tea, or coffee, or something else?" he asked, his manner easy.

"Coffee, please," I responded without turning round. "It's beautiful. Does all that out there belong with the house?"

"Yes. This is their summer house, but well, now I'm on my own. My parents let me live here."

Surprisingly I could smell real coffee. *So, Mr. Cole, you're not an instant man...*

"Sugar?..."

"Two, please. It must be lovely to live here."

At first, he didn't respond. I turned to look at him.

"I'd rather be with my wife and kids." He finished stirring the coffees, and brought them over to a glass-topped wicker table.

"Sorry. I didn't think." I sat down, feeling awkward.

"It's okay, you don't need to apologise."

I felt sorry for him nevertheless, and I genuinely felt his loss.

"I don't mean to pry, Lawrence, but was it your job?"

He laughed sarcastically. "No, she always wanted me to work my way up, but I'm not my father. I'm happy where I am. She left me for a Greek attaché. They live in Greece, with my two kids..." He stopped to swallow a big mouthful of coffee. "Anyway, I don't want to load you up with all my baggage shit." I was surprised again. "The only thing is, I'd appreciate you not letting people know who my father is. It's a matter of security really, only my colleagues in the force know."

The coffee tasted delicious. "Of course I won't, but then why bring me here and tell me then? Some people might say I'm a bit of a bubble-head. I wouldn't be any good under torture."

That made him smile. "I don't think it'll come to that, and I just feel I can tell you."

I was getting the feeling there was a lot more to Lawrence Cole than I'd previously thought. I hadn't thought of Nick for nearly one whole hour, and I silently thanked Sergeant Cole for giving me that respite.

We finished our coffee, and he asked me if I wanted to look round the house and grounds. Considering my clumsiness, it was a complete danger-zone. Priceless vases balanced on priceless sixteenth century tables. The water and the boats I was staying well away from. I refused, saying I needed to get back.

He walked me back to my car. Now it was awkward. After what he had done for me with Maisie, just shaking his hand seemed much too informal, whereas hugs or kisses might be construed as something else. I mistakenly pulled a pair of tweezers from my bag instead of my keys, which made us both smile. I kissed him quickly and lightly on the cheek.

"Thank-you Lawrence, you've been most kind."
"Anytime... I'm always here if you need anything."
Smiling, I got into Maisie, and drove off.

I got lost on my way home, but didn't care, I was just driving for the love of having my car back. I parked her safely outside my flat, and that night I started mulling over the day's events. Lawrence Cole had definitely surprised me, and I decided I did like him, a bit, so he could stay in my life for the moment. I went to bed with no idea of the huge shock I would have the next day.

Everything about the day began normally. I got up with enough time to eat some cereal and stare at Nick's photo. The journey to work had me feeling relieved that it was Friday. Same chair, same staff, everything was normal. It was now thirty-four days without Nick, and still I was nowhere near normal. I wondered if I'd ever get over him, though I knew I would never stop loving him, I just wanted the heavy lead weight I carried inside to diminish, even slightly.

It was just after lunch - Ten past one. I picked up the phone again.

"Hello, Hunt and Chapman. Lauren Bowman speaking. How can I help?"

No-one replied.

"Hello?"

I was just about to put the receiver down when he spoke. At first, I thought I was having pseudo-hallucinations.

"Hello?..." I said, timid now.

He said my name again. There was no hesitation, misunderstanding or faltering. My whole being knew this voice.

Scared, I responded quietly - "Nick."

IN TURMOIL

It had been a very brief, official sounding call. He said he was coming to London the following day. He had my address, and said he'd be there by about five. He hung up leaving me stunned.

Nick... Nick is coming...

I couldn't put the phone down, my hand was shaking so much. A light sweat came over me.

I can't work, there's no way I can work...

Finally, I put the phone down and went to Mr. Forrester's office. He was filing files in filing cabinets, and I made him jump.

"Sorry Mr. Forrester, but I'm feeling a little unwell. Would you mind if I left early?"

After my glowing month, he took me seriously.

"Actually, you don't look that well. Yes, go home, and hopefully you'll be fine by Monday."

I headed for my desk, turned off my computer and fetched my bag.

The journey home I don't remember, as if I were drunk. I only became aware where I was once I was in my front room, staring at Nick's image on the wall. Tomorrow he really was going to be here. I lay back on the sofa, not really grasping reality.

Maybe I dreamt it, zoned out, had a mirage?...

I stared at the ceiling, daring to believe it was real. Suddenly I sat bolt upright.

What if it is real?...

I looked around me. I hadn't cleaned since my mother had last visited. It looked as if I'd asked a gang of teenagers to move in and use everything, with the proviso that they clean nothing, then leave. I didn't want Nick to see me in my own home when it looked this way, but what if it was all some cruel joke? Then again, why would he do that though? It wasn't his style.

I went over to my music collection, and once again chose the *Communard's ~ Don't leave me this way*, fuelling myself for the clean. Once again, I sang loudly, feeling happy, truly totally happy. Nick was coming, that was all that mattered. I danced and span as I gathered three weeks of clothes from the floor and the furniture.

My mother would have a fit... Who cares!...

I'd never been so happy to clean in my life, though it took me four hours. I filled my thoughts with what I was going to wear. I didn't even care if he was coming to spit at me a few times, or even urinate on the furniture. He was coming. Nerves and excitement stopped me sleeping, and I snatched mere minutes, as if I were five years old again on Christmas eve, hoping to catch Santa in my room with all the pressies.

At eight, I couldn't stand it anymore, and I got up to make coffee. After three cups for my nerves, I ran myself a bath and spent an hour scrubbing every part of my body, twice. I chose the most scented products I had, and shaved every wisp of hair that was out of place. I even tidied up my Brazilian, though I doubted that I would need to do that if he was just coming to spit on me.

However, I wanted to be perfect. After the bath and hair-wash, there came the dreaded plucking of eyebrows, then blueberry body lotion, before I dried my hair, using straighteners for the final touch.

So, clothes... I faced the open wardrobe, thinking; *What did I decide yesterday? - Nothing...*

I chose a few different options, laying them out neatly on the bed.

First outfit - no, second - no, third - no, fourth - No... Arrghhhh!...

Something was also wrong with the next six choices as well. They made me look too pale, too clubby, too sensible, too shitty, too short, or too wintry. I flung the clothes haphazardly into heaps.

At first, I'd been careful with my hair, using my hands to protect it. Now, I was like a supermodel on speed, pulling each outfit off wildly, as my hair became more and more statically charged with each change. Every time my hand touched my hair, fine strands stuck and followed, leaving a trail of fine fan-shaped hair. The more clothes I pulled on and off, the bigger it got. Light from the window diffused through it, giving a surreal blonde glow.

A giant dandelion clock shone back at me from the mirror.

Great... Just how I wanted Nick to see me looking - with an albino afro...

I'd amassed a huge, jumble-sale like pile of clothes on the bed. I'd been at it for three hours and I was getting nowhere. I was sweating with the exhaustion.

Shit... I probably smell again, now...

So, I had another bath, just wetting my hair this time. I made another coffee, and took it with me into the bedroom. Nerves and caffeine buzzed heavily in me, and I wasn't paying attention.

As I rushed into the room, I tripped over my own foot and flung the contents of my mug forward, covering all the clothes and the bed with stain-able coffee.

Screaming, I tried, futilely to catch the liquid in my hands, and just ended up with sticky coffee running down my arms. I got down on the floor and added some vomit on the carpet for the final effect, then just sat there, not even having the energy to cry.

I imagined Nick coming and finding me sitting in my own sick, looking at the contents of my mind displayed in front of me. An installation like that would probably have won the Turner prize.

Minutes ticked by, and finally the stench powered me into motion. I got a mop, bucket, and scrubbing brush, and after I'd dealt with that, I dealt with the clothes by picking the whole lot up and throwing them back into the wardrobe in one great heap. I changed the bed, and realised that now I smelt of vomit, coffee and sweat again.

I took another bath.

This is obsessive compulsive, Lauren...

However, during this Third holy cleansing, I decided what I was going to wear. Once more, I returned to the bedroom, this time picking out a dress with daisies on. The one I'd last worn on the magical day of the picnic. As soon as it was on my body, I felt better. I took my time with my make-up. It was nothing I needed a steady hand for.

Finally, I stood, looked at myself in the mirror, and decided I was ready.

Back in the front room, I glanced at the time.
Four-thirty. OMG! - Where has the day gone?...

Barely minutes to go, and I began to position myself around the furniture; Lying back casually on the sofa, sitting perched on the edge of the armchair, then sitting back. Next, I tried cross-legged on the floor. None of them felt right. I needed a pose to get straight into when he was here. I lay back with my legs open in the air, giggling, more from nerves than anything else.

The doorbell rang, and I screamed a light scream. Glancing at the time, I realised I'd been rolling around for forty-five minutes. I stood up on wobbly legs, coughed, then coughed some more. My breathing increased and my stomach turned over. My mouth was totally dry and my palms were sweating. I went down the hall, grasped the doorknob, and willing myself not to cry, I turned it.

He had his back to me. I couldn't speak. He turned to me in slow-motion and our eyes locked on each other's. The breath caught in my chest. He looked pale and haunted, yet still song-inspiringly beautiful. I slowly let my breath out, trying to moisten my mouth enough to speak.

Nick snapped the spell. "Are you going to ask me in, Lu -" He stopped himself.

It felt so good to hear his voice.

"Yeah, sorry," I managed to reply, and stood aside to let him pass.

As I shut the door, he looked at the poster of himself on the wall.

I started babbling. "We took them. The night, the night we were drunk..." I shifted about nervously. "on my phone..." I went to the lounge door. "Please, come in."

He looked like he was lost. I wanted to run to him and offer him every part of me. Soothe our pain. Instead, I just showed him through. He'd lost some weight, as had I. As he removed his backpack, he noticed the other two prints of him. Blue, sad eyes looked questioningly at me.

"I liked them, it felt like... like you were here," I explained, my voice crackling. Tears welled in my eyes. "I, I missed you, Nick."

He sat down heavily and put his head in his hands. I didn't know where to sit.

I want to sit next to him, but does he want that?...

I decided on an edge of the armchair pose. As he looked up, his hands rubbed down his face.

"It's a mess," he said quietly, his voice as shaky as mine.

He'd not been sleeping well by the look of the black under his eyes.

"I'm a mess..."

My mouth opened, just about to pour out how awful it had been for me as well, but I shut it.

Just let him speak in his own time...

"Lucy - now, see? I don't even know what to call you. That's not your name, but well..."

I looked down and slumped forward onto my knees, sitting on the floor. I leant against the coffee-table, trying to be more at his level.

"I like you calling me Lucy. Why can't you call me that?... I'm still the same person, even if my name was Dave."

He stared wryly at me. "So, if you're still the same person, are you holding any more secrets?" It was my turn to look down. "Sorry, Lucy," he said, softly.

I returned his gaze. "There are to be no more secrets."

He sat back and closed his eyes, momentarily.

"Would you like a coffee, Nick?" I stood, and his blue eyes followed me.

"Yes, that'd be good." I busied myself making it as his voice floated over to me. "You're wearing the dress you wore for the picnic," he remembered.

"Yes," I replied, modestly.

"You still look fantastic in it," he said.

A huge lump in my throat made swallowing difficult. As the traitor, I didn't know how to act in this moment. Verbal defence seemed futile, too late. To leap onto him and hold him tight would be inappropriate. Loose chit-chat would be ineffectual.

Just be totally honest, Lauren, lay it out there...

I brought the coffees through and put them on the table. Nick was absorbed, looking at the larger photo of himself. I sat in my previous position on the floor.

"Nick - I'll be completely honest with you. I'm scared as hell of what's going on, I didn't know anything, and now you're here. Please don't take this wrong, but when you called yesterday, it actually gave me a real reason to get up this morning. But tell me, are you here for a showdown? ...Or to tell me you're going to marry Jenny?"

He held both hands up. "Woooah there! Lucy, breathe."

I loved the way he called me Lucy so naturally, but I'd already decided that only Nick could call me by that name. I breathed deep and picked up my coffee, and as he leaned forward to get his, I noticed his face was already regaining some life.

"I'm here because I want to be. I need to be here - this is where you are..." he began.

I wasn't able to stop the tears that filled my eyes.

"It's not easy though..." He sat back, mug in hand, thoughtful. "You came back here, you *could* run away. I was full of anger, left with this whole bunch of... fucking mess. Not being able to tell anyone, listening to all the terrible things people said; '*Good job she's gone*,' and well…" He looked at my tearful face. "Stuff. Me and my dad are hardly talking, both of us secretly in love with the same woman. I had to move out, it became impossible for us to be in the same house. I stayed at the cottage."

I started to cry for real.

"My mum knows something's wrong. We told her it's about work, but she's not stupid..." He paused. "I hate lying to her. I'm angry at my father for Loving you. He should love *her* like that. Angry at both of you for putting me in this position. If I'd stayed, well, her knowing the truth would make everything much worse..."

I dared not say a word. *Both in love with me...* That meant Nick did still love me. *There is hope...*

As he finished his coffee and leaned forward to put it down, I ached for him.

"But..." He looked intently at me again. "everything about the cottage reminded me of you. I've been trapped in a twilight zone, forced to be in the world we made."

His words began to falter.

I've always thought that the word '*Sorry*' is so inadequate for many things. If you bump into someone in the street, sure, a simple, '*Oops! Sorry*,' is appropriate. Buggering you on a date-rape - '*Sorry…*'

well, it simply doesn't cut it. '*Sorry, I didn't mean to ruin your life,*' seems so inadequate.

I felt conscience-stricken, and guilt-ridden. Daring it, I moved over next to him. He didn't move away from me, just sat back resting his head on the sofa.

"It wouldn't matter if I went to the moon, I'd still wish you were there with me. There's no escape, I'm irrevocably in love with you. It's too tiring to fight it, so I got your address and phone number from Stan."

I'd forgotten Stan had my details, but not my work number, only my mobile. I was just about to speak when Nick continued.

"We can all look at Facebook, Lucy. Your page tells everyone where you work. I simply looked the number up."

Only two hours here, and he's already reading my mind...

I assumed David had told him how I found out where he was.

"Maybe you should secure your information?" he said, with an edge of sarcasm.

I probably should...

I'd been tracked down, the same way I'd stalked them.

"Does anyone know you're here, Nick?"

He closed his eyes. "Stan does. That's it. I left a note saying I was going on holiday."

"Do you think they'll worry?"

He opened them again. "I'm a grown man, Lucy. No-ones snatched me. Please give me this - I'm running away, just like you."

"You can stay here as long as you like," I said. *Forever, in fact...*

"Thanks, I'll crash on the couch if that's alright, Lucy. My head's a mess. All I know is I cannot be without you. When you left, this candle in my life was snuffed out. You're not someone I can relinquish lightly. I had a choice and I made it. You shouldn't have come looking for my dad, but if you hadn't, I wouldn't have met you. He shouldn't still be in love with you, but I understand why he is. Everything is double-sided..."

I acted involuntarily, placing my hand on his knee.

He looked down at it, then up at me. "I'm so tired, Lucy."

Okay, so now it was my turn to look after him, as he had me before. I jumped up. The time was nine-fifteen.

"Nick, look, you can have my bed. I don't have work tomorrow, I can watch TV, and the sofas comfortable."

His eyes closed again. "No, I..."

I grabbed his hands, and pulled him up. "No arguing, it's my turn to nursey you..." I lifted up his rucksack and took his hand, leading

189

him to my room. "The bathrooms the next door along. If you need anything, let me know."

He saw the picture of us together, and tears strained from his eyes.

"So, you did miss me, then?" he asked.

I squeezed his hand. "More than life itself..."

He turned quickly so I couldn't see his face. "Thanks Lucy. There's one thing I need, although I'm too tired right now."

"Yes?"

He took his top off. As he showed me his sculptured back, unrequited lust rose in me.

"I want you to tell me about you and my father. I need to know, to be able to understand more. It'll hurt, but you know I think it's better to have everything out in the open."

The least I could do was give him that. "Tomorrow, Nick. I'll tell you tomorrow."

"Goodnight, Lucy."

"Goodnight, Nick."

I closed the door slowly so I could keep looking at him. I floated back to the sofa, mesmerized by his photo.

"Now you're really here," I whispered to the image.

You must tell him the truth, Lauren. Don't fuck this up, start as you mean to go on...

Nick deserved the truth. He'd done nothing wrong, other than to fall in love with me. I needed him in my life, so honesty had to play a major role. No little grey lies or embellished stories, or saying what I thought he wanted me to. I'd have to filter my thoughts and only reveal the best. Honesty could be cruel, but it's best to be true. I wanted him be to be armed with all the information, ugly and pretty, then at least he could make his decisions based on truth. Delving into and bringing up the past would always be hard for me. I too squashed it down, or remembered it with rose-coloured glasses. To tell the tale of the man that totally broke me, to his son, made it a difficult story to tell. I hugged my knees. He was here, in my bed, near me. That fact alone was enough to give me joy that warmed my cold body.

My mobile rang as I switched the TV on. I looked quickly - it was Nora. If I didn't answer, he'd just keep on trying, or even worse, come round. It was Saturday night, but if I answered, there was no way I could tell him Nick was here, or he'd definitely come round. Nick wasn't yet strong enough to meet him.

I answered with a light and cheerful tone, and Nora was immediately suspicious.

"Okay, so what happen, que?"

"Nothing... Well, I got Maisie back."

He screamed. "Darlink!... And she's good? - Buena?"

"Yes, she's perfect, Lawrence Cole did it for me."

"Aiieee!... I tell you, he have a big fat purple stiff one for you."

I started laughing, my mood was the best it had been since post-Nick.

"Maybe, yes, but actually he is quite nice."

"Oooh!..."

"No, no, but I don't see any reason why we can't be friends."

"Darlink, of course, are you loco? You get busted, you can have your leedle friend come and sort it all out..." I just giggled. "Okay, so I hear you have your mojo - we go fiesta tonight in that shiny car?"

I thought quickly. "Nora, sorry I can't, my parents are coming over tomorrow, and well, I have to clean, but I do feel good. Maybe next week?.."

He sniffed. "You big party poo poo, but you promise?"

"Well..."

"Promeese?"

"Okay," I conceded, smiling.

"Yee-hah!... Good, darlink. Say hello to Dolores and Lionel for me." (My parents.)

"I will. Have fun."

"Are you crazy? - of course! Besos, darlink." He hung up.

So that will keep him away from the house tomorrow under the pretence my parents are here, and on a sexed and drugged Sunday comedown, I can guarantee it. After tomorrow, I can deal with him. Maybe Nick will leave when I tell him everything, maybe he'll be unable to digest the information?... But I've got to let him decide that, just be totally honest...

I lay contentedly back on the sofa, suddenly feeling very tired, and my eyes closed for the entire night.

THE TRUTH

Nick woke first, coming into the front room. I stirred when I felt his presence.

"Sorry, didn't mean to wake you..." he said, sounding more like the old Nick; Relaxed.

I stretched. "That's fine, fancy a coffee?"

He walked into the kitchen. "Don't worry, I'll do it, I'm sure I'll find everything."

Laying there listening to him opening and closing cupboards was like a symphony to my ears. The occasional tutting, or '*Shit!*'

I had a feeling of complete contentment, almost equal to the feeling of just having had sex. I was even craving a cigarette.

He carried the coffees in and put them down. His boyish smile was back.

"Errr, I think I made a bit of a mess."

At that moment, I wouldn't even have cared if he'd poo-ed in the sink.

"Don't worry, thank you for making it." I couldn't help smiling as I sat up.

He sat on the floor, with his back against the armchair, and legs extended. He wore jeans and a short-sleeved dark blue shirt, which was open, exposing his torso. Even seeing that small amount of bare flesh left me feeling like a Victorian, getting stiff over a lady's ankle. My leg twitched involuntarily.

Probably my vagina limbering up... I sat up and tucked my hair behind my ears, sipping my coffee. *God, he makes a good cup...*

"I really needed that sleep," Nick said, in-between sips.

"Well, I don't remember falling asleep, but I didn't wake up once," I said, feeling very pleased about it, and knowing it was because *he* was there.

The TV was still on, but it was helping me at that moment by providing background noise.

"Ahhh..." he said as he tilted his head back and forward. "it's quite odd, seeing yourself that big."

"That's my favourite one. How do you think you look?"

He turned his head to look once more. "Okay, I guess."

"Okay?...mmm." I drank a mouthful.

"What?"

He genuinely didn't know how exquisitely alluring he was.

"Nick, you are spectacular."

He blushed and ran his hand through his hair. It made me feel like crying; just a simple gesture that I'd missed so greatly.

"Well, I don't think..."

"You are," I interrupted, insistently.

Both of us sipped quietly for a moment.

Nick cocked his head slightly. "Do I..." He paused, clearly finding it hard to say what he wanted to. "...look like my father, when he was young?"

I didn't want to avoid his eyes. "A little. But only a little."

"We've only got a coupla pics of him when he was young."

Because your mother ripped them all up... I didn't feel there was a need to say that out loud.

"He was very, very confident. Unshakably sure of himself. It added to his charm," I said.

Nick raised his eyebrows. "Funny, I can't imagine him like that. He's so easy going."

I remembered back, and I could still smell the leather, and hear motorbikes being revved. That big house, always so full of life, and people coming and going. I smiled at my reminiscences, and sat up so I could talk properly.

"

I lived in Surrey, just on the outskirts, a very upper-middle class area. My family moved there when I was fourteen, early spring 1981. I was excited. New kids to play with, boys... At fourteen, I was feeling a full sexual revolution, rising up within me. My mother had wanted to move to a better class of neighbourhood to protect me and my brother, Jonathan, who'd just been born two months previously in April. Unwittingly, she'd actually put me right in the middle of a sexual lion's den.

We lived in *Moorlands Road*, and it was like a retirement village. At first, I was disappointed, us being the only family in the street, but my mother liked that very much.
'Don't worry darling, you'll meet other children once we choose a school for you to go to,' she said.
That had been the only sadness about the move - leaving my old school. It had been familiar, and I knew most of the kids there, where all the classrooms were. I'd known which teachers I could play, and the ones I'd had to knuckle down with.
My father, Lionel, pointed out to my mother at the time that I was in the middle of studying for my CSE's, as they were called, then.
My mother retorted, by saying it was character-building for me, and, 'Good gosh, what is all the fuss about? - Anyone would think we were moving to a foreign country, forcing her to speak Russian!'
No, for the health of the baby, they would go. The health of my brother, Jonathan, dominated all their major decisions from then on.
So we moved, and my mother, to my sheer horror, enrolled me at Saint Francis all-girls school. In addition, now I had to get two different buses to get there, making it a forty-five minute journey each way. I sulked for a short two days.
My mother stopped giving me food, saying 'Anyone can sulk,' before she stopped speaking to me in return.

For a month, I suffered the journeys, and then, as it was May and the weather was better, I began getting off the first bus and walking the rest of the way home. Cutting that second bus meant I could pocket the money. My mother was totally preoccupied with the baby, and didn't notice me coming home late each day.

One street in particular began to stir interest in me on these walks home - *Giles Lane*. Every time I passed, it was bursting with life. Teenagers on skateboards propelled themselves as fast as their feet would let them... Quads were massively popular - the four-wheeled skates that these kids were practising on. They had a huge rubber stopper on the front of each skate to help you brake. On a few occasions, I had to wait at the kerb while motorbikes turned into the lane. Music was changing, and I could hear different tunes filtering from the houses. I wondered why we didn't live in a street like this.

Anyway, I began hanging around at the top of the lane. I didn't really know why, except I wanted to be a part of some action. I began to notice a lively girl with dark chestnut hair who played there. One day, as I stood there, a ball flew through the air towards me and landed at my feet. The chestnut-haired girl ran up to me, panting, with this big, warm, happy smile.

'Thanks,' she said, as I handed her the ball. 'want to join in? We're playing rounder's...'

And that was how I met Shannon McCormick.

After the game, we went to her house at the end of the lane. It had a huge front garden full of old push-bikes, children's toys, a car shell and motorbike parts. There was a blow-up paddling pool half full of black water, with things growing on the surface and a plastic duck in it. All surrounded by waist-high grass.

As soon as she opened the front door, a barrage of noise hit me. When I opened our front door at home, all I ever heard was the sound of a ticking clock. As she led me through the hallway, music from upstairs blared down the staircase on my left. The TV was just as loud in the room we passed on the right. I heard lots of voices, that got louder the closer we got to the huge kitchen, which had the biggest dining table I'd ever seen.

Shannon had led me to the candy store. Boys were everywhere, eating and drinking, their crash helmets laid around. Some boys were in casual wear, others in tight black leather with splashes of colour. Boys, some of whom were already turning into men. I was stunned, looking round I could see they were all around seventeen or eighteen, a couple were a bit older. None of them paid the slightest bit of attention to us at all.

'Like a drink? er...'

'Oh, Lauren!'

She beamed at me. 'I'm Shannon McCormick, and...' She indicated towards everyone in the busy room. 'some of them over there are me brothers.' She went over to a woman who appeared to be speed washing up. 'Ma... This is Lauren, can I get us a drink?'

She didn't stop washing, but nodded her head.

'Ah, but don't feckin' touch yer father's beer.' She had a thick Irish accent.

Beer?..., I thought. *We're not likely to drink beer...*

My mother had let me have a sip once at my Uncle Jerry's fiftieth, but that was all. I had a feeling I was going to like this house.

That day I found out that Shannon's parents were both Irish, but only her two eldest brothers, Patrick and Ted, were born in Ireland. The rest of them were born here in England, although their father said they were all Irish, through and through. The rest of them consisted of Darrah, who was seventeen and Shannon's only sister, away in Ireland training to be a doctor eventually. Declan was twenty, Mickey was eighteen, and my favourite. Patrick and Ted, the eldest, did not live there, although they seemed to eat all their meals there.

Flynn was her father, and Margaret her mother. Shannon was thirteen, and we got on well from the moment we met. Her brothers ignored her, her sister was away, and her mother was forever dealing with the barrage of people the boys brought round. I loved being there. We were left to our own devices, and I was free to stare at all their good-looking friends. Mickey was the one who used to talk to me, simple chat like - 'Hi, Lauren. How are you?' He had dark chestnut hair and dark green eyes just like his sisters. A few freckles added to his mischievous air. Mickey was the one into sports bikes. He was the only one I would ask if he wanted a tea. Having no friends at my new school, Shannon and I bonded quickly.

I think it wasn't until about my sixth visit before, well, before I met David. The McCormick's had a very big, long back garden, even busier than the front. The lads used to bring their motorbikes round the side entrance into the garden to work on them, or just polish them up.

It was a beautiful day, and I knew Mickey was out there. So, I was putting on the kettle for the boys, and Shannon was playing Dancing Queen by Abba, for the millionth time. I had to get away from *that*, so I went out into the sun and walked towards the bikes. As I approached, Mickey was talking to Kevin Lawson, and had his back to me. Kev, as we called him, was the joker of the pack, and I liked him.

A chestnut haired boy with huge blue eyes and big full lips squinted and put his hand over his eyes so he could see me better. I stopped walking and just stood there.

He smiled. 'Hi, love.' And in that one moment, everything changed. 'I'm David.'

My body felt strange, like my blood had started running slowly. My stomach was flipping over.

'Tea?' was all I could manage to croak.

'David...' Mickey called, and saw me there. 'Oh. Hi, Lauren.'

David looked at me. 'Well, Lauren is here to offer tea.'

Mutely, I nodded.

'Yes ta,' said Mickey.

'Me too,' chipped in Kev.

David stepped towards me, making his leathers squeak. 'Yes, please.'

Turning, I scuttled back into the house, ran upstairs, and was promptly sick.

I became a very good tea maker, especially when David was there. He was training to be a motorbike mechanic, and worked away in Europe. I tried to spend every moment at the McCormick's house when he was there. I told my mother I'd taken on lots of extra-curricular activities at school, which pleased her, as she assumed I wouldn't lie.

Shannon wasn't stupid. 'Which one of my brother's friends do you like then?'

I would lie, and she would try and guess. Her favourite was Harvey. I didn't like him, he was cheeky, but rude, and ignored me mostly. He made a fuss of Shannon, but only because she was Mickey's little sister. Declan had his friends over too, but he was more quiet and broody, taking his mates to a large TV lounge that was upstairs next to Shannon's room.

When I knew David was there, I began leaving school early so I could spend more time at the McCormick's. David always made time to talk with me.

'Hi love, been to school?' he'd ask, making me feel too young.

'Yes,' I would pout in reply.

Eventually Shannon said, 'Okay, that's enough now, who do you like?'

197

I was bursting to tell her by this time. 'David,' I blurted out.

She laughed. 'But everyone likes David. He's always got a girlfriend. I've seen him here with three different girls in one week. My sister liked David, but my brothers told him not to even think about it.'

I sighed. 'The trouble is I'm not old enough. All that lot sees us as babies. David will never take me seriously.'

'Even if he did, he'd dump you within a week.'

She was right of course, but I thought about him all the time nevertheless. He went away again, and I had to live with not seeing him for a while. On his return, Shannon was proved right. A stunning Italian girl accompanied him on the back of his bike, whom I hated instantly. Jealousy raged through me. I made him no tea while *She* was there.

A month or so later he changed, turning up with a different girl. For him, charm came naturally, and along with his looks, the world of women was at his feet.

One day, it was just me and him alone in the McCormick's garden. I was watching him fix something on his bike. It was three months before my fifteenth birthday, the beginning of August, very hot, and no school.

'Pass me that wrench please, Lauren?' Quickly, I did as he bade, leaning down to give it to him, my eyes meeting his. 'So, how come you never make me tea when I bring a girl here?' He took the wrench and continued his work.

The question surprised me. 'Well. Well, I...' As I stood up I had no answer. 'Would you like a cup?'

He smiled and wiped his hands on a rag. 'Yes, that'd be nice.'

I skipped away quickly and made him one. When I brought it back, he was sitting stretched out in the grass. I took it over, placed it down, and turned to go.

'Lauren, why don't you sit next to me? I don't bite.'

I sat looking at the floor.

'You think I don't notice things, but I do. When you make tea, you always bring mine out first.'

'Do I?' I murmured, still looking down.

'Look, I'm shit with girls. A bastard heart breaker, anyone who knows me will tell you that. It's not that I mean to be, but I like girls, what can I say? - Guilty...' He sat up to drink his tea. 'Lauren?' I looked at him. 'You're a very pretty girl, why don't you have a boyfriend?'

'I don't like boys my own age. I like...' I stopped.

'Well just don't like me, I'm no good, honest.'

He got up, threw the last bit of tea from his cup, and went back to his bike.

Too late... I more than liked him and my teenage hormones were going mad. *He must like me or he wouldn't talk to me...*

At home, I was having trouble eating or sleeping. My mother said it was because I needed more exercise, and that gave me a reason to spend more time away from home, but it was actually because of David. I tried to tell Shannon, but she said it would pass, that it was just a schoolgirl crush.

A couple of weeks after I'd spoken to David in the garden, I was in my own back garden. My father had constructed a tree-house as per my mother's wish, to be for my brother when he was old enough to play in it. Two years too early, but I loved the space up there, just sitting in it - getting away. My mother called me from the house, and I jumped down and came in.

'Someone called David, on the phone for you,' she said, looking disapprovingly at me.

David?..., I thought. *Who do I know that would call me here?...* I picked up the receiver. 'Hello?'

'Hi, Lauren. Its David. Sorry, I got your number from Shannon...'

I nearly fell over. Unable to talk, a silence lay between us.

'Mmm? Maybe I shouldn't have called.'

Speak, quickly... 'No, no it's fine,' I managed to say. I played nervously with the curly telephone cable, twisting it into bigger curls.

'Well, I just wondered if you were doing anything tonight?...'

My head spun. 'Now?'

'If you want. Just tell me your address, don't forget I have my motorbike.'

Oh, his sexy machine...

David wanted to come to my house, and probably didn't understand what the hell was going on. There was no way I was going to refuse, but there was also no way my parents would allow him to come to their house.

Suddenly I had a brainwave - 'Don't come now. Later, but you'll have to go round the lane at the back. Don't park your bike there or my parents will hear you. There's a red bin by our back gate - I'll meet you there,' I looked round furtively to make sure no-one was listening.

'Er, okay, but you have to give me a time.'

I thought for a second. 'Nine O'clock?'

'Sounds good,' he said, and we said nothing for a few moments.

'...I'll need an address to meet you at this time.' Now he sounded amused.

I told him where I lived and replaced the receiver, the cable now just one big curly knot.

Almost peeing myself with excitement, I ran to my bedroom. *The tree-house... That's where our secret rendezvous will take place...*

My mother came in.

'So, who was that boy on the phone?' she demanded.

Mmm, yes, who was he?... 'Oh, he's the minister's son. From the church near our school. I've been helping out there.'

Her attitude changed immediately. 'Oh, that's lovely, darling.' She left the room then, and didn't require any further information.

I washed my hair and painted my nails. I put sparkle lip gloss and eyeliner on, and I was ready. Those strange feelings returned with full force; sweating, stomach rumbling, giddiness and sexual explosions throughout my body. I thought maybe I had some illness. I was completely sheltered by my parents, and the 'Sex talk' still hadn't happened. Everything I knew, I had learnt from my mates at my old school, and from a porno movie, found hidden when I was twelve.

Even when I got my period, I told my mother I was bleeding and she just informed me;

'We all have it. Every month till we're old,' and gave me a big long white pad.

Apparently, nice girls did not use the 'other ones' which I later found out were tampons. With no instructions, I had to navigate the sanitary towel. Finally, I got it in place but I hated it. I felt as if I had a rolled up hand towel in my underwear. That week, my walking had taken on a different form - an intense horse rider's walk, legs wide, and toes pointing outwards. John Wayne would have been proud. From that moment on, I switched to the loose girl option - tampons. I had to keep them hidden away, while displaying the huge white bricks I was meant to be using in the bathroom.

Sex so far had been lots of kissing, grinding, some finger-games and one wank job. That was it. So, I was getting myself into a complete state thinking about all this.

He's only coming to see me, not to have a sex orgy..., I thought. *On the other hand, is he?...*

I knew already I would give David whatever he wanted.

Dangerous, sexual liaisons within a small tree-house perhaps? My attire certainly said '*Come on - It's all here, take it!*' - A small light blue cotton dress. Blue always matched my eyes, which everyone used to remark on. It wasn't even necessary to wear mascara on my long, long black lashes. At fourteen, I wore no bra on my plump, developing bust, and dresses clung to me.

9PM came around and my breath became rapid, excited gasps. I sneaked out of the back door, shutting it very quietly, and ran lightly down the garden to the wooden gate. I calmed myself for a moment before I opened it.

Don't forget to breathe, Lauren...

The gate creaked as I popped my head out and saw he was there. Casually leaning against the fence, decked out in motorbike gear with a crash helmet under his arm. Smiling.

'Hi, love.'

A lamb to the slaughter..., came to mind.

I even loved the way he said; 'Hi, love.' and assumed it was special, meant only for me. Sadly, I later realised it was simply because he couldn't remember all his girl's names, but for a while, it was special.

I said nothing, just beckoned David to come in. I closed the gate carefully behind him, and placed my finger on my lips to signify stealth. We stole through the garden as the summer sun was saying its last goodbyes. As he followed me up the wooden stairs to the tree-house, I knew David would be able to see up my short dress.

I closed the little wooden shutters and lit the Tilly lamp, listening out as he sat down on the floor.

'Is it okay to talk, yet?' he whispered.

I turned to look at him and noticed an expression I'd not seen on his face before.

He hates it here, probably wondering why he's come to visit a child in a Wendy-house...

David was eighteen that month, on 31 August. A Virgo. His favourite drink was tea, and it had to be very sweet. His most prized possession was his black and red Honda CBR 600cc. His favourite hobby was seducing girls.

I gulped, sat down, and straightened my legs.

'Yes, it's okay to talk,' I finally replied, but my whisper betrayed my nervousness and embarrassment.

'Sorry, Lauren, will I get you in trouble if I'm caught here?'

Baby, stupid young baby... 'You probably want to go,' I said, leaning forward as much as I could in that small and intimate space.

'I don't want to, but am I worth the punishment?'

Yes, yes, stick pins down my nails, yes!...

His eyes sparkled even in the half-light. He leaned back and pulled a packet of John Player Special's from the breast pocket of his leather jacket. The sound of the tightness of his attire made my vagina pucker.

'Do you mind?' he asked.

'No,' I replied, thinking; *You can do whatever you like....*

He lit his cigarette as if he was James Dean, the flame from his silver Zippo illuminating his divine face. He clicked it shut and took a puff, letting it dangle from his full lips.

I just sighed. *Oh, Cupid, I think you've shot your arrow...*

David exhaled the smoke. 'Kinda like it in here,' he said, looking round at the small, twee room.

'My father made it for my baby brother,' I squeaked.

'How old is he?' he asked, but I didn't want to say. He kicked my foot playfully. 'hey, how old?' There was amusement in his voice.

'Seven months,' I confessed.

He began to laugh. It was infectious, I joined in, and we both sank more easily into the atmosphere.

'Seven months? - Shit, it's better than my place.'

Shannon had already told me how bad his place was, on the numerous occasions that I'd pumped her for information on David. She had no idea *where* his flat was, and I dared not ask her brothers.

Without any control over my next sentence, I was horrified to hear myself say; 'You can live here if you like.'

His smile was gentle and real. 'Lauren, you're very sweet. You look different tonight,' He surveyed me. 'Can't say how, but you definitely don't normally look this...' He stopped to let a long line of smoke out across the room.

Like what?...., I thought, frantically. *Terrible. I look terrible...*

He stubbed his cigarette out slowly on the floor, keeping me in my un-confident suspense.

'Well, let's just say, you look good. I'd probably get put away for what I'm thinking.'

Put where?..., I wondered. I didn't understand. 'So you'd have to go away somewhere, to think I look good?' I was seriously clueless.

He tittered. 'Are you serious?' I figured he was probably appalled by my sheltered upbringing. I didn't respond. 'Sorry, I didn't mean to snigger, but well, most people know that. Put away means to get put away in prison.'

Then I understood, and felt the need to explain. 'My parents are very protective. They even choose which TV programs I'm allowed to watch,' I pouted.

'Little Miss Innocent,' he said, and his eyes flashed.

Too innocent for him. David needs someone older than me..., I thought dejectedly.

He lit another cigarette, just as sexy as the one before.

'I suppose I'm here because you seem like you'd be cool to talk to. Mickey told me you were only fourteen, but you seem okay...'

Talk to little old naive me?...

'To be honest, all the girls I begin to make friends with, well, I end up shagging them. I don't mean to, but sometimes it seems as if I'm doomed not to have a girl as a mate. All the lads... well, they're lads, and it's different.'

So he wants friendship, that's all, and it's only because I'm young and not worthy of shagging... I was experiencing a crushing disappointment mixed with realization; *Of course that's all he wants...* Still, I felt I could do friendship if it meant I could still be close to David. *I'll accept whatever he needs...*

I wet my lips and pulled my knees up, exposing more of my legs, goading him. David did the same, mirroring me. Without taking his eyes from me, he placed his elbows on his knees.

'Mmm...,' he said, as he closed his eyes for a second and then coughed.

'Okay, friends then,' I agreed.

'Good, but its better if it's secret - Just us.'

He's embarrassed of me, I'm sure...

'I know that sounds bad, but it's just the lads. They'd take the piss, they wouldn't understand.'

Well, that I *did* understand. All the lads thought I was a baby - of no consideration. It would ruin his street cred. Again, I agreed, and he had me in the palm of his hand.

He told me he'd been seeing two women... well, one was definitely a woman, a Mother, and the other was her daughter. A seventeen year old girl. The Mother had caught him out, but she wanted to keep seeing him. He didn't know what to do. In addition, he had a girl from Sweden coming over, only now he wasn't sure he wanted her to, because he thought she was getting a bit clingy after six dates. I sat listening, grinding my back teeth with jealousy.

Still, he's here with me... I just listened.

He left at Midnight. He kissed me on the cheek, told me how nice I was, and he was gone.

For the next few days, I was on cloud nine, convincing myself he was pretending to be friends because he liked me. Over the next few weeks, we had seven secret meetings at the McCormick's, having to keep up the pretence. David remained the same in that environment, 'Hi, love,' being his standard acknowledgement. I wanted to tell Shannon, but I was scared that if I told her, and David found out, it would all be over. That was very, very hard.

Food had become a challenge to me, and my mother, who was worrying about my drop in weight, took me to the doctor. He said it was normal teenage hormones, and gave me a vitamin prescription. I didn't need a doctor to tell me what was wrong. I was in love. I thought about David every day, from the moment I awoke, until I finally got to sleep.

It was almost David's birthday, and the McCormick's were throwing him an eighteenth birthday party. Declan had declared it to be fancy-dress, and anyone not wearing a costume would not be allowed in. Personally, I was dreading it. I knew David would be bringing his latest conquest with him.

Shannon was excited, but not amused that I didn't care what I wore, or that I had the enthusiasm of a dying gnat. I'd asked my mother if I could go out camping with the church group. If I had said I was at a friend's house she would have wanted the phone number to check. At first, she wasn't sure, but my father said it'd be good for me, and that he'd drive me to the church. Then she agreed, and I proceeded to start panicking.

Now I'll have to look for a church near my school...

I wore my school uniform, which was perfect, as Shannon and I were going as St. Trinian's schoolgirls. The rest of the costume was at her house. I had mixed emotions about having to get a bus or walk from the church as well.

I got into the car as my father started the engine.

'So, where are we going?' he asked.

I slung my overnight bag on the back seat. 'St Augustine's church.' I turned to face forward and fiddled with my seat belt.

My father looked at me. 'Lauren, where are you really going?... I think its best one of us in the family knows.'

I thought about lying, but he was right. I told him where the McCormick's lived, and everything else on the journey, but of course, not about David.

My father said that he wasn't stupid, even if my mother thought so, and he knew something was going on. He told me that it wasn't my mother's fault, she was wrapped up in the baby, but that someone had to keep an eye on me.

We pulled up outside, and opening my door for me, he said;

'We all deserve to have fun, Lauren, but please, just be careful?'

I nodded as I got my bag, and kissed him on the cheek, grateful to have him.

'Shall I pick you up tomorrow?' he asked as he got back in the driver's seat.

I held the door open and bent down to talk - 'That might be good. Is the afternoon okay?' I wanted to spend as much time near David as I could.

'Course it is. I'll come by about Two-ish.' His kind, fawn-coloured eyes flashed at me.

'Thanks, Dad...'

I watched him drive away, ran through the front garden and knocked hard on the front door. Loud music was already playing, and I was relieved to see Shannon open the door. We both went directly upstairs to her bedroom. Excited to be getting ready, we put our hair in bunches and put on torn fishnet tights. With great delight, we wrote rude obscenities on each other's school shirts.

Shannon had drinks ready for us, they were yellow, and foamed like sherbet. I could hear *Adam and the Ants* playing *Stand and Deliver* downstairs.

'What's this?' I asked, holding up the glass of liquid custard.

'It's a Snowball, you'll like it,' Shannon gestured at me to drink.

'Is it alcohol?' I asked pensively.

'Course it is.' She slurped it confidently.

At first, I sipped, then I drank it hungrily. I put my glass down. 'Mmm, that's nice.'

Shannon giggled.

'What?' I asked.

'You've got a foamy moustache.'

I licked it off my top lip and applied some deep red lipstick.

'Is David here yet?' I asked, trying to sound casual.

Shannon tutted. 'I don't know. You *know* he'll bring someone.' She applied the same colour to her lips.

'Yeah...,' I muttered as I picked up my snowball for comfort. It was making me feel warm, and my cheeks felt prickly.

'Here,' she said as she handed me a hockey stick to complete the look.

We clinked our glasses together, and finished our drinks. Now we were ready.

We went downstairs, and headed into the huge kitchen/dining room.

I whispered in Shannon's ear - 'Can we have another snowball?'

'Course, I'll get me Pa to make us another one.'

I was stunned. 'What?' I stopped in the doorway.

'Don't be silly, it's a party!' She laughed, and led me to a big table, covered with every type of alcohol.

Shannon's father, Flynn, was tending the bar, dressed as a leprechaun. When he saw us, he beamed.

'Ahh, girls. Excellent costumes. Come...' He beckoned us over and placed a loving arm around his daughter. 'So, me darlin', what'll it be?'

Shannon looked up at her father, proudly. 'Two more snowballs please, Pa.'

He released her from his grip. He was a huge man of six foot five inches, with jet black hair and dark, dark eyes. Yes, he sometimes scared me, but his heart was good and kind. I watched him pick up the bottle of runny custard and fill the glasses halfway. Next came the lemonade, which fizzed it up.

Fascinating...

I was eager to take my glass back when he offered me my potion.

Depeche Mode was playing -

> *I just can't get enough,*
> *All the things you do to me,*
> *And everything you say,*
> *I just can't get enough...*

Looking round the kitchen, it seemed we were the only ones there.

'Where is everybody?' I asked.

'The music's in the front room...'

Just as Shannon said that, a giant pickle came to the table, grabbed a beer and shuffled back in the direction it came from. I looked in amazement at Shannon.

She raised her eyebrows. 'Declan.'

We giggled.

'He's so silly,' I said, as she linked her arm in mine.

We walked together, hockey sticks tucked under our arms and snowballs in hand, following the music. We opened the door to the lounge, and disco lights flashed in the semi-darkness. Liquid red globules travelled along the walls. A projector sat behind a lava lamp in the corner of the room. A penguin stood behind two record players on a wallpapering table. Snowball happiness was making us giggly. A woman was walking round with a tray of snacks. She had big blonde hair and a white halter-neck dress.

'Who's that?...' I pointed.

'It's me Ma,' said Shannon through a mouthful of drink.

'Who is she dressed as?' I was confused.

'She's some dead film star called Marilyn Monroe.'

I didn't have a clue who that was. Mickey was a punk, talking to Kev, who was a priest. There was a gorilla with a fairy and a pretty girl dressed in 1920's dress. The giant pickle, of course, and Harvey had donned a big bouncy afro and seventies garb.

About an hour and a half, and two more drinks later, a lot more people in funny outfits were making us both laugh, but there was still no sign of David. My body felt light, and my head was jiggling. Shannon and I started to dance, and *Donna Summer's, I need love* came on. Both of us loved that song, and the alcohol was helping us to lose our self-consciousness of youth.

In the middle of the song, the door opened, and in He came; dressed as a Roman, with a beautiful dark-haired girl as Cleopatra on his arm. The alcohol took on a bitter taste in my mouth, and my stomach started to bubble much as the drink had done. Everyone cheered, and Flynn came through and made us all sing '*Happy Birthday.*' I just mouthed the words, entranced by the girl.

She looks more like David's age. How could I compete with that?... I bet that round her house, he can go in through the front door... be in a real room, not one that's up a tree...

David looked magnificent with his new haircut, short dark chestnut completing the perfect Roman. He even had the laurel round his head.

The party went on with full force. Mickey came over to say 'Hello!' safety-pins stuck through his ears, before quickly retreating from the children's corner. David acted as if I didn't even exist. My costume looked like a dirty dish rag compared to the stunning-ness of his date. Everyone was drinking a lot, and more people were arriving. Shannon and me switched to Martini, even though the taste made me squint. Kev, now as the drunken priest, came over and asked us if we had any schoolgirl confessions we wanted to make. At least *that* made me smile.

As Kev turned to go, out of the corner of my eye, for the first time, I caught David looking at me. He was across the room, and he looked away as soon as I noticed.

Probably wondering what on earth he'd been doing with me… boredom, of course. When he's got nothing to do, he comes to me…

Suddenly the room went dark, and a candle-lit cake was brought in. All the guests, maybe fifty in all, came in and we all sang '*Happy Birthday*' again. David blew out the eighteen candles, and then he kissed her, at which point I left the room and ran upstairs to the bathroom. Nausea engulfed me, and I just about made the toilet before I threw up.

My head was spinning. I flushed the toilet and put the seat down, ran some cold water, splashed it onto my face, gargled with it and finally drank some. There was a banging on the door. I gathered myself and staggered to open it. I wanted to lie down.

I opened the door and David stood there. I hiccuped. He took my hand and led me across the hall and into Shannon's room. As he switched the light on, he stood swaying slightly. I held my nose in the air, trying to act as if I didn't care. I was fourteen, dressed as a schoolgirl, while the Head of Empires confidently stood in front of me.

'I'm going to bed,' I announced.

He took one step forward. 'Is that a proposition?'

I took one step back. 'No.'

He surveyed me. 'Aren't you even going to wish me Happy Birthday?…' He pulled an unhappy face. 'Are you angry at me?'

'No,' I pouted, quick to answer.

He took another step. This time I stood firm, mainly because I could no longer feel my legs. I needed to sit down. I went to the bed and sat down in the same little pleated kilt that I had to wear for school. It was far too short, and I had a replacement for when I went home.

David came over and sat next to me. I couldn't look at him, his body was so close to mine.

'Now why would you be angry at me, if you're just my friend?'

Goosebumps ran all over my body. 'A secret friend,' I whispered.

His hands turned my face to his, and tears filled my eyes.

'You're so pretty – just like a doll, dressed like that…'

Honey dripped from every pore in his body, and I was the small, hungry bee. His searching eyes took in all my features while his hand gently stroked the side of my face.

'So, you haven't asked what I wished for when I blew the candles out.'

I was starry-eyed. 'A new bike?'

He laughed. 'That'd be nice. No, it was something more simple. Just a kiss.'

I didn't know what to do, but he leant forward and kissed me softly on the lips. My head was spinning with joy and alcohol. The door to the bedroom flew open and we separated joltingly. Shannon entered, looking suspicious.

'I wondered where you were…'

David stood, 'See ya.' He skipped out, effortlessly.

'What's going on here then?' Shannon asked, as I flopped down on the bed and lay there, delirious.

'Nothing,' I replied, not even trying to sound convincing.

'You're playing with fire, Lauren. He'll use you like a tissue.'

'Maybe he wouldn't.'

She lay down on the bed with me. 'Don't be so naïve, Lauren. Maybe Harvey will come in and ask me to get engaged to him as well!…'

I closed my eyes, disbelievingly. With me, it would be different. I would make a special effort. We fell asleep then, both of us feeling like drunken little girls.

When I opened my eyes, I saw we were both still in our fancy dress, cuddled into each other, sisters in arms. We slept till Midday, then filled the room with our teenage chatter. I knew David would have gone home with Cleopatra.

By the time my father came to pick me up, my head was hurting. I didn't say much on the journey home, and blissfully, my father let me be. I just sat there knowing He had kissed me.

Over the next two months, I saw him only once, at the McCormick's. Only the 'Hi, love.' Life was becoming intolerable. My weight was still too low and my fretting was playing havoc with my digestion. It was coming up to my fifteenth birthday, and my parents asked if I'd like a small tea-party, and to ask my school-friends.
What school-friends?...
I hated the thought of it, and I asked if I could stay at a friend's house instead. Shannon and I could stay up late, drink and eat a huge bag of sweets. For once, my mother said I could. I told Shannon, and suggested a birthday sleepover with a horror film.
'Great,' she said, and we arranged all the supplies we would need.

On the morning of my birthday, I went downstairs to gather my cards from the mat, flicking through them as I walked to the kitchen. One envelope caught my eye, because it had no stamp. Just my name. I carefully opened the birthday card, without even looking at the caption on the front.

> Lauren,
> Meet me in the tree-house 8pm.
> Happy Birthday, Beautiful.
> David x

I threw the others unopened onto the kitchen table, re-reading what he'd written. David was coming here, on the night of my birthday, seemingly forgetting he'd been out of my life for two months.

The day passed in a dream like a soft-focus haze. I forced myself to eat my birthday food to please my parents. I opened my presents ungratefully, preoccupied.

That afternoon, I picked out a little light-pink tennis dress, with blue edging and a small pleating on the side. It was very short. I covered it with a long winter coat that I planned to remove upon entering the tree-house After tea, my father asked me if I'd like a lift.
Wouldn't take long to drive to the tree-house...

I accepted, knowing I would have to take his lift to Shannon's, and then walk back and come in the back gate, sneaking into my own home.

He dropped me off, gave me a whole five Pound note, and asked me not to tell my mother. I watched him drive away slowly, then I started to make my way back home.

As it was the Second of November, the weather was beginning to get cold. I pulled my coat tightly round me, and hoped the tree-house would be warm enough. I felt bad that I hadn't even bothered to tell Shannon that I wouldn't be there, but my only thoughts were of Him.

As I crept through my garden, I spied a faint light coming from the tree-house

We must close the shutters…

I removed my coat at the foot of the ladder, and folded it under the bottom rung. Now I was shivering to pay the price of vanity, but I felt exhilarated as I climbed up.

As I reached the small door, a strong, sweet floral perfume hit me, and as I opened it, I gasped. Different flowers were arranged all round the small dwelling, and candles flickered, illuminating the myriad of colours. David was closing the shutters, and turned upon hearing my gasp. He had me - his puppet on a string.

'Hi, love…' He grinned.

He came over and kissed me again on the lips. I closed my eyes and he released his mouth.

'Happy Birthday.'

I opened my eyes again quickly. It was unusual to see him in normal clothes. Dark-green Fred Perry shirt and jeans. His hair had grown slightly, but now it reminded me of Paul Weller from *The Jam*, who every girl had a thing for at that time.

'David, you've gone to so much trouble…'

He sat down, and I followed suit.

'…and I'm going to be in so much trouble,' I said, light-heartedly.

Reaching behind some red roses, he produced two glasses and placed them on the floor in front of us, followed by a small bottle of champagne. He popped the cork and it hit the ceiling as foam gushed from the bottle. David quickly tilted it, filling the glasses with the bubbling golden liquid. Romantic heaven enshrouded me.

211

He made the toast - 'To the prettiest girl ever!'

Oh!...

I already loved him. I would be as easy as pouring the drink was. It was the second time I'd drunk champagne, but this time I drank it properly. The bubbles went up my nose, and made me splutter and cough.

'Do you like it?' he asked.

'Yes, it tickles.'

That made him laugh. 'Sorry I haven't seen you. I've been in Norway...'

He could have been away on the Moon, I didn't care.

'So what did you get for your birthday?'

I told him about my sensible parents, but boasted of my five pounds.

'Wow. A whole fiver...'

He was making fun of me. Our glasses were empty. He filled them again and his eyes scanned me.

'So, did you miss me?' he asked casually.

'Every minute,' I replied truthfully.

He moved closer to me. 'I missed you too. I tried not to, but it didn't work.'

He missed me, He missed me..., my mind sang.

His hand lay on my leg. I put my glass down because my hand was shaking so much, and turned to face him. Before I even had time to blink, we fell upon each other. Kissing as never before, his hands explored my young body.

This is it..., I thought. *It's going to happen... I want it to happen, it's going to be magical, fairytale-like...*

It was a comical disaster. First, I stood to take my panties off, but being slightly tipsy, lost my footing, and fell on the roses. Their sharp thorns pierced my legs and bum. David helped me up, and even though it hurt, I was giggling from the effect of the champagne. I let him lead, not knowing what to do. Twice we banged our heads together. We rolled around the small floor until we heard a small breaking sound, accompanied by a sharp pain in my shoulder. I sat up quickly.

'Ow. That hurts...' I turned to show David.

'Ooh, you've rolled on one of the glasses – don't move...' His hand came up and pulled something out.

'Owww!'

He showed me the shard of glass he'd just pulled out. He had my bright red blood on his hand.

'Better take your dress off, then I can see better,' he said.

But then I'd be naked... Self-conscious of my developing body, I didn't want to. 'No, I,I...'

He kissed me on the lips again, halting my sentence. He made me stand and helped me to take my dress off over my head, throwing it to one side.

'God!..,' he said, slowly and deeply.

I knew it, he thinks I'm disgusting... I put my arms across myself.

'What are you doing?' There was shock in his voice. He took my arms down gently. 'You are perfect,' He spoke softly, and my whole body blushed. He turned me around, looking for glass damage. 'It's okay, it just pierced the skin.'

He began to kiss down my neck and all my pain drifted away. I lay back down and David undressed as well. It was the first time I'd ever seen a man or a boy naked. I tried not to sneak peeks in case I might giggle. David skilfully slipped a condom on, and took my Virginity, Heart, and all my rational thinking. It was painful, uncomfortable, sensational, and over.

After laying there in a confused, crumpled heap for a while, David informed me he couldn't find the condom.

'Where could it go?' I asked naively.

He smiled at me. 'Well, where do you think it could be?'

I hadn't a clue.

'Still inside you?' he suggested.

Disgust projected me into a sitting position. 'What?'

He was putting his jeans back on. 'It's okay, you can get it out with your hand, but it's no good for stopping baby sperm now...'

Oh no, no, no...

Now he was putting his top on. 'It's probably okay.' He shrugged. Tears stung my eyes. He crouched next to me. 'Sorry, but I've got to go...' Now they fell down my face. 'Ahh, babe. Don't cry. You'll see me soon.'

He kissed me on the forehead as he stood, then he descended the little ladder and left me sitting there, with a condom stuck up me, on my birthday. I cried hard, knowing I was a fool, and that Shannon was right, but still I would have given anything for him to come back.

I retrieved the remains of my first sexual encounter, and coughed a lot, hoping it would get the baby-makers out. Then I lay on

213

the floor and covered myself with my coat, eventually falling to sleep, unable to go in the house.

I spent the next two weeks praying for my period, while my weight continued to plummet. I locked myself in my room, mostly crying and praying that I would hear from David. Of course I didn't. I was too depressed to go over to the McCormick's, and I supposed that Shannon probably hated me by now. My parents fretted, forcing me to eat small portions of food at mealtimes and telling me it was unhealthy to spend all my time in my bedroom. Finally, some relief came with my menstruation, at least I could semi-return to the cruel, outside world.

The first thing I had to do was go to the McCormick's and explain myself to Shannon. I wanted to tell her everything, I wasn't able to keep it all inside. When I knocked at their door, Declan answered. I was stuttering with nerves.
'Hi Declan, is... is...'
'- Shannon in?' He completed my sentence.
'Yes.'
He tutted. 'Yes she is, but she's pissed at you.'
I bowed my head in shame.
'Come in, she's in her room.'

I went sheepishly up the stairs, and tapped lightly on Shannon's bedroom door.
'Come in,' she called, cheerfully. Her face dropped when she saw me. 'Sorry, David isn't here,' she said, snootily.
'So am I, Shannon. Sorry, I mean...' I started to cry. 'I'm in love, and it's horrible.. painful. It's eating away at me incessantly.'
Big sobs started to escape from me. Her face softened, and coming over to me, she placed a comforting arm round me. She led me to the bed and sat next to me while I poured everything out to her.
When I'd finished, she said nothing for a moment, then she angrily pronounced -
'What a fucking bastard!...'
My mouth fell open at her swearing.
'Oh, Lauren. I don't want to say I told you so, but...'
There was no need for her to finish the sentence. Still, I defended him, as I would do for the next four years, but being with Shannon helped to share the burden, and particularly to take my mind off David.

I didn't see him for another two weeks, a month in total. Then, at the beginning of December, as I was leaving school on a Friday, I saw a black and red motorbike with rider astride, waiting outside the gates.

David!...

I should have been angry, walked off, but first love had me, and I ran excitedly over to him.

His big smile warmed my heart. 'Hi, love.'

'What are you doing here?' I panted.

He produced a second helmet. 'Taking you for a ride.'

I didn't believe he was going to take me on his baby. I took the helmet shakily.

'not scared are you?'

'No,' I answered defiantly, even though I was a bit. I'd never even sat on a bike before.

'Just hold tight on to me, that's all you need to do.'

He put his helmet on and started the bike. The beast roared into life, and I got on, trepidly. I put my arms round him, my school satchel on my back. As soon as I was astride, a new and erotic sensation ran through me, like I'd mounted a big, purring, dangerous tiger.

He turned his head to the side. 'Ready?' he shouted, above the engine.

'Yes!' I shouted back.

My very first ride gave me a lifelong passion for bikes. The jolting acceleration made me squeeze tight as he moved with ease between traffic-stuck cars. Both of us leant as one with his magnificent machine, as tangible life flashed past, giving me the feeling I could reach out and grab things. I'd never had these urges in a car.

I shouted out with the pure thrill of it - 'Whooo-hoooo!' As we moved through country lanes, David increased the speed, opening the Honda up.

I will explode before we get anywhere..., I thought, with excitement.

The whole experience was a combination of emotions, as I had to hold David very tight. I never wanted to get off.

He finally pulled into a collection of small, new looking country cottages. Slowing down, he stopped in front of one. They all looked the same to me. I wondered where the hell we were, and why we were here.

He removed his helmet and rubbed his hand through his hair. I took mine off as well, and as I lifted my leg over to get off, my legs went all wobbly. The way he swung his leg over, that simple gesture just made me think how sexy he was. With no questioning, or even words, I followed him like a puppy.

David opened the door to reveal a small entrance hall with a door on each side. He opened one and motioned for me to come in. I closed it after myself, and realised we were in a one room apartment with only one other door. There was a kitchenette, a telly and a sofa-bed with a giant playboy bunny on the quilt cover, which was fully extended, ready for any action. In awe, it dawned on me that I was in David's flat. All past indiscretions seemed instantly forgotten.

Well, I bet he doesn't just bring anyone here - I must be special...

He went to the tiny kitchen area and threw his keys down.

'So, just take a seat,' he said, and removed his jacket.

It looked like the only seat was on the bed. I sat. He ran over and flung himself next to me, lying on his side.

He ran his fingers down my side. 'I've missed you.'

I stayed sitting up, not looking at him, and trying to retain some sliver of resistance.

'Did you like the ride?'

Okay, you've caught me now... I turned to him enthusiastically. 'Yes,' I flushed. 'I loved it.'

His arm lay across my lap. 'Sorry I haven't seen you.' He blinked his big blue eyes. 'I've been away.' He squeezed my pelvis bone. 'Have you lost weight?' he enquired.

'Yes. Did you know I was a virgin until that night?' I blurted out.

'Baby...' He pulled me down and wrapped his arms around me, kissing my face. 'If I'd have known, I would have stayed.'

How many boys does he think I've seen?...

'I spoiled it. I'm flattered you chose me.' He kissed me hard on the mouth. 'Let me make it up to you.'

The second time was what I thought it should have been like the first time. Star-burstingly, room-spinningly, fantastic. David unlocked my libido, only making me love him more.

Afterwards he smoked a cigarette and made us a cup of tea, while I sat with the playboy bunny wrapped round me, my whole body tingling and my face burning up.

'David?'

He was once again next to me. 'Yes?'

'Do we still have to keep Us a secret?'

He lit another cigarette and the smoke stroked his face. 'Best to babe... for now, anyway. It's more romantic if it's a secret.'

I supposed it was.

He kissed me and got up. 'Better get ready to go,' He stubbed his cigarette out.

'David?...' I was scared I wouldn't see him for a while. 'Are you working away again?'

He was rinsing the cups. 'No, I'm here until just after the New Year.' He dried his hands as he turned to me. 'Why?'

I was trying to dress myself under the duvet. I was still so conscious of my naked body.

'Just wondered. When will I see you next?'

He pulled on his leather jacket. 'I don't know. You know how I am, a free spirit. Don't like committing myself too much.'

I was almost dressed, and glad I was bending down to put on the trousers David had given me for going on the bike, as tears stung my eyes. Lastly, I put my trainers on, as David waited for me, keys in hand, before passing me his spare helmet. I didn't understand how I could feel so sad, after such elation. My young mind did not have any answers.

'Don't look so sad, Lauren. It won't be long, I promise.' He kissed me on the cheek, which cheered me a little.

He dropped me off two streets away from my house, and waited for me to take off the armoured trousers, revealing my school skirt.

He took the lid from me. 'Well, see you soon. At least the condom stayed on this time...'

Closing his visor, he pulled away.

I visited Shannon, telling her what had happened every day. She thought I was a fool, but she was a good friend, listening to my constant babble about David. Two weeks went by and no one saw him, until one Saturday morning at the McCormick's.

I knocked on the door and Flynn opened it, with a 'Morn', Lauren.'

'Hello, Mr. McCormick.'

He ushered me in. 'Flynn, call me Flynn...'

At this point, Shannon flew up the hallway and pulled me into the front room.

'Hey.... What's going on?' I asked.

Shannon seemed very agitated. 'David's here...' she whispered.

I smiled.

'I think we should go upstairs to my room.' She looked round as she spoke.

I sensed there was something wrong. 'I don't want to, Shannon. What's going on? Please tell me.'

A big sigh escaped from her lips. 'He's here, in the garden with a girl.'

I started to blink rapidly. 'I want to go in the kitchen. Can we get a cup of tea?'

'But then you'll see him. Don't do this to yourself…'

'She might be a friend.'

Shannon laughed sarcastically. 'When has David ever had a girl as a friend?'

'Well, I'm his friend.'

She stared at me, pitifully. 'No, you're his secret shag.'

Why is she being so mean?... 'Tea – is that okay?' I asked quietly.

Exasperated, she turned and led the way out of the room. I could hear David's voice, he'd come into the house now. Shannon put the kettle on. Kev and Mickey were at the table, sitting and chatting playfully with David and a beautiful girl with short, bright, pillar-box red hair.

The happy couple were both decked out in leathers, standing with their arms around each other, laughing. The boys looked over to see who'd come in. David glanced over, then turned away and they continued as they had been before this minor interruption. I was there forty-five minutes before they left together. He didn't even say hello.

Shannon consoled me as I wept on her bed, only offering support instead of condemning me for my crime of Loving a complete bastard. When I got home, I curled up in my bed for the whole weekend, telling my parents that I didn't feel well. I even managed to get Monday off school.

During the next two weeks, leading up to Christmas, I went to see Shannon once. She told me she was worried about me, and that my weight was too low. I told her I just felt tired a lot and was finding food a struggle. She invited me to a party at their house on Christmas Eve, and told me her father had said that year all the men had to be dressed as Santa, and all the ladies Mrs. Santa. I said I might come, but I thought my parents probably wouldn't let me stay out that night.

'I know David's coming,' she said in an attempt to cheer me.

I hugged her before I left. She was my best friend in the whole world.

On the evening of the twenty-second of December, my father popped his head round my door.

'There's a phone call for you, love... A boy.'

I jumped up and ran down to the telephone.

My voice trembled. 'Hello?'

'Hi, love. I was just calling to find out if you're coming to the Christmas party?' David asked, as if nothing had happened.

'Why? do you want me to?'

'Yes,' he said simply. 'I miss seeing you.'

I missed him too, and I knew I'd go. 'I'll see you there then.'

Blowing a kiss down the phone, he hung up.

My walk back to the bedroom was different - lighter somehow.

He's gotten fed up of her, and now he's realised he only wanted me all along...

The next day I made my outfit as sexy as possible without being slutty. White hold-up stockings with red garters. I folded it carefully and hid it in my rucksack. Then I asked my parents if I could go to midnight mass, after staying at friends of the church group. My mother wasn't pleased.

'But darling, then we won't be waking up on Christmas morning as a family,'

I gave her my most disappointed face. 'Please, Mother. It would be nice to wake up with kids my own age.'

She relented, but said, 'Well, if we can have the number of the parents, just to check if that's alright.'

She had me humped there.

My father cut in; 'Well, Dolores, I could drive her to the church and meet the parents myself?'

My mother smiled. 'Even better, Lionel. Good idea.'

Slyly, my father winked at me.

Christmas Eve came, and my father and I were in the car on the way to the McCormick's. I had normal clothes on, the others were in my bag.

'Your mother would kill me if she found out,' My father mused.

'Thanks, Dad.'

When he dropped me off, he said, 'I'll pick you up at ten O'clock, and Lauren? - If you do have a fella, just make sure he treats you good.'

I didn't say a word in case I gave anything away. *He does...,* I told myself.

Shannon and I changed excitedly in her bedroom, and she exclaimed how risqué she thought my Mrs. Santa outfit was. We were both drinking what was by then our only tipple, the dreaded snowball. As we came down the stairs, we saw the whole house lit up with fairy lights, and decorated with tinsel and mistletoe. A Santa stood at the bottom of the stairs and whistled loudly as we passed. It was Kev.

Shannon and I were giggling as we went into the front/party room. This time the room was truly full. We'd been mucking about upstairs, as girls do, for a couple of hours. There was a sea of Santa's before us. *This Old House by Shakin Stevens* was playing. Kev came running in with mistletoe, and came straight for me, holding it above my head.

I giggled.

'Well, it is Christmas,' he said.

I nodded, and he placed a quick kiss on my lips.

Next thing I knew, David was the other side of me.

'Hi, love.'

I turned as if I'd been caught doing something naughty. 'Hi!'

Kev went off with his mistletoe.

'Hi, Shannon. Merry Christmas,' David said.

Shannon flounced. 'You too, David.'

David placed his hand on my back and leaned in, whispering to me. 'Do you have any idea how totally desirable you are?' before he pulled away discreetly.

The outfit had worked. I wanted him, even dressed as Father Xmas.

It didn't help that my sexual needs were attacking my sanity every waking moment at that age.

Mickey came over and whistled. 'Wouldn't mind if you were in my stocking,' he said, kissing me on the cheek.

I just carried on giggling, having a great time with so much attention lavished on me.

David's face was looking tense.

Mickey slapped him on the shoulder. 'Drink, mate?'

David loosened up a bit. 'Yeah, why not?'

They both left the room to get drinks from the huge, biggest

Daddy of all the Santa's - Flynn, serving the bar as usual.

The party was great fun, boys I'd never seen before paid attention to me. This time I was careful with the alcohol, not wanting to spoil my night. After I'd danced for a while, David returned and whispered in my ear that he wanted to meet me upstairs. A few seconds after he left, I followed.

We went into Shannon's room and he closed the door, before hugging me tightly and kissing me passionately. I responded equally, I needed him to want me.

Finally, our lips parted.

'You look so good... I felt jealous of boys talking to you,' he growled softly, still hugging me.

I felt delirious with happiness. *He does care, he does....*

As our passion increased, he discarded his costume, and we were laid on the bed when the door was flung open and two drunken Father Christmases fell laughing into the room. David and I sat up together and both Santa's stopped dead. It was Kev and Harvey.

'So...' said Harvey, eyes half-closed. 'we seem to have disturbed something here.'

David was completely cool, while I scrambled to pull my shirt down.

'Though I wouldn't blame you, mate,' Harvey continued.

'Don't even think about it, Harvey. Lauren's with me,' David said.

'Don't worry, Mate. I'm not into kids,' Harvey sneered, but you could hear the jealousy seeping through.

David pulled his clothes back on, and held out his hand to me. I took it, and feeling nothing but total pride, we walked out of the room and down the stairs - together. That magical Christmas Eve, We made it official.

For the next three weeks, David was a perfect boyfriend. My eating got better, pleasing my parents, who remarked how happy I seemed, and I *was* happy, deliriously so. Everyone at the McCormick's knew now. David let me sit on his lap, kiss him, and hold his hand. I noticed a few raised eyebrows, and Mickey said, 'So, you two, ah...' and that was that.

New Year's Eve was brilliant. David was attentive and fun. We danced together. He loved dancing as much as me, and he was good at it. The whole room sang the words to *Don't you want me, baby?* by *The Human League*, a brand new tune, just released. Everyone loved it. David kissed me passionately as Midnight struck, lifting me up, and spinning me round. I thought we would be together forever.

Kev kissed me on the cheek. 'Happy New Year, Lauren.'

I flushed with joy. 'Thanks, Kev. You too.'

His brown eyes looked into mine. 'I just hope he doesn't hurt you,' he said in a low voice, before going off to kiss someone else.

How could he? This is IT, even David knows that now...

He acted as openly with me by then, as he had with his other girlfriends. There was no more need for secrecy or hiding... well, except in the tree-house occasionally.

After the Christmas Holidays, I had to return to school. David picked me up every day, affording me an older girl's superiority as I climbed on the back of his bike. Some days we went to the McCormick's together, and he would be with the lads while I hung out with Shannon. Other days we went to the tree-house to make love. I knew he was going to go away soon, but only for seven days – I could hold on that long. The night before he left, we lay in each other's arms, the heat from our passion warming the cold little space of the tree-house

'David?'

'Mmm?'

My voice became very small. 'I love you.'

He shifted his pose slightly so he could look at me. 'I like you… very much.'

He kissed the tip of my nose. Now I was wishing I hadn't told him, but I had.

He sat up and lit a cigarette. 'I'd better go soon, I have to get ready to go tomorrow.'

I've scared him, Oh why did I say it?... 'Where are you going?'

He held the cigarette in his mouth while he pulled his jeans on. 'Holland.'

As usual, he was fully dressed while I was still naked.

He crouched down to meet my eyes. 'I'll call you when I'm back.'

I wished with all my being that he wouldn't go, but he kissed me goodbye and rode off into the night.

The week hummed along, and I missed David like mad, but my appetite came back full force, pushing me over the seven and a half stone mark. School was bearable, only because I was excited that that summer it would all be over. I was only doing the necessary classes that would get me into Dotty Lombridge's School of Dance. It was pretty hard to get into, but luckily for me, right on our doorstep in Surrey, or else my parents would have said <u>No</u>.

My mother wasn't keen on the idea of this choice of profession at first, but all I'd ever wanted to was to teach dance. Since I was two, Ballet was thrust upon me. Fortunately, I loved it, and later progressed to Jazz, Tap, and Ballroom. The classes had stopped when we moved, but my mother wanted me to resume them, so I was hopeful that I'd go to Dotty's.

On the eighth day after David had gone away, I rushed home from school and asked if anyone had called.

'No,' my father informed me.

Good, I haven't missed his call then…

By the third day, with still no call, I was stricken with worry.

What if he's had an accident on his bike?…

After school the next day, I went to the McCormick's. Having not eaten for two days, the walk made me quite light-headed. As I neared the house I saw his bike outside, and the sight filled me with relief. I began to run, and was still knocking breathlessly as Kev answered the door.

'Lauren!…,' he said, sounding shocked.

I was panting with excitement.

'…are you here to see Shannon?' he asked, sounding unsure.

'No, David,' I sang, as I skipped past him straight to the kitchen.

I stopped dead, and a sharp pain speared me. David was sitting at the table, with a dark-blonde girl sitting on his lap. Mickey was making tea. Harvey was sitting at the table with *Them*.

He saw me and smiled cruelly. 'So, where do you live in Holland, Maaike?'

I couldn't hear her answer for the loud, static noise in my ears. I felt nauseous, and frozen to the spot.

Shannon came in from the garden then, and took my arm. Still, I couldn't move.

'Lauren?' she prompted quietly.

David looked over. 'Oh. Hi, love,' he said, and returned to his chat.

Kev sat back down, and looked at me with pity.

I turned, and ran. Out of the door, down street after street, not caring where I was going. I stumbled over, grazed my knees, and crying, that's where I stayed.

I heard a motorbike, and hoped it was David, but the colours on the bike told me it was Kev. He pulled up, stopped his engine, and came over to me. He sat down and hugged me, letting me lean my head into his neck as I sobbed.

He stroked my hair and soothed me. 'Shush, I'm taking you back to the house - you can't go home in this state.'

I pulled away from him, sniffling. 'Please, I don't want to…'

'Well, you've got no choice. I'll take care of you.'

My bottom lip trembled.

'Look, Lauren. David's my best mate, but when it comes to girls, well, he's a complete Cunt…'

I was stunned he'd said that, and at least it stopped the waterworks temporarily.

He helped me up and gave me a skid-lid. – 'Just hold on.'

The short journey felt weird, holding onto Kev instead of David. It almost felt like I was cheating on David. We went up the path and Kev banged on the door. Horrifically, David answered.

'Everything alright, mate?' he asked Kev, and then he spotted little old disheveled me.

'Mmm…' Kev muttered as he passed him, then turned his head back to me. 'Come on, Lauren. I'll make some tea.'

I let him walk on for a moment, wanting to be with David, thinking he would plead my forgiveness.

Instead, he was pissed off. 'What's going on, Lauren?'

'Oh, you can remember my name then?'

He slammed the door. 'Don't be childish.'

Kev called to me from the kitchen.

'Don't you care, David, that you're here with someone else?' I asked him.

Blue eyes can sometimes be so cold. He leant towards me. 'I didn't tell you that I love you. We're not married. Did I sign a contract?'

Salty tears stung my eyes. Pushing him away, I went into the kitchen, and straight through into the garden.

Kev came out. 'Look, Shannon's upstairs…' He handed me a cup of tea. 'It's freezing, why don't you go up to her?'

'Thanks, Kev,' I said, my voice breaking. He was so nice.

Once more, Shannon comforted me, something she would get used to doing a lot. She got her father, Flynn, to drive me home under protest. She told him it was girl's personals, knowing he wouldn't question me about those things.

For the next month, David was a ghost. I existed in limbo, trying to concentrate on my schoolwork.

Love… , I thought, *Love can go fuck itself…*

My weight went down again, along with my enthusiasm for living. I told my parents it was just nerves about my exams, and school. They took me to a counsellor, thinking I was anorexic or bulimic. He gave me some bog-standard advice, but I knew all I really needed was David.

A couple of days into March, on a Saturday, the doorbell rang unexpectedly. I was in my room and paid it no attention, lying on my bed, studying.

There was a knock at my bedroom door.

'Lauren…' My father called.

'Yes?' I answered in my monotone accent.

The door opened to reveal my father holding a big bouquet of flowers. I sat up.

'These came for you.'

I jumped up and took them from him. Twelve perfect red roses. He shut the door and I looked at the inscription on the card.

Lauren, I'm sorry.
Please meet me in the tree-house tonight.
Love, David x

I turned it over to see if there was a time, but there was nothing. I smelled the roses and they gave me back the scent of Life.

Love, David x.

Had he meant to sign it like that?…

For the first time in four weeks, a light smile played at the corners of my mouth. I went to get a vase, and placed the roses in it one by one.

He Loves me, He Loves me not…

I ended in a not, took them out again, and started with Loves me not...

As I placed rose number twelve, He Loves me..., I vowed not to tell him I loved him again. That had scared him away from me.

I put my books away; No way I could study then. He was sorry and I'd already forgiven him. The day went faster than usual, without David they dragged on.

I chose the kind of jumper dress that was all the rage at the time, with tights, readying myself for him.

I won't have sex with him…

I needed to know if he really was sorry, but I definitely didn't intend to have sex.

At eight-fifteen, I went down to the tree-house He wasn't there, so I covered myself with the blankets that we'd put in there in December. Time ambled by, and my face felt cold.

Just as I thought he wasn't going to show, a movement below told me he was there. He climbed up, blowing on his hands as he bent to get through the small door.

I sat up, pulling the blanket up around me.

He pointed next to me. 'May I?'

'Yes.'

He got under the covers and turned to me. 'You probably think I'm a bit of a shit…'

I didn't say a word.

He continued. 'I panicked. You know?... Telling me you loved me? Heavy stuff.'

There, I knew it… My voice was almost a whisper. 'I'm sorry I said it.'

He put his arms around me, and hugged me. 'No, I'm sorry for treating you like that. I want you back. I'm all yours.'

He kissed my neck, and I pulled away slightly.

'But for how long, David?... A day? A week?'

He curled himself into me. 'I'm not going away for three months.'

My body was still stiff.

'Lauren, I love you as well.'

Those three little magic words seemed to cover everything. We made love and I melted into him, handing my fragile self over.

For the next three months, he was perfect once again. We saw each other nearly all the time. If I could have had my way, it would have been every day, but David said that would ruin things, so I embraced the days we had. He took me out on the bike, and we travelled around visiting romantic locations.

I bloomed under his love and did well at school, reaching a glorious eight stone in weight. He also ended up meeting my parents. I'd broached the subject of him meeting them a few times, and David had said that it was way outside his comfort zone, but maybe one day…

It turned out he had no choice. At the end of May, as the weather was getting warmer, I'd arranged to meet David at five O'clock in the tree-house.

I wandered dreamily down there in my flip-flops, and called up to see if he was there.

'Hi, love,' came his voice.

I climbed the wooden stairs too quickly, in a hurry to be with him as usual. My foot slipped, and one of my flip-flops caught on a rung. I screamed as I fell backwards, and then there was a soft *thud* as I landed, sprawled on the grass.

David jumped nearly all the way down from the top.

'Lauren, my God…. Are you alright?'

I honestly didn't know. There was no pain.

'Yes, I'm fine. That was lucky…'

I tried to sit up and saw my left hand dangling, a piece of bone jutting out through the skin.

'Oh, that's not right.' Giggling, I showed David.

My head began to spin as nausea took hold.

'Fuck! No that's not right,' he said. 'I'm taking you to the house. You've got to go to hospital.'

Now pain began to encase me. 'No! You can't, how are we going to explain this?'

His arms went round me and lifted me.

'I don't give a shit, Lauren. Look at your hand.'

I looked, and saw it had already swollen to the size of an orange. I tried to put weight on my legs and it made me scream with pain.

David looked down. 'Oh no! Your ankle's massive as well.'

He swept me up into his arms and started up the garden. I pleaded with him to take me round to the front door, and though he did as I asked, he tutted, saying, 'I'd rather have taken you up the back door.'

I was still oblivious to the joke, as he rang the doorbell with his head.

My mother opened it and yelled. 'Oh my God! – Lionel, Lionel, Oh my God!...'

Pain was clouding my thoughts. *Think, think…* 'Mother,' I rasped. 'I was hit by a car, and this boy saved me.'

David's eyes snapped towards mine, and my eyes implored him to go along with it. The door swung open, and David carried me through heroically.

My father rushed up the hall. 'What's wrong?.. What's happened?'

My mother was flapping her arms about. 'Go through there, young man. Oh my God, Lionel, our baby's been hit by a car.'

David placed me on the sofa.

My loving father looked wrought with worry. 'I'm going to take her to the hospital, Dolores.'

My mother was wringing her hands. 'This brave young man rescued her.'

My father shook David's hand vigorously. 'Thank you, thank you so much, er?...'

'…David,' said David, his voice tight.

'Did you see the filthy swine who did this?' My father asked him.

'No, sorry, I didn't.'

My hand, by then, was the size of a small melon. David stood waiting while my father fetched the car keys.

'I assume you'll want to come to the hospital, so you can tell the police everything you know?'

I groaned. 'No, no…'

However, my father insisted. 'It's a hit-and-run, Lauren. A very serious crime…'

Colours danced before my eyes, and I remember nothing until I was on a hospital bed, with a doctor examining an X-ray beside me. He held it up to the light, turning it one way, then the other. *Perhaps the picture changes when you do that?...*

There was no-one else in the room.

'Where's my father, and the man that's with him?' I asked the

228

doctor.

He continued to study the x-rays. 'They're with the police,'

Alarmed, I tried to sit up. He put the X-ray down and stopped me with a bony hand that matched his face.

He got a small light out and shone it into each eye. 'How do you feel?'

Great. Oh, just great, couldn't be more swell... 'Okay,' I answered sulkily.

He raised one thin bony eyebrow. 'You've shattered your wrist, you won't be using that for some time. Also, you have a fracture in your ankle, but that will heal quicker...'

He took my good wrist and held it limply. No-one spoke for a few seconds, then he released his cold grip. '...The police will want a statement soon.'

Then he left me alone, and I started to panic about what I was going to say. The minutes went by as slowly as the drip that was attached to me. Eventually a policeman and a policewoman came in, and took a statement. I told them that the only thing I remember was crossing the road, and nothing else until David carried me into my house. They asked if I'd ever met him before, and I gave a firm 'No.' in response.

After they left, I was taken to have my injuries set in plaster, worrying about David all the way. Then after what seemed like ages, they eventually allowed my father and David in to see me.

David didn't look happy. My father fussed round me, proclaiming what a wonderful man David was, and that he should get a bravery award.

David's tight smile didn't soften under his praise.

'...So, I'm just going to have a quick word with the doctor, Lauren. Need to check some things, is that okay with you, David?' My father asked.

David simply nodded.

As soon as the door clicked shut, I spoke. 'David, I'm sorry. Are you angry?'

His blue eyes were now the colour of dark steel, to match his mood.

'Yes, I'm angry.... I've had to give a statement to the police with all my details. I'm totally lying to them, and your parents, just because you can't tell Mummy and Daddy the truth.'

I was speed-blinking to stem the tears as I tried to reason with him. 'But if I told them the truth, they would have forbidden me from seeing you, especially with the sneaking around in the tree-house. At least now they'll accept you.'

He took an angry step towards me. 'I don't fucking care if they do or they don't. I don't like being forced into things.'

I bit my bottom lip in a futile attempt to stop crying.

He turned away from me. 'Older girls are much less hassle. Say goodbye to your father...'

David opened the door and stepped out of my teenage, rule beset life.

When my father returned, I was crying. I told him it was the pain, and that David had had to go, and relayed his goodbye. I cried the whole way home, my father unaware that it was the pain of not knowing if I'd see David again.

In fact, for two whole months I didn't see him or hear from him, not even a message. It seemed that as far as David was concerned, I had died in the fall from the tree-house. I wished I had. The doctor told my father my wrist would be in plaster for a minimum of two months, and my ankle for six weeks. Confined to the house, having my schoolwork sent to me, I wished it had been my right hand so I could have been rendered completely useless.

Shannon called, and for the first time in our friendship came to my house. I told my parents she was a friend from school, and my mother was just happy that I finally had a friend. Shannon came twice a week, and it was her visits that kept me sane. To all intents and purposes, I seemed normal - talking and breathing, but inside my body was withering as fast as a burning crisp packet.

Each visit I asked Shannon about David, and each time the tale grew worse.

'I'm only telling you this because I'm your friend, Lauren, and I want you to know what he's really like...' she would say.

David had gone back to Holland and brought back the Dutch girl I had seen him with before.

'He's telling everyone how in love he is, and that they might get engaged. She's living with him at his flat.'

I contemplated the quickest way to end it all. 'It's my fault, Shannon. I drove him away. He thinks I'm too young.'

'He didn't think that when he shagged you,' she almost shouted. 'Let him go, Lauren, he's no good for you.'

I was up to my neck in David-quicksand. That June and July were extra warm, but I hid pallidly indoors. School was over, and I had all the necessary passes to get into dance school. The cast on my leg had been taken off, though I was still carrying round the one on my wrist.

Gaining entrance to Dotty's made me feel jubilant, along with the absence of that itchy, dead plaster cast, allowing me to walk properly. Well, wobble like a duck anyway. But nothing gave me salvation.

A few days into August, and I was already wondering what David would be doing on his birthday at the end of the month. I heard the front doorbell ring, and a few moments later, my mother opened my bedroom door without knocking, holding a huge bouquet of flowers. She was flushed and breathless.

'These...' she beamed. 'Are for you.'

I didn't move from my position on my bed.

'Lauren, did you hear what I said?'

They're probably a parting gift from David before he gets married... 'Yes,' I pouted.

'They're from that lovely young man that saved your life.'

I raised my eyebrows. She always did like to be dramatic. *So, I was right, they are from him, she must have looked at the card...*

'Yes,' I said again, in one low note.

'Lauren, please. I want you to go to the door and thank him,' she said, curtly.

I sat forward. 'What! - He's here, at our door?'

'Well whose door do you think I would be talking about?'

I got onto my wobbly legs.

'That's it, darling. What a charming man, he brought me one as well,' she said, pointing haughtily at the bouquet.

He has her in the palm of his hand. Is it a gift, or something you learn - having people adore you, obey all your whims, and trust you implicitly?...

I tried not to duck-walk down the hallway, and I quickly put my arm behind my back. I didn't want him to see me looking any worse than I already did. That year's summer fashion was the slowly

231

dying look, black bags under the eyes and limp, lacklustre greasy hair. I had the skin tone of a sixty year old asthmatic, and an insipid colour, complimented by the graceful walk of a hip replacement candidate.

I stood in front of him assuming I must have looked like a discarded laboratory rat. Of course, *he* looked sensational. He was tanned, and wearing his hair longer again. It was a dark chestnut turned autumn gold with the sun. He seemed genuinely agitated, blowing his fringe away from his face. His eyes seemed to be a paler blue, drawing me into them.

'Hi,' he said, his voice low, not full of the usual confidence.

'Hi,' I said, meekly.

'Can I come in and talk to you? – Your mother said that would be fine...' He cleared his throat.

'I'm sure she did,' I retorted blandly, stepping aside.

I took him through to the front room, hiding my arm as I went, and gritting my teeth with the pain of trying to walk normally. I sat down, lay my giant hand on my lap, and covered it with a pillow. I sat on the couch, probably because I knew David would sit next to me, which he did. He took my good hand in his.

'You probably think I'm an arsehole, and I am. I'm a fool for leaving you. Lauren, please, you can have me forever. The storytelling about the accident pissed me off, but well, real love scares me even more, and with you, well, it *is* real...'

I blinked tired eyes that would soon shut that night, as I slept normally with David back in my life. I didn't even need forgiveness.

'Sorry I lied... I'll try to be more grown up,' I said, looking down at the cushion.

He put his arm round me. 'I don't want you to. I love your innocence.'

My head snuggled into his neck, and he was back in my life once again.

This is how it was to be for the next three years. David ending it, and me always taking him back, believing his lies and promises of change. He had a talent of always making it seem as if it was *my* fault his dick had strayed.

He was scared of commitment, he'd fallen in love with someone older, he needed space, I was dedicating too much time to my dance at college, he was bored, I was still living at home, his job was taking him away, and many more.

During this time, I was still friends with Shannon, visiting the McCormick's whenever I could, even when I was with David. Of course , everyone told me I was crazy, but you must have heard the expression 'Love is blind,' because it is. It's blind to indiscretions, and fake proclamations of love and honour. Blind to the fact your spiritual health is fading away.

In the beginning, my parents adored him, saying how good he was for me. My self-esteem appeared to rise as I took care of myself so that I always looked good for him. They even let him take me away for the weekend on my sixteenth birthday, one of the magical times with David. In the end though, they hated him, eventually realizing he was the reason for the changes in my health and mood.

I never knew how long we'd be together, or when the excuse would come for him to disappear out of my life and continue seeing whoever it was he was cheating on me with. He completely forgot my seventeenth birthday, he was in Italy with his latest. He tried to make it up to me by getting engaged a month later with a Cubic Zirconia gold-plated ring.

Meanwhile my dancing suffered at Dotty Lombridge's Dance School. I always worried that David was bored of me, and I missed a lot of classes when David complained that I hardly saw him. My life was simply set in two realms, Heaven and Hell.

Just before my eighteenth birthday, I discovered I was pregnant. David and I were having one of our more '*together*' times, a whole five months. I told him my news, and he did his usual disappearing trick, leaving me to deal with it all.

I spent my eighteenth at home, crying once again.

Shannon was horrified when I told her I was planning to keep my baby. I missed more classes at Dance School, feeling sick and hoping David would come round. I didn't see him until three months later. And then it was just the usual;

'I'm sorry, babe. It just freaked me out, the responsibility of it.'

He told me he was happy about it. My parents hated to even let him into the house, but they hoped I'd eventually see sense.

One week later, I lost the baby. I called David and left an

emotional message on his answer-phone. He never came. I lay alone, curled in a fetal position on my bed. I wished my mother could comfort me, but I was alone in my utter misery.

Shannon came round three days later, and was shocked at my appearance. I told her what had happened, and she took my hands in hers.

'Lauren…' She sounded serious. 'David's been at our house, with a girl, while you've been going through all this. Please, when will you see? People are laughing at you behind your back. He can do anything he likes, and you, his doting puppy, Lauren, you take it all. You are worth so much more than David. You're very pretty, you're funny, and you're intelligent. As your friend, I can't bear to see you suffer like this anymore…'

When she finished, her hands squeezed mine tightly, and the expression on her kind, freckled face implored me. After she had gone, I lay still for a long, long time, thinking over and over what she'd said.

Poor pathetic sad Lauren…

Shannon's speech was mixed with disbelief that while I was mourning the loss of our baby, he was at the McCormick's, having fun with yet another girl.

For three days, I didn't eat or come out of my room. My mind was opening, expanding and examining. My parents threatened to take me to counselling. When I emerged, they were frantic. I asked my mother if I could go and stay with Aunt Patty, in Norwich. I needed to go away, and distance seemed the only option. I thought it was a shame we had no relatives in Australia.

So it was all arranged, and they were pleased I was going to be away from David, but not about the fact I was dropping out of Dance School, which I didn't have the strength to continue, even though my finals were only four months away. I couldn't even have presented a toilet roll, let alone my final Dance thesis.

Staying with Aunt Patty did me good. For three months, I lived with her in her beautiful thatched cottage. My mother and my aunt were like chalk and cheese. Patty, or Patricia, as my mother insisted on calling her, had wild, long, dark-auburn hair and wore loose hippy clothes. She loved everyone, and everything. A thin, petite, dead ringer for Janice Joplin, she showered me with healing stones, reiki, and Buddhist chanting. She walked barefoot round the garden for fresh grass healing, and sat cross-legged outside on a blanket at sunset, her smile on constant orgasm setting. She told me to listen to the birds, because, yes, it was birdsong therapy.

With all her healing, and at last being able to confide in someone older, it took my mind off David. My mother called to inform me about a card, flowers and one visit from David.

'…But Daddy nearly punched him,' she blustered.

Being in beautiful Norfolk soothed me, and allowed my thoughts to finally rationalize. I could see that David was a '*psychic vampire,*' feeding off my low self-esteem. I had been in the grip of young love. I was saddened that I had to release that grip, but I was finally waking up.

Love? Ha.... Love is a sick, cruel joke, invented by people who want you to do their bidding… It was twisted, contrived, and it left me mournfully delirious. I never want to have it again…

David had throttled the love out of me.

I wrote to Shannon every week I was away. She never mentioned David, and I was relieved. She wanted to be a vet, and had nearly completed her preliminary courses at college. Her sister Darrah was back home from Ireland, and was completing her Doctorate in a hospital near Surrey. She had brought a friend home with her, who was living at the McCormick's.

At the end of three months, I felt and looked considerably more human. My cheeks bore a natural flush from the fantastic country weather from May to July. My blonde hair was almost white, and my skin was lightly kissed by the sun. When I looked in the mirror, I remembered Shannon's words; '*You're worth so much more…,*' and I knew I was.

I set my Heart-o-meter to 'stone' setting, ready to go back and get on with my only just started life. I said a tearful goodbye to Aunt Patty. Her parting words; 'Chamomile makes the best vaginal douche.'

It was nice to see my parents. They said how well I looked. Then I stood in my room, observing all the cards, flowers, (most of them dead) letters, and cuddly toys. Care bears with love hearts told me they loved me, but my heart had gone to the dark side. I got a rubbish bag and threw everything into it, not daring to open David's cards, which I knew, said '*Sorry!*'

Shannon came over to my house, excited because she'd passed her exams. We greeted each other as sisters, both speaking too fast and laughing. The new, older, Lauren asked nothing of David. Our small, happy world in my room felt so precious, I didn't want to spoil it. We hugged and chatted and chatted. She told me how good I looked, and I told her I felt much better.

The hardest thing will be when I see that devil's minion; David...

When she asked, I told Shannon that a part of me would always love him. It's not an emotion one can simply cast aside, but I wasn't In Love with him any longer.

My big test came at the end of August, when the McCormick's were holding a Twenty-first birthday party for David. It was the usual mandatory fancy-dress. Now that my heart was stone, I refused to skulk away. Quite the opposite. My body had settled into something very pleasing, being nearly Nineteen. My blonde-white hair reached the middle of my back, and caused a lot of comment. My clear-blue eyes shone brightly.

I will be Lauren the Bitch, who always has the upper hand...

Shannon and I got ready in her room, just like the old times. Her sister, Darrah was working until midnight, as was her friend, who had trained to be a nurse. We had the room to ourselves as we drank the traditional Snowballs. Shannon was a vampire, and I was a biker chick. Full black leathers hugged my body, and I had racing boots with red trim. The zip was undone enough to see my plump cleavage. I put a black-visored helmet on to finish it off, and tucked all my hair into it.

We went downstairs, visors down, and Shannon led the way to the kitchen. There were a shitload of people everywhere, and I could feel eyes on me.

Don't look for him..., I told myself.

The huge gorilla serving at the bar could only have been Shannon's father; Flynn. So I ordered a Bacardi, while Flynn told me how fantastic I looked.

'If only I were younger,' he said, and Shannon told him off.

I turned, and He was there, dressed as a Marine officer, all in white. His hair was cut short again, but his usual sparkle didn't accompany him that night. I removed my helmet and shook my hair down like I was in a shampoo advert. He opened his mouth slightly as his eyes took all of me in.

'Lauren,' he exclaimed, coming over to me.

'David,' I said, coldly. '...Shannon, let's go over there,' I asked, as I pulled her away.

I planned on shunning David all night, and I was enjoying myself. Lots of boys were dancing round me. Whenever I saw him, his mood looked dark. After the cake, and the blowing out of candles, the DJ announced the inevitable slow dances. Two girls came into the party, one dressed as nurse, the other in a doctor's coat.

Shannon called over; 'Darrah!' and her sister came over to us, with her friend, who had bright-red hair.

Shannon introduced me. 'Darrah, this is my best friend, Lauren.'

Darrah beamed the same smile as her father. 'Hi,' she said in a strong Irish accent. 'This is my friend, Angela.'

'Hi,' Angela said in the same accent. She turned to Darrah. 'I'm just going to wish David a happy birthday,' she said in a low pitch, and left us.

The slow songs started to play. After a while, David came up, and without even asking hustled me to where the others danced and smooched.

I tried to push him away. 'I don't want to.'

He was pulling me about. 'You have to listen to me... please, Lauren.'

He wrapped his arms around me, and momentarily, his familiarity dented my resolve. He tried to talk.

'I won't listen,' I said.

A new song came on; *The Thompson Twins – Hold me now*, and we just turned on the spot, neither of us saying a word, as we let the lyrics say it all for us.

I have a picture pinned to my wall
An image of you and of me and we're laughing, we're loving it all
Look at our life now, tattered and torn
We fuss and we fight and delight in the tears that we cry until
dawn

Hold me now, warm my heart

Stay with me, let loving start, let loving start

You say I'm a dreamer, we're two of a kind
Both of us searching for some perfect world, we know we'll never
find
So perhaps I should leave here, yeah, yeah go far away
But you know that there's nowhere that I'd rather be
Than with you here today

As the song finished, I looked into David's tear-filled eyes.

'Please, Lauren. Please, will you let me talk to you for just five minutes?'

Okay, I'll give him five minutes… To face the future, I have to resolve the present…

As we left the room together, I saw the startled look on Shannon's face.

She thinks I'm going back with him…

Darrah's friend's green eyes had narrowed like a cat's.

She's jealous…, flickered across my mind as we went into the hallway.

He went as if to go upstairs.

'No, David. We'll go in the garden.'

I wasn't about to test myself that much by sitting on a bed with him. We found a quiet spot and sat down on the grass. He took my hands. I removed them.

'Lauren, I've been a fool. I'm sorry…' His eyes implored me to believe them.

I flicked my hair. 'Is that all you could come up with? I did think you'd have the time to dream up something more original…'

His mouth opened slightly. I'd never spoken to him like that before. He got a packet of JPS from his pocket, and pulled out a cigarette.

'Not going to offer me one then?' I asked.

He looked from the packet to me. 'Since when did you start smoking?'

I helped myself to one. 'Since right now. I'm not a child, David.'

I really did want to try and smoke. It fitted the character I was playing. The *I don't give a shit* Lauren seemed to be working well for me, hiding all the scars he'd left inside me.

I began to cough violently from my first puff, and then my head felt light, in a pleasant way. The second puff produced only minor spluttering. By the third puff, my body had accepted the poison and my head was enjoying that cotton-wool feeling.

David was waiting for me to give him the usual *'No, it's my fault,'* speech, but none came. I quietly enjoyed my first cigarette, while he tried to think of ways to win me back.

'Lauren, I will change, I swear. Please, let me show you... Truly, I love you, and yes, maybe before I just said it, but now I *know* it's real...'

I blew smoke into his face, signaling boredom.

'Lauren, I didn't bring anyone tonight, I didn't want to. For fucks sake, it's my Twenty-First, and I want you with me. See? I do love you, can't you see it?'

His eyes didn't leave my face as I stubbed my cigarette out. Still I said nothing. It was making him slightly angry.

'Lauren, see? – I've already started to change...'

I simply stared into space.

'For fuck's sake, say something.'

I tilted my head very slightly. 'What? Don't you like it, David? Maybe I *have* changed. Don't you like what you've created. You can thank yourself for that. You...' I prodded him with my forefinger. '... taught me a valuable lesson. Not to be reckless with my heart.' I stood and looked down at him. 'Stay away from me, David. I don't care if you change or not, you're no longer any concern to me.'

He called after me as I walked off, back to Shannon and the party. We had a great night, hardly seeing David. Angela, the red-haired Irish girl stayed by his side, flirting with him.

Later on, I had a small cry, but soon resolved not to shed any more tears over David. He bombarded me with poems, rose petals strewn up our path and a fresh bunch of flowers every day. Baskets of fruit arrived, accompanied by tokens, already paid for, to go on a Health weekend, which I tore up. Shannon told me he hadn't been seeing anyone, and that he really did look like he was suffering.

'Good. – Now he knows what it feels like,' was my attitude.

She also told me her sister's friend, Angela liked him, but he had said he didn't want anyone.

I got on with my life and did an intensive secretarial course, paid for by my Parents. I had a couple of dates that went very wrong when it became apparent that David was stalking me. He waited outside the house and followed me when I went out in the car. He constantly called on the phone, and my Parents had to change our number. It got so bad the police had to go round and warn him to stay away from me. He sent love notes with Shannon, which I tore up.

'Look, Lauren, I do think he was a complete wanker to you, but I've never seen him like this. I think he's a broken man. He really is in love with you.'

'You reap what you sow,' I replied.

'You've become hard, Lauren,' she commented, wistfully.

'Yes. Yes, I have. I'll always protect myself now, Shannon. It's the only way I know.'

I needed to get away again, so I took my secretary's diploma to Norwich, and Aunt Patty's. I found myself a job with a small family solicitors, and worked for ten months there, saving all my pennies, until shortly before my twentieth birthday, I set off to travel around Europe for eight months, and replace my anger with some new relationships. This included girls, as I felt vehemently disillusioned with the male of the species.

I sent Shannon postcards of all my travels. She wrote back to me, saying she was going to start a four year apprenticeship at a veterinary practice in Scotland. Apparently, David had been seeing Angela for a few months, but he was a changed person, subdued and quiet. Privately, I wished him luck, thinking I would never see him again. I was so wrong.

About two years later, I was living in a small apartment, still in Surrey. I was working for a local building company as a secretary. Life was good and simple. I was living with Rachel, who I'd met on a night out clubbing. We had clicked instantly, and she moved in with me for six months.

Rachel totally took my crap. I'd always be playing the bad hard-ass, and I'd argue and give her loads of shit. Of course, it wasn't fair on her, it was always misplaced anger, meant for David. She accepted my bubbly clumsiness, my forgetfulness, and my nastiness. It was during this time that I saw David again.

It was on a Saturday morning, both Rachel and I were in bed. Nine-thirty, and the doorbell rang, rousing us. Then it rang again, more impatiently.

'Who the fucks that?' Rachel groaned.

'How would I know?' I croaked, as I got up to answer the door.

I opened it and my mouth fell open. I rubbed my eyes.

I must be dreaming...

Standing before me was David, dressed in full Top hat and Tails.

'Hi, Lauren,' he said softly.

He looked amazing dressed like that, but all I could feel was sadness.

'So, you're real? I'm awake?'

He smiled vaguely. 'Yes, you're awake.'

My whole body was frozen to the spot.

'Is it okay if I come in?' He took his top hat off.

How the hell did he know where I live?... 'Yes... yes of course.'

I took him into our tiny front room, and he sat, nervously playing with the rim of his hat. I sat down too, still in shock that he was there decked out in wedding attire.

'So, David. It would appear that you are going to a wedding?'

He couldn't look me in the eye, and just kept staring down at his hat. 'Yes.'

One word answers. The situation began to un-nerve me.

'David, I'm a bit spun out by all this. Can you tell me what's going on?'

The door opened, and Rachel's beautiful elfin face appeared. She squinted sleepily at David, then directed her question at me.

'What's going on, babe?'

David looked from her to me.

'Its fine, Rach. Go back to bed. I'll be there soon,' I said.

Her gaze still fixed on David.

'really, it's fine.'

She blew me a kiss and closed the door.

'So, I scared you so much, you've turned gay?' David blurted out, shaking his head.

'I hardly think you're in the position to ask questions about my life, when you turn up here after two years, at nine-thirty in the morning, dressed in top hat and tails.'

He sat forward, still playing with the damned hat. 'I'm the groom.'

For a moment, I was stunned.

'In three hours. I'm marrying Angela.'

'And you're here?... Why, David?'

He placed the hat down carefully and looked at his watch. 'Do you have a radio?' he asked.

It was too early for cryptic clues. 'Yes, but why?'

'Can we listen to it for ten O'clock?... Please?'

I sighed, and not knowing what was going on, I switched the stereo on.

'Station?' I asked, without turning round.

'Globe 103.'

I typed in the frequency, and a DJ's voice enthusiastically informed me it was Saturday.

For some of us it's a fucking weird one...

I returned to my seat and perched on the edge.

'Okay, now what?'

He said nothing.

'David, what's going on?'

Creases of concentration arrowed his forehead. 'Just listen please, Lauren. To the radio.'

I threw my hands up in resignation. 'Okay!'

A song was ending that I didn't recognise. The over-awake DJ was saying -

'*Now it's ten O'clock, it's dedication time.... This is from David, to Lauren, and David says - Sorry for the way he was, and he will love you forever. Ahhhh... The song he has chosen is Hold me now, by The Thompson Twins...*'

The song began to play. I knew every word, and ancient tears collected in my ducts. When it had finished neither of us could look at each other. When I spoke, my voice shook, and for one solitary moment, I softened.

'David, why?... Why couldn't you have been like this when we were together? Things could have been so different.'

He stood, and raised his voice. 'Don't you think I know that! It's something I'll always have to live with. I'm here to say goodbye, but I'm also here wishing you'd take me back.'

How the tables had turned, a complete reversal of roles.

'Then why on earth are you getting married? Why are you saying all this two hours before your own wedding?... We said goodbye, David, a long while ago.'

His big blue eyes widened. 'I'm getting married to Angela because she's good, and kind, and I can't pine my life away for something I'll never have.'

'You did have it, David, but you gambled, and you just don't like the price of losing. Look...' I got up and sat next to him, getting eye

242

contact. 'David, I'm still getting over us. Rachel *is* my Lover, but I'm not a lesbian. You hurt me, destroyed me. I'm putting myself back together, making some adjustments. It'll take me a long time to trust anyone, and forgive you, but I will.' I took his hand. 'I hope it works out for you, David, and that in the end we'll both be happy. One day I hope we'll be friends.'

He placed his other hand on top of mine. 'That's a nice thought, but I can't see Angela allowing that. She knows how much I think of you, well, thought of you. She burnt every photo I had of you.' He laughed hollowly. 'As if that would erase you from my mind... No, it's goodbye. Friendship isn't an option.'

We hugged, embracing everything we didn't have.

David stood. 'I'd better go. If I'm late because of you, I don't think things will go too well.'

I smiled at him. 'Who's your best man?'

'Kev.' He chuckled nervously.

'Wow. You two are still mates. Say Hi for me.'

Good old Kev...

I wished I could see him and say Hi in person. I was still in touch with Shannon, albeit infrequently, or I'm sure she would have told me about this marriage plan.

'Oh yeah, I'll say; Hi Kev, just popped round to see Lauren today, and she said Hi...'

'Mmm. Yeah, I see your point.'

I took him to the front door, opened it, and kissed him on the cheek.

His eyes took all of me in. 'How can you look so fantastic dressed in an old shirt?'

'Oh this? It takes days to perfect this look,' I joked, trying to lighten the parting.

'Take care, Lauren. I hope you get the person you deserve.'

He turned left, and went off to get married.

Tears irritated my eyes as I closed the door, and a small piece of the stone fell away.

Rachel and I drifted apart, athough we stayed friends. For the next two years, I travelled round Europe, working in bars and having fun. Over time, my heart began to soften. I saw many people trying to love, pretending to love.

243

When I met Perry, he was twenty-five, rich and full of life. I did try to love him, I liked him very much, but when we married after only two months together, the trying quickly turned to pretending. It lasted a year.

It was while I was with Perry, living on a brand new housing estate, in a tiny one bedroom flat that cost a fortune, on the outskirts of Surrey, that I bumped into David. By sheer chance, we were both out shopping in the same place. Both of us were shaken and shocked, so we went for a drink to catch up.

He was still married to Angela and they were trying for a family. I told him about Perry, trying to make myself sound more enthusiastic than I felt. It was good to see him. We chatted about old acquaintances, and our air was relaxed, happy, and friendly. He took my phone number and we parted.

Over the next few years, we met only as friends, maybe three times a year. David became a father, while I saved up and got a visa for Australia. I was planning to travel for a long time. Not long before I was due to go, he called me asking if we could meet. I said I would, but I never saw him again. He didn't turn up.

I travelled for about twelve years, periodically visiting England to see my parents. I worked my way round many different countries. When I was Forty, I came back, and for the last three years, as you know, I've been working as a secretary for a small firm in Woolwich... **"**

When I was about to finish talking, ten hours later, my mouth was bone dry and my head hurt from the memories, and the fear of what might occur next. Nick came back into my field of vision, his face unreadable despite everything I'd told him. He was still glowingly beautiful.

I felt fifteen again, thinking those same old useless thoughts; *I'm going to lose him, it's all too much...*

"and so, for the last few months, I've been totally, obsessionally, uncontrollably in love with his son. I am not looking to replace anything, rather that I've been looking for the real thing. I've not accepted false prophets, nor met anyone else who made me believe it was real. That happened for the first time with you, as it should have. With you, it *is* the first time for me. I want to experience us for the rest of my life. You would cherish and nurture, it could be love as it should be... Yes I admit, it is a twisted tale of fate, but if I hadn't looked for David, I would never have found you, and even if you don't want to see me, I'll always be thankful that you gave me that short time of what I so longingly wanted."

Nick didn't move. I hung my head, I thought I had lost him.
"Lucy. Lucy, look at me..."
I looked up.
"That's what I want to call you, if that's alright..."
It sounded like he might be staying around.
He ran his hand through his hair. "It's a bit of a shock finding out my father was such a complete bastard, and that he didn't tell my mother he was seeing you..." He took a deep breath. "But that's my father's fault, not yours. It won't be easy, but..." He leant closer, across the coffee table. "I'm in love with you, Lucy. I don't want to walk away."

Fresh tears ran down my face, and I un-tucked my legs from underneath me. They'd been in the same position for all those hours. I tried to stand up and they gave way, no feeling left in them whatsoever. I fell hard across the table, my chest taking the brunt, and winding me. Luckily, I'd clamped my mouth shut to avoid biting my tongue. My head was now resting on Nick's genitals, and I was hyperventilating.

He grabbed my shoulders. "Are you alright?"
I looked up at him, trying to smile.
He smiled back. "Well, if you wanted to give me a blow job, why didn't you just ask? It might not be the best moment, though."

I rolled onto my back, and joy and laughter instantly healed my bones. Nick helped me up, and we lay in each other's arms on the sofa, a new, honest love beginning.

NICK MEETS NORA

For the next three days, Nick and I submerged ourselves in each other, no longer afraid to communicate. We decided he would move in with me and try to find a job. We were still sleeping on the sofa together, only embracing. The truth was still too raw for us to make love.

My phone kept ringing, and I'd told Nick it was Nora, and that he wouldn't be put off for much longer. Nora had texted me to say that the song was ready, and that I *had* to listen to it – I would simply die, apparently. I called in sick to work, but my boss told me to take care of myself, and have the whole week off if I needed it. As I hung up, I knew already that I would.

Lawrence Cole rang once and left a short 'Hope you're okay' message.

My mother just left a beep, and no message.

I told Nick how much I loved his poem, but I left out the part about turning it into a song.

He asked me to take down the pictures of him - "It's a bit creepy being in a room where all you can see is yourself."

"With pleasure..." I took them all down and stacked them against the wall in the bedroom. "I don't need them with the real thing here," I answered, gaily.

Nick wanted to talk about his family, and I loved his need to talk about everything, hiding nothing away.

"I'm telling them the truth about being here with you, but I'm not going to tell my mother who you really are, as much as I hate to do that. I don't want to upset my mum at the moment. You are Lucy to them. My dad, well, he's got no choice, but he *is* my father and I still love him. I'm also angry with him, because for years he probably loved you far more than he loved my mum. I won't ignore him, but it definitely helps that we are here in London."

I admired the way he thought things through, trying to make the best decision that caused the least hurt to anyone. Every minute I was holding back from telling him I loved him. I just let it all settle around us. He said he would call at the weekend to let them know what was happening.

Nora called five times in a row.

"It's no good, Nick. He won't be put off anymore."

"Well, then I think it's time I met your best friend."

I pouted purposefully. "It's only because I'm being selfish and keeping you all to myself."

He came to me and embraced me, allaying my fears. "You can be selfish for the rest of your life then," he said, and kissed my forehead.

My life will be very short at this rate..., I thought, as I exploded in one giant orgasm of delirium.

"Call him. I'm making us a coffee."

So, I did. Nora complained about my disappearance again, but quickly forgave me when I said I had a surprise, and he could come to my flat today and see what it was.

"Darlink, you sound so 'appy. Yes, sí, sí, I come soon!..." He gasped, shocked at his own double entendre, and excited.

"Okay, you asked for it, get ready for Nora," I said, after I'd hung up.

"I'll be fine," Nick said, with a playful smile.

Three hours later, I would be wondering why I had worried. Two hours after my call, Nora presented himself at the door dressed in an Issy Miyake dark green khaki gamekeeper's outfit, including the hat, which was jauntily cocked to one side.

"Lauren. Darlink!..." he sang as he air-kissed me on both sides.

Nick had been taking a shower, and at the precise second Nora stepped into the hall, Nick stepped out of the bathroom wearing only jeans and holding a towel. As he dried his hair, he looked like a Greek God, with a body tuned to perfection.

Nora's mouth dropped open, and his eyes expanded bigger and faster than I'd ever seen them do on drugs.

Nick walked towards us, flinging the towel over his powerful shoulder. He had a big, full smile as he held his hand out to Nora, whose mouth still hung open limply.

"Hi, you must be Nora. Lucy's told me so much about you."

Nora screamed a long witches scream, then he placed the knuckle of his index finger in his mouth, biting down on it. All this time, Nick held out his hand patiently.

"Nora!" I cut in.

"Oh! Yes, Lo siento..." he said, shaking Nick's hand as a Lady would.

I led Nora through to the living room, not the easiest of accomplishments, as he was clearly still in shock. I placed him on the sofa and turned his hand into a fan, waving it furiously in front of his face.

"Would you like some water, Nora?" Nick asked.

"Oh the shock... So naughty, Lauren! You should have told me... Yes, sí, por favor." He feigned faintness as he turned to Nick in answer.

Then Nora's dark Cuban eyes flashed at me and one of those perfectly waxed eyebrows arched high, the sign for - '*You?... Darlink, please!...*'

Nick placed Nora's water in front of him, and asked if anyone wanted a coffee.

"Oh, yes." I did.

"Sí, also I'm going to have a joint, for the shock, darlink..." He opened his bag and retrieved the requirements. "So, you really here? The boy from the pictures?" he shouted.

"Yes, I'm Nick," he shouted back.

Nora leant forwards to roll up, and spoke under his breath. "My God, darlink. He is magnifico..." He was purring like a cat. "I want to know todos, everything." He pulled a Rizla from a silver case, giggling.

"I will..." I whispered.

Nick brought our coffees through and returned to the kitchen to fetch his.

"But please, Nora. Don't tell Nick about the song yet. I want it to be a surprise."

Nora's eyes narrowed, and he tapped the side of his nose.

"Come, come, darlink." He tapped the seat next to him as Nick approached.

Nick smiled, and did as he was told. Nora put down his freshly rolled joint, leant towards Nick, and gently stroked his hand down his torso.

"Nora...." I gently reprimanded him.

Nora threw his head back and shook his hand out. "Oh, aiieee! So nice..."

Nick reacted as if a thousand gay men had stroked his chest before. I loved him even more, if that were possible. No drama, no jitteriness, and no pretense. He took Nora completely in his stride.

"Tu eres muy perfecto," Nora was saying as he finally managed to light the joint.

"Muchas gracias, equalmente," responded Nick.

The coffee mug stopped just short of my lips, and Nora coughed on his joint.

"Ahhh... Habla Español?"

Nick blushed, shrugged, and looked at me. I had no idea what had been said, or that he even speak Spanish, but it was obvious Nick held many surprises for me.

"Oh well I'm not great, but I did a bit at school," he explained.

Nora handed the joint to Nick, who took it and inhaled a huge lungful. He began coughing hard, and quickly progressed to stomach-tearing coughs, his face turning red with the exertion.

"My throat's burning!" His voice was squeezed out between reaching sounds.

He was still clinging to the joint, not passing it on. Nora was looking shocked again, staring at him.

"Nick, Nick, are you alright?" I asked, as he performed a final lurching cough at me across the table.

He took a sip of Nora's water. "Yes," he said, and started toking again.

A similar episode ensued, only not as violent.

Nora splayed his hand on his chest, as Nick passed me the joint.

"Darlink, don't you smoke?" He placed his hand on Nick's thigh.

"No..," Nick replied, his voice still husky.

Nora looked at me. "Ahhh, Lauren, so naughty! I like this one,

249

Sí, mucho."

As I passed the joint back to Nora, Nick was wearing a silly grin. I got up, needing the loo.

"So, Nora, be nice to Nick, but not too nice," I said, wagging my finger playfully.

Nora slapped Nick's thigh. "Sí, nice..."

While I sat on the loo, I recalled how Nick hadn't even flinched when Nora passed him the joint. He'd just wanted to try, without hesitation or agitation, absorbing life's new offerings. Very different from the usual reprimand - 'Oh you smoke pot, do you?' asks the man who drinks a bottle of whisky a day. I wondered how Sergeant Cole would react if he was fondled by a gay man, who then passed him a joint. I amused myself thinking of all the possible scenarios and outcomes.

As I came back into the room, Nick was passing the joint back to Nora. They were sitting closer than when I'd left, and Nick was only coughing mildly. Nora stubbed the roach out and Nick looked up at me. His face looked as if he were five years old again, Santa was still real, and he'd just discovered the train set he'd wanted so badly, ripping off the paper.

"Lucyyy!..." he cried, holding his arms open.

Nora giggled. "Okay, I wanna know, que pasa? Why you call her Lucy?"

Nick slapped his legs, motioning for me to sit on them, then wrapping his arms around me.

I coughed. "Nora, you know why."

"It's the name I met Lucy with. So that's what I call her," Nick answered. He pulled me back with him into the corner of the sofa.

"Ahhh, but that's so romantic - a special name." Nora mirrored us and descended into the opposite corner of the sofa.

Nick began to giggle, raising a smile from me.

Nora joined in with small, light ladylike giggles. "I'm not sure what's funny, but it just is..."

A tree of laughter began to grow, expanding all the way to mild hysteria. Then bit by bit, it subsided, interjected by the odd giggle.

Nora stood up. "Oh, so funny!" he said, wiping a tear away.

He went over to the CD's, lightly humming as he made his choice. Nick and I gazed at each other.

"Sí...," Nora crooned, as he selected a disc. Then he grabbed his bag. "Must powder my nose," he said, and left the room quickly, as the first few notes of **Take That ~ Back for good** began.

How does Nora choose such apt tunes?...

We let Take That say everything for us, perfectly. The music built up on the piano, and the crescendo came as the door opened to reveal Nora, arms wide open and singing loudly -

"Whatever I said, whatever I did, I didn't mean it, I just want you back for gooood..."

Nick and I jumped out of our skins, and Nora mounted the coffee table to sing the rest of the song.

"...if you come back for good!..."

He bowed when the song finished, while Nick clapped and I cheered. Then he fell onto the sofa.

"Ahhh, so hot and sweaty, but I think it is Nick doing that to me." He laughed, and fanned himself with his hand again.

"Sorry, Lucy, I need to get up," Nick said.

He grabbed my hips, and his powerful hands sent a jolt through me. His blue irises were set in lava-red eyes, and he wore a big, dopey grin. Standing proved to be difficult.

"Wooaahh!..." He splayed his arms out to the side, in an attempt to balance himself. "I can't really feel my legs," he said, giggling.

Nora leant forward and placed his hands at the top of Nick's thighs, running them all the way down. "I feel them for you... Darlink, they're fantastic."

I slapped Nora's hand away. Nick, still chuckling, leapt up and navigated the room like a flightless bird, only just making it out the door. Nora let out a huge breath, as if he'd been holding it the whole time, and I joined him on the sofa.

"Oh, darlink. I can see why you're in love with him. I think me, too."

I smiled. "No, your dick is in love."

Nora giggled. "Yes, sí, sí. So naughty!"

I lay back and sank into the sofa. "Nora, he's moving in with me. I'm so happy, more than I ever have been. Life feels rich, and decadent. I could CONQUER THE WORLD!" I shouted.

"So what about the song? When can I bring, for you to listen? It is estupendo!" he exclaimed, clapping his hands.

"I'm not sure. Things need to settle first, Nora. He's only been here four days..."

Nora's bottom lip pouted.

"Okay. It won't be too long, but I want it to be a surprise for Nick, so mums the word, okay?"

Nora placed his hands together as if in prayer. "You know I am an angel."

"Mmm, of course."

The door flew open, and Nick stood there, white as a sheet and sweating profusely. I stood quickly and went over to him.

"Nick, are you alright?"

He held his hand up. "Yep. I'm fine now. Just need to sit down."

He progressed unsteadily back to his place beside Nora.

"I'll get you some water..." I said, and went to the kitchen.

I could hear Nora saying - "*Don' worry. It happen to us all...*"

I returned to find Nora standing in front of Nick, fanning him with a drinks coaster with one hand, and feeling his brow with the other.

"Yes, thank-you, Nora, I can take over now," I said, handing the glass to Nick, who still looked ghostly pale.

He drank the whole glass down and then sat back. I resumed my previous position on his lap. Nick kissed me on the cheek, and his silly grin was back. My face must have shown concern.

"I feel good, Lucy. Really good. So relaxed, so don't worry, I feel good, so good, because I got youuu..." He sang the last word in the style of James Brown.

Nora and I burst out laughing, and Nick joined in.

All the time his hand was caressing my back, which in turn caused my vagina to begin shouting at me - '*HELLO!... REMEMBER ME?... There's cobwebs all the way down this corridor...*'

I began to fidget, adjusting myself in an attempt to tone down the shouts to a whisper. Under the squirming of my bottom-cheeks, movement had begun. I could feel Nick's cock growing beneath me, exacerbating my efforts to hide my sexual desire.

"So, darlinks..." Nora interrupted. "We all go clubbing this Saturday, sí?"

My eyebrow arched up.

"Sí, yes," said Nick, enthusiastically.

I turned to him quickly. "Are you sure?... You only just got here."

Nora tutted. "If the man wants to shake his tush, darlink."

Nick tried to shake his tush, grinding his hard cock into me.

The doorbell rang, short and sharp, three times. Gasping, I looked at Nora, who was looking back at me open mouthed.

We both knew that my mother was at the door.

Shit!...

I jumped up, and total panic set in. We were all stoned out of our minds, and Nick was there.

"Nora, come with me please..." I said, gesturing with my head.

"Who's at the door?" Nick asked, innocently.

"I'll tell you in a minute," I answered, as I led Nora into the hallway. "Nora...," I whispered. "I sort of told my mother a little white lie."

He tutted. "Okay, what you say?"

"That Nick was a model, and a friend of yours..."

He sucked in his breath.

"Well I didn't know he was coming here – Please, Nora?"

"Lauren!" my mother's shrill voice called out.

"Okay, darlink. I do it. Nick is a model and my lover." He smiled.

"No, Nora. Your friend. You open the door while I tell Nick."

I gave his clothes a quick straighten, then ran into the front room and over to Nick, who tried to pull me down and kiss me. His cock was still ramrod hard.

"Does this stuff normally make you horny?" he asked, then managed to kiss me passionately.

I was finding it hard to pull away. I was surrendering to him. Delaying the moment of telling him that I'd lied once again. Hearing my parent's voices in the hallway jerked me back to reality.

"Nick, my parents are here, I..." was all I managed to say before the door opened.

I bolted too fast to my feet, and fell down directly, like a plank of wood. My mother and Nora both gasped simultaneously. My father rushed over to help me, as did Nick.

253

"Lucy, are you alright?" Nick asked, as he helped me up.

"Fine, fine, it's nothing," I answered, trying not to show the pain.

My mother surveyed the scene suspiciously.

"Hi Dad," I said, kissing him quickly, then going over to do the same for my mother.

"You're not drunk are you darling?" she asked me.

"Of course not," I flushed.

Her eyes went to Nick's face, which was close behind me.

Nora stepped forward. "Dolores, this is Nick." He held out his hand towards Nick. "And Nick, this is Dolores, Lauren's mother, and this..." He turned slightly. "...is Lionel, Lauren's father."

Nick stepped from behind me, went over to my mother, and hugged her. My father smiled, but I saw her tense up.

"Lovely to meet you, Dolores," he said as he squeezed her tightly, stoned off his head.

"I think you will find, young man, that my daughter's name is Lauren, not Lucy." said my mother in irritation.

Then, as he stepped back and turned to my father to shake his hand, my mother screamed, visibly swaying as if she were going to faint. For a moment the rest of us were stunned at this outburst. Nick turned to me and I saw what she had seen. His proud, erect cock was sticking up and forward through the waistband of his trousers. Nora's hand went over his mouth. My father coughed, and went to support my mother.

Nick's beautiful innocent eyes glistened, his face was asking - '*What?...*'

"Er, Nick...," I said, and pointed down as tactfully as I could.

My mother shrieked again. "Oh, Lionel!"

Nick looked down. "Oh, fuck!"

Oh no, that's swearing, now Nick loses 101 points...

"Please excuse me, I need to go to the toilet," he said, and left the room at greyhound speed.

Poor Nick...

Nora took charge, taking my mother's hand and leading her over to the sofa.

"Dolores, darlink. Sit down. Such a shock. Lionel, could you please get some water? Gracias, darlink... Lauren, maybe a cold flannel for your poor mother's head?" he asked, winking at me.

Clever Nora, the flannel happens to be in the bathroom...

My mother was breathing hard. "Oh, I never... I, I feel as if I have been violated..." she gasped out.

Nora patted her hand and my father brought the water over, looking very uncomfortable. He handed it to my mother, and I slipped from the room to look for Nick.

He wasn't in the bathroom, but lying on the bed.
I approached him. "Nick?... Are you alright?"
He said nothing for a moment.
"Nick?"
He rolled over to face me. "Yep, I'm great. I thought that went really well, that first meeting with your parents. Me, totally stoned, waving my cock around. Hugging your mother and thus pushing it against her. Swearing, and then leaving the room, apparently to finish myself off. Yes, I'm just fine."

I couldn't help it, but as Nick spoke, my smile broadened and spread.
"Well, when you put it like that... at least she won't forget you."
He tried not to smile but he couldn't help it, either. I kissed him on the lips.
"Don't worry, I'm sure they won't stay long now," I said, jumping up and giggling.
"It's not funny, Lucy."
I blew him a kiss. "Oh, but it is. Very...," I said as I skipped from the room.

I quickly wet a flannel in the bathroom, laughter bubbling up within me, then returned to the front room to find Nora still chatting to my mother. I handed him the flannel and he held it gently against her forehead. My father sat nervously.
"I was just telling your mother, Lauren," Nora said. "That Nick is very jet-lagged, and models can be so excitable."
I suppressed a smile.
"Disgusting...." My mother complained. "I won't be staying long, not with a pervert in the house."
"Nick's not a pervert," I countered. "All men get erections."
My mother screeched loudly. "The only reason I haven't walked out is courtesy to Nora. After all, he is a friend of yours..." she directed her speech at Nora at whom she smiled weakly.

"You are very kind, Dolores. A real Lady," Nora cooed, patting her hand, while my mother bathed in his praise.

"Nick's gone for a sleep, Nora," I said, tightly.

I wanted to defend him, and shout out how special he was, that I was in love with him. That he was David's Son, even. But I knew all that would have to wait.

"I'm feeling better now, Lionel, and I would like to go," my mother proclaimed.

My father rose, and Nora helped my mother up.

"You haven't even said why you came round," I pointed out, my exasperation obvious.

"Your brother called..." my father started to explain.

My mother took over. "Yes, he's coming to England in two weeks, so please make an effort, Lauren, to keep your place tidy."

I didn't want to argue, so I just sighed.

Nora kissed my mother on both cheeks. "Hasta luego, Dolores."

My father simply said goodbye, and I walked them to the front door, giving my mother a peck on the cheek.

"Please be careful of the company you keep, Lauren," she said, before summoning my father and descending the steps.

My father hugged me quickly and kissed me on the cheek. He had a playful smile on his lips.

"Your mother hasn't had a reaction like that in years," he whispered, and winked at me before he turned and departed.

I closed the front door and ran to the bedroom where Nick lay on his stomach.

"They've gone, you can come out now," I said.

He sat up slowly, looking pained. I went to him and put my arms on his shoulders, kissing him lightly on the forehead. He moved back, catching and holding my hand.

"If it helps, this incident will pale into insignificance when they find out who you are..." I said.

He smiled, self-mockingly.

"And should I be jealous that you're so turned on by my mother?" I teased.

He grabbed me, threw me on the bed, and straddled me with his strong legs.

"I love you, Lucy Bowman," he said, determinedly.

It stoked the flames of hell within me, and I wanted him there and then. I pulled him down onto me, crushing my lips against his.

But, I could hear coughing. Yes, it was definitely coughing.

"Is this a private party, or can anyone join in?" came Nora's voice from the doorway.

Caught up in the moment, I'd totally forgotten he was still there. We broke apart, breathing hard.

Nora came over and sat on the corner of the bed.

"Okay, okay darlinks, so Nora no really understand. Nick gets a stiffy for your mother, then you both come here to fuck?... Es loco, but one of the funniest things I ever saw." He screeched in delight. "Nick, so naughty!" He leaned over to pat Nick's leg.

Nick turned bright red. "It's not really like that, Nora."

I stood. "Okay, let's go back in the living room, and Nora, don't tease."

Nora fluttered his eyelashes and led the way out of the room. Nick held my hand, his look telling me he hoped this would be a small interlude, and his words confirmed it.

"I want you, Lucy."

"I'll get rid of Nora," I whispered.

Nora sat on the sofa, cross-legged and humming. "So, where we go clubbing this weekend?..."

Nick went to the kitchen whilst I sat closely next to Nora.

"What about The Back Door?"

"No, we're not going there..." I flushed. "Anyway, Nora..." I lowered my voice.

"Okay, okay so we go to Frenzy."

"Nora, please!"

He raised his eyebrows. "Que pasa?"

"Could you go? We would like some privacy..." I nodded my head towards the kitchen.

Nora's eyes widened and he smoothed his hair thoughtfully.

He stood slowly. "Okay, so, Frenzy, Saturday night."

He air-kissed me nonchalantly, and spoke Spanish to Nick, before saying in English, "Keep it warm for me."

Nick laughed. "I will, Nora. It was fantastic to meet you." He came over and hugged him.

257

Nora sighed. "So lucky, Lauren. I see myself out."

Nick and I watched him go, and listened for the sound of the front door closing.
Slam!
We pounced on each other like wild animals, crushing our mouths together. The desire was by now too much to bear. He threw me down onto the sofa, undoing his jeans and tugging them down halfway. I pulled my knickers off frantically, throwing them across the room.

Nick thrust into me immediately, and I gasped as I finally had him inside me. His cock felt perfect as we bucked and thrust, and I was beginning to lose my control completely, when Nick shouted – "NO!..."

For a moment, I thought he'd had a cramp, or perhaps envisioned Jenny's face, but then he pulled out. He looked down at me, obviously mortified.
"Fuck, I'm so sorry, Lucy, I've come..." He ran his hand through his hair.
I smiled gently, and sat up, giving him a tender kiss. "It doesn't matter, we've got all the time you need."
"This doesn't usually happen, but I've imagined this moment so many times, well..." He sat back without finishing his sentence.
"So have I, Nick, but I couldn't have imagined *that* scenario of having my parents here, you getting a stiffy and exciting the hell out of my best friend, whilst scaring the shit out of my mother! We *are* stoned on a Thursday afternoon, but I do think we should keep bashing away at it, so to speak." I finished my sentence with a grin, as his sperm glided out of me.

Nick grinned as he pounced on me again, and bash away at it we most certainly did. We spent all of Thursday night fucking in bed, and jungle-fucked on every available surface and floor in every room, all day Friday. Nick seemed to have an amazing gift for constant production of sperm. However many times he came, very shortly afterwards he would be ready again for action in the field. I thanked the Goddess I'd been working out, and was able to keep up.

By early Saturday morning though, my poor vagina was so puffy I could have held a toothpick with it. We both lay spent for a while, Nick cuddling into me.

He kissed my neck as he slid out of bed.

"I'll go get us a coffee. You'll need an ice-pack for your..." He pointed down at my throbbing red labias and giggled.

"Mmm, coffee sounds nice, but we've got no ice."

"Just rest it here then, and relax," he said, leaving me to think about just how disgustingly good I felt, now that our love was completely official.

CLUBBING TO LIFE

We were still in bed late Saturday afternoon. Nick had made us a very late breakfast in bed. Nora called to finalise arrangements. I was to drive, picking him up around ten, and then we were going on to *Frenzy* in South London.

Sergeant Cole sent me a text asking me if I was all right, and asking if he could maybe take me to lunch one day. I told Nick all about Lawrence, and he said he sympathised with him.

"How do you mean?" I asked, genuinely not understanding.

"He likes you a lot, silly. Why else would he have got your car fixed, or helped with that lollipop man incident? Lucy, you are oblivious to the power you yield. You make men fall for you."

I pulled a face. "Oh yes, that's definitely my special power," I said, self-mockingly.

He jumped on me, pulled me down, and kissed me with molten passion. As he pulled away, he left me breathless.

"But that's why I love you; you're totally unaware of it."

He made me smile as always. "Well, I'm just glad that works for you, then."

He sat on the edge of the bed, his beautiful olive-skinned back to me, saying nothing for a few moments.

"I mean, I hope Lawrence Cole hasn't worried you. I've not intentionally led him on, but I don't want to avoid him either."

He turned to face me, his expression troubled. "It's not that, you can be friends with who you like, Lucy. I was just thinking that I have to phone my family, and I can't put it off any more."

BANG! I fell straight back down to earth. I sat up and moved closer to him, placing my hand on the small of his back.

"It's not a phone call I'm looking forward to, but they'll be worried." His voice was heavy, and he was obviously in pain.

"I'm putting you through this. I just hope I'm worth it."

"I will fight for you as long as my heart beats..." he began.

My damn tear ducts began production.

"Like I said, I don't think you realise the power you hold, with the way you look, and the things you say. You make people fall in love with you." He smiled weakly. "Is it okay if I give them your address? They need to know where I am. Although I don't think everyone back home will be so in love with me at the moment."

A mild panic burned within me. *Angela and David, knowing where I live? Well, hello Lauren, you know where* they *live. Yes, but I didn't want to go there and* kill *them...*, I argued with myself. *Shit, but it's important to Nick, so why am I even thinking like this?...*

"Of course you can," I replied finally, smiling more confidently than I felt.

He stood up and went to the door. "I knew it wasn't going to be easy... I'll take whatever's going to come."

I stayed in the bedroom and let him have some privacy. His voice travelled faintly down the hallway, and for a while, it seemed calm. Just as I started to think that maybe everything was okay, Nick's voice rose and he started shouting.

Actually, no I don't think everything is okay. Poor Nick, having to go through all this...

I hoped he would tell me what had happened. Then there was only silence. A nervous sweat crept over my body. Still nothing. I couldn't stand it in the end, so I got up and went into the front room.

He was sitting on the sofa, beeping phone in one hand and his head in the other. I stood still, my breathing short and shallow.

Sensing my presence, he looked up. "Fucking stubborn woman," he muttered.

261

So, he got Angela then. She's probably getting on her broomstick right now...

I slid into one of the armchairs, too scared to ask questions.

Nick put the phone down on the coffee table. "I know she's my mother, Lucy, and she only wants the best for me, but fuck!... She can't command me. I'm not a fucking dog!" He stood, shouting.

I gave him the most sympathetic look I could muster, and his whole demeanour changed. He softened visibly and sat back down.

"I'm sorry, Lucy. I don't mean to be so angry. She's telling me that if I stay here I'll break her heart, just as I have already broken poor Jenny's, who is apparently devastated and waiting for me to return. She even used Maggie against me, and well... Fuck her, she went too far." He took a deep breath. "I told her to go fuck herself, and if that's how she feels, then she won't fucking see me."

My heart was bleeding for him. "Nick, I'm sure when she calms down, she'll see sense. You *are* her Son."

He smiled, mockingly. "Thanks, Lucy. But you know her. Do you really believe that?"

No, not for one second... My silence answered his question. *Jesus, if Angela's like this now, how will she be when the truth comes out about who I really am?...*

Nick was reading my thoughts again. "Fuck knows what she'll do when she finds out... well, that you're Lauren."

I was about to say that we didn't have to tell her, but I knew by now that Nick hated lying, so that wasn't an option.

"How will she find out?" I broached the question.

"Well, at the moment I don't know. I'm hoping my father will find his balls and tell her. After all, he did know who you were."

I looked down at my feet, and felt ashamed. "I should have told you," I whispered downwards.

He came over and knelt in front of me, lifting my face up with his hand. "I'm sorry, that wasn't meant to be a jab at you. I don't want to be anywhere else, or with anyone else." He smiled a beautiful smile. "Anyway, bollocks to it. I'm glad we're going out tonight. I haven't even thought about what I'm wearing yet. I don't have much choice."

And that was that. He didn't dwell on it, or let it spoil the rest of the day. He seemed genuinely content, and he allowed himself to move on. He was going to be so good for me.

We started to get ready. Firstly, we had a romantic bath together, both in a playful mood.

"So, where are we going tonight? I haven't really asked you much about it, though I do trust you," he said.

"We're going to *Frenzy*, which is a small club, under the railway arches in South London. It's fantastic."

Nick repositioned himself, having been gallant enough to take the taps end. "Is it a gay club?"

I blew soap bubbles at him from the palm of my hand. "No, not really. Why? Would that bother you?" I quizzed him.

He chuckled. "No. I just don't have the right outfit," he explained, making me chuckle as well.

"If Nora had his way we'd be going to the gayest clubs in town, where even I feel out of place, but no, Frenzy is a real mixture of people. Gay, straight, trannys, drag queens, lesbians, bisexuals, all races, and all party people."

"Sounds great. I've only been to London three times before."

I raised my eyebrows. "Country boy," I teased.

Nick blew a handful of suds at me. "So, you think we can get some decent drugs?"

His question totally threw me. I could only gape at first.

"Not as much of a country boy as you thought, eh?" He winked at me with those innocent blue eyes.

Shit. I want him again. Do we have time? Who cares?....

As I pounced on him again, he yelled out – "Arrgghh! Shit!"

My full bodyweight was on him. "I'm not that scary, am I?"

"It's the taps, Lucy. They're sticking in my back."

I jumped back and water splashed over the side. "Oh Nick, sorry. In my passion, I forgot you'd got that end."

He leant forward, groaning slightly as he did so. I stepped out of the bath to get a better look. There were two deep red indents, and just above them, a perfect 'C' for Cold on one side, and a 'H' for Hot on the other. It looked painful, and I put my hand over my mouth to stop myself from laughing.

He turned to look at me. "It's not that bad, is it?"

I could only shake my head.

"So what's wrong?"

I took my hand away. "Well - you've got a perfect set of taps," I said, grinning.

"They've never been called that before," he said, grinning and wincing simultaneously as he got out.

"I am sorry."

"Really... So when you're sorry you always grin like a Cheshire cat?... and what were you saying about passion?"

He grabbed me and took me down to the floor, rampantly making love to me. It was nine before we even got dressed. However, both of us were like excited teenagers, eager to go out. Nick wore big baggy jeans that hugged his fantastic arse, and a red vest-top clung to his toned torso.

"This is all I have...." he exclaimed, holding his arms out and looking slightly embarrassed.

I went over to him and ran my hands up his arms. "A gay man's dream, Nick. My dream, too."

I kissed his doubts away, and had to make myself pull free, or we never would have left the house.

I chose a white boned corset edged with black, that pushed my breasts to a sensational plumpness. I loved the way they jiggled with every little motion. Small black hotpants and knee-high leather boots with low heels completed my outfit.

Nick whistled. "Holy shit! You look hot."

I blushed.

"...No bullshit, you're not going out like that," he joked. Pride emanated from him.

"I love you, Nick," I exclaimed loudly, and proudly.

Now it was his turn to blush.

It was ten-fifteen by the time we finally set off in Maisie. Nora called as we were on the way to pick him up. Nick answered, assuring an impatient Nora that we wouldn't be long, and due to the recent congestion charge that made Central London easier to get across, we weren't.

However, once we entered Kensington, trying to find a parking space was a nightmare. I drove round and round, near to where Nora lived.

"Shit. At this time of night we could be here till dawn," I moaned.

Nora called again, and Nick told him of our predicament. I could hear Nora babbling in Spanish on the other end of the phone, making Nick grin.

Finally, Nick spotted someone pulling out of a space, and I swooped in, claiming my prize. We both cheered with joy. As we got out, I fitted the only security device that Maisie possessed, an ancient security clamp, which fitted round the gearstick.

Although I probably won't be needing you round here...

I locked the doors as Nick whistled.

"Nice area," he said, as he looked round at the huge Victorian houses.

"Nora's only two blocks away from here, and yes, it's very nice. Makes me sick to my jealous stomach, every time I come here."

I smiled at Nick, and we linked arms, walking as if we were travelling down the yellow brick road. We stopped in front of a typically large, white, fantastically elegant twentieth-century house. Large white steps ran up to the entrance with plant pots on both sides, that led up to big bay windows and were filled with lavender and lilac, which created a very heavy scent as we ascended.

"Which floor does he live on?" Nick asked.

"He lives on all of them. The whole house is for Nora."

Nick looked astonished.

I rang the bell. "I told you, it makes me sick."

A flustered looking Nora opened the door, wearing a gold and white Jean Paul Gaultier suit over a caramel yellow silk shirt. He looked like a high-class pimp, especially with the gold-topped cane he held.

"Darlink! Where have you been?"

"Parking, Nora."

Nora air-kissed me, eyes sparkling and pupils swollen, before shoo-ing me inside and greeting Nick. He closed the door and led the way to the main lounge - his second favourite room of the house.

"Purleese, darlinks. Sit." He pointed to a lilac two seated sofa.

Nick sat as if he was scared to breathe, as if his breath was a potential weapon that could break things. We had entered Fabergé egg country.

"So, darlinks. A quick drinky?" Nora was animated and flushed with excitement.

I had a sneaky suspicion he already had more than a drink in him.

"Yes please, but just a small one. I still have to drive to the club." I sat back, enjoying the feel of the soft expensive fabric against my skin.

"I'll have whatever Lucy's having," Nick announced, looking distractedly around the room.

Nora went over to the bar to fix us Bacardi and colas, knowing that was my choice of tipple.

"Lovely place, Nora. Muy spectaculo," Nick said.

Nora tutted as he brought the drinks over. "Sí," he commented, sounding bored. " but it comes at a high price, darlink."

He put the drinks down, went back to the bar, and returned bearing a small mirror with a wrap on it.

So, I was right...

"Time for a little cheeky one?" he asked, grinning naughtily.

For a moment, I was torn, and I glanced quickly at Nick.

So, how will he react to this? Oh well, no pretence... I was determined to be myself.

"Yes, I'm up for a cheeky one," I said, trying not to sound too keen.

Nora began to chop out two small lines, hesitating when it came to the third and raising an enquiring eyebrow at Nick.

"Chop away," Nick responded, casually.

Nora was unflinching, absorbed in his task.

We all did our cheekys and finished our drinks. Nora preened his last preen in a huge gold-framed mirror while the magic powder worked its charm on Nick and myself. Our eyes were big and full of lust. We looked at each other intently, and tried to telepathically convey our dirty thoughts to each other.

"So, darlinks..." Nora began dramatically. "Now we vamos!"

He picked up his small handbag, without which he never travelled.

At nearly midnight, we set off again, destination - *Frenzy*.

Nora chatted incessantly all the way there, while Nick and I pretended to listen. Nick's hand rubbed up and down my thigh as I drove, his gaze burning into me. I sucked constantly on my bottom lip, trying to contain the longing inside.

"Hello, holá? Anyone listening to me?"

I started from my passion. "Oh. Yes, of course we are." I smiled at him in the mirror.

"So I said to them, well, you can cuppa my balls if you feel like that..."

I didn't have a clue what he was talking about. The streets became smaller and darker as we reached the arches. I headed for the space I always tried to claim - just three streets away from the club, in a small no-through road. It was dark and looked ominous, but this meant there was nearly always a space there, and that night it didn't let me down.

As I reversed into it, Nick looked about concernedly.

"Do you think it will be alright down here? There's no cameras. It looks a bit moody."

I retrieved the security lock from the boot. "Don't worry, I've parked here dozens of times," I reassured him, as I fixed it firmly into position on the gear-stick.

Then we all linked arms. Dorothy, the scarecrow, and the tin man. All we needed now was a lion. At the front of the club were just two big metal doors. No flyers, posters, or advertisements.

The only clue, apart from the throbbing bass-line leaking out, was Mick and Gary, the two faithful doormen, who stood outside. They made impressive figures with their all-in-black '*I'm a bouncer,*' look.

Nora gasped. "Ooooh, gentlemen, you can deliver me chocolates anytime."

Mick and Gary smiled faintly in unison.

"Evening, Nora," said Gary, as he opened the door for us.

A wave of heat and music hit us. Nora went first.

"Hi, Lauren. You look good tonight," said Mick, blushing.

"Thank you, Mick. Always the gentleman," I responded, flashing my baby-blues at him.

I took Nick's hand as the door shut behind us. Nora paid the entrance fees and led the way, the fine gold thread in his suit glinting under the UV lighting. We all headed for the bar and Nora ordered tequila over the huge noise.

"Salud!" he toasted, and we downed them.

Nick was squeezing my hand tight and his blue eyes were dancing already, scanning the room, and taking in the sights and delights before him. Hard house music pumped out, and the crowd was gyrating, swaying, and stomping as they danced to the beat. People of all nationalities and every style of dress were here to relieve the tensions of Life, enraptured by the positive energy in the hot space.

Nora quickly skipped off with someone; Probably doing the cheeky. Huge glowing mushrooms hung from the ceiling, that month's theme being Enchanted Forest. Fake vines and foliage surrounded the bar, and the staff were dressed as fairies and gnomes. Sparkling green fabric covered the walls, which gave the illusion they were alive.

Nick looked at me as if he had discovered a secret. He was about to say something when Gerald bounded up to me.

Gerald was a cross-dressing accountant who was there every Saturday, without fail. Dressed in a green gingham check dress edged with lace, low cream heels, and pearl earrings, he also sported a full hairy biker's beard, laced with a nervous smile.

"Hello, Lauren," he greeted me, giving me a kiss on the cheek, and flicking a quick glance at Nick.

"Hi, Gerald. This is Nick..." I hesitated. "My boyfriend?" I said as if it were a question.

"Hi..." Nick beamed, shaking Gerald's hand. "And yes, I am her boyfriend," he said, looking intently at me.

Gerald's big brown soulful eyes looked down at himself, then back to me. "Too much?" he enquired.

"I think you look great. Green suits you."

His nervous smile settled for a moment. "The earrings are my mother's. She'd kill me if she knew." He grinned like a naughty boy. "Anyway, Christmas is here, so open your hand for a present."

I did as I was told, and he dropped something into my palm and danced off. I opened my hand to look and three tablets sat there. I closed it quickly.

Gerald mouthed to me - "One for Nora."

I smiled and nodded my thanks to him.

"What is it?" Nick asked.

"Ecstasytablets," I replied, so quickly it sounded like one word. "Nice. Shall we do half each?"

I was surprised again. "Well, only if we can get a taxi home?"

His face was soft and glowing with perspiration, totally relaxed. "Taxi it is then," he concluded.

Ten minutes later, Nora returned with a feather-boaa'd young boy who was all pouty and sulky looking. His bleached-blonde hair was set in spikes that matched the rubber ones he wore round his neck.

"Aaaiieeee!" Nora's cry rang through the air. "Darlinks. This, is Matt."

He presented him with his arms spread wide, as if bored Matt was the new messiah. Matt just about managed to curl the corners of his mouth in response.

"Hi!" Nick and I said in unison.

"Nora?..." I leant into him, handing him his little pressie, which made him squeal with delight. "From Gerald - he's on the dance floor." I looked at Nick. "Tequila?" I mouthed.

He nodded, and then we stood at the bar raising our glasses, ready to lick the salt from our hands.

Nick coughed. "To all my dreams - I'm finally here..."

His deep blue eyes rested on mine for a moment, then he slung back the shot. I followed suit and we slammed our glasses on the counter. His body shook slightly as the tequila ran down his throat.

"So, shall we dance?" he asked, stepping back and bowing.

I curtsied. "Why yes, kind sir."

And dance we did. Nick, as I already knew, was a badass mover. His broad smile never left his face the whole night. He was a whirling dervish of afro soul energy, throwing his tribal gift out all around. I basked in it, bathed in it. His intoxicating wavelength drew people to us all the more. So many people came up to us, or around us, just to say '*Hi!*' or to be in the magic sphere.

Nora joined us occasionally, unable himself to stay away too long from our magnetic attraction. He shimmied on the spot, both hands splayed open at his side, moving back and forth, and often grinding up against Nick. He was always accompanied by '*I've got good drugs,*' Matt.

Eventually, at about 5am, Nick and I found ourselves a small corner to sit down. By now, sweat covered both of us. Nick's chestnut-brown hair was sticking to his scalp. I'd pulled my carefully straightened hair back in a band, and my fringe stuck together in long points, which dripped moisture from the tips. We sat on the floor, not caring what we were sitting on.

Nick was the first to speak.

"What a fucking brilliant night. Great place, I love it here. Thanks, Lucy."

"For what? Pumping you full of drugs since you came to London?" I exclaimed. Though my tone was playful, a tiny part of me had worried about that.

"Yes, it's been great. You holding me down and pumping me full of heroin. Straight into the eyeball..." He poked me in the ribs. "Thanks for just letting me be me." He put his arm around me.

"That's just how I feel."

"So, its official then, we're soul-mates... Partners in crime." He squeezed me close to him.

Yes..., I thought. *Yes, we are...*

Nora came over, saying; "We all leave together. Darlink, my jacket is in your car. Matt is coming with me... Aaiieee! We all come together. Come! You know, Lauren? - Man-jam!..."

269

He cackled with laughter and raised his hands in the air. He was totally fucked, but his hair was still immaculate. He squeezed Nick's thigh, whimpered, and bit his knuckle again.

"Oh. So sexy, sexy. Guapo, Nick. You make Nora's heart bleed."

He skipped off, shouting Matt's name and something about marching powder.

"He's great," Nick said, sloppily.

"I love you for that, Nick Palmer." I kissed him on the cheek. "The club'll close soon. Do you want to have another boogie?"

Nick whispered in my ear - "Hell, yes."

We deposited our positronic rays once more, as everyone's energy culminated in a dome of euphoria.

As the lights came on, a long queue was already forming at the cloakroom. There were lots of hugs and goodbyes and running make-up; the top signs of a great night out. A light murmur trickled round that the police were outside the club. I was glad we were going to get a taxi. The state I was in I could just about handle walking, let alone summon the brainpower to drive.

I spied Matt and Nora before us in the coat queue, Nora groaning that we would be in for a long wait. Nick stood just behind me, holding my waist.

Sex jumped right to the front of my brain. Top of the list. My labia's unfurled and ripened, calling out a soft sea chant to lure the sailors that served aboard the great ship Penis.

I closed my eyes and subconsciously released a small moan.

Nick pushed into me from behind, no need for words, his hard cock doing all the talking for him.

Nora came over and neither of us moved.

"Okay, darlinks. The car for my jacket, then taxi..." He clicked his fingers in the air.

A flying taxi crossed my mind. *The quickest thing to get us home - a rocket...*

Many people were still leaving the club, spilling out like vampires into the dawn light of Sunday morning.

"Aren't we waiting for Matt, Nora?" I enquired.

"Of course we are, darlink. I'm taking the little sulker home." He sniffed airily.

"Are you sure, Nora? He's not your usual type," I said, sounding as normal as I could considering I had a loaded cock pointing at my back.

Nora leaned into me confidentially. "He's got fantastic coke, a fantastic cock, and for a hundred pounds an hour he'll do whatever I want." He grinned sadistically as he stepped back.

"Oh, even better," I began sarcastically. "Take a young male prostitute back to where you live."

Nora clapped his hands triumphantly. "Sí! All night, darlink. So naughty."

"And I take it your parents will be paying for all this?"

Nora straightened, arching one eyebrow and patting his hair. "Don't ask silly questions, Lauren. Of course they are. My father will have a fit." He turned smartly on his heel and rejoined Matt, who was almost at the front of the queue.

I sank into Nick's arms.

"Did I hear right? That's a hooker with Nora?"

"Yes..." I sighed. "He loves to push it sometimes. Even if Matt robs him blind, he won't care. Anything to piss his parents off, especially his father."

"Are they rich then?"

"As Crœsus."

Nick motioned to something behind me, and I looked and smiled as Nora, dragging Matt, descended on us.

"Vamos!" Nora shouted.

We were reaching for our sunglasses and shielding ourselves from the daylight with our arms as all four of us burst out. We linked arms again, only this time we were complete with the '*I charge by the hour*' cowardly lion. We stumbled on the yellow brick road, vaguely aware of police cars lurking in the background.

I wasn't really looking where I was going, and Nora was chatting non-stop, so as we came to the street corner, I floundered, and fell into a man in uniform. He caught me, and I grabbed round his neck with my arms to save myself.

Nora cried out and Nick jumped forward to help.

I looked up into the face of the man who had lightning reactions to catch me, and saw - Sergeant Lawrence Cole. In my happy loved-up state, I hugged him and kissed his cheek.

"Lawrence...," I cooed girlishly.

He straightened up and coughed, as he turned red. "Er, Sergeant Cole, Lauren," he said, glancing over to the other police officers.

I took a step back and twirled. "Nora, Look! Look who it is."

Nora's jaw fell open dramatically. "I know! I can't believe it..."

271

Bored Matt looked mildly surprised. Lawrence Cole coughed again, and Nick put his arm around me, talking quietly -

"Lucy, your breasts have come out."

For just a split second, it didn't register, and then I looked down and gasped at my escaped cleavage. My pert nipples were perfectly balanced on top of my Basque.

I looked up quickly. "Oh dear," I said, trying to stuff them back in a completely undignified way. "Oops! Escaped tits - better call the police..."

I giggled at Lawrence. He did not seem amused.

"I'm sorry - Nick, this is Sergeant Cole." I introduced him, very pleased at myself for saying it right this time.

Nick offered his hand to Lawrence, who shook it briskly.

"So you're the boy from the pictures?" he asked Nick, as if he were interrogating him.

Nick pulled away, shifting and unsure of himself.

"Yes..." he said, and ran his hand through his hair.

"OOOOEEEE! Sargent Cole!" Nora shouted, and waved at him.

Lawrence simply nodded his head.

"So, Lawre...erm, Sergeant Cole, what are you doing here? I didn't know you liked clubbing," I said.

That brought a small smile to his serious business face. "I'm working, Lauren."

"Oh. For missing people?"

"No. Today it's another department - drugs mostly."

My drug-addled eyes widened. "Well, I haven't got any," I pronounced, defending myself guiltily.

"No, she took them all." Nora sniggered.

I flashed Nora a '*Shut your face*' look. "Anyway, we're going to the car, Lawrence. It was lovely to see you." I kissed him on the cheek.

"You're not driving are you, Lauren?" he asked, sounding concerned.

"In this state? You must be joking," I said, grabbing his arm to support myself.

Nick put his arm round me. "You okay, Lucy?"

"Lauren," Sergeant Cole corrected him.

"To me, she's Lucy." Nick asserted, staring into Lawrence's face.

"Come along, children. Adiós sexy policeman..." Nora blew a kiss as he walked off with Matt sewn to his arm.

We trailed after them. "Bye, Lawrence," I called, over my shoulder.

Nora was ahead of us as we walked.

"Well, he definitely doesn't like me." Nick stated.

"Oh, Nick, he's on duty. It's not like he can be himself."

"You can defend him, but I can feel it. He doesn't like me."

"So you won't be sucking each other off then?" I was giggling.

"No. I can safely say that's not on the cards."

As we rounded the corner, I could see Nora standing in the middle of the road, open-mouthed. Matt stood stock-still, his face in apparent wonder.

"Something's wrong." I looked at Nick, and our pace became faster before both of us stopped dead with our mouths hung open.

None of us moved and time seemed suspended to me, an ultra-reality there to replace it. I don't know how long we all stood like that before Nora's high-pitched scream cut through us all.

He screamed again, clutching his heart. I could see his eyes were wild and he was gasping for breath.

"Nora, please, this isn't helping... unless you're having a heart attack?" I told him shakily.

"I can't believe it," Nora wailed.

I couldn't believe it either. I was looking, once again, at what had once been Maisie. The wheels were gone, now replaced by bricks. The bonnet was still propped open, but all the doors were gone. The seats, lights, windscreen wipers, steering wheel, and dashboard were all gone.

Ironically, the security lock was still attached to the gear-stick, which was minus its knob.

Great... Managed to save something...

Nick went over and looked under the bonnet, then looked baffled. "Even the engine's gone," he reported.

Nora screamed again.

"Nora, please, get a grip... after all it is my car," I said, losing patience slightly.

He left '*I couldn't give a fuck,*' Matt's side and came to me, clutching my arm with his hand.

"Lauren, darlink. It's my jacket, it's... Gone!" He ended dramatically on the last word.

I looked over at what had once been a car, and then back to Nora.

273

Nick walked over to us, shaking his head. "I don't know how they did it. There's a car in front and behind." He shook his head again.

"Darlink, you didn't see a jacket?" Nora asked tentatively.

"Nora!" I shouted at him. "My fucking car's been dismantled, and you're worried about a jacket?"

He let go of my arm. "No need to shout, darlink. It's not just any jacket, it's an original from a Vivienne Westwood collection, probably worth more than your car." He sniffed.

"So why leave it in the fucking car then?" I continued to shout.

"Your car is still there, my jacket is not," he shouted back at me.

My mouth fell open again. "Well, I'll just get the fucking keys out and drive us all home then."

Nick began to faux-cough, and both of us looked at him.

"Nora, Matt's gone," he stated, calmly.

Nora looked, gasped and began to gently weep crocodile tears. Beautiful, kind, loving Nick went to him and placed his arm around him. Nora said something to him in Spanish, and Nick's eyes scanned me.

"Sorry this has happened, Lucy... I don't really know what to say."

He brought Nora back over to me.

"Sorry, darlink, but it's all too emotional," he whimpered.

I kissed him on the cheek. "I'm sorry I shouted, but... but I still can't believe she's gone."

I resumed gazing at Maisie's remains. That fucking security lock was mocking me.

"Lucy, you'll have to report this to the police," said Nick, soft and un-panicked.

My eyes widened. "What, now?"

"Yep. Best to..." He released Nora from his powerful grip, and slipped his arms around my waist. "Don't worry, we're in this together."

I snatched his words of reassurance, I felt like I knew he meant it.

"So as much as I don't want this to be my idea, I think we should go back and see your friend, Sergeant Cole?"

A glimmer of hope sparked in my brain. "Yeah, of course. Lawrence."

"Well there's no need for all of us to go back. I'll go and get him, you and Nora can wait here if you like?"

I nodded. Even though Nick was dubious, and had suspicions about Lawrence, he was still willing to help. He kissed me tenderly on the lips before running off.

"I want a hero like that..." murmured Nora beside me, as if in a daydream. "Does he have any brothers?"

He was so blatant that I smiled despite myself. "Yes, two, and you're not meeting them."

He pushed me gently. "So croooell to Nora."

"It's a complicated enough situation already, thanks, without any more added attractions."

"So, he call his parents yesterday?"

I nodded.

"and not so good?"

I shook my head.

He leaned close to me. "Sooo, darlink, you know what you must do?..."

I waited for the pearls of wisdom.

"You must tell them to stick their fingers up their culo's." He proceeded to snigger.

I should have known that everything could be solved with arse and cock.

"Of course, that will definitely warm them to me."

Nick came round the corner with Lawrence and I saw how different they were. One with his life all mapped out, the other with a scribbled drawing as a picture. I was totally betting my life, my love on the scribble.

Lawrence Cole walked up to me as only a policeman would. "Lauren?"

I could only point towards the problem.

For a moment, even he was stunned, turning his head from side to side like a confused bird.

"I see what you mean..."

He turned to look at Nick, then back to what once was a car. He spun sharply round, making me jump.

"Not technically taken and driven away, but definitely stripped."

"Raped, more like," I interjected.

"You'll have to go to Vauxhall Police station to report it, Lauren. I can come with you, then drive you home if you like?"

Even though I was wearing my heels, Lawrence towered over me, taking control as usual though his amber eyes betrayed concern.

"Well, we can get a taxi from the station," Nick added.

"I'm coming, darlink - I have stolen property also," Nora piped up.

"With all due respect, it will be a lot quicker and easier if it's just Lauren. She has all the vehicle details. Only one person need be there, and she'll be fine with me."

I noticed Nick's eyes narrowing as Sergeant Cole said that.

Nora patted his hair, vainly. "Well, if you think I'm staying here on my own then you are all loco."

I sighed, not knowing what was best. I wanted Nick with me, but I knew Nora would be a nightmare, only prolonging the whole situation. I opened my bag and pulled out my house keys, handing them to Nick.

"You and Nora can go back to mine. Hopefully, I won't be too long. Get a taxi."

I smiled at Nick, hoping he knew how much I needed him. He took the keys graciously, but I got the feeling this was not what he wanted.

I took his hand and kissed him. "I won't be long..." Then I looked at Nora sternly. "Be good."

"Darlink, are you crazy? I am in mourning." He placed his hand reverently on his chest.

We all walked back to the club together, and Nick and Nora carried on to the cabstand round the corner. Lawrence escorted me to the front passenger seat of a police car. As soon as we were less than a minute from the arches, Lawrence turned to me.

"Lauren, are you alright?"

He didn't sound like Sergeant Cole any longer, just Lawrence. He seemed to be genuinely concerned.

"Yes, I'm fine..." I hesitated. "Lawrence."

He smiled, and his smile lines complimented his grey hair at the sides, along with the two-day-old stubble.

"You should smile more often, Lawrence. You're far more..." I couldn't finish the sentence, it felt like I was flirting.

"You've gone red, Lauren. And I'm far more what?"

"Nothing," I answered, feeling like a child.

We drove a few streets without speaking. I thought about Maisie and Nick.

"Lauren?"

"Yes?" I eyed him sideways.

"Is that the boy who broke your heart?"

I looked straight ahead. "Yes, but there's a lot more to it than that."

"And you're back together?"

"Yes," I answered, resoundingly.

Lawrence had no chance to ask me further questions before our short journey was over. He parked with the other pandas behind the station, and led the way in through the back. In the fatal light of day, my fantastic night attire took on the look of a prostitute's day attire. As I followed Lawrence up to the duty desk, I felt like I was his arrest, about to be sent down for having a brilliant night, and enjoying some of life's little pleasures, oh yes, and for being dressed like a tart.

Sorry, yes, I'm guilty...

Lawrence presented his badge to the young constable behind the desk.

"Yes, Sergeant Cole, how can I help?"

Lawrence presented me. "My friend here…"

The officer looked me up and down, slowly.

"…had her vehicle stripped last night, and needs to fill out a report."

"I'll just go and get the form, Sir." He scurried off.

Lawrence smiled. "Won't be long here, Lauren."

"Thanks, Lawrence. For helping."

He shifted slightly, looking down, then forced himself to face me.

"This boy… do you think, well, he's a bit..."

He didn't finish, but I immediately knew what he meant.

"A bit what, Lawrence?... Intelligent? Too good-looking? Too well hung for me?..."

He detected my sarcasm and didn't answer.

"...Young? Is that the word you're looking for?"

He shrugged. "Well, he is a *bit* young."

I stepped away from him a pace. "So, what you're saying is that this decrepit old hag here, who's nearing the end of her years, isn't entitled to a toy boy?"

"That's not what I'm saying, Lauren," he countered, speaking low as the constable returned.

"So how would you say I look?"

"Good?" the desk constable remarked, and we both looked at him. He coughed slightly and began shuffling papers.

"Yes, thank you, constable..." Lawrence took the forms and pen and handed them to me. "Ask if you're not sure," he said, in his Sergeant Cole voice.

I was having trouble concentrating.

277

He's right though. It's what people will think - that he's too young for me. I've lived half my life, and he's just beginning his. Damn Lawrence Cole, planting his shitty seeds of doubt...

I filled out the forms as quickly as possible, Lawrence just had to help me to describe the actual offence. I signed it and handed it back over the desk.

"I'll just make a copy of this, Miss."

By now, my feet were killing me, and I was flagging.

"So, what do you think the chances are of piecing my car back together?"

Lawrence looked doubtful. "To be honest, it would have been better if they'd stolen it. I've countersigned the form, so there shouldn't be any problems with insurance. What remains will be photographed, then taken away for scrap."

My eyes moistened. "So, once again you've stepped in and helped me."

He stepped forward, taking my hands, his voice almost a whisper. "That's what I want to do, Lauren - Help you and look after you."

Anger rumbled within me and I shook his hands free with annoyance.

"I don't need looking after, Lawrence. For God's sake, I can look after myself."

I whirled around to flounce out, and smacked hard into a cop, who was bringing hot coffee, a plastic cup full in each hand. The hard impact threw hot liquid into the air, whilst I stumbled backwards. Most of it rained down onto the floor, but the rest of it found my cleavage precisely.

Lawrence jumped forward and stopped my backwards descent, while I screamed with the pain and shock of burning hot coffee on my breasts.

"My breasts! My breasts!..." I shouted out.

Lawrence held onto me. I glanced out of the corner of a tear-stained eye and saw a piss-stained tramp with his week's food allowance stored in his beard, staring at my cleavage and sucking his gums noisily. I regained my balance, but not my dignity as I quickly checked that my breasts were still undercover.

The shocked policeman came forward, still holding the cups. "Are you alright, Miss?"

He was middle-aged with fine blonde hair and matching beard

and moustache. He reminded me of Shaggy from Scooby Doo.

"Yes, I'm fine," I answered, looking from him to the tramp.

"I'm Sergeant Cole, from Holborn." Lawrence introduced himself to Shaggy. "I need to take this lady to a quiet room somewhere, and could you get us a first aid box?"

"Sir," Shaggy affirmed, and led us through some double doors into a small, seemingly airtight room.

He left us alone and went off to fetch the medical necessities.

"Really, Lawrence, I'm fine... it was just the shock."

"It looks like you have some scalding. You'll need some antiseptic on there."

I looked down at the red patches on my chest. Luckily, the drugs I was still on were numbing any pain.

"Oh, yeah." I looked back at Lawrence sheepishly.

"I have to say that was a brilliant demonstration of looking after yourself." His warm smile was infectious.

Shaggy came back, handed the first aid kit to Lawrence, and left quickly. Lawrence placed it on the table and opened it carefully. He spied what he was looking for and handed me a tube of Savlon.

"I think you should apply it," he mumbled.

As the cool unguent sank into my hot skin, Lawrence looked away.

Is he a perfect gentleman, or is he getting turned on?... As I replaced the cap, I still couldn't decide.

He packed the stuff away, and my phone rang. It was Nora, wanting to know if I'd reported his jacket stolen, and how long I was going to be. I decided not to mention the hot breasts incident just yet, and told him not much longer. I asked if Nick was all right.

"Of course he is darlink, it wasn't his jacket," he sniped, and hung up.

Lawrence was waiting by the door. "We can go now. Are you sure you're alright?"

I stood and went over to him. I didn't know if it was right or wrong, but I placed a gentle kiss on his cheek.

"I'm good. Thank you, Lawrence, really."

I stared up at him, and the amber of his eyes turned a deep brown. I saw sadness emitted from somewhere deep down.

Even if I weren't with Nick, I'd still make Laurence sad, eventually...

Lawrence didn't know that little old clumsy Me, could be a bastard when it came to my men. He just looked into my baby blue eyes and saw a helpless female. Nick saw beyond all that and our flame was still burning high.

We got back into the same car in which we'd arrived. The air inside smelt sterile and new, like a giant plastic capsule. Lawrence did a quick check - seatbelts on.

"Please can you open the window, Lawrence?" I asked.

He opened the passenger window a couple of inches. Personally, I would have liked more, but I couldn't be bothered to ask again. Lawrence stayed quiet.

Outside the car, it was 9:30am, and even on a Sunday, London was just waking up. Luckily, we had no rush hour to impede us, but cars were going a respectful speed with a cop car nearby. I knew the journey would take longer than I wanted if everyone was driving under the speed limit. Lawrence still wasn't talking, and I felt the need to babble and fill the silence, something I never felt when I was with Nick. I didn't want to defend myself, but I did want to explain. The babble began.

"Lawrence?..."

The only sound was the hushed muffle of the police radio, faint voices I couldn't decipher. All kinds of things were occurring to me.

Maybe he's listening for that special code that will make him slam the blue light on and break the speed limits through London... What if there's a high-speed chase after robbers with guns?...

"Yes, Lauren? I thought you were going to ask me a question," he said without taking his eyes from the road.

"Are you allowed to do high speed chases with me in the car?"

I saw the edges of his mouth turn up. "So that was your question?... And no we are not allowed to with civilians in the car."

Whew. Good... I relaxed a bit. "No, that wasn't my question, but then I thought of that, and anyway, it wasn't going to be a question."

Full babble was commencing. I too was keeping my eyes ahead, where the black BMW in front was desperately trying to keep to the speed limit. The driver was shitting himself with the police on his backside.

I couldn't help myself and the words came straight out. "Do you like it that people are scared or nervous of you?"

His hands tightened on the wheel.

"That's also not what I was going to ask."

"I try not to." The tightness in his voice told me I was on shaky ground.

"Anyway, it was about what you didn't say earlier."

"The age thing."

I softened my voice purposely. "I know he's young, but this has never happened to me before, so at forty three, I'll take it while I can. He's my Neo, Lawrence. Nick is The One…"

Lawrence sighed and said nothing.

"…but that doesn't mean we can't be friends."

I smiled at him and he changed gear clumsily, made the gearbox scream, and tutted.

By now we were nearing my apartment and the full light of day was streaming down. I thought about what a shit end to a good night it had been. Poor Maisie gutted like that, me getting a lift home in a police car driven by a man who thinks he likes me.

I had scalded tits, and dancing feet that felt like they'd turned into eagle's talons. The sexy time I thought that Nick and I were going to have, seemed to have been replaced by the absolute opposite.

Lawrence pulled into my street, stopped in front of the building, and turned the engine off. He twisted round in his seat and his earnest, ocean-green eyes were wrinkling at the corners with concentration.

"The trouble is, Lauren, I do want more than friendship, so it's probably best that we don't see each other." For a moment his eyes blinked quickly in succession. "I was too late."

I placed my hand on his leg. "Lawrence, you're not. Even if I'd met you before him, he would still be The One, and the situation would be even worse. Thank you for driving me home. I wish you all the best, Lawrence Cole."

He started the engine as I opened the passenger door.

"If you need me, Lauren… you know where I am," he said, without looking at me.

I closed the door without reply and watched him drive away. A slight sadness flashed through me as I realised Lawrence had done the decent thing and been honest, which surprised me. As I climbed my front steps, I knew it was for the best.

Nick opened the door, with Nora hovering behind. Nick hugged me, but that squeezed my breasts and a little cry escaped me. I pulled away slightly.

"Sorry, they're a bit sore."

Nora gasped, and Nick raised his eyebrows.

"Darlink, what happened?" asked Nora, genuinely curious.

"Oh, you know, kinky sex, hot coffee on the tits…" I offered

Nick a feeble smile. "Anyway, can I get into my flat please? It's been a long night."

Nora went back through and poor Nick looked a bit concerned.

I put the palm of my hand on his cheek. "Everything's fine. I missed you."

His beautiful young face softened. "Sorry, Lucy. To be honest I was a bit jealous, you being with Lawrence Cole. Well..." He looked down. "I hate jealousy. I'm not used to feeling it, and now I'm even less calm - your breasts were fine when you left..." He faced me full on with searching eyes. "That makes me sound like I'm questioning you, but I don't mean to."

My hand slid down his neck and rested on his chest. "Usual me had another accident, and honestly, I like the fact you're a tiny bit jealous."

"I've only just found you, Lucy, and I don't want to lose you."

His hand ran up my neck and a tingle ran through me.

Nora called out; "Hellooo, darlinks. I am still here you know?"

Nick smiled at Nora in acknowledgement.

"It's funny," I said. " I'm the one who's scared of losing you, and you're here worrying about what I'm doing."

He pouted those big red lips and that simple gesture made me ache for him.

"Anyway, you don't have to worry about Sergeant Cole. You were right, he does like me. He told me. He said it was for the best if we didn't see each other again."

Nick looked surprised. "Well, Lawrence Cole has gone up a bit in my estimation. Most men would just pretend to be friends and then try and get into your pants."

"HOLA!" Nora bellowed from the door, making us both jump. "You are not here alone, how can you leave Nora?"

We postponed that conversation and went into the front room. I joined Nora on the sofa while Nick made tea in the kitchen.

"So did you report my..."

"Nora," I cut in. " If I hear the word *jacket* once more, I'll scream. And yes, I did."

He retained his composure. "Jacket..," he remarked, bitchily. Too tired to bite, he sat back, happy he'd had the last word.

Nick brought the teas in and lounged on the floor by the coffee table.

"So, what have you two been up to then?" I asked.

Nick was about to answer when Nora cut in. "Oh, no. You first, you go away with the lovely Sergeant and when you come back, you claim you have sore boobs. Darlink, it's too good *not* to ask."

Great, let's bring it back round to that. Thanks, Nora...

So I quickly relayed the story, mainly to please Nora, who found it most amusing. I removed my boots as I spoke, and my feet pulsed with pain and relief as I freed them. "...So, now it's your turn."

Nora flicked his hand dismissively in the air. "Oh, we just chat." He sat back and nursed his tea.

"Apparently, I've written a song," Nick said, casually.

The mug that I was lifting towards my mouth stopped dead, and I turned my head slowly towards Nora. His left eyebrow arched highly, and smugness emanated from him. Right at that second I could have smacked him across the face. I put my mug down and concerned myself with Nick.

"Sorry, Nick. I wanted it to be a surprise. I hope you don't mind?"

A smile slowly spread over his face. "No, Lucy, I don't mind. It's kind of flattering. Nora's going to bring it over Tuesday so we can listen to it."

I returned my, by now slit-like cat eyes to Nora.

"Darlink. I've been here hours, what can I say?" He threw me a look of pure innocence.

Nick stood. "Mind if I take a quick shower?" I found myself pouting at the thought of not joining him. He blew me a quick kiss and left the room.

I turned to Nora immediately. "I have a slight memory, Nora, of asking you not to tell him about the song. I should have been the one to tell him, after all, it was me he wrote the poem for."

Nora uncrossed his legs and smoothed his trousers carefully. "I'm sorry, Lauren, but I didn't know what to talk about. I told him about a couple of my latest fucks, and then I didn't know what to say. It's not as if I'm going to tell him my Life story."

He re-crossed his legs as he finished his defence. I sighed heavily and softened, placing my hand on his knee.

"It's probably best. I don't want any secrets between Nick and me. Thanks for looking after him."

I feigned a smile and clasped his hand with mine. He suddenly looked all secretive, and lowered his voice.

"Darlink, his phone - message, message, message. Send me loco. Nick turned it off." He raised an eyebrow of mystery.

"Probably his family," I explained, sighing again.

283

"I hope no trouble comes from this, Lauren." For once, Nora was sincere.

"It's normal, I suppose, under the circumstances. Nick will handle it, I'm sure."

The door opened to reveal Nick, in his Calvin's, toweling off his wet hair. Nora and I both stared at him.

"Oooh!..." Nora exclaimed, fanning himself with both hands. "Nick, darlink, can you stop this? It's sooo bad for my sundial."

He crossed his legs with the smile of a hungry cat, amusing me, although inwardly I was purring myself with the smugness of knowing that this stunning creature before us was truly mine.

Nick threw his towel onto the back of the chair, his muscles working with perfect synergy, and I too crossed my legs.

"Anyone for more tea?" he asked, as he turned and walked slowly into the kitchen.

Unable to help myself, I stared transfixed at the contents of his underwear until it was out of view. From the corner of my eye, I could see Nora was doing the exact same thing. We faced each other quickly, both caught out. For a second our faces defiantly dueled, but we both ended up wearing sneaky smiles.

"Almost makes me want to be a woman," Nora whispered. Then his mouth opened slightly as his face showed a process of enlightenment. "Aaiieee!" He shook his hands either side of his head.

"More tea?" Nick called out.

"No thanks," I answered.

"Oh, Sí. Yes, yes." Nora accompanied himself with clapping hands.

"Okay, I'll bite. What is it?"

"I can roll a joint, but the weed was in your..." He looked at me as if a lubed finger had just been inserted into him. "...The thing that you keep your tampones in."

I smiled sarcastically. Nora never took drugs into a club. Not through fear of getting caught, but he didn't see why he should bring his own, when in ten minutes he could get someone else to give him some of theirs.

Nick brought in the teas and sat in the armchair with his legs slung over one arm. I loved his boyish ease.

"Lauren, please can you give me your bag?" asked Nora.

Puzzled, I looked round to see what he was pointing at and saw the little white satchel I'd taken out sitting on the floor next to Nick.

"Nick, can you throw me that please?" I asked.

He leant down and threw it over with good aim. I caught it and passed it to Nora.

"Do you mind?" Nora asked.

"Go ahead," I said, utterly clueless.

He opened it and instantly pulled out a rolling tobacco pouch. Now the penny slowly started to drop, - I was virtually a non-smoker. He closed the bag and put it on the coffee table. Nick and I were enthralled. He opened the pouch and inhaled deeply, sniffing its contents. The penny was dropping fast now. Nora's eyes glinted as he extracted a huge bud of weed. Penny dropped. My eyes came out on stalks and I sat bolt upright.

"You fucking didn't?"

Nora shrugged slightly as he removed some rolling papers.

"I've just been to the fucking police station with that." I said, in my pissed off voice. "I opened my bag, Nora, right in front of Sergeant Cole. Why is it even fucking in there?"

Nora was rolling a joint coolly. "Darlink, how was I to know your car would be dees-membered? My bag was with Matt's jacket... anyway its fine, you're here."

I was flabbergasted at his casualness. "But, but..."

"Lauren, it's hardly midnight express," he said, as he lit the joint and inhaled long and hard.

"You are fucking priceless, Nora," I commented.

He nodded in mistaken acknowledgement.

We all smoked and then I went for a shower, leaving Nick and Nora chatting in Spanish. On my return, Nora informed me there was a message on my phone. It was from Lawrence.

"It just says I've got to wait for the photos to be taken of the car, then I can send the insurance claim in." *Oh no, my poor car...* I remembered she was dead.

Nick tuned into me again. "It's a shame about Maisie, but with the insurance money you can get a new car, to fill with adventures."

Only he can make me smile... "That's a lovely way to look at it. Yes, you're right - adventures filled with you and me."

Nora made a disgusting throat clearing noise.

"Okay muchachos, this is too lovey-dovey for Nora. Lauren, I'm calling a cab."

Within minutes, we heard the bibb-ing outside, and said our goodbyes, confirming that we'd meet up on Tuesday.

Nick and I listened to the taxi drive away and fell on each other hungrily, the vampires finally able to feed.

The light of the day merged subtly into dusk as we fell exhausted on the living room floor. We were naked in each other's arms, with a solitary cushion under our heads. Our skin glowed with Life and Love and we were stultifyingly happy. We gazed at the ceiling, neither of us able to talk while we allowed our worlds to re-assimilate.

"I think it's illegal to feel this good in most countries," Nick eventually commented dreamily.

"Can I bottle it, and take it to work with me next week?" The thought of going back to work filled me with revulsion.

"I wish you could take me with you. I'm not really sure what I'm going to do with myself."

"Well, I've always fancied a manservant with great cooking skills..." I said, elbowing him in the ribs.

"Hmm, will my devotion take me to that level?" he joked.

"I'll get you a key cut, and then at least we'll have mobile contact..."

He didn't answer.

"Nick?"

"Sorry. That reminded me of my mobile. I've had to turn it off, Jenny keeps texting me…"

Ahhh, so it's Ms. Snetterton herself plaguing him...

"…anyway, I don't want to think about her." he said, as he deftly rolled on top of me.

We made love until the early hours and ended up in bed, expended.

INTERVIEWS AND SONG

I slammed my hand down hard on the snooze button of the alarm clock that was screaming time to get up. I rolled over, cuddled into Nick, and pretended it wasn't happening. Five minutes later, I repeated the ritual.

Nick stretched lazily. "Do you want me to help?"

I yawned mildly. "No need for both of us to get up."

He pulled me towards him and kissed me passionately. "Er, I think I'm already up," he teased, pushing his hardness against me.

I giggled. "But, then Mr. Morning Cock will make me late... "

He flung me onto my back. "But it's a great excuse."

Half an hour later I was running around trying to wash, do my hair so it didn't have that '*I've just been shagged*' look, apply some make-up and drink the coffee Nick had made for me. He came into the bathroom as I was brushing my teeth, drinking coffee in between brushes.

"Never seen it done like that before," he said, smiling.

"Watch the professional," I retorted, spitting out the concoction.

He pulled a face as if he was eating a sour sweet. "Think I'll leave that one."

Finally, at eight-thirty, I was ready. I knew I'd be late for sure, and after a week off sick that didn't look good. I felt physically sick when I had to part with Nick, wrenching myself away and travelling to work. He promised to put his phone on and deal with the texts from Jenny.

It was nine-twenty when I arrived at the grey depressing building.

Mr. Forrester's probably going to have a fit...

I took the stairs, and felt completely unfit. I hadn't worked out since Nick had been in my Life.

I'll start again tomorrow...

Of course, the first person I saw when I pushed open the door was Gladys. Her smile and her hair were particularly rigid that morning.

I flashed her a look, which I hoped said - '*Don't fuck with me today.*'

Conceited tightness radiated from her as I walked by.

I knew I couldn't go straight to my desk because I'd been off sick. There was no getting out of going to see Forrester. After being a real human being for a week, breathing real air, the office's artificial dusty version was constricting my throat. I was coughing violently by the time I knocked on Mr. Forrester's door.

"Come in!" he shouted.

I grabbed the door handle for support and opened it slowly, putting on my best smile.

Mr. Forrester looked up from the papers that lay before him on the desk. "Ahh, Lauren, please sit down." His watery eyes gave nothing away.

Without meaning to, I scraped back the wooden chair, recreating perfectly the sound of nails going down a blackboard. He clamped his eyes shut whilst clasping his hands together. I sat down meekly, sinking low to give the impression of smallness and frailty. After all, I was supposed to have been sick, when in reality the only thing that was unwell was my happily sore and weeping vagina.

"I'm sorry I'm late, Mr. Forrester - I'm still feeling a bit fragile." I wasn't exactly lying.

His sigh was accompanied by a wheeze from his blackened peanut lungs below. "I expect you to be a perfect employee from now on, Lauren. I have been more than accommodating, but…" He leaned over the desk to emphasize his point. "…this is where it ends. Do you understand?"

I nodded.

"Do, you, un, der, stand?" he said slowly.

"Yes, Mr. Forrester. Perfectly."

"Good." He sat back and allowed himself to relax a little. "Right. There was a memo last week, but seeing as you weren't here, I will inform you about it. Maureen Little, as you know, is pregnant…"

I scanned my memory frantically for a face. *The woman who*

sat next to Janice?... No, I don't know her. Is she?...

"Well, she's on maternity leave in three weeks, so for the next two consecutive Fridays, I'll be interviewing for her job. There's an advert going in the Gazette today and Wednesday. I'll be interviewing those applicants on Friday, and it'll be the same procedure next week." He paused to take a breath of office air.

God, just let me out of this oversized coffin...

"As your desk is the nearest to my office and the window seats that will be placed there for the interviewees, I expect you to offer them tea and coffee while they wait."

A huge groan rumbled silently within, but I dared not offer any resistance. Instead, I smiled thinly.

"That's all, Lauren," he said, dismissing me.

I went to my desk, glad it was over. I was happy to submerge myself in work, I just wanted the day to be over, so I could be back home with Nick. I ignored the lads as I acted like the perfect worker. Nick texted me three times telling me how much he ached for me. I texted him back and told him I felt the same. The morning passed quickly, but by 3pm, I was ready to pluck out my eyelashes with boredom. I had no desire to look at Facebook, previously my normal boredom backup. By the time 5pm came around, I'd been playing Ms. Pacman for two hours. I rushed out of the building like a bull on crack.

As Nick opened the door, a fantastic smell of food came from behind him. It reminded me of his cooking at the cottage.

"Hi honey, I'm home." I greeted him, putting on an American accent.

"Gee, it's great you're here. Just swell," Nick responded, and followed it up with a full on kiss.

Bet the curtains are twitching, along with mine...

I had to take deep breaths on the way to the lounge.

"It's not often my flat smells this good," I commented, as I sat down gratefully on the sofa.

Nick sat next to me. "Well, don't get too used to it..."

I rolled my bottom lip at him.

"But then again, I have tasted your cooking." He smirked.

His eyes were pure diving pool aqua blue. I stuck my elbow

playfully into his ribs. I felt like I had my own private elixir of youth.

"Would you like anything?"

His question made my tongue slide slowly over my top lip. He didn't ask again, our fires rose, and Nick almost burnt our dinner.

He served it on a tray, completely naked, and caused me to have a fit of the giggles.

"Maybe I should ask my mother over to dinner?" I quipped.

He grinned. "Maybe I should ask mine?"

"Not funny, Nick." The thought of having Angela here for dinner almost put me off my food.

"My dad called."

I really did stop eating then. "Did you answer?"

"Yes..." He paused.

I wondered if talking about David would always make me feel so uneasy.

"...Best to face it. Otherwise how the fuck can anyone move forward?" Annoyance crept into his voice. "He told me it's best if I go back. He said it's just an infatuation, which is a bit rich coming from him. He told me how upset my mum is. The trouble is, Lucy, I can't tell if he's saying all this because it's genuine, or because he's jealous."

I stared at my plate. "Has he, well... told her who I am?"

He shook his head. "No, not yet. He said there was no need if I came home. Blackmail again." He softened his voice. "But I'm not going home. Not yet, anyway. The day will come, though, I'll want to see my brothers and my sister."

He took a mouthful of food and winked at me.

I was scared to ask, but I had to; "Did you deal with Jenny?"

Nick swallowed hard. "Yes, I called her. I told her to give up, and that I love you."

"How did she react?"

"Oh, the same as always, totally calm."

"No tears, or anger?"

That made him smile. "Jenny doesn't do those emotions. In the beginning, I liked it that she was so together, but I grew to hate it. It's not normal to be like that all the time. I think we've got a range of emotions for a reason, and not to use them is like strangling your spirit."

I loved listening to Nick and his wise words. I told him about my soul sucking, dying heart day.

"I hate it. It's one of the easiest firms, and now I'm a fucking trolley dolly..."

He let me rant, until I realised for myself the insignificance of it all.

"...Sorry, moaning's not very sexy, is it?"

"You could be covered in horse-shit sucking a tramp's balls and you'd still be sexy."

I choked slightly on a Brussels sprout. "Remind me never to act out your sexual fantasies."

"I have an idea, though, if you hate your job so much. We could go travelling?" He sat back, staring and gauging my reaction, which was utter surprise.

"So, you've been here nine days, and you think we should go travelling, like running away?"

"No, like travelling. We wouldn't be able to go straight away. We'll need money, and that takes time, but there's nothing stopping us from planning. I've been putting some money away so we wouldn't need too much."

The idea was crazy, but I loved it.

"Yeah, why not? Really, we could. I'd love to visit places with you, have someone to share the memories..." I felt myself becoming more excited. "I could use the insurance money, instead of buying a car." I got up to take the plates. "Fuck, this is brilliant. I didn't even think about it before, but what a way to start!"

Nick came to me and held me round the waist, his blue eyes earnest.

"We really can do this," he said, and kissed me passionately, thus sealing the dream.

I floated over to the sofa while Nick insisted on clearing away.

"So, if you don't mind me asking..."

"Four thousand," he called through.

I blew a low whistle.

"So, now you're only after me for my money..." He came back in and threw the tea towel at me. "But you're washing up."

"As you command, Mr. Rich." I submitted, hugging into him.

Both of us spent the evening excitedly talking about the countries we wanted to go to, effectively shutting out our external world. We made love most of the night, only falling asleep as the first light gleamed from the sky.

Somewhere in the distance, I could hear a ringing. My eyes opened like a long forgotten treasure chest.

What is that noise?...

Nick was sound asleep next to me. Slowly, body parts were beginning to move, and I sat up violently.

Oh, fuck! It's the alarm. How long?... I looked, and saw it was 8am.

"Shit! Shit!" I shouted, as I sprang from the bed.

Now I was fully awake and wild-eyed, with barely time to get dressed and go. Nick roused sleepily, leaning up on his forearms.

"What's wrong?" he asked, his voice thick with sleep.

"Late. Very late," I replied, frantically opening my wardrobe to reveal my clothes, piled and stuffed into every available space.

I began to pull everything out, grabbing items madly and throwing them aside.

"Can I help?... I could make coffee?" Nick's concerned voice filtered through into my demented brain.

"Sorry, ahh, not this morning. No time." *Summer clothes, summer...*

I screamed. It was the middle of September and Autumn coldness was creeping in.

"Where's all my fucking clothes?"

Angry and exasperated, eventually I found a pair of striped green tights, a green and black self-knitted hoodie, and a small black wraparound skirt that fastened with Velcro. To me, the outfit looked hideous, but by now, it was eight-fifteen.

Nick had remained quiet, enjoying watching the show before him.

"Sorry I've got to rush, but if I'm late Mr. Forrester will go mad." I grabbed the chance to speak, kissing him quickly.

"Be careful. I love you, Lucy."

I took his words with me and rushed out.

On the tube, my eyes started to close slowly, and I luxuriated in the daydream of travelling.

Nick and me, swimming with dolphins, making love under waterfalls...

A voice way off in the distance was saying the names of the stations - 'Woolwich... Woolwich...'

I gasped and opened my eyes. *Oh, shit. That's my stop....*

I looked at the doors, which were just starting to close, and bolted. I just about managed to squeeze myself through them before they clamped tightly shut, literally as I stepped onto the platform. I was panting, relieved that it had been such a close shave, and thanking God.

Slowly, the train behind me began to pull away.

"Phew," I murmured, quietly.

A woman with a small child in tow scuttled quickly past me. The infant stared intently at me, turning to look as the woman pulled harder and reprimanded for staring.

A bloke in his mid-twenties wearing a cheap suit whistled, and winked at me.

"Love the look, girl," he said. His thick cockney accent matched his threads perfectly.

I was perplexed, and looked down at myself, round quickly at the commuters, then down again.

What the fuck?...

Then I started to feel round my waist where the skirt once was. *I'm sure I remember putting one on...*

I began to panic, and my eyes scanned the floor frantically as I turned my head back and forth. I looked up and saw my train slowly rumbling down the tracks with something black billowing from the clamped shut doors.

It's hard to describe the feeling of watching your dignity disappear into the distance. I stood, unbelieving, watching, until I could see it no more.

Reality crept back and I realised I was still standing in the exact same place. I felt mortified as I noticed the stares.

Think, Think... The station toilets!...

I moved as fast as I could, running manically down the concrete steps, fuelled by a need for a safe haven. I could hear giggles and gasps as I descended, but I spied the door, flung it open and rushed inside.

By now I was pacing, and the ludicrousness of my attire mocked me, aided by the mirrors. I couldn't take off my jumper/top - all I had underneath was a bra.

Oh no, no! Must go to work..., my mind screamed repeatedly.

I fruitlessly searched my bag, as if it were by some miracle storing spare clothing. There was one empty folded up Lidl carrier bag, one empty purse and some make-up. I paced some more, and came up with a brilliant idea.

Unfolding the Lidl bag, I carefully tore the bottom open. Then I stepped into it and slid it up my legs until it was at my waist. I tucked the handles in, and it barely covered my bottom. I tried a couple of steps, and although it made a noise like the opening of a sweet wrapper magnified, luckily it didn't rise up too much. Checking the time, I saw I had eight minutes to be at my desk.

I left the toilet and walked as quickly as I could considering I didn't want to rip my precious new-age clothing.

Crunch, crunch, crunch, every little quick-step went.

I knew people were looking at the loony spectacle.

As I neared the office building, I slowed down and peeked ahead. Luckily, the entrance was quiet.

Crunch! crunch! I scuttled through the doors, and frantically pushed the elevator button.

No stairs today...

Ping! - And the doors opened. I stepped inside, and as I turned to face the buttons, I saw Dave running through the lobby straight towards me. I groaned, and held the door open for him.

"Thanks, Lauren," he panted.

The doors slid shut as I fixed my eyes front.

"Er, you do know you're wearing a plastic carrier bag?" Dave asked, sounding bemused.

"Your powers of observation are astounding. Perhaps you should work for the police?" I retorted, my words steeped in sarcasm.

We passed the first floor, and I began to sweat nervously.

"Woah there, bag lady!" Dave quipped.

I turned to look at him. "Look, I mislaid it, okay?"

His wide grin shone big white teeth at me. "Must have been a hell of a journey to work."

My bottom lip trembled and my eyes turned into Bambi's.

He put down his briefcase, took off his suit jacket, and handed it to me. "Wear this - I'll get it back off you later."

Timidly, I reached out and put it on. The sleeves totally covered my hands, but it covered the bag.

"Thanks, Dave," I said, as the doors opened and I wrapped the jacket protectively around me.

I crunched my way to my desk, causing a few raised eyebrows on the short journey. I sat as carefully as I could, and got to my desk at one minute past nine. Mr. Forrester popped his head out of his door to check I was there, then retreated again. I turned on the computer, knowing I'd have to spend the entire day at my desk, even lunch, and wait for everyone to leave. I just prayed that Forrester wouldn't call me into his office.

Dave came over at midday.
"I'm going to lunch now, is it okay for me jacket?"
Phil hovered in the background.
Thank God, it hadn't been him in the lift...
I took the jacket off the back of the chair and handed it over.
"Thanks, Dave. I owe you one."
He winked. "Well, if you ever want to share the contents of your carrier bag... bet you've got a great sandwich in there."
I couldn't help grinning. "Yeah – tongue."

He winked again and left. Mr. Forrester always ate his lunch in his office, but other than him and me, it was deserted. He came out and jumped when he saw me there.
"Oh ho, not going out today?"
"No, Mr. Forrester, there's some work I need to catch up on."
That lie made him crack a smile. "Well done, Lauren."

In reality, I'd been playing Ms. Pacman all morning, my bladder was starting to ache and I wanted to go to the toilet badly. Mr. Forrester went back into his hutch, and with no one else there I began to rise slowly, when the double doors opened, and Bernard Hugh and his eyebrow ambled in.
I sat back down quicker than I meant to, and felt the bag rip down the side.
Shit! Now I'm trapped... I crossed my legs, stupidly believing that that would help.

By three-thirty that afternoon, I could have wept at the pain of needing a pee. Phil had been grinning at me from his desk since the moment he'd returned from lunch.
You shithead, Dave...
Eventually he sauntered casually over to me, every twitch of his

being, cocky.

"Well, a little bird tells me you think your fanny's so fresh you keep it in a bag."

"Even if it was rotting dead flesh I wouldn't give it to you," I spat out venomously, without taking my eyes from my monitor.

"Think I wanna fuck a bird who fuckin' dresses in a carrier bag? What's tomorrow, dustbin liner?" he replied, his chirpy Essex accent full of wit.

"What makes you think that girls want to fuck a guy after his mother's been there?..."

I was met with silence.

"...Hit a nerve, have I?"

"Fucking slag," he hissed, as he walked off.

That was the thing with Phil, he could dish it out, but he couldn't take it.

At about 4pm, just as I began to seriously consider peeing into a cup under the desk, the phone rang.

I picked it up; "Hunt and Chapman, how may I help?" I tried to sound mildly bothered.

"Lucy Bower?" a female voice asked.

My spine turned to ice as I recognised Jenny Snetterton's voice.

"Y-e-s?" I answered slowly.

Suddenly queasy, I began to look round psychotically, as if she were in the room.

"I think you've taken something that doesn't belong to you," she said.

My shackles rose. *Nick isn't a possession...*

"Did you think I would just give up, do nothing? My dear Lucy. You have seriously underestimated me." Then she hung up.

I was left clasping the phone with paralysis from the shock.

She's got my fucking work number, how?... She doesn't even know my real name. Jenny Miss fucking Marple...

I put the receiver down, feeling haunted. Ten or more minutes passed as I sat and stared into space. The doors to the office opened, and I started up, bug-eyed, terrified it was Her.

Lawrence Cole appeared like an apparition.

I'm having a hallucination...

As he strode up to my desk, my eyes were full of wild fear and my mouth hung open slightly.

"Lauren?"

I didn't even breathe.

"Lauren?" he repeated, coming round the desk to where I sat, a waxwork figure.

He spun my chair around and crouched down, placing his hands on my shoulders. Then I realised he might be real.

"Lawrence?" I asked disbelievingly, my hands resting on my carrier bag.

He looked down, then back to me with very concerned eyes. He put his hands on mine and I offered no resistance, just glad he was here.

"Jesus, Lauren. What happened?" he whispered urgently.

I took a deep breath and tried to summon some sanity. "What?... Oh, oh nothing."

He furrowed his eyebrows together with concentration. "You're sitting here in a Lidl carrier bag looking like you've seen a ghost, and nothing's wrong? Even if I wasn't a copper, the evidence clearly points to the fact there is definitely something wrong... Lauren, please, I can't bear to see you like this."

I quickly relayed the morning's events, about my skirt and I parting company. He tried not to smile, but he couldn't help himself.

"What?" I demanded, and the tone of my voice said - '*Well I don't find it so funny...*'

"Sorry, Lauren, but for a moment I thought someone had done something to you."

It took a minute for it to register, and then it dawned on me.

"Oh. No, nothing nasty's happened."

He let go of my hands and stood up to remove his jacket before handing it to me.

"I'm going to talk to your boss, and then we're leaving," he declared, before striding officially up to Mr. Forrester's door.

I put on his jacket and was just switching off my computer, when he reappeared with Mr. Forrester, who fiddled nervously with his shirt and kept his voice low.

"Lauren, Sergeant Cole has explained the situation, and I'm quite happy for you to leave now."

What did Lawrence say?..., I wondered, smiling fraily I picked up my bag and we walked out together. I also wondered what Lawrence was doing there in the first place.

In the car, we began our drive across London. Lawrence was driving his own car, so the cars in front could carry on with their over the speed limit journeys.

"Are you taking me home?" I asked.

"Where else would you like me to take you, with only half your clothes on?" He was concentrating on tutting at the other reckless drivers.

"Thank you again, Lawrence. But I don't understand why you were at my work after, well, what you said..." I softly broached the question.

"I've got the photos for your insurance. I thought it'd be quicker if I brought them straight to you." His eyes flicked at me as he spoke.

"Oh. That's nice, thank you. I can't pretend I wasn't pleased to see you, though."

"What else happened? I know it was more than just losing your shirt, something spooked you."

Silently, I contemplated whether to tell him about Jenny for a few moments. I needed to tell someone, so I decided to tell him. The story took almost the whole journey.

"...So you see, I am understandably a bit, yes, spooked."

We turned into my road and parked a few doors down from mine. Lawrence cut the engine and turned to me.

"That explains why he calls you Lucy. So, his Ex is a potential bunny boiler."

I raised my eyebrows and pouted slightly. "That's a technical police term, is it?"

The lines around the eyes of his eyes and mouth relaxed, and he took my hands. "Look, Lauren. Don't worry. If anything else happens, contact me immediately and I'll deal with it."

I sighed. "Lawrence, I don't want to get you involved, especially after what you've said. It would be unfair."

"I'd only be doing my job, just like I do every day."

I removed my hand from his, sensing that on this occasion however, his interest was personal. I attempted to give his coat back and he stopped me.

"You can't walk in that split bag."

I thanked him with my baby blues and he walked me to my flat. I buzzed the buzzer, returned the jacket to Lawrence, and stood in my split bag. He put it back on and retrieved something from the inner pocket. I realised it was photos as he handed them to me. Nick opened the door and couldn't hide his surprised expression.

Lawrence flicked a glance over Nick and turned briskly to leave.

"Goodbye, Lauren," he said, and took the steps, rapidly.

I gave Nick a kiss and slid into the hallway. "I'll explain in a minute."

I wondered if I should tell him about Jenny, and decided since I'd told Lawrence it would be abhorrently wrong not to tell Nick. As I entered my flat, I ripped the only remaining part of the bag that still held together, and it fluttered to the floor.

I fell into Nick's arms and he stroked my hair and kissed my forehead. The tenderness of his touch started the tears.

"Lucy, baby. What's happened?"

I was clinging to him, holding on to what seemed like my one sanity in an insane world. As he took me through to the front room, I began to babble as I relayed my day. At first, he was mildly amused, but as the story went on, his face changed; light blue eyes misted into dark blue, and his mouth set into a hard line.

"...And here..." I waved the photos at Nick, concluding my story. "Here are the pics, as proof."

The same darkness descended over Nick that I'd seen that day in the cottage.

"Fucking bitch!" he spat, full of murderous intention.

He stood, and began to pace the room.

"Why?" he shouted, trembling. "Why can't that fucking bitch get it through her thick head that I don't want her... Aaaghh!"

He picked up his mobile from the coffee table.

"What are you doing?" I asked, standing.

"I'm going to fucking call her, and warn her to back the fuck off."

I took the phone from him. "Nick, don't play into her hands. That's what she wants. Lawrence is right, if it happens again, I'll call him. Don't give her any more power."

Nick softened perceptibly. "I thought you said *I* was the wise one."

He came to me and slid his arms round my waist.

"Don't get me wrong, Nick, I would love to see her drown in her own conceitedness, but it's not going to happen. I won't lie, it has un-nerved me, and I hate to say this, but I'm glad Sergeant Cole's on board."

He sucked on his bottom lip and I knew he wasn't comfortable with that.

"Yes, for some reason, Lawrence Cole is inexplicably in your life. You can't blame me for being slightly paranoid about the man - every time you're with him something happens. Last time you came back with sore breasts, and this time with no skirt."

I hugged into him and tried to kiss his worries away, pulling him back onto the sofa.

"No-one, absolutely no-one, Nick Palmer, could replace you."

Even in jeans and a plain T-shirt, he looked amazing. I wondered if my adoration would fade over time, and I doubted it would.

"I hate to admit it, but it's probably a good thing that you can count on him," Nick conceded, bright red lips bursting with passion.

I leant into him, wanting, needing. We pushed our mirrored insecurities aside, and replaced them with love, and lust. Once again, we roamed my apartment naked. I'd never felt so uninhibited before, and both of had forgotten that Nora was coming over when the buzzer rang at seven-thirty.

Nick threw on some boxers, and I grabbed my daffy duck dressing gown.

As I went to answer the door, I said to Nick; "Please don't mention about today, it'll only make him highly excitable."

Nick grinned, and I went to open the door to Nora, who raised an inquisitive eyebrow at my attire.

"Is it the wrong moment? You lucky thing," Nora said, air kissing me as he entered.

Nick was in the kitchen, already making drinks.

"Buenas tardes, gorgeous," Nora called out.

"Holá, Nora," Nick replied.

Nora sat down carefully and pulled a CD from his bag. He looked at me intently as he handed it to me. I took it as Nick called through - "Coffee?"

"Sí, darlink."

My eyes were studying the cover. "Yes, please..." I answered absently, engrossed in the image.

The text read; DESIRE in delicate gold lettering. A man with a hauntingly gaunt and beautiful face stared out, a ravaged cigarette dangling from his wide lips. I didn't need to see the name of the singer. It was the living legend of electro blues - *Frankie Bubbles*.

"SHIT!" I exclaimed loudly to Nora, before looking back at the CD with a low whistle.

"Aaiiee!..." Nora screeched, clapping his hands together. "Darlink, can you believe?"

I shook my head to indicate that no, no I couldn't.

Nick came in with the coffees. "Okay, what's the excitement?"

I handed him the CD and he studied it quickly, then looked at me, then at Nora and then back to the cover.

He held it out before him. "Holy shit, this is Frankie Bubbles."

Nora squealed, holding his hand out. "We play it."

He took the CD and put it in the stereo. Nick joined me on the sofa and all of us sat transfixed, listening to Frankie's brilliant voice, and the way he'd transformed Nick's poem into these amazing lyrics.

Listen by scanning the code or go to
trixiebloom.com/frankiebubbles

DESIRE

I breathe too deep when I think of you,
My heart explodes, this is something new,
Driving me crazy, what am I to do?
Valentines spin in my brain.

Without you, there is only pain
I know now on I'll never be the same.
Something that I can't explain
Desire in my soul spills over again, over again.

Real Love in Life is fleetingly grasped,
I will not let this moment pass.
As long as you are right there by my side,
You build up my foolish pride.

Without you, there is only pain
I know now on I'll never be the same.
Something that I can't explain
Desire in my soul spills over again, over again

I breathe too deep when I think of you,
My heart explodes, this is something new,
Driving me crazy, what am I to do?
Valentines spin in my brain.

Without you, there is only pain
I know now on I'll never be the same.
Something that I can't explain
Desire in my soul spills over
Without you, there is only pain
I know now on I'll never be the same.
Something that I can't explain
Desire in my soul spills over again over again
Over again...

When it had finished, all of us sat hardly daring to breathe. Nick's head was laid back on the sofa, eyes up. He moved slowly, and his deep eyes darted between Nora's and mine.

"I, I..," he stuttered, clearly in utter shock.

Nora sat earnestly forward, gripping his knees. "Darlink, do you like it?"

Nick floundered for words, opening and closing his mouth before finally managing to say;   "Yes..."

Nora screamed, and raised his hands in the air, before producing a bottle of champagne from his bag. "Cost my parents a fortune," he chirped wickedly. "But worth every penny, darlink."

I fetched some glasses, in a daze.

"So is this the only copy?" Nick enquired, timidly.

"No, Nick, darlink. It's going on release next week. Leonard said probably Monday," Nora said, and released the cork, which flew across the room at full speed, hitting my Japanese dragon teapot, a present from my parents.

The teapot wobbled slightly, then miraculously regained stability, whilst I held my breath and the bubbles exploded, gushing from the bottle.

"Reminds me of some of my boyfriends," Nora jested as he poured.

I spied Nick running his hands through his hair and knew he was in absolute shock. He went quietly over to the stereo, got the CD cover, and returned to his seat to inspect it.

Nora handed each of us a glass, and raised a toast. "Here's to fame."

In mute dumbness, we followed suit before Nick became immobile again.

"Nick?" I asked quietly, pulling a face from the taste of champagne.

"Eh?" he muttered, clearly residing in another realm. "Oh!...," and he took a sip of his champagne before returning his attention to the cover and turning it over.

After another sip, he began to choke, putting the glass down and coughing loudly. He slapped his chest to try to ease it.

"What's wrong?" I asked, putting my drink down.

"Fricking hell!" he coughed out. "Says on the back - '*Lyrics written by Nick Palmer.*' That's me."

"No shit, Sherlock," Nora interjected.

Nick's eyes appeared to be re-enacting every drug he'd ever taken.

"But, that's me!..." he muttered again, making my smile wider.

"Yes, darlink. That's you, and next week it's going to be on National release - Radio, TV, internet - Leonard is one of the best in the business."

The excitement of prospective fame mounted me like the beast with two backs, as I downed the rest of my champagne and poured out some more. Nick held his glass out for a refill before repeating the feat.

"Nick, I have a valium? - Nora can see it's a big shock."

Nick shook his head in refusal but he filled his glass again. "Frankie Bubbles, singing *my* words," he muttered, before taking another gulp of champagne.

Nora got up and put the song on again. I decided I loved it. My horrible day faded away, replaced by magic. I held Nick's hand, squeezing it tight.

"I'm sorry, I'm definitely in shock," he responded.

"Darlink, it's natural. It's not every day you hear your words published for the world to hear," Nora said, and Nick darted a terrified look at him.

"Stop it, you're scaring him." I scolded Nora, who shot me a venomous look in return.

My mobile rang, and I jumped. I looked at the number and though I didn't recognise it, the code was definitely from abroad. Tentatively, I answered, and relief rushed through me as I heard my brother's voice.

"Jonathan!" I gushed.

Nora squealed, waving frantically at me. "You say hello, holá, to Jonathan," he shouted.

I raised my hand and cupped the mouthpiece. "I'll just take this in the hall…"

While I chatted with my brother in the hall, I could hear Nora talking excitedly at Nick in Spanish. Ten minutes later, I was back in the room, the call having cost Jonathan a small fortune from the Maldives. Both men's gazes rested on me expectantly as I sat back down.

"He's coming home next week. He'll arrive here Thursday, and he wants to stay here for a few days before he tells our parents that he's back."

Nora clapped his hands in glee. "Aaiiee! - Jonathan, he comin' home."

Nick still looked shocked, except now it was shock tinged with worry. "Is it okay with me here, will there be room?"

I smiled. "Of course, and don't worry, my brother's great. He's nearer your age than mine."

"Darlink, Jonathan is fantastico. Party animal."

"There's so much going on," Nick said.

Nora took Nick's drink from his hand and smoothed his hair with the other.

More than he knows…

We finished the champagne and Nora went home, leaving the CD behind.

I cuddled into Nick on the sofa. "My life is full of surprises since you came into it."

"I think I could say the same," he said, bemused.

We went to bed shortly afterwards, still in shock, and fell immediately into a deep sleep.

The next three days at least passed without incident. Nick received no texts, and I no further threatening phone calls. I sent all the paperwork in to my insurance brokers, and I wasn't late for work. Nick and I luxuriated in each other's company.

That Friday, I dutifully did the hostess act with the interviewees. I hated the way they sat staring at me nervously while they waited to go in. Nervous smiles tried to engage me in conversation, and I ignored them all. One of the applicants was a stunning brunette with a fantastic smile and even better legs.

"Rachel Hewitt?" Mr. Forrester called from his office door.

She beamed at me as she sashayed across the floor.

God, I hope she gets the job...

The thought of doing this again next Friday bored me to the bone. Jonathan would be here by then and there was no way I could pull a Sickie. I started to think of a way out of it, and by the end of the day, I had it.

I knocked on Forrester's door.

"Ah, Lauren... Come in. What can I do to help?" he asked, smiling weakly.

He never seemed to have the guts to manage a full beam.

"Mr. Forrester, I'm sorry to ask, but would it be possible to have next Friday free? My brother's home from abroad, and it's only for the day. It'd be lovely to spend it with him..." I tried to look as angelic as possible.

His blonde eyelashes fluttered with concentration. "But I did need you for the second round of applicants."

I acted as if he'd reminded me something I'd forgotten, and followed it with a sad face.

"I suppose Janice Croft could take your place for the day. And seeing as you've come to me with the truth, instead of taking the day off with some trumped up reason, I'll allow it."

I gave him my biggest smile. "Thank you so much, Mr. Forrester."

I was relieved that I wouldn't have to perform again, and I ended my working week on a high, returning contented to my knight in shining armour.

JONATHAN

Nick and I enjoyed the whole weekend without many outside distractions. My mother called, but I ignored it, so she followed it up with a text message informing me that Jonathan would be coming home on the Twenty-eighth of September. That day was the Sixteenth, which meant he planned to stay a total of eight days.

No more fucking in the front room for a while.

Nick's response to that - "Oh well, we'd better make up for it then," and being the one man sperm bank that he was, we did.

Even Nora was ominously quiet.

One of the best things about Nick was his sense of humour. When we weren't making Love, he was making me Laugh.

"I think that even if my cunt fell out, you'd still be able to make me smile."

"Yeah, but I wouldn't fancy *that* trip to A&E," he quipped, proving my point.

That Sunday Nick cooked a mouthwatering roast, and we spent the rest of the day in each other's arms watching films. Rain began to drum lightly on the windows, recreating that day at Warbling Cottage. I kept stealing glances at Nick, still in awe that he was really there with me. His perfect body radiated heat and Life. Fate seemed to have granted me an anomaly.

I left Nick at home on the Monday morning. His mission - to look on the internet and plan our travels. Both of us liked the idea of a three-month holiday visa in Australia, and he wanted to look into it. As much as I hated it, I told him I'd be two hours late from work. It was workout time for me as I felt like a slob.

"You have to work out twice as hard when you reach my age," I informed Nick, shamefully.

"We could step up the sexual Olympics," he suggested, grinning.

"My pum's not that fat," I replied, with faux indignity.

When I came home later that day, I felt recharged, and endorphins coursed through my body. I ignited sexually the second I saw Nick, pouncing on him as soon as the front door clicked shut.

I gorged upon him until we lay in a heap, a cool breeze from under the door tiptoeing down the hallway over our semi-naked bodies.

"I think it was a brilliant idea of yours to go back to the gym." Nick's voice was husky and lust-laden.

I sat up. "Well, I like to go five times a week."

He grinned like the cat that'd got the cream. "Great!" he said, pulling up jeans that had only got down as far as his knees.

We spent the evening excitedly discussing our plans. Monday turned into Tuesday, which quickly ticked into Wednesday. Our small and simple way of Life was remarkably sensational.

As I mounted the front steps on Wednesday evening, the remnants of sweat still clinging to my hair from a particularly grueling workout, I thought about how I was looking forward to Jonathan's arrival the next day.

We got on exceptionally well despite the thirteen years between us, and more than anything I was looking forward to his unknowing, unbiased opinion of Nick and I.

Jonathan had been a toddler in my David years, and was blissfully unaware of it all.

As soon as Nick opened the door, I knew something was wrong. He still kissed me in greeting, but it wasn't the same as the other nights. He said nothing at first, but just went through into the front room with me following anxiously.

"Your mother and father were here..." he said, his voice giving away no emotion. "And it turns out I'm a male model, best of friends with Nora and I'm living in your flat."

I looked at the floor, my favourite pose when I'm about to be told off.

"I'm not angry, Lucy, but I didn't know what to say. You have to tell me these little white lies, or just give them up altogether." He began to pace absently.

"Nick, I'm sorry. I was just about to tell you that day, but there wasn't time, and we were all so stoned, and then with the... well, the cock incident I totally forgot."

"To tell them I'm a neurotic model, though?" He stopped to look at me, lifting my head so that my eyes met his.

"Truly, I'm sorry, Nick. That's the only thing I haven't told you. They can't know who you are, they'll have me committed, put away. In their minds, it would look like I was trying to turn back the clock and replace what was missing. They'd never get it in a million lifetimes, and I know you hate lying, but please?..." My voice took on a note of frantic pleading. "Please?"

He came closer to me, one arm going round me, and the other moving my damp hair tentatively out of my face.

"Lucy, it's alright. I went along with it, but your mother asked me outright if I was living here. I told her it was best if she spoke to you."

"Oh, I'm sure she will."

"Anyway, they didn't stay long, not with the Cock-ness monster here."

Nick was doing his thing spectacularly again, weaving his magic and humour.

"Thank-you," I whispered, kissing him delicately on the lips.

We both relaxed and flopped onto the sofa.

"Did you have to tell many porkies?"

"Well, she's not backward in coming forward..." Nick said, frowning. " She asked me which modelling company I worked for. All I could think of was Calvin Klein, so I said I worked exclusively for them." He shrugged his shoulders.

"And how did she seem with that?"

"Okay, I think. It's hard to tell when her look is that of permanent disgust."

I pouted. "Oh baby. I'm sorry, I'll talk to them tonight."

"Your father even asked me what my intentions were towards you."

I had to smile inwardly. "Yes, you can hardly say, to fuck her brains out..."

A muffled sound cut into our world, letting me know I had a text message.

"That's probably her now," I joked as I got up to retrieve my mobile from my bag.

Surprisingly, it was Nora.

"The song's being released tomorrow morning. If we listen to 104FM, the morning show with Ricky Babcock, we'll hear it played."

Nick gulped visibly. "I still can't believe all this is happening."

I dive-bombed him, landing fully on top and tickling him. "Wow. A male model turned song writer."

Nick wriggled underneath me, and clasped his strong arms around me. "Very funny," he said as he squeezed his prey tightly.

As he loosened his grip, his lips found my neck and he bit me gently. My hold on my phone released and I dropped it to the floor. Animal Lust was stampeding through us. This time, all our clothes were torn off, thrown around, and abandoned.

We ended up somehow on the kitchen floor, where the coolness felt good against the heat that was being projected from my body. Nicks arm was across my stomach, and we both lay on our backs, waiting for the earth to stop shaking.

I turned my head slowly. "If this feeling never ends, I'll have to get re-constructive surgery on my pink bits."

He turned to look at me, and in the clear light, his blue eyes sparkled. His voice was clear and deadly serious. "It will never end."

He took my hand, his touch so soft and gentle he almost made me cry.

We lay in each other's arms until my mobile rang.

"I'd better get it..." I said, rising to fetch it. "It's my mother."

I steadied myself with a deep breath, and answered.

Finally, after half an hour listening to her berate me at length for my lack of responsibility, I hung up.

I filled Nick in. "Mostly about the age thing, and that the way you look, you wouldn't be with me for long. Full of compliments isn't she? Oh yes, and she thinks, really, as you are a male model, you are a friend of Dorothy's - only you're in denial."

Nick raised his eyebrows. "Who's Dorothy?" he asked innocently.

I suppressed a laugh. "Really? It means you're gay."

"Oh..." he mused. "Would it make it confusing if I did have a friend called Dorothy?"

I let out the laugh in a guffaw. "Yes. It would."

"Fancy a shower?..." he asked.

I nodded. "I told her I love you, you know."

He stopped still and stared at me. "And what did she say?"

"She told me I was being naïve and childish."

He kissed me on the shoulder, then took my hand.

"You should have told her..." He pushed against me. "...that my world now revolves around you."

It was another forty-five minutes before we actually made it to the shower.

That night, after I successfully cooked beans on toast for us both, my brother text messaged me, saying he'd be there around Two-ish the next day.

"Sorry, Nick. That means you'll be here on your own when he arrives."

"Well, as long as I know What, and Who I am."

"You're my boyfriend... but, sorry, you're gonna have to remain a Calvin model. I won't go to the gym tomorrow, I'll come straight home," I assured him, taking his hand in mine.

We both fell asleep on the sofa, waking naturally with the morning light. I switched on the radio and tuned it into Dicky Babcock's show for Nick. Then I took my Mp3 player, which had a radio built in, and stuck the headphones in my ears, determined to keep them in until I'd heard Nick's song played.

I set off for work, happy to leave Nick playing house-husband again. He planned to pop to the shops, get a few bits, clean the flat, and make dinner. I kept randomly pinching myself to make sure it wasn't just one long incredibly vivid dream.

The song played at nine forty-five, when I was sitting at my desk. I looked round excitedly, as I squirmed in my seat. Afterwards, Dicky waxed profusely about how much he liked it.

Nick called me, excited, and still saying he couldn't believe it. He paused in mid flow, just for a second, but I could feel something wasn't right.

"Nick?"

"Mmm?"

"What's wrong?"

"Nothing," he lied.

"I might not be with you, but I can feel it from here."

"See? We *are* soul mates, and okay then, a part of me wishes I could call my family and tell them, but..."

He didn't need to finish the sentence. Guilt seemed to saturate me, coming out of every pore.

"I'm sorry, Nick. If it wasn't for me..."

"Then none of this would even be happening in the first place," he cut in. " I do love you, Lucy."

"I love you too," I replied.

They were the same words I'd said before, to others. Except then the words hadn't had any weight, any depth, or truth to them. They had slipped easily from my mouth, without a sliver of integrity.

With Nick, I felt the words physically. My heart beat faster and my stomach rolled. Each syllable seemed ripe with emotion.

"I'll see you tonight, don't worry," he said, and his voice was replaced by the dial tone.

At twenty past one, Jonathan called to tell me he'd arrived and was on his way to my place. I took the opportunity to tell him that Nick would be there, and told him I'd spill the beans later.

That afternoon I was consumed with hoping that Nick and Jonathan were getting on. I told myself I was sure they would be.

At 5pm, I departed quickly, saying 'Goodnight,' and 'See you Monday,' to Mr. Forrester.

I rang the doorbell almost an hour late, stamping with impatience and hunched against the chilly air. Jonathan answered, looking disgustingly healthy. His short, normally dirty blonde hair shone almost white from the sun against deep brown skin, intensifying the glare. His pale blue eyes twinkled at me.

"Sis!..."

He opened his arms and flung them round me, bear hugging me tightly. Then he pulled away and examined me up and down before returning to the hugging, making up for all the months he'd been away.

Finally I prised myself free, shaking him off like a dog drying itself.

"Okay, okay! It's good to see you, too."

Jonathan was still young enough to produce a huge boyish grin, which crinkled the freckles scattered on his face.

I lowered my voice. "So, everything been okay with you and Nick?"

"Great," he whispered back. "You sly old slut." He winked at me, conspiratorially.

"Oi!... Not so much of the old."

"Nick's cooking. You've got him trained well in such a short space of time, I must say," he teased.

"He's full of surprises," I replied, smugly.

We went through and Jonathan slumped down in a chair. A suitcase was on the floor and clothes were scattered everywhere. A damp towel lay on the back of the sofa. Three used coffee mugs, a can of beer and an ashtray with at least ten butts in. Yes, Jonathan was definitely there.

As my mother had spoilt him rotten, he didn't have a clue how to look after himself. Barely armed with the basics of eating food that came out of ring-pull cans, he was pretty much clueless. I wasn't even sure if tea and coffee making were on his skill list. If he couldn't eat it immediately or put in in a microwave, it wasn't happening. His private world involved sinks full of washing up, dirty mountains of clothes, bins that spilled over and beds forever left unmade.

That all stood in total contrast with his high-pressure working career. Luckily, earning the wages of a small continent enabled Jonathan to employ a series of invaluable maids, which he worked his way through quickly. He always said the fact that they were all young and pretty had nothing to do with it, but I suspected that if they'd been old and fat they might have remained.

Whenever Jonathan visited however, generosity abounded. He never let me pay for anything.

I went to Nick, and he hugged me, kissing my neck.

"You okay?" I asked, cautiously.

"I am now," he said, smiling gently. "And you're right, your brother's great."

I stroked his face with the palm of my hand. *You're going to be all I ever need...*

"Drink?" he asked.

"Another coffee, cheers," Jonathan called through.

"Me too. Thanks, Nick. So you already know my brother's main diet is coffee and cigarettes." I walked into the lounge. "Apart from when he's with our parents," I said, loudly enough for Nick to hear.

"They know I smoke," Jonathan said sulkily, putting his feet up on the coffee table as Nick brought the coffee through. "Thanks, man."

"Thought I'd have a shower, Lucy," Nick said, winking at me. "Give you two a moment to catch up."

Jonathan leant forward, picked up the mug, took a gulp, and burnt his mouth.

"Aargh! Shit, that's hot."

"Have you not drunk enough coffee in all these years to realise it's made with boiling water?" I teased.

Jonathan poked his tongue out at me. "Anyway, why do you call her Lucy?" he asked Nick.

"Erm... "

"Take your shower. I'll field all questions," I said, smirking at Nick as he left us alone.

"And?..." Jonathan blew into his mug expectantly.

"Well, Nick's a friend of Nora's, and we met at one of his modelling jobs. When Nora introduced us, Nick thought my name was Lucy. He kept calling me Lucy and it felt rude to correct him. Finally, of course Nora did, but the name stuck."

I ended my explanation with a big, lying smile.

"Uh... okay," Jonathan said in between sips. " Although I must say, Sis, he's a hell of a looker, and it looks like you've fallen in love."

I preened myself, flicking my hair. "Can you tell?"

"Yep. You're glowing. You look at Nick like a sick puppy. Every bit of you screams that you're in love."

I sat forward and began talking profusely. "I am, I am.... This is It, Jonathan, my future is through there, taking a shower. I'm alive, I feel like a teenager, like together we could conquer the world."

He smiled. "Wow. I've never seen you like this. I'm happy you've finally found it. He does seem like a nice guy... Has he met Mum and Dad yet?" His left eye twitched slightly, a nervous childhood habit.

"Yes... it wasn't the best of meetings."

I quickly retold the story. Jonathan slapped the arm of the chair rapidly, emanating a dull thud, which echoed round the room as his amusement escalated.

"Oh, fuck, man!" He was laughing so hard he was almost crying. "I wish I'd fucking been here."

I could detect a subtle American accent from all his time spent working in the states. I took a moment and waited for his mirth to abate.

Nick strolled in, languidly, wearing jeans and no top. He sat next to me and placed a perfect arm round my shoulders.

Jonathan lit another cigarette. "Speaking of Nora, any chance we could pop over his in Maisie and get some green?"

I pouted my bottom lip.

"What?" Jonathan inquired, and   exhaled a succession of smoke rings.

"Maisie's dead."

I quickly and truthfully ran through *that* story, which also told him about my newfound acquaintance with Sergeant Lawrence Cole.

By the time I finished he'd lit another cigarette. "Can't be mates with the fuzz, Lauren. Shit..." He spilled the contents of the ashtray on the floor as he reached for it. "Can't you give Nora a ring to come here with some? I'm hanging for a smoke."

"But it's your first night back, and Nora will stay for most of it," I whined.

"Exactly, big Sis, it's my first night back, and I wanna get fucked. We're not on our own anyway... No disrespect, Nick..." He shot him a reassuring glance. "And you're not at work tomorrow, so what the fuck?"

He shrugged his shoulders and held his hands out in supplication.

Sighing, I got my phone and called Nora. A small part of me was hoping he'd be out, but he picked up, and shrieking with excitement, said he'd love to come over and bring Mr. Green.

"And a bottle of whisky," Jonathan shouted. "I'll give him the money when he gets here."

I rolled my eyes and took the rest of the call in the hallway, telling Nora that as far as Jonathan was aware, Nick was a male model I'd met on a shoot.

"Sí, sí, darlink. Secret's safe with me," Nora drawled.

I returned to Nick's side on the sofa and gave him a quick peck on the cheek. Jonathan was in the kitchen, clanking and banging his way through the fridge.

"Any more beer, Lauren?"

"No, but there's half a bottle of red wine in the cupboard."

He found his prize. "Anyone want one?"

314

"No," Nick and I answered simultaneously, whilst smiling conspiratorially at each other.

Nora arrived just as my brother finished the wine. Apprehension flicked at the edge of my emotions as I realised that mine, and Nick's tranquility was about to be busted wide open.

"D-a-a-r-r-l-e-e-nk!" Nora shrieked in greeting, dragging every syllable out.

That night he wore a dark green musketeer's hat with an emerald feather in it. He had a matching two-piece suit in dark green with a fine emerald thread running through it. The hanky protruding from his pocket bore a peacock motif.

Jonathan hugged him tightly as he came in. "Nora!"

Nora merely smiled and raised an eyebrow, before stepping out of the embrace and using his hands to smooth his immaculate suit. As always, he sat on the end of the sofa, opening his handbag and producing a huge baggie of sweet smelling weed. Jonathan clapped his hands loudly. Nora went a step further and pulled a bottle of expensive whisky out. I knew which one I'd be sticking to that night. Jollity's commenced, with Nick and myself sticking to the joints while my brother and Nora devoured the whisky.

Two hours later, they were drunk. Nick had been faithfully passing the joints along, and we were on about the fifth round. Both of us were happy to listen to the drinkers, every now and then interjecting with a word or two.

"Sooo, darlinks, did you hear the song then?" Nora suddenly asked, giving us his full attention while swaying slightly.

"Yes," Nick said, with a sloppy grin slanted across his face.

"Errr, and?..." Nora shrugged, his palms upturned either side of his head.

"Er, I'm still a bit spun out by it all to be honest."

Nora clicked his fingers. "Well, darlink, you'd better get with the program."

"Okay, okay..." Jonathan slurred. "What's all this about a song?"

Nora gasped, and shot Nick and I a look of disgust. "You no tell him about the song?"

He placed a hand on his chest, and told Jonathan the story, including telling him Nick had written it for me after we met at the modelling shoot.

Phew... Thank you, Nora...

315

Jonathan made me play it again while he sat back and puffed on a joint. I was struggling to keep my eyes open.

When it had finished Jonathan flicked his hand out, snapping his fingers.

"Wicked! Seriously. You wrote that, man," he said, pointing to Nick and stating the obvious.

Nick merely smiled and nodded.

"So, Jonathan, how long you home for?" Nora asked, slurring a bit himself.

"Dunno. I fancy spending a bit of time in the UK, but I'll be fucked if I'm staying at my parents, and I can't crash here?" He made it a question.

"No, you can't," I told him flatly.

"Darlink, you could stay with me."

Jonathan smiled. "Thanks, Nora. However, I'm a slob, and you don't even allow dust to settle. I've always found it best not to crash with mates, but I appreciate it." He passed Nora the joint.

"Well, maybe, when Nick and I go travelling, you can stay here. It'll be for about three months, maybe more," I offered.

Nora stood and screamed, shaking his hands in front of his face. "Que?... Whaa...What you say?"

"Travelling," I repeated.

"You not say nothing to me." His voice was loud and high.

"Well, we only just started talking about it, Nora."

"You leave me, Lauren…" He sniffed. "…all alone, Nora. I cannot cope." He sat back down, the back of his hand resting on his forehead. "You're leaving me. Where you go?"

"Not sure," I said.

"Maybe Australia," cut in Nick, making Nora scream again.

"All those bronzed Aussie men... I'm coming with you both, darlinks."

Too tired to fight him, I didn't respond.

Jonathan leant forward. "Well, I don't care who goes, but I'll definitely house-sit. Another joint, Nora?"

I took Nick's hand. "Feel like going to bed?" He nodded. "We'll leave you two to it," I said, and we stole away to the bedroom, both of us so stoned that we fell straight to sleep.

Unusually, I was the first to wake up, and I wanted to make

Nick coffee for a change. I tiptoed from the room and down the hall, where all I could smell was acrid cigarette smoke.

I opened the living room door to what appeared to be Armageddon.

Nora was still there, sleeping on the sofa in his suit. Jonathan had favoured the floor, with his head in his suitcase and still clutching his empty bottle of whisky. Mugs and glasses lay everywhere on their sides. One of the rolling papers was stuck in Nora's hair, and the rest were strewn about with a liberal sprinkling of tobacco.

I picked up two mugs as I crept through to the kitchen and made coffee, trying not to wake the living dead. My mission was successful, and I made it back in time to kiss Nick gently on the lips and wake him. That made him twitch his nose, so I kissed that as well. He lifted his beautiful eyelashes and blinked rapidly, then a huge smile spread across his face.

"God! You look good first thing in the morning," he said.

"That's because you're still stoned. Rose-coloured glasses," I replied, unable to hide a tiny smile.

I got back into bed and sat up for my coffee.

"You made coffee?" Nick sounded as shocked as I felt.

"Yep."

He pushed himself up with his hands and took his mug from the bedside table. "Is your brother okay?"

"Him, and Nora will be fine I think, but it's probably safer if we hide in here for a while."

As I watched his red lips pucker to blow on his coffee, I knew it would be easy to stay put.

"So, do you think Nora was serious about coming with us, or just drunk?"

"Who knows?" I took a slurp from my mug. "He's prone to hysteria, so we'll see."

"And what if he is serious?... Would you let him come?"

"Would you want him to?"

"You can't answer a question with a question."

I sighed. "Hopefully it was a spur of the moment comment. There's already enough going on without that... Let's just see what happens." I smuggled down into the duvet. "Anyway, I want to enjoy a morning in bed."

"And enjoy it you will." Nick smirked and put his mug down.

Our sexual exploits that day made us feel like teenagers under the covers, giggling, trying not to make any noise in case '*the parents*' caught us. Nora knocked on the door but didn't enter, and sounding terrible, he told us his cab was there, and he'd call.

When we heard the front door close we upped our noise level before falling back into a dreamy sexual sleep.

When I awoke, Nick was gone from my side. I put on my daffy duck dressing gown and padded down the hall towards the sound of the TV.

Jonathan sat watching while eating Rice Krispies.

"Mornin' Sis, just woke up meself."

I looked at the clock. It said two fifteen. My brother Lived to sleep, he Loved it.

"Afternoon," I corrected him.

"Whatever," he said, allowing milk to trickle down his chin as he took another mouthful.

The front room looked spotless, and I knew Jonathan hadn't done it. I went through to the kitchen, where Nick was at the sink tackling a huge mound of washing-up. I kissed him on the back of the neck and slipped my arms round his waist, making him jump.

"You don't have to do that - you've done enough already."

"Hello, Sleeping Beauty... I don't mind."

"Let's get a Chinese takeaway tonight, so no-one has to cook," my brother shouted through.

"YEAH!" I shouted back, putting the moka pot back on the stove.

"I'm going clubbing tomorrow night with Nora. Fancy it?"

I leaned back and raised an eyebrow at Nick, who shook his head.

"NO," I replied.

I made us all a drink and joined Jonathan.

"Oh well, at least you and your Lover can have a night alone. I'll crash at Nora's," he said, grinning.

I stuck my tongue out at him, quietly pleased.

All of us spent the rest of the day and the next morning eating, chatting and watching mindless TV, until Jonathan left to go to Nora's.

Our simple, two person world returned and both of us revelled in it. Jonathan didn't return until Monday when I'd already left for work. Nick texted me to let me know he was back safely, while I sat on the train, relieved the interviews were over and hoping the redhead had got it.

It seemed everything was returning to normality, but I had no idea just how wrong I was.

CHAOS

The week bumbled along, one day falling hardly noticed into the next. There were endless rounds of tidying up after my brother. Nick and I had stolen sex sessions, grabbed wherever possible. Jonathan arranged with our parents that he would arrive at their house on Friday afternoon. Work had returned to the same boring routine. Mr. Forrester informed the staff that the applicant had been chosen, and would be arriving Friday to meet us all, including Maureen Little, whose job she would be doing.

Nick and myself were falling more and more in love, churning the stomachs of all around us. On the Thursday night, Nick cooked a fantastic meal for us all, Nora included. It was more civilised than our previous meetings, though still mostly spent laughing. All of us were in great spirits, and my brother made a toast;

"Thank God I'm going. I love you both, but it's disgusting watching, and hearing how happy you both are." He raised his glass.

I went bright red, and shot a look at Nick, who was wearing a small pink glow himself.

Nora tittered, raising his glass as well. "Salud!"

Only moments later, Nick's song was played on the radio, which we were keeping switched on most of the time.

Nora raised his glass in perfect time with an eyebrow, directing his gaze at Nick. "Here's to infamy," he sung.

"What's that mean?" I asked, having no clue.

Nora tutted. "Infamous is when you are famous, but nobody knows exactly who you are."

"I like the sound of that one," Nick said, softly.

I could see Jonathan looking at Nick, inquisitively. He took his last mouthful and pushed his chair back. "Great meal, Nick."

"Thanks."

"Although there's something that's been puzzling me, do you mind if I ask?"

My brothers question was directed solely at Nick. I stopped eating and looked at my brother.

"It's just you seem nervous about this song, and the attention it could bring to you, as if you don't want to be in the limelight, but…" He paused while his cognitive processes caught up. "I would have thought that being a male model, you are constantly getting attention and in the 'limelight'." He held his hands up, using his fingers as inverted commas as if to illustrate that word.

Nick had stopped eating and was flicking his eyes to mine in a cry for help.

"Well, Nick, he," I began, but my brother cut me off, holding up his hand.

"Sorry, Sis, but I was asking Nick."

I knew Nick didn't have the lies in him to quickly invent a plausible story as I watched him running his hand through his hair. I could feel his discomfort palpably.

"Okay, he's not a male model, I mean, we didn't meet like that," I blurted out.

Bitterness tinged my words. Jonathan was a clever bastard.

Nora let out a huge breath. "Thank God that's out," and carried on eating.

Looking at Nick, I could see his eyes sparkling with a layer of fine moisture. It seemed as if I'd said the magic chant, releasing him from the wicked spell.

'Thank you,' he mouthed to me.

Jonathan lit a cigarette. "Okay, so why the big story? What's going on?" He threw the question out to all of us.

"Don't worry, I'll tell you, Bro. After dinner." I got up to clear the table.

Nora left shortly after, sensing it best on this occasion. Nick said he was going for a long bath and left me with a passionate kiss.

I told the story to Jonathan. Not everything. for there was no need to tell him all about David, only that he was my first love, and that he broke my heart. I explained that Mother and Father had hated David, so we'd gone for the male model story when Mother had seen the photos everywhere. "...and so here we are, up to date."

My brother chain-smoked throughout my explanation, and when I'd finished he got up and poured himself more wine, returning to the exact same position. He took a huge gulp of wine and finally spoke.

"That's one hell of a fucking story. I can't believe you did all that, and now Nick's here. Un-fucking-believable." He took three big gulps in a row. "I love it. It's great. I'll go along with the story with Ma and Pa, if only for the sheer satisfaction of what they don't know. Hell, even I looked up my first love on Facebook; *Samantha Brown*..." He shuddered. "Well, I wanted to know, and it turns out she now looks like she needs shooting in a game park."

I wasn't able to suppress a smile.

"Fuck. How can people let themselves go like that?" He sat closer to me. "Lauren, who gives a fuck what happened in the past? It's obvious you're both in love, so fuck everyone else."

I kissed him on the cheek and hugged him. "I'm so glad to have you, Bro."

He reached for his cigarettes.

"One for me?" I asked, and he handed me one already lit.

"It does make the whole '*Lucy*' thing more understandable... Mm-mmm." He blew his smoke out long and slowly.

"Very good, detective smart-ass."

"Well, one of us had to have the brains," he said, smirking.

I knew I was going to miss him when he left the next day. I'd told him the story, but omitted to tell him about Jenny Setterton. I didn't want to make him worry unnecessarily.

"You will come over to Mum and Dad's soon, eh?" Jonathan asked.

"Of course, but probably on my own. Nick will definitely have a modelling assignment that day, you know what Mum's like. It will take her at least two years to get over the cock incident."

The corners of his mouth rose, and he slapped his leg.

"It's not funny," I said unconvincingly.

"It is."

"Hey you, by the time I get home tomorrow you'll be gone." My words were tainted by sadness.

"Yep. Look, you two don't need me around."

It felt like we had talked for hours, and a sudden thought made me jerk rigidly. "Where's Nick?"

"Errr..."

I raced through to the bathroom which was steeped in darkness. I frantically searched for the light switch and flicked it only to to find it empty. I peeked into the bedroom, and found Nick laying sound asleep on the bed.

I went back to the front room.

"So, still in the flat is he? Slipped in the shower?... Fucking hell, Sis. You have got it bad..." Jonathan said, amused. "Worrying about him while he's still in the flat! I think you could get him fitted with some sort of tracking device - '*Nick is now in the hall, Nick is now in the kitchen*'..."

I ran over, laughing, and karate-chopped him in the stomach.

We said our goodbyes, and shortly afterwards I joined Nick in bed. I cuddled into him and breathed in his smell. Recharging from his energy made me feel even more alive in the dead of the night.

I woke up just before the alarm went off, and got ready quietly, letting both men sleep. As I slipped effortlessly into the day, I was glad it was a Friday. On the journey to work my hazy thoughts were random and scattered.

As I approached my desk, I noticed two silhouettes projecting from the doorway of Mr. Forrester's office, caused by the sun streaming through the window.

At least it's a beautiful autumn day..., I thought, as I started my daily rituals.

Take off jacket, place on back of seat. Sit. Turn on computer. Think about coffee. Look up as Forrester's door opens wide. Scream slightly. Turn green and throw up in waste paper bin.

I brought my head up slowly and wiped the sick from round my mouth. Mr. Forrester stood before my desk, his look of incredulousness definitely apparent. I focused my pupils a millimetre to the left of him, my mind screaming over and over; *BUNNY BOILER! BUNNY BOILER!...*

Jenny Setterton stood behind Mr. Forrester, her whole demeanour Holier than Thou. She was dressed perfectly in a two piece with a skirt in sensible brown. An Alice band was set in advert-perfect hair, and her hands were clasped before her. Her dark, dark, soul-less, brown eyes were offset by her terrifyingly egotistical smile. She didn't even blink as she viewed me down her nasal cavities and I shrank away, leaving the chair and sliding to my knees, holding on to the bin for support and staring upwards in disbelief.

"Lauren, what on earth is happening?..." Mr. Forrester asked, coughing and fiddling with the knot on his drab grey tie.

I glanced uncomfortably at Jenny. *BUNNY BOILER!...*

"This," he said, holding his hand out and presenting the Bitch. "is Miss Jenny Setterton, who will be taking over Maureen Little's job."

"UURRGHH!..." I began to violently puke.

BUNNY BOILER, FULL FULL ALERT!...

Loyally, Mr. Forrester apologised on my behalf. "I'm very sorry about this, Miss Setterton. Not the introduction I'd imagined."

He shot me a look of pure murder as rays of sun shone through his thin hair, giving him a pretty weak Jesus look, enhanced by my perspective from floor level. I bit my lip to suppress hysterical laughter. It seemed like he was an Angel bringing the Devil to me.

"This, Miss Setterton, is Lauren Bowman." Mr. Forrester completed the introductions even as he turned away in embarrassment.

"Lauren, Bowman," Jenny repeated back slowly. "Oh dear, poor Miss Bowman. You seem to be ill." She sounded perfectly concerned.

The rays of light formed an almost-perfect halo round Mr. Forrester's head, and giggles escaped my clamped lips. Mr. Forrester's skin turned a colour I'd never seen before, a purple-red shade.

"I think you should go home, Lauren," he commanded, anger popping on his tongue. "Miss Setterton, could you just give us a moment, please?"

"Of course, Mr. Forrester." Jenny's smile was wide, but the corners of her mouth were not turned up. "I do hope you feel better soon, Lauren Bowman. I'll see you Monday." She turned, and walked off.

Mr. Forrester's stare wasn't weak now. "When you've finished your impression of a midget who pukes their words, we will conclude this conversation in my office. You will wait if I'm not there." He stormed off.

My muscles had forgotten how to work. I sat, holding my

vomit and listening to Jenny fucking Setterton being introduced to everyone, each time giving a perfect reply.

AARRRGHH! How the fuck is this happening? Have I banged my head on the way to work, and now I'm in the Matrix?...

Gradually my motor-neurons began to function, and I put the bin down.

Rising unsteadily, I wobbled into Mr. Forrester's office keeping my head down. I sat down and waited, though the nausea hadn't abated and I'd lost all concept of time. I looked up slightly as he entered, went silently to his desk, and sat down.

"You are to go home, get better, and have a good think about your job here. You are erratic, and there's not a shred of continuity about you. I hope you noticed how the new girl is dressed? Impeccably, not in a Lidl bag."

That made me look up. *How the fuck?...*

"That's how I expect you to dress from now on. No more excuses. One more incident and you'll be on a written warning. It's time you grew up, Miss Bowman. See you Monday."

I gathered my stuff and switched off the computer. I walked past Jenny, being instructed by Maureen, who was no longer Little.

She should be Maureen Big now..., I pondered.

Jenny paid no further attention to me whatsoever.

I ran down the stairs and into the toilets, sitting on the floor as tears of anger and fear fell, unstintingly. I felt haunted and invaded, plagued and tormented. With shaking hands I retrieved my mobile and dialled the number for Batman.

Lawrence knocked on the door of the ladies in which I sat in one of the cubicles.

"Lauren?" he called nervously.

I unlocked the door and went out to meet him. He was casually dressed in a deep turquoise shirt with three buttons undone, hinting at his chest. He had dark blue jeans on and his thick hair was gelled slightly.

Must be off work, he looks good...

He held the door open with a reprimanding, '*what is it now?*' type of stare.

I took his arm and quickly dragged him out of the building.

"Lauren, what's going on?"

"Tell you in a minute. Where's your car?"

I was looking about madly and acting deranged. I pulled him over to the blue Audi he pointed out, and waited impatiently on the passenger side as he unlocked the doors. I flung open the door and flung myself in, slamming it shut. Lawrence got in and just looked at me warily. I allowed my breathing to become normal before I spoke.

"I'm sorry, Lawrence," I said, speaking to my lap.

"It seems that you're always saying sorry to me, and I'm always rescuing you."

"Sorry." I sighed.

"Okay, where are you going, home? You can tell me on the way."

"No!" I shouted.

I didn't want to tell Nick yet. I knew this would make him angry.

"Oh God, this is all my fault..." I held my head in my hands. *How can I go and tell him his ex is stalking me?...* "I need time to think, Lawrence."

He started the engine and began to drive. I wasn't taking much in until the scenery became beautiful and the houses screamed of money.

"Are we in Richmond?"

"Yes, my father's house if you don't mind. He's away again."

That made me smile. "No, I don't mind. It's a beautiful house. Could we walk down to the lake, where the boathouse is?"

Lawrence smiled back. "Yeah, of course we can."

The house may have been beautiful, but it was devoid of a soul, in sharp contrast with the gardens, which were breathtakingly beautiful and tended with love.

"It's thanks to the efforts of my mother, but mostly the gardener," Lawrence said as if he could read my mind.

I gushed at the magnificence of it all. By the lake there was a big stone bench. I sat down and looked across the calmness, thinking how much Nick loved to be near water. Lawrence sat next to me and we both sat thinking our own thoughts for a few minutes.

"I do hate this lake though," Lawrence said, sounding

surprisingly wistful. "When I was a boy, all I ever wanted to do was go out on the boat, and jump off into the water and go fishing like normal boys did. My father never allowed me to, he said it was much too dangerous. So, every year I would merely bathe in the shallows at the edge, as obviously swimming out of my depth was considered too dangerous. My parents had already planned out my future, and they didn't want to risk anything.

One day, I couldn't stand it any more, and I took the boat out. My mother had a small Pekingese dog at the time, who jumped aboard with me, then as soon as I set off, jumped overboard and drowned in an apparently suicidal bid for freedom. I don't know why I was to blame, but I was never allowed in the lake again. The boat was chained up and probably still is, rotting away... So since then, no matter how hot the summer's been, all I could do was stare. I've not been in since - it's such a fucking waste."

He picked up a small stone and threw it into the water. I had a feeling that that latter comment was referring to his Life.

"Got no idea why I just told you that." His calm amber eyes held a touch of sadness and regret.

"Maybe cause you're sick of listening to me all the time?" I suggested.

He hadn't yet asked again about what happened to me.

"If you had a map of your fate, would you look at it?" I asked, inquisitively.

Turning to face him, I watched the thought-lines crinkle on his forehead.

Eventually he answered; "Yes, I'd look. And you?"

"Before, no. But after everything that's been happening recently, maybe yes."

"What *has* been happening, Lauren?"

So I told him about Jenny.

"So, I was right!" he exclaimed, triumphantly.

"Yes," I replied, snapping briefly. " You were right. I can't have her there every day. It's insanity. Can't you do anything?"

"Well, I could arrest her on the grounds that she's got a job?..." he quipped.

I stuck my tongue out.

"Lauren, at the moment she hasn't actually done anything, but if she becomes threatening, then that's different."

"I still don't know how she found out where I work. She must have been following me, surely that's illegal?"

"But you'd have to prove it," he countered.

327

My eyes fluttered.

"You've got beautiful eyes..."

I pulled away a bit.

"Shit. I just said that out loud didn't I?" he joked, forcing a smile from me.

"Lawrence, I'm sorry I relied on you yet again. I just thought maybe you knew something I could do."

He sat back and crossed his ankles. "She'd go away if you broke up with Nick..."

Eyes full of poison looked at him.

He held his hands out. "Okay, okay, just throwing it out there."

"That'd be just what she wants. Shit, I'd love to punch her straight in that smug face."

"That's just what she wants, too, and then you're the one who gets arrested..."

I shivered suddenly as a mild breeze chilled me.

"Cold?"

I nodded. He pushed closer to me and put his arm round my shoulders.

"Sorry, I've not got my jacket," he explained.

That act alone, made me feel like I was physically cheating on Nick.

I stood quickly. "Can we go back to the house?"

"Of course."

I rushed up the garden, though Lawrence's long legs and big strides easily caught me up. I opened the kitchen door and went through to the breakfast bar. Sitting down, I wondered what on earth I was doing there.

It's Nick I should be with...

"Lawrence, sorry, could you drive me back home? I shouldn't have called you and involved you. Shock, that's it, I was in shock."

Lawrence stood in front of me, forcing me to look up. "It's very hard for me to stay away from you when you call me for help. I'm not a bastard." He picked his keys up. "So. Home, Miss."

"Thanks. I'll try hard not to need your help again," I promised, smiling feebly.

Lawrence pulled up right outside my front door. "If anything changes, let me know."

I leaned over and kissed him lightly on the cheek. "You are a star."

Getting out, I ran up the steps and pushed the buzzer as I checked the time; Ten to three. No answer. I pushed the button again.

Fuck. What if she came here?...

The door opened to reveal a perplexed-looking Nick. I threw my arms around him and held him as close to me as I could.

"What's wrong?"

"I'll tell you inside."

And I did. I was right about him being angry, telling him flicked a switch. Shouting and swearing, he punched the wall.

"Right, Monday I'm coming with you."

"And then what, Nick?... You march her off the premises? Kill her? She's proving it's not going to be easy to get rid of her."

Nick was pacing, and shaking his right hand, which had started to swell slightly. "I don't know, but she can't do that."

My eyes darted from side to side, following his progress. "Nick, please. Come and sit down."

He stopped, looked at my imploring expression and relented, sitting on the sofa. "Lucy, I'm sorry. It must have been horrible."

"Not one of my best mornings," I replied, tears filling my eyes.

He took my hands, wincing at the pain in his own. "So, if this all happened this morning, where have you been all day?"

I gulped guiltily. "Well... I was distressed, not thinking straight."

"And?"

"And I rang Lawrence Cole."

Nick's hold loosened. "So that's where you've been, with him all this time. Pouring out your stress... to him."

Hostility sliced his words. He stood up.

"No. No, it wasn't like that, Nick. He's a policeman, I thought he could help."

"So you called him before me. Finding comfort with fucking Sargent Cole."

"What would you have done then, Nick?" I demanded, my voice raising. " If I'd called you? You're angry now, what would you have been like earlier? Not thinking with a clear head, acting on passion. Lawrence does have that clear and logical way of thinking. I told you, it was all so fucked, and No, I wasn't finding comfort in him. Stupid me thought I might get that here, from YOU!" I shouted the last word.

"Yes, of course I'm fucking angry... Swooping in all the time, being the fucking hero. I bet he Loves it."

329

"Nick, that's hardly the bigger picture here. Do you think it's an appropriate moment for a cock fighting display?" I stood myself.

Nick stopped pacing for a second, wild-eyed.

"Look, Nick. Look at what she's already doing to us. Please? I hate this."

That nauseous feeling was returning as the row began to brew.

Nick's eyes shone out, glazed with hatred. "Fuck!..." he said, drooping his shoulders. "Shit, Lucy. I'm sorry..." He came and hugged me. "I just feel so powerless to do anything. My frustration is showing itself in my anger. I wish it was me that could swoop in and save the day... It *should* be me. What kind of man am I if I can't even protect you?"

I was touched by the powerful words of this twenty-three year old. I hugged him tightly.

"Nick, you have all the power, which is why Jenny wants you so much. Why I..." I pulled back a bit to look into his eyes. "...want you so much. You can't control the uncontrollable."

He kissed me. "I only want you to be alright."

"I will be, as long as you're here."

Kisses of comfort turned into kisses of need and desire. We made love, confirming to the world our impenetrability. Nick's hand was even more swollen afterwards, so he put it in the freezer, while I made coffee.

"What are we going to do about her then, Lucy?"

"I don't know. Work was unbearable before, but this brings a whole new meaning to it. Also, I don't know if you've thought of this, but she also now knows my real name." *Judging by the way his mouth just dropped open, he hasn't....* "So now the shit's really gonna hit the fan."

Nick groaned. "Fucking Lies - this is what happens. Everyone not knowing what's going on. Who said what to who? In a way I'm glad. Now my mum will find out the truth and the decision is taken away from my dad. He's there and I'm not, he'll have to handle it." His voice fell cold.

Of course he was right, and I made a decision right then.

"I suppose it's for the best, and if it's alright with you, would you come with me on Sunday to my parents? I'm going to tell them the truth."

Nick took his hand from the freezer and came over to me, sliding it under my shirt and round my waist, making me jump with the cold.

"I'd love to..." Our hips crushed together. "Sorry I was such an arsehole earlier." He lowered his thick lashes.

"Even arse-holes need to spout shit sometimes," I said, grinning.

"Very good."

"I'll make dinner - you can't, with that hand."

He replaced it in the freezer. "So, where did you go with Sergeant Cole?"

I faced him. "Is this a trick question?"

One corner of his mouth perked up. "What?... Why is it a trick?"

He genuinely didn't understand.

No more lies, Lauren..., floated through my head. "We... Shit. This is difficult."

Nicks eyes opened wider.

"I think I'm allowed to tell you this. We went to his father's house, who's a very important man. Lawrence swore me not to tell anyone. It's a very expensive house, in a very nice part of London."

"Oh, even better, his dad's some big cheese."

"Aww..." I pouted. "I feel sorry for him, Nick. From the few things he's told me, his upbringing was hard. All his choices were made for him. The thought of never having any freedom makes me shudder."

"Well, it's just as bad for poor kids, Lucy. They get too much freedom, no decisions made for them." He withdrew his hand and shut the little freezer door.

"Nick?"

"Yes?"

"If you'd been given a fate map, would you look at it?"

"No," he said vehemently. "I wouldn't want to know, and you?"

I smiled broadly. "No, although I asked Lawrence the same question. He said Yes."

"Of course he did. So, is that the trick question then?" Nick teased.

"No!" I shouted, and threw a dirty tea towel at him.

Passion enveloped us and we forgot our worries. Eventually, I rolled off him, gasping and waiting for the eye wobble to stop.

"Shit. You're so good! especially what you can do with that tongue."

Nicks chest rose heavily. "I love doing that. It makes me horny when you love it so much."

331

"Hits the jackpot every time. Most men look, and sound like a pig searching for truffles."

Nick let out a laugh and rolled onto his side, propping his head up with one hand. "You know, I think we should put *Her*..." He wasn't even able to say her name now. "to the back of our minds. Let's not do anything. Perhaps she'll go away, or we'll see what her next move is, but one thing I'm insisting on is that from now on I'm meeting you every day after work."

"Nick, the journey's shit, and..."

"Lucy, please. It's the one thing I *can* do."

I relented. "Okay, and I agree with you about Her."

We submerged ourselves in each other again, and shut everything else out.

I called my mother and told her we were coming that Sunday, and could dad pick us up?

She wanted to know where my car was, and I told her I'd tell her when I got there.

Nick and I spent long hours shagging all over the flat, a luxury previously denied to us. Our shadows lifted and we began to discuss our dreams again.

At one-thirty on Sunday, both of us were ready and waiting for my father, equally nervous. Nick dressed casually in jeans and a shirt, while I opted for a long-sleeved, brown woollen knee-length dress. Nora would have hated it just as much as I did.

I heard the beep-beep of the horn outside and opened the door. My mother always hated beepers, so that was my father's small rebellion in her absence.

Nick and I held hands as we descended the steps, ready to enter the gladiator's arena.

DECEPTION ENDED

The journey to my parents was fraught with anxious tension. Nick sat in the back, and I rode shotgun. My father tried to be sociable, even asking Nick how the modelling was going, but Nick, not wanting to confirm the Lie, simply replied - "Fine."

I babbled in an attempt to fill the gaps, asking how it was to have Jonathan back, what had they been up to, how is the garden, *blah*, *blah*, until I was sick of the sound of my own voice. Then I shut my mouth and gazed out the window, wishing I was with Nick in the back.

When we arrived, the outside of the house looked as if it was being entered for a competition. All the plants shone, and the grass looked as if it had been trimmed with scissors. Little name-sticks informed us what each plant was. No weeds dared to grow here.

The pure white gate was set in a pure white fence, and opened onto a perfectly white crazy-paved path. I took Nick's hand as we walked down it, following my father, and wishing we'd brought flowers.

My father opened the door. "Erm, we're in the drawing room, Lauren."

The room designated for formality. My dad showed us in, said he needed to change, and departed quickly.

Nick sat tensely, his back straight and both legs firmly together. I squeezed his good hand.

"If it's any consolation, I'm just as nervous as you," I whispered.

"Are you going to tell them now, or later?" Nick asked quietly with big dark blue concerned eyes.

"Now," I just managed to say, before Jonathan bounded into the room and slumped into an Edwardian style armchair with plums and apples patterning it.

My brother was smiling, but there was a touch of crinkling at the edges of his eyes. "Shit. Is there any seat in this house that's comfortable?" he moaned, before putting his hand up in salute. "Hi guys."

I thanked God he was there, as I felt my tension loosen.

"Hi, Jonathan," Nick responded.

"Hi, little Brother. How's it been?" I asked, quietly.

"Great... spoilt rotten." He grinned even more as his eyes glanced towards the door and he lowered his voice. "but I'd kill for a smoke."

"Where's Mum?"

He raised his arms and shrugged to signify ignorance. "Probably in the kitchen, polishing the roast potatoes."

"Actually I'm here, darling." My mother's voice came from the doorway, wiping the smiles from our faces.

Nick jumped up, and I tried to stand gracefully, while my brother simply picked at a tooth with his nail. My mother was dressed in a pale blue chiffon dress and looked good enough to go to a fancy tea party. She floated over to me, ignoring Nick, and tickled me on the cheek. At least I'd been deemed worthy of a kiss.

"Lauren, lovely to see you."

"You remember Nick?" I placed my hand on his arm.

Nick held out his hand. "Lovely to meet you again Mrs Bowman. It's very kind of you to have me to dinner."

My mother flicked her eyes over him and offered a limp hand, before pulling away quickly.

"You'll all have to excuse me for a while. There's some touching up to do on the dinner. Your father will be along in a moment to serve drinks." She raised her eyes in supplication.

As she turned to leave, she stopped dead facing my brother, who had his leg over one arm of the chair. "Jonathan. Your father and I do not live in a minimum three hundred and fifty thousand pound property area, just so you can put your leg over the chair." She stared intently while he slowly removed the offending article.

Jonathan pulled a face as she walked from the room. "Welcome to the family," he said to Nick, with more than a touch of sarcasm.

My father entered the room looking red and flustered, and wearing a shirt and tie that I knew my mother had made him wear. I could hear her voice in my head; '*He may be a pervert, Lionel, but we'll still dress for the occasion.*'

He fiddled with the knot on his striped bow tie. "Drinks. Nick, what would you like?... Ah yes, but there's wine being served with dinner, so I suppose you could have that if you like, but maybe Dolores doesn't want that opened yet." Now he was talking to himself.

"Dad!" my brother shouted.

"Mmm?" His bushy eyebrows bristled. "Oh yes, Nick?"

Nick and I sat holding hands. "Just a coke if you have one, Mr. Bowman."

My father's brow was set into deep lines. "Yes, I think we do."

"I'll have the same," Jonathan cut in. "But can you add some whisky to that?" He placed his leg back over the chair arm.

"I'll just have a water thanks, Dad."

He turned and smiled at me warmly, rubbing his hands together. "Good, good."

"Lionel!" my mother's high-pitched voice called out.

My father turned on his heel, and hurried out. "Yes, dear."

Nick and I exchanged glances that meant; '*This is going to be a long afternoon.*'

I didn't get the opportunity to tell my parents anything very quickly. I didn't see my mother again until we'd sat down for dinner in the dining room. My father poured us all a tiny glass of wine each, before helping my mother in with the serving dishes. They did all this without one word being spoken. My father carved the meat while we handed round the different bowls of vegetables and potatoes. All the while, I was feeling for Nick, having to go through this, knowing the worst was yet to come. It wasn't until everything was served and ready that the first word was spoken.

"So, Nick. Whereabouts do you come from?" My mother's voice cut through the air.

He finished his mouthful before replying. "At the moment my family live in Devon, Mrs Bowman. But originally I was born and brought up in Surrey."

My mother raised her eyebrows at that. "Oh. Did Lauren tell you we lived there once?... When Jonathan was a baby." She looked across at her son as if he still was a baby.

"Yes, Mrs Bowman, she did."

My father took a sip of his wine. "We went to Devon on holiday once, didn't we, dear?" He put his glass down, catching the edge of his plate and making a clanking sound.

"Do be careful, Lionel," my mother chided. "Yes, we have been there, but I must be honest, I found it a little too earthy for my taste..." She sipped her wine as if to wash away the memory. "When you say family, what does that consist of?" she asked Nick, resuming her questioning.

"My mother, my father, two brothers and one sister."

While Nick struggled to answer, my father and brother ate systematically.

"Do your parents come from Kent?"

"My father does, but my mother's from Northern Ireland."

The mention of Northern Ireland caused my mother to cough slightly and look round the room, whilst fiddling with her necklace.

"It's alright, Mother. She's not a terrorist."

Why I was defending Angela I didn't know, except that it was for Nick, who was handling the Spanish Inquisition perfectly.

"Really, Lauren. As if I thought such a thing," she protested, knowing that was exactly what she had thought. "And how do your mother and father like your choice of career?"

She picked up her wine again, and this time I joined her, taking a huge gulp as I realised the truth wouldn't wait until after dinner. Nick looked at me, and I smiled back reassuringly.

"Nick's not really a male model, Mother. So his family don't have to worry about it."

The fork that was about to enter my brother's mouth stopped, and his head jerked up to look at me. My father just continued to eat, apparently oblivious.

Mother pulled her puzzled face. "I don't understand, Lauren." She dabbed at the corners of her mouth with a linen napkin.

"Well... I - I met Nick in Devon, Mother. On holiday..." I paused to drink more wine. Nick's hand lay on my leg under the table. "So, when I came home I missed him, and then I had the photo's done."

Jonathan had finished his mouthful, put his knife and fork together and was sat back, arms folded, ready to enjoy the show.

My mother masticated slowly as she thought. "So, why the need for deceit? And why tell us he was a male model?" My palms felt sweaty and my mouth was painfully dry. She gave me no time to answer before turning to Nick. "So, what is it you do for a living?"

Nick gulped hard on a mouthful of food, on the verge of choking.

"Is this really necessary, Mother? Couldn't the questioning wait until we've finished our food?"

She answered me without taking her eyes off Nick. "They're simply questions, Lauren. Only common people don't make conversation at dinner."

Nick spoke up. "My parents own a bed and breakfast, so I help a lot there, and me and my father have a firewood delivery service."

My mother began to play with her necklace again. The real diamonds glinted madly in contrast with her pale skin, which was protected from the sun at all cost. I had only ever seen my mother's skin with a light pink glow. She always said only working class people have suntans.

"Bed and breakfast," she repeated with mild disgust, twisting the big diamond ring on her index finger. "I still don't understand the need to lie."

I slipped my hand under the table with Nick's and gathered my courage. "Well... You know Nick's father." My voice was shaky. I took another gulp of wine.

"Do we?" my father asked, sounding surprised as he rose to clear the table.

"Yes. His father is David Palmer."

My mother's eyes were raised in recollection as Jonathan poured more wine, offering the bottle to me. I took it gladly and filled my glass to the brim. My mother gave us a look of distaste.

"Is that the boy that used to clean our windows?" My father raised his voice to compete with the sound of the plates clattering together.

"No, but that name is somehow very familiar. Oh, Lauren. This isn't cluedo. Tell us," she commanded sharply.

"Nick is David's Son. David, who... who was my first boyfriend."

Mother glanced at Nick. At first it didn't register. She reached for her glass, and then stopped as she realised. Her eyeballs plumped out, widening to their fullest extent. She was blinking rapidly.

"Lionel. I would like a sherry." She turned a deathly shade of white and stared dead ahead into space.

My father, who was putting down plates on the side dresser looked bemused, and obviously didn't know what was going on. He poured the drink and placed it in front of my catatonic mother.

Jonathan was smiling, enjoying himself, but probably wishing he had something to smoke.

"Dolores?" Even my father's strong tone failed to rouse her. He looked to me. "Lauren? Who's David?"

My mother recovered suddenly and snatched at her sherry, raising her voice. "Oh for God's sake, Lionel! David. How can you not remember that barbarian? A disgusting excuse for a human being."

Slowly, my father sat down. Nick squeezed hard on my leg.

"Yes, I think that's quite enough please, Mother. Nick *is* David's son."

My mother's mouth opened.

"Da-vid?" my father said inquiringly, looking at me sideways.

Mother pushed her chair back. "I... I don't quite know what to say, Lauren. After everything he did to you, and now, now his son is living with you. Oh dear. Oh dear..." She clasped her head, breathing hard. "Oh my Goodness. It's... It's disgusting. It's almost incest." She swayed perceptibly as she shut her eyes.

"It's not incest, Mother. How could it be? We're in love."

A small cry escaped my mother as I heard my father's weak tone. "David's son..."

"Mr. and Mrs Bowman, I realise this is a big shock, but I really do love..." Nick paused briefly. "Lauren, and I'll take good care of her."

My mother laughed sarcastically. "You are a boy. How on earth are you going to look after her?... Maybe you are with her so that you may atone for your father's sins."

Nick's jaw tightened as he clenched his teeth.

I stood. "Sorry, Mother. I've heard enough. I won't have Nick being spoken to like that."

Her neck slowly receded and her fingers massaged her temple. "Lionel, I'm getting a migraine. Please get me some pills."

I looked at Jonathan. "Can you drive us home, please?"

He shot me a sympathetic glance as he stood. "I'll just go and check with Papa."

Nick stood up, obviously glad to leave the room.

"Lauren, I don't understand why you are doing this to us," my mother whined. "You need to grow up."

That was the second time I'd been told that in as many days.

I took Nick's arm and led him from the viper's pit, without even saying goodbye. My father was in the hall holding a glass of water and some tablets. I felt sorry for him, I knew my mother would take it out on him. He moved his mouth as if he had a boiled sweet in it and didn't know what to do with it.

Finally he settled on - "Lauren, your brother has the keys." He managed a weak smile.

"Thanks, Dad. Sorry."

Nick held his hand out, but then realised my father's hands were full.

"Lionel!" came my Mothers voice, impatient in more ways than one.

My father bristled past us. "Coming, dear."

Jonathan was already in the car and the front door was open, as if waiting for the heathens to leave. We stepped through and I closed it behind us and hugged Nick.

"I'm sorry, that was horrible."

He placed a hand gently on the back of my neck. "You don't have to apologise. You're not responsible for your family."

As soon as we had turned out of the street, Jonathan opened the driver's window and lit a cigarette. Nick and I sat together in the back this time.

"Well, that went well," Jonathan volunteered. " Probably as well as if you'd both gone in there, squatted, and shat on the carpet." He banged the steering wheel with mirth.

Anger gripped me. "Yes, thank you, Brother. That's really fucking helpful."

Nick put a calming arm round me.

"Hey, don't take it out on me, Sis. You must have known that would be the reaction."

I sighed softly, knowing I had indeed known.

Jonathan flicked his cigarette out of the window and got another from his pocket. "Shit, man. This means she's going to be a fucking nightmare at home."

"So there is some small consolation," I joked.

"Maybe I could come over to yours?"

"No."

He swerved to avoid a cyclist, beeping his horn and shouting "FUCKER!" at the poor man. "Nora. I'll stay at his for a couple of nights."

Good, that will occupy the two of them... "Great idea."

Jonathan smoked four more cigarettes in the time it took him to drive us home. We said our goodbyes but I was just desperate to be alone with Nick.

We fell into each other's arms as soon as we entered my apartment. He covered my face with kisses and pulled my head onto his chest, stroking my hair.

"I'm sorry, Lucy. That it didn't go better."

Sweet, adorable, sensitive Nick. My damn tear ducts again... "Why are *you* sorry? She was awful to you, especially the things she said. *I'm* sorry. I should have gone alone and not subjected you to that." I tilted my head back and looked up into his beautiful face.

"We're together, Lucy. So that means we do things together."

His words made my pain and embarrassment slip away.

"Nick, I still can't believe how much I'm in love with you. Your words always sound so right, but so much is against us as well. It scares me."

He kissed me gently. "Lucy. It doesn't matter, because it's you and I who are strong."

I wanted him, and I took him. The aggressor in me came out as I directed assertively, and Nick submitted to me. Hours later we were sore, content, and happy. As I lay in bed, cuddling into Nick, one hand idly stroking his six-pack, a small yawn escaped me.

"You'd better set the alarm. Don't want to be late," Nick murmured.

"Oh yeah, I can't wait." I rolled slowly over to reach the clock.

"Just ignore her, like we said. And I'm meeting you." He put his arm around me and pulled me towards him. "Shit, Lucy. You've got such a fantastic little body."

I giggled, and gave myself up to him again, pushing all other concerns to the back of my mind.

PERFECT

I thought Monday would be just another normal day. Jenny was concentrating on being taught the job, and enjoying all the attention from the males in the office as they introduced themselves. I kept myself to myself. Babs came over that morning to tell me which herbs and plants helped with being run down, which did nothing for the way I felt, but rather left me wondering if I looked *that* bad.

An hour before we finished I was already getting excited at the prospect of Nick meeting me.

I quietly gloated; *Fuck you, Ms. Setterton...*

At five sharp I was flying down the stairs, straining my eyes to see through the misted glass doors, sure I could see a figure beyond them. I pushed them hard and flew through them.

Nick turned and smiled with perfectly white teeth. The wind was blowing his dark chestnut fringe. My heart beat faster and I ran to him, crushing myself into his arms.

"You're a sight for sore eyes... and everything else as well," he said as he pushed his shlong against me.

I smiled and looked up into his aqua blue eyes.

"Come on Mrs Palmer. I've got a surprise for you."

He took my hand, and I glowed a rapturous red inside. I was delirious because he'd called me *Mrs Palmer*. I didn't want to grow up if it meant giving up this feeling I'd waited so long for. I resolved to rebel and remain youthful at heart.

Cocooned in that droplet of love, neither of us mentioned *Her*. We giggled together on the tube, spoiling the sombre pallid atmosphere. Nick gestured for us to get off at Piccadilly Circus. I accompanied him with tiny squeals of excitement, enjoying the mystery of our destination.

He took my hand as we came up into the street, and I looked round at the throngs of different people. There was always such variation. Nick's pace slowed as we passed an amazing hotel. Huge white pillars stood atop marble steps, leading to a red carpet, and ending with an immaculately dressed doorman, replete with top hat and tails in cream and burgundy, and white gloves on his hands which were clasped in front of him.

Looking higher, I saw the name in nineteen-twenties style lettering, white on black. It said; REGENT PALACE HOTEL.

I'd glanced many times from afar at this beautiful, but seemingly untouchable hotel, never before daring to get this close.

Nick stopped.

"It's beautiful, isn't it?" I said in awe.

"It is. Let's go in," Nick said, and began to lead me over to the steps.

I pulled him back. "Nick, don't. We can't go in there."

He pulled harder. "Yes, we can."

I was as meek as a mouse going up the steps, smiling at the doorman as if I had toothache. He looked us up and down imperiously.

This is it... He can see we're imposters, smell our lack of money...

But he produced a curt smile and opened the door for us.

"Good afternoon, Sir. Madam."

My bottom lip hung limply. *Okay, so we made it in...*

Nick took me over to the front desk which was in keeping with the beautiful original nineteen-twenties design.

"Nick?..." I whispered imploringly.

An impeccable man who looked to be in his fifties wearing a black suit stood behind the desk. To me, the expression on his face said; *'Oh dear God, am I going to have to deal with this?'*

He lifted his head and addressed Nick down his nostrils. "Sir?"

"Yes, I have a room booked in the name of Nick Palmer."

The concierge's eyebrows rose to the centre of his forehead and stayed there.

Mine followed suit as I stared disbelievingly at Nick.

Behind the desk, he was clicking a mouse and glancing down as his eyebrows slowly lowered.

"Yes, Mr. Palmer. You've been upgraded by personal request of the manager."

He raised his finger to summon a bell boy, just as an elderly jewelled lady holding a small yappy dog entered the reception area. The bell boy came over rapidly, and the concierge had to raise his voice to be heard over the yapping.

"Do you have any bags, Mr. Palmer?"

I stood stock still in stunned disbelief, staring at the noisy little dog.

"No," Nick answered.

"Would you take Mr. and Mrs Palmer to suite 205?" He handed the bell boy some keys.

The small dog lurched up and over the desk, taking hold of the concierge's suit cuff in his teeth and shaking his head from side to side. The concierge looked horrified.

"Rufus!" The lady reprimanded.

We were led away listening to the scene. I felt like we were in a movie as we entered the lift. The bell boy stared dead ahead. I stared at Nick, who was still smiling. The bell pinged and the doors opened on the fourth floor, and we were led down the posh corridor until we stopped at the door marked **205**. The boy used the key and opened it to reveal a small slice of heaven. We walked slowly in, looking around us in awe.

"Will that be all, Sir?"

"Yes, thank you," Nick replied, tipping him.

The door closed, and I turned to Nick. "Is this a dream?... Can you pinch me?"

"I can do a lot more than that, Mrs Palmer." He drew closer to me.

Gorgeous cut flowers adorned the cream and mint coloured suite and their fragrance filled the air.

"Are we... Are we..." I didn't really know what I was trying to ask.

"Yes, we are staying the night. You can lay in a bit in the morning and go straight to work. Dinner is served at eight." He bowed slightly.

"I... okay, but I can't wear this." I panicked, as I looked down at my drab work attire.

Nick curled his index finger, beckoning. "Follow me."

Across the room, he opened pale mint double doors to reveal the bedroom. A huge king-sized bed featured in the centre of the room. I ran over girlishly, stopping straight away when I saw the two outfits laid out on each side.

For him there was a black tuxedo with a white shirt and black tie. On the other side lay a beautiful dark blue dress. Simple and elegant, the material looked exquisite. I gasped and looked at Nick, as I tentatively reached for the dress. Cool, pure silk slid through my hands. It had a daring low neckline on the front, and the back was exposed and open. I held it against me and stared at Nick, who was leaning against the door frame, enjoying my reactions.

"I don't get it... All this must have cost a small fortune. Why?"

"Because you deserve it. We need a treat, you've been through a lot lately. I wanted to make something nice."

I blinked rapidly, attempting to stem the tears. "I think it's a bit more than nice..."

Nick ran across the room and threw me on the bed. He ignored my half-hearted attempts to complain he was crushing the dress, and made passionate love to me. His young but expert hands found the exact places to transport me amongst the clouds.

Afterwards, I ran naked to the en-suite bathroom, gasping "Wow!" as I got there. The oversized room was totally decked out in cream marble. A round bath sat in the corner and gold taps glittered. Tons of complimentary products surrounded the toilet and bidet. A vase full of white and mint-green flowers was balanced on a tiny circular marble table.

"Phewww..." Nick let out a low whistle behind me and slid his arms round my waist. He pressed his flawless, soft skin against me and kissed my shoulder. "Let's have a bath. I think we've got time."

"Yeah." I skipped over and began to fill it.

Nick quickly checked the time. "We've only got twenty minutes, so it'll be a bit tight."

I bent over to feel the temperature in the tub, smiling. "Not as tight as my poor Minnie."

Nick joined me and we poured all the complimentary bubble bath bottles in, watching as the bubbles rose higher, and higher. Then we slipped in, our toes touching in the middle. As the bubbles bobbed just below our necks, Nick spotted a small panel of buttons on the wall. He reached up and pressed one and the faint sound of a motor somewhere was accompanied by jets of water round us.

"Wicked! It's a jacuzzi."

"Oh, Nick. This is so unbelievable. I don't know what you did to get an upgrade, but I'm loving it."

He pursed his kissable red lips together. "Well, Lucy. This..." He raised his hands in the air. "Could be a sign of things to come." He brought his hands back down under the water and ran them down my thighs.

"Okay, Mr. Mysterious. Spill it."

His boyish excitement was clearly visible as he lowered his voice. "I couldn't believe it myself, Lucy. When I came in this morning to book a room, I was feeling way out of my depth too. The guy on reception looked at me as if I was a stray dog who'd accidentally got past the doorman. I thought; *Fuck him, my money's as good as anyone else's...* So I asked for what I wanted, and as he was taking my name down, another older guy behind the desk, who was talking to one of the maids, turned round when I repeated my name. He said; 'Excuse me, Sir, but did you say Nick Palmer?' 'Yes?' I said, puzzled. 'I'll deal with this personally,' he said, and dismissed the other guy. 'Mr. Palmer, please let me introduce myself. I am Mr. Cohen. I'm the manager of this hotel, and I'm very good friends with Mr. Bernstein...'" Nick paused for breath. "Well, Lucy. I didn't have a clue what he was talking about, and that was apparent to Mr. Cohen, who then elaborated for me and told me he'd already bought the song and he liked it very much." Nick sat back a bit, shaking his head in disbelief at it all. "I never knew writers could get the rock star treatment."

My heart swelled with pride for him. "See? You *are* amazing. He upped your room. It's like a fairytale."

He slid over to me, cutting a valley through the bubbles and kissing me passionately, before releasing me reluctantly. "We'd better get out and get dressed for dinner."

"Yes darling. One had better," I said, putting on my poshest accent.

We dried ourselves off and I went through to get the dress and my bag, which luckily held my emergency make-up and hair clips. My work shoes were black with a slight heel, so they went with the outfit. Nick was changing in the bedroom, and both of us shouted the odd comment between rooms.

I pinned my hair up and applied neutral make-up. Cool, exotic silk slid slowly over my skin, over my head, and down my body as I carefully slipped the dress on. The feeling was sexual, as if two sets of the softest hands were skimming my sensitive skin. The material clung provocatively to me, ending halfway down my thigh where it tickled me faintly.

I could hear Nick cursing in the other room. "Fucking things..."

"What?" I called through.

"These ties. I never can seem to do them properly," Nick said, his voice behind me.

I spun to face him, and a cold tingle ran through my body when I saw how good he looked. I'd never seen anyone look *that* good. My eyes slowly beheld the vision before me.

Nick stopped playing with his tie. "Oh my God!"

I started and looked down at myself, crinkling my eyes with concern. "Oh no. What's wrong?"

"Are you joking? - I've never seen anything look so right," he said, smiling.

"Snap. But if we don't leave in two minutes, we won't be." I went to him and did his tie up. Our eyes were swimming with pride and love for each other.

"Nick, I don't know if you're aware of this, but you hold my whole life in the palm of your hand..."

Nick said nothing.

"I know that's a ridiculous statement for a woman of forty-three to make." I immediately felt embarrassed that I'd said it.

"Lucy, I feel exactly the same. Since you came into my Life, I feel alive. That sounds like such a cliche, but it's true. It scares me shitless, the thought of losing that energy." He took my hand and gallantly kissed the back of it. "Shall we go?"

I nodded my head, unable to speak.

We got into the lift where a porter pressed the button, taking us up two floors. As we stepped out, a Maître D holding a menu came over to welcome us.

"Name please, Sir?" Nick told him and he nodded his head servilely. "Right this way, Mr. Palmer."

As we ascended the marble steps, Nick and I exchanged looks of shock. The massive roof was made completely from glass. Huge potted palms climbed towards it while a man played a white grand piano below. We followed silently up a small wrought iron spiral staircase, which led to an oval balcony that overlooked most of the other tables whilst being totally private.

Our chairs were pulled out for us, the Maître D pulled the champagne out of the ice bucket and turned over our champagne flutes, popping the cork and expertly pouring. "Courtesy of Mr. Cohen."

Nick and I sat dead still. Personally, I was afraid of what I would be like in such a delicate space. For someone as clumsy as me the whole environment was fraught with danger. We were each handed a menu.

"Your waiter this evening, François, will be over presently to take your order." The Maître D bowed promptly and departed.

"Shitting hell!" Nick whispered. He took his glass and held it up.

We clinked our glasses together. "Shitting hell!" I toasted.

Both of us grinned as we sipped the exquisite bubbly. My nose wasn't crinkling much so I knew it was a very good champagne.

"You do look like a star," I said, blushing faintly.

"Then let's pretend we are, Mrs Palmer."

I dissolved every time he called me that. We clinked our glasses together again, and the rest of the evening blurred into a conveyor belt of culinary delights. The plates that arrived were arranged like such works of art that it seemed a shame to destroy them.

By the time coffee, chocolate, and mints were served, I was quite tipsy, and very full up. Some time during the course of the meal, Nick had reinvented us as Lord and Lady Fobbsbury, from a stately home in Buckinghamshire. We giggled throughout the whole thing, behaviour quite unbecoming of almost royalty. We decided we'd acquired our fortune from the pickle business, all kinds of pickles. We had two children attending public school - Bertie, and Larup. I almost spat my expensive drink out when Nick said that. Both of us were very good at adopting posh accents.

I sat back, sipping my coffee. "Nick?..."

He smiled, knowing our charade was being put on hold.

"Thank you. No-one's ever done anything like this before. It's truly special."

Nick leaned forward and the light from the candle danced across his face, catching his eyes. "Then they were fools."

I took the hand he had hurt, now that the swelling and bruising had gone down. "I know what I want. I've just never had anyone else know what I desire." The coffee suddenly became completely insignificant. "Can we go to our room? - I need you."

Nick rapidly signed the bill without letting me see how ludicrously expensive it had been, but it was worth every single penny to me. Our love-making was torrential, insane and consuming. We ravaged each other all night, and everywhere possible in the suite, finally falling asleep exhausted in each other's arms on the giant bed. I was blissfully unaware that I hadn't set an alarm. My dreams were full of magic and fantastic fairy tales, always with Nick as the prince, rescuing me from every swooning scenario.

When my eyes eventually fluttered open, I looked around quickly to make sure it had all been real. The prince still lay asleep next to me. I propped myself up with one hand and felt a tinge of heaviness. While I stared at the unconscious Adonis, perhaps five minutes passed before I realised I had to go to work.

Shit!...

I rolled over to the edge of the bed and grabbed my mobile, trying to focus my eyes on the time. The digits '*8:50*' floated together, and I blinked.

Oh no! I'm late...

I groaned quietly and replaced my phone.

Oh well..., I thought, as I rolled back over towards Nick, *If I'm going to get a written warning, I might as well make it count...*

I wasn't about to spoil everything by rushing away from the nicest thing that ever happened. I cuddled into Nick and allowed myself to doze off again, listening to his soft breathing.

Untold time passed before I felt Nick's body stirring. His heavy eyelids flinched with the movement as his gorgeous thick lashes fluttered open.

"Morning, Beautiful."

"Hiya, Handsome." I touched his face gently. "I'm a bit late for work..."

Nick tried to rise, but I pushed him back down.

"But I don't care. I'm ordering breakfast in bed, and this one's on me."

Passion overtook us, and it was more than another hour before I was able to pick up the receiver and order room service. Fresh strawberries and croissants were brought along with the coffee. I answered the door in my complimentary robe which had deeper pile than the shag rug on my living room floor. I signed the bill without peeking, before discarding the robe in order to serve breakfast in bed naked.

Clutching a rose stem between my teeth, I entered the bedroom carrying the tray and swaying my hips slowly. Nick was sitting up, both hands behind his head and a white sheet draped across his groin. His perfect biceps twitched. Michaelangelo himself probably turned in his grave with a yearning to be resurrected, just so he could paint this Greek God.

I placed the tray across from him. "Breakfast, your Highness?"

As I slid carefully next to him he brought his arms down, gently stroking my arm and giving me goose bumps.

"God, Lucy. You look so youthful. No-one would ever think you're forty-three. Never..."

He poured the coffee while I blushed.

"And your body is better by far than all the girls I've ever been out with." He handed me a cup.

I had been mildly curious about where I rated, but I didn't really care about his ex's.

"Have you been out with that many, Nick? You were with Jenny for a long time." I hoped he didn't mind me asking.

"I'm not the kind of man who keeps count, but honestly, a few." He shot me a sideways glance as he put his cup back on the tray. "Jenny and I went to the same school together, but we were in different classes. We also took the same bus every day. In the beginning I didn't really notice her, and she didn't seem to see me either. By the time I was fifteen I'd already gone out with about six girls in my class and I knew it couldn't continue. I could feel the hate emanating from all of them, along with the realisation that I wanted older women, not manic, giggling schoolgirls. So at sixteen, I was hanging round in the local pubs, meeting older women..."

It was his turn to blush as he cut the croissants and continued talking without looking at me.

"Sorry to say, but I have got my father's genes."

I leant forward, and kissed him on the cheek. Never in a millennium could Nick be as bad as David had been. I sipped my coffee smugly.

"Don't get me wrong, Lucy. Everyone always knew my intentions. I didn't want anything serious, I was far too young. But I was driven by a massive sex drive, so I dated, and had a few one-night-stands. Thinking back, it was actually only a couple of months before school finished that I noticed Jenny. She started to stand out against the other girls. Always quiet, controlled and very neat. So I began to make a point of smiling at her, smiles to which she reciprocated in kind. Then I really noticed her, her smile brought out her prettiness. When school ended..." Nick turned to look at me while he handed me a croissant.

"Go on," I urged.

He twisted his body round so he could face me. "After that summer, in the September, I started a one year diploma in forestry at the local college. Well, Jenny was there doing secretarial."

Aha! - Hence why she got the bloody job...

"So, we were on the bus together again twice a day. For a year we just exchanged little pleasantries and occasionally I sat next to her on the bus, but I had no idea she liked me. College was great though, let's just say I had a Good time." He shrugged his shoulders and tried to look innocent. "But when I was seventeen, one day as she sat beside me, I just thought - *Why not?...* Immediately she said yes, and for the next year we saw each other casually, although she knew I was sleeping with other girls, so nothing really sexual happened between us. I'll be honest, Lucy..." He closed his eyes momentarily, pausing. "it was that which made me finally commit to her. We were definitely an item by my eighteenth birthday. At first I loved her control, her knowing exactly what she wanted made her appear much more mature than her years. She very much had that girl-next-door look going on, which at first, again, I found very appealing. We went on holiday to France, and it bowled me over that she could speak the language so fluently, being sociable with everyone. My parents loved her. Everyone loved her, but I did not. For two years it seemed like we were permanently together. She told me countless times that she loved me, and well, in the end I felt the pressure was too great *not* to say it back, so I did. But I never meant it." Nick chewed slowly for a moment.

I could feel a small part of him really regretted it.

"Nick, we're all guilty of that. - Saying we love someone when we don't."

"But it doesn't excuse it, Lucy."

I sighed, knowing he was right.

"Anyway, at twenty, I knew it had to end. By then I hated her trying to control everything, never wanting the same adventures I wanted, and always saying I had to grow up. There was no way I wanted

350

to live my life like that, so we broke up. It was hard telling her the truth. We'd meet for drinks and she would say we had remained good friends, but in my heart, it didn't feel like Jenny wanted that. Occasionally, shamefully, we would sleep together, and on my twenty-first, we did, which pushed us back together on and off for the next year. Just after I was twenty-two, I decided enough was enough. On the face of it she seemed to take it well, which I know was just an act, but since then she's put herself in my Life as much as she can. Even though she saw me taking girls back to my parent's... " He shook his head. "And now she's put herself in the life of the woman who I *do* love." He chewed his bottom lip.

Picking up a strawberry, I rolled it along his lips. "To be honest, Nick Palmer, I'm relieved you were a bit of a slut. If it'd only been Jenny before me, I would have felt like I was the re-bounder..."

I popped the strawberry in my mouth and sucked it suggestively, to make him smile.

"Did she lose her virginity to you?" I managed to ask with a mouthful of juice.

He nodded.

I took another berry and did the same thing again, Nick put the tray on the floor, and nothing more was said about Jenny.

We had to rush to make it out of the room by midday. I was wearing yesterday's old dull work clothes as I packed the beautiful dress carefully into my bag. We held hands in the lift and walked together to reception. The same man was looking neat as usual behind the desk, accompanied by a younger, but equally immaculate colleague. The man who'd dealt with us the previous day was smiling curtly.

"Mr. and Mrs Palmer. I do hope you have enjoyed your stay with us?"

"Very much," Nick answered.

"Would you like to attend to the account, Sir?"

"Yes."

"Oh," I interjected. " But I'd like to pay for breakfast, please?"

"Certainly, Madam." He signalled the other man, who was clicking away on a computer. "Mr. Lewis, if you could attend to Madam's bill?"

Nick shot me a look.

"No argument," I reiterated.

"No, Madam," Nick said, and grinned.

"Room two-O-five?" the older man asked Nick. "Sir, if you would?"

He moved towards another computer at the far end of the desk.

Mr. Lewis carried on typing with his manicured hands and nails. He had dark auburn military cut hair and a long thin pointed nose, under which sat a mouth with no lips to speak of, just thin lines in an insipid pale pink. He looked as if he had been birthed right here behind this reception desk, and brought up by the staff. I would have preferred being weaned by wolves myself, although I was sure Mr. Lewis could lick his own balls clean.

I tranced out staring at Nick, who was handling the bill adroitly.

"Madam?" Mr. Lewis's nasal voice cut in.

I turned my attention day-dreamily back to him. "Yes?" My eyes were still glancing sideways as I held Nick in my field of vision.

In a low voice, Mr. Lewis said; "In total, Madam, your bill comes to two hundred and sixteen pounds."

"Yes?..." I answered vacantly.

Mr. Lewis coughed slightly, gaining my attention.

"Oh, sorry. Can you say that again?" I was thinking - *Two... sixteen... Two pounds, sixteen pence? That's an odd amount...*

Mr. Lewis raised his grey-green eyes to the ceiling. "The bill, Madam, is two hundred and sixteen pounds."

For a second, it didn't compute. "Oh, I'm sorry. I'm just paying for breakfast."

Mr. Lewis tried to purse what lips he had. "That *is* for breakfast, Madam."

An allergic reaction spread through my nervous system as I grappled with my disbelief, the effort making me twitch. I eyed him as if he'd just slipped his hand down my knickers. I slapped my hand on the counter and leaned over, darting my eyes left and right.

"Could you... Could you just check that for me please?" I asked in a low voice.

Mr. Lewis's right eyebrow arched perfectly as he stared at me and wished he didn't have to deal with this commoner. He looked at his screen. "One bowl of strawberries. Two croissants and a pot of coffee..." He looked back at me. "Yes?"

Wild-eyed and puzzled, I repeated it back slowly like London's prize idiot. "Strawberries... croissants... coffee..."

His colour dropped a shade as if this incident was draining his soul. "Yes."

"Nothing else?" I whispered.

"No, Madam. Nothing." He sighed deeply with the frustration of having to deal with this pathetic earthling. "Well, there were two mints, but they were complimentary." He threw me a patronising smirk.

"Two hundred and sixteen pounds?" I repeated again.

"Yes, Madam." He was becoming impatient with me.

People were hovering in the background, waiting for service and enjoying the show.

It was almost everything I had in the bank. I wondered if they'd flown in Jamie Oliver to make a breakfast that would normally cost me a fiver. We hadn't even eaten it all. All in all it seemed like an expensive fuck.

"Two hundred and..."

"Madam," Mr. Lewis interjected. " The amount will not reduce if you keep repeating the figure."

My eyes narrowed in order to view better the serpent before me.

"Everything okay?" Nick's voice came from beside me, making me jump.

"No," I answered quickly. "I'm, I'm paying the breakfast bill."

"Madam hasn't actually got to that part yet, Sir." Mr. Lewis said, his nasal scoff rising a notch.

I fixed a look of hatred upon him as I opened my bag to get out the dreaded credit card. "It's fine, really. Here..." I offered it to the insipid creature over the desk.

He curled his fingers round and pulled, but I didn't seem to want to let go. His eyebrow arched as he pulled harder. Finally I let go and heard his fingers on the keyboard.

I looked at Nick, making my eyes cross and poking out my tongue. I was trying to show that it didn't bother me. Nick guffawed, causing Mr. Lewis to shoot us both a look of loathing as he handed me my card back.

"Ms. Bowman?" His eyes glinted like a guillotine's razor edge. "And if you could just sign here?" He handed me a pen and an invoice.

I signed it without looking and handed it back. The machine made some noises, and Mr. Lewis tore off my receipt.

The thin line of his mouth didn't move as he handed it to me. "Good day to you both."

I snatched it from him and before we turned to leave, unable to help myself, I leant over the counter.

"Cocksucker," I said, low under my breath and directed straight at Mr. Lewis.

He smiled slightly. "Thank you, Madam. Did you work that out from the way I type?" and turned his back to me.

Linking arms, Nick and I exited from a fairy tale that even Mr. Lewis couldn't spoil. When I thought how much breakfast had been, I shuddered to think how much Nick had just spent, although not even that had spoiled it. I decided nothing and nobody would be able too steal this feeling from me. Nick walked me to the tube platform so I could get to work by about 2pm. I let one train go, not bearing to be parted from Nick.

When the next one came, Nick said; "Look. Go, Lucy. I'll be there when you come out."

"I love you," I called out, as I jumped on. "I don't care what happens."

And it's a good job that I didn't.

My entrance into the office was perfectly timed to receive my bollocking, as all the staff were returning from lunch. As soon as I walked in, Jenny walked past with Maureen Little. Maureen was panting and grunting as she hauled her heavily pregnant body up the stairs.

"Good morning, Lauren," sang Jenny, in a convincingly chirpy voice.

"Good afternoon, ladies." I beamed back, my performance equally as good.

I let them go ahead of me, not caring while I was still re-living last night in my head.

Still in a dream-world, I knocked on Mr. Forrester's door.
"Come in."

He sounded easy, but as I opened the door his face changed immediately.

"Close the door, Miss Bowman. Take a seat."

His tone had changed completely now, as he played the baddie, the 'He's behind you,' type in a pantomine. He pulled his chair in and opened a drawer, retrieving a form and placing it ominously in front of him.

"I don't even want to know your excuse for being late today, Miss Bowman." He eyed the paper.

354

"I have no excuse, Mr. Forrester," I said, with maybe a touch too much happiness.

"I must say this bravado attitude is surprising, considering I am about to give you a written warning."

I shrugged my shoulders. "I know, Mr. Forrester. But truthfully, I just don't care. I've just had the best night of my Life, and I'm emphatically in love."

Sitting forward, he began to write immediately, and slid it over to me. "So I see you haven't taken my advice to grow up, then?"

What a stuffy old fart.... I took my warning and stood up. "What, and turn into something like you?... I'd rather drink Maureen Little's baby flavoured piss."

As I walked out, I thought maybe I'd gone a step too far. I felt the looks as I walked to my desk, but I didn't care. I was too high for any of them to reach. I settled in my chair and texted Nick, once again professing my love. I thought about how I'd changed into one of those putrid love-sick people, the people I'd normally run a mile from but now I wanted to run towards, gushing and proclaiming about how wonderful love can be. I viewed those who did not have It with a kind of smug contempt. Nick texted me back, saying he'd gone to a friend's place, as it was only three hours until I finished.

What friend? Who does he know round here? No, nothing can spoil this...

Ms. Pacman kept me company all afternoon, and once again I flew from the building at five on the dot. My Prince Charming was standing, chatting to a couple of people. I ran over and realised it was Nora and Jonathan, who were both laughing.

"Darlink!..." Nora called, opening his arms and drawing Nick's attention to my presence.

I walked into his hug.

"Can you believe who came to see Nora?" He released me and grabbed Nick's arm, patting his hand. "Ahhh..." Nora sighed.

"Hey, Sis." Jonathan put his hand up. "I'm crashing at Nora's. Couldn't stand it at home."

I smiled as apologetically as I could by way of reply, and went to Nick and kissed him, just as Jenny walked by with Janice Croft. Jenny's demeanour seemed unchangeable, and I shuddered at her control. However, I felt strong with my three musketeers to accompany me to the train.

"So, Nick says he was coming to meet you, and we think okay, let's come," Nora said, chatting away.

"We're going to Soho," Jonathan commented sneakily.

I asked Nick if he'd told them what he'd done for me and he modestly admitted he hadn't.

So I managed to relay most of it before they had to get off at their stop. Nora said it was the most romantic thing he'd ever heard of, and that he was going to kidnap Nick and take him to a desert island to exist on a staple diet of Rohypnol and Viagra. That sent us all into hysterical laughter.

"Dude! Sounds like it cost a fortune," was all Jonathan could say.

"I don't care about the cost," Nick answered, shyly.

"Hope you got your money's worth, man," Jonathan said to Nick whilst grinning and winking at me. "That's one expensive fuck."

"Jonathan, please. I *am* your Sister, not a high class Ho."

Nora caught the giggles and still hadn't shaken them when their stop came. "Adios!..." He sang.

Jonathan's departing word; "Laters..."

"You are full of surprises... Going round to Nora's?" I teased, as soon as we were alone.

Nick shrugged. "I like Nora, he makes me laugh. Also it's great practice for my Spanish."

I hugged him tightly all the way home. I felt so safe I was oblivious to the set of eyes that followed us as we went up the front steps of my building.

STARK REALITY

That Wednesday I was still floating, but I made it to work on time. Still glowing inside, I'd got up early and made an extra effort to look good. Not for anyone else, just for me. I wanted to look as good on the outside as I felt on the inside. Nick saw me and said he thought none of the men would be able to work. My hair was straightened and smelt fresh. I wore sheer tights underneath a small blue pleated skirt and a white shirt with a high collar and turned up cuffs, one button too many undone to show my wonder-bra. High heels completed the look. Nick tried to grab me, but I regretfully resisted him, knowing then my luck would end.

Nick was right, my look did cause some stares. Even Phil couldn't help himself, coming over to my desk on some trivial matter so he could stare down my top and call me '*babe*'.

"Have you finished?... Or would you like some popcorn?" I asked, indignantly.

Phil looked up into my face, grinning. "I wouldn't mind unloading some pram jam in-between those beauties."

But even Phil's coarseness couldn't spoil my mood. I attempted to get some work done, staying at my desk for lunch despite Dave's pleading to go for a drink.

Around three-thirty, Nora texted me to say that Desire had entered the Top 40 charts, and adrenaline flowed through my body.

Just past four, the doors opened and in strode Lawrence Cole. I smiled and waved from the coffee machine.

"Lawrence!" I called as I went over.

"Good day, Lauren. It's Sergeant Cole today though." He was holding a sheaf of paper.

"Oh." *It's an official visit...*

But he still looked me up and down slowly. "I'm..." He coughed. "just going to see your boss."

"About me?"

He smiled softly. "No. It's police stuff."

Lawrence knocked on Mr Forrester's door, while I returned to my desk.

Only moments later, he re-emerged and handed me a MISSING poster. It was a girl called Helen Cuttering, *Fifteen years old and last seen leaving Stonehill Secondary on the tenth of September, in the Forest Hill area. Anyone with any information to call this number. All calls strictly confidential.*

I stared at the picture. She was a pretty, smiling girl with chestnut-brown hair. My mood ebbed slightly as I looked back up at Lawrence, feeling sorry for him and the darker side of his job.

"Poor girl... I hope she's alright."

"I'm giving these to everyone. We have to broaden our search. I wonder..." He looked down, momentarily unsure, just being Lawrence. "If you could help me hand them out to all your staff? Maybe introduce me to *Miss Setterton*?" He whispered her name.

I stood and smiled for a second as I contemplated his cunning, before we went round together so Lawrence could introduce himself, and ask everyone to be aware and on the lookout for Helen. He was very professional, almost dashing. He left the best for last, going over to where Maureen and Jenny sat at their workstations, awaiting their turn with the mystery visitor.

"Mr. Cole, this is Maureen Little..." I held out my hand. "And this is Jenny Setterton," I said, in the most neutral voice I could muster.

"Miss Little." Lawrence nodded in greeting and then faltered for a second as he looked at Jenny. "Miss Setterton... er..."

The corners of Jenny's mouth turned up slightly and her rosy cheeks blushed even redder. Her eyes lingered upon Lawrence a fraction of a second longer than she intended, and she quickly turned back to her computer screen.

"I'm Sergeant Cole, from Holborn station. I deal with missing persons..."

He had both women's full attention as he handed them each a MISSING poster.

"So if you see or hear anything at all, please call this number and it'll go straight through to me."

Maureen placed her poster carefully on her desk, and rubbed her hands over her swollen belly.

"I'm sorry, officer. I need to go to the ladies room. Since baby's got bigger he's pressing on my bladder... Pee-ing for England, I am."

She rolled off, leaving all three of us with a vivid image in our heads.

I was wondering why it is, that as soon as women become pregnant they feel the need to inform everyone about every personal gruesome detail; 'My vagina's grown huge since I've been pregnant.' 'I'm getting this brown discharge, but the doctor says it's normal.' 'From seven months on I had huge blue veins all over my breasts.' 'My clitoris is like a bruised grape.'

Pissing always seems to feature prominently, and it doesn't even stop with pregnancy. From the birth onwards the obsession is transferred to the new mini-me, and we are informed about baby's first word, first hair, first tooth and first piss in a potty, shortly followed by the inevitable first poo. My mind was going off on a tangent, wondering what was next.

Jim's first wank? Jim's first fuck? A sample of Jim's first ejaculation? Perhaps a frozen stool from when little Jim first mastered the alchemist's riddle and operated a toilet? Jim's first pube?...

359

Jenny's voice floated into my psychedelic consciousness, and I heard Lawrence say;

"Well, that would be most helpful, Miss Setterton."

I had no idea what was going on. "What would be?" I asked no one in particular.

Maureen waddled, puffing, back to her desk.

"Miss Setterton lives in the area, so I'm going to give her a lift," Lawrence said.

For a second I didn't know what to say. "Are you allowed to take civilians in a police car?" I asked, sounding almost sulky.

"I have my own car, Miss Bowman. This is my own time now."

"Oh." I was vexed until a light-bulb glowed dully. *Ahhh, then he'll know where the witch lives...* I smiled broadly. "Great idea. I hope Miss Setterton can help."

I walked off leaving him there. It was nearly five so I switched off my computer and got ready to go. Lawrence stayed at Jenny's desk, chatting. For once, she was ready to leave before me, and exited briskly with Sergeant Cole.

I allowed a couple of minutes so I didn't catch them up, before I went downstairs and peeked through the smoked glass on the double doors.

Just Nick...

I pushed the door open with fresh vigour, sped out, and kissed him hard before he could speak.

"Wow!... Thanks," Nick said when I released him. He sucked his lips for a second and ran his hand through his hair.

"What's wrong?"

"Did I just see Lawrence Cole and Jenny leaving together?"

"Yeah. I'll tell you about it while we walk."

And I did.

"Did she say anything to you then?" I asked.

"Nah, she totally ignored me. But Lawrence nodded his head in my direction."

We were still chatting as we walked in to my street.

"Wouldn't it be great if Lawrence and Jenny got it together." I laughed, ironically.

Nick put the key in the door and turned it. "Then somebody's heard my prayers."

As he opened the door, out of the corner of my eye, for a split second I thought we were being watched.

Don't be so paranoid...., I thought, as I stepped through the entrance.

Light rain became heavy and torrential. We got the duvet from the bed and pushed the coffee table out of the way to make a lounge bed in order to watch movies in all our naked glory. While I made tea, previews on the telly showed Frankie Bubbles face behind the presenter. *"Tomorrow at eight, our interview with... Yes! The king of Electro Blues - Frankie Bubbles!... He's here to talk about his new single; Desire. Only on Four Digital."* A sample of the song played before the next set of adverts cut in.

Nick looked up at me, while I stood dumbfounded holding the teas.

"Wow. Wouldn't it be cool if we got to meet him?"

I bent down and put the tea on the floor. "I know our lives seem like a Hollywood movie sometimes, but I don't think it'll come to that."

"Ahhh, a pessimist," Nick said, pushing his plump bottom lip out.

I lay down next to him. "No, okay, you're right. I can see him here now - Alright, Frankie? Fancy some fish fingers and chips?"

Nick poked me in the ribs and we carried on watching TV and drinking tea until we both fell asleep.

The TV was still on when I awoke.

Time! Time! What's the time?... I searched frantically for my mobile. *Six-thirty. Whew...*

I turned the telly off and continued with my favourite pastime; staring at Nick. I wanted him, and I pulled the sheet off gently. My lips teased over the golden sacred cock. Nick moaned slightly, stirring from his slumber as I intensified my worship. His crescendo mounted and he bucked up, arching his hips as he came. I kissed all the way up his stomach and gazed into his face.

"Shit!... Can I order that every morning?" He was panting hard.

I rolled next to him, content just to watch his chest rise and fall.

"My God, you're good at that," he said.

I was ridiculously pleased with myself.
"Most girls suck it like a senile porn star."

He made me giggle, and after five minutes of kissing and hugging Nick was ready to make love to me.

I just about made it to work on time, by running from the tube station. As I rounded the corner I stopped dead. There in front of the building sat Lawrence's car, and Jenny was getting out of it. I held my breath and waited for her to go in and him to leave. I dared not hope they had got on as well as it appeared.

Rushing to my desk, I texted the gossip to Nick, who texted back;
yip yip, let's fucking hope so! :-)

The rest of the day passed slowly. In the afternoon I had a highly uncomfortable but mercifully short meeting with Forrester, however at least it took my mind off Nick's absence for a while. Throughout the day I stole occasional glances in Jenny's direction, but she always seemed to be hiding behind her computer screen.

I got ready to leave at five forty-five and sat in my coat hoping Forrester wouldn't come out. While I sat there my phone beeped to tell me I had a message. It was from Lawrence;
sorry Lauren, I did intend to have a quiet word with Jenny, but she is a lovely girl. I think you have nothing to worry about. Lawrence.

I left the building five minutes early, on a high, knowing Nick would be there to elevate my soul as soon as the double doors closed behind me.

That night, instead of going straight home, we explored the West end of London, getting off at Piccadilly Circus and walking up Old Compton St. into the heart of Soho. We drank too many shots of tequila and had so much fun that we didn't get in till it was gone 1am. We fell into bed, both happily drunk, and shagged sloppily.

362

I woke with the alarm, glad it was Friday, and lay in bed holding Nick, as always feeling a wrench with our parting. He was sleeping so heavily I didn't want to wake him, so I grabbed my clothes and took them through to the front room to get ready.

As I shut the front door quietly behind me, there was no way I could have known what was about to happen.

Rushing as usual, I rounded the corner of the street and banged hard into a man coming the other way. Slightly winded, my eyes were on the floor at first.

"Oh, Oh dear!" I grabbed for breath. "So sorry..."

I looked up and pulled my head and shoulders back sharply, hyperventilating more from shock than from the collision.

I'm hallucinating... David? David?... "David?" I said, disbelievingly, shaking my head and trying to straighten up.

David stood, eyes blazing, glaring at me.

"David!" I shouted.

"Yes, Lauren?"

"Wha... What... I..."

He took my arm in a firm grip, and marched me along with him.

I started to pull and resist. "David, where are you taking me?"

He squeezed my arm harder. "You're coming with me. We need to talk, Lauren." He yanked me on. I'd never seen seen him this physically aggressive.

"David! You're scaring me." I managed to pull my arm free.

His face softened subtly and he didn't attempt to grab me again. "I just want to talk, please? There's a café nearby, we can go there." His eyes were steely grey with tiny flecks of blue in them.

"David, I have to go to work. If I don't I'll..."

"Fuck your fucking job!" he shouted. " After everything that's happened. I've come a long way. The least you can do is join me for a fucking coffee... I won't go away, Lauren. I'm not going to conveniently disappear, not this fucking time."

I sighed as I silently said goodbye to my job and went with him. David strode angrily, and I found it difficult to keep up with him. Rage spewed out behind him and encased me in its cloud. I consoled myself that at least I would be able to tell him that Jenny was here, and what she was up to. That day's grey sky began to spit rain, which only made David walk quicker. We rounded a corner and I spied a dishevelled greasy spoon café on the other side of the road.

David crossed the road and the rain became heavier.

The sign above bore the name of this high class establishment;
FRANNIE'S.

FRANNIE'S

We went inside and David headed for a small plastic table near the window. We sat down on the matching plastic chairs, I with my back to the counter, gawping at the faded, threadbare yellow checked curtains. Dust and oil was thickly encrusted along the top of the dark yellow gingham. Once they might have been vibrant curtains, luring customers in with their sunniness, but now they were the complete opposite, a warning that germs were having a huge party in there.

A stick-thin hag descended upon our table. In fact, that's not fair, a stick would have been fatter. She had jet black hair with at least three inches of grey roots showing through the grease it was stuck down with. Glimpses of skin weaved between the deep lines that covered her face. She wore a green woollen dress which was at least two sizes too big, and American tan tights which ruffled and crinkled round her ankles. The final touch of glamour was the pink fluffy mule slippers. I figured her approximate age must be somewhere between twenty-five and ninety-five. I wondered if this actually *was* poor Frannie, and felt the urge to give her some money.

"Yes?..." poor Frannie asked, clutching her notepad, her voice thick with gravel and apparent stupidity.

"Tea please," David said, without taking his eyes off me.

I smiled at her. "Coffee, please."

She clicked off in her mules without writing anything down. *Please won't someone adopt this odious minion?...*

"Lauren?..." David's voice brought me back down to earth. "Lauren?"

"Yes, David. I heard you," I snapped.

Looking at the Elvis Presley clock that hung above the door, I could see that The King's leg was telling me it was eight fifty-five, which meant I would be getting my second written warning in ten minutes.

"You looked sexy on Wednesday, when you went to work."

My head snapped straight back to David. "What did you say?"

"Got your attention now have I?"

Frannie returned to dump two cracked mugs on the table. On top of my coffee, what looked like cigarette ash circled slowly, but I was more concerned with what David had just said.

Frannie clacked off and he had my full attention.

"I see you've already got my son spending his hard earned money on fancy hotels." Venom soaked his words.

My mouth opened as I blinked, rapidly. "Have... have you been following us?"

"Yes, I have. I want my son back, Lauren."

I was dumbfounded. "Oh that's just great. Now we've got two stalkers, how popular we are." The sarcasm in my voice matched my face.

"No, you only have one. Me. I was the one who brought Jenny down here, and I'm paying for her to be here."

My mouth flapped open. "I... I..."

"It worked out better than I thought. When we looked in the paper for somewhere to stay, we saw the advert for that company you work at. I knew where you lived because Nick told me, but I simply looked up your name on Facebook, and voilà!" He held his hands up triumphantly. "It told me where you worked. I already had your work number off Mr. Warbling from when you booked the cottage." He pursed his lips as he supped his tea.

So, I was getting the old David here, with his cold, calculating *'Do as you're told'* tone.

"Please, don't let me stop you, Mr. Detective. You seem to be having so much fun."

366

He slammed the palm of his hand into the table with a THUD and leant towards me, his face close to mine and his eyes boggling. "No, it's not fucking fun, Lauren."

"Well, fuck off then," I hissed.

"You came back into my life, but I suppose it's different rules for me, I can't come back into yours?" He sat back, arms folded.

"I don't suppose Angela knows you're here, or anything about all this?"

I needed air suddenly. I pushed my chair back, and fiddled with the mug that now held lukewarm coffee I had no desire to drink.

David's forehead crinkled. "No, she doesn't. It was my idea, and I suggested it to Jenny. I had to act surprised when she told me your real name. Jenny can see there's no point involving Angela, it'd only upset her further."

"So, what was your next move, David? To have her take me out gangland style?... Maybe poison, or running me over?"

I smiled wryly at him from what seemed to have become my witness stand. I was scared to think what outcome all this could achieve.

David sipped his tea and pushed it away from him. "Nothing quite so dramatic as that. All I want is for Nick to come home."

His eyes portrayed a great sadness and I let my vexation drop a little. The rain outside pistolled down, ricocheting off the street.

"David..." My tone softened and my syllables became non-antagonistic. "I'm sorry this has happened between us, but Nick's in love. I'm in love. He wants to be with me, and he's happy." I tried to appeal to him with my blue eyes.

"I've no doubt that he is... for now. But Nick's my son, and that won't change. He's extremely close to his family, who miss him very much. His sister, Maggie, idolises him, but she doesn't understand. She's crying for Nick."

That made me look down. "But..." I raised my eyes back up slowly. "If he'd met someone else and moved in with them, he wouldn't be at home either."

David moved his thick fringe away from his forehead with a brown weathered hand. "Don't be so naïve, Lauren. If he was with someone else, he could bring them home. They could be a part of the family and Maggie would understand. What?" He raised his voice. "You think we could all sit around at Christmas, laughing and joking? Or spend quality times on bank holidays? Maybe you could bring your parents down to stay at the bed and breakfast? I'm sure they'd love to see me again..." He paused to inhale. "And as to what they'd think of me as their new Son in law's Father." He laughed ironically. "Can't you see the fucking ludicrousness of it?"

The café door opened and two old men stepped in, soaking wet. Water poured from their flat caps as they stamped their shoes, making squelching sounds. They glanced at us for a split second, before scuttling quickly to a table near the counter. They both looked how I felt.

I hated that what David had said was true. No birthdays, no Christmas or joyous gatherings. Nick was excluded because of his love for me.

I fiddled sulkily with the teaspoon. "You want him to be with Jenny. Are you jealous of us, David?"

He leant on the table with his elbows, keeping his voice low. "I don't care who he's with as long as it's not you." He licked his lips the same way Nick did, making me feel unbearable. "A tiny part of me *is* jealous, but it pales into insignificance compared with how I feel as his father. I want to protect him, stop him from making the biggest mistake of his Life."

I went to protest, but he held up his hand.

"Sorry, Lauren. There's too much riding against you both. You're twenty years older, okay we both know you don't look it, but at this age, are you thinking of children? You've avoided them so far with good reason. Nick loves children and he's always said he wants them. So not only will he sacrifice all of us, but his future kids as well... Please, Lauren. Don't be selfish. Even if you do love him, this is torture for the rest of us. Even Angela's quiet, not saying anything, and I've never seen her like that. The boys miss their brother..." He paused and his hand fell on top of mine, his eyes pleading. "I miss him. I love him. Please, Lauren. If you're in Nick's Life, you're in mine and I don't want you to be."

Tears filled my eyes and they clouded over to match my head and my heart. David was right, even if magnificent things happened to Nick they would be empty and soulless if he couldn't share that excitement with his loved ones. I was alienating him from all that, and No, I didn't want children as I didn't really like the darling creatures, but I remembered how Nick was with Maggie. He adored her, and I was keeping him away. Tears slowly dropped from my cheeks onto my lap, and David's heart softened as he wiped them away with the back of his hand.

"Sorry, Lauren. I hate seeing you cry... but there's no way out. Angela would never accept you, and with her foolish pride she'd ignore her eldest son."

I closed my eyes and wished he wasn't there to bring the rain and wash away my Life. My eyelids creaked back open. "I love him..." was all I could muster. "He wrote me a poem... that turned into a song. They play it on the radio."

David's mouth opened and closed, as Frannie clacked warily down to our table.

"Drinks?" she croaked.

"Tea," I croaked back.

"Same," David said.

She shuffled off and David shut his eyes tight, pinching his septum on his nose. He was tired, widening and rolling his eyes as he replaced his arms on the table. Thunder cracked ominously above, the Gods were on David's side.

"What song is it?" he asked.

"Desire, sung by Frankie Bubbles."

His head flicked. "I've heard that... Jesus! Nick wrote that?"

He shook his head, his face sad but his voice full of pride. Which just seemed to illuminate to me even more just how right David was.

Nick should be able to tell his family about this...

Sadness filled my cells and guilt ran through my veins. Frannie hovered in the background and both of us sat like statues as she plonked two even more foul looking mugs down. Lightning lit up the street outside, and I could hear water cascading down the gutters.

"Lauren. It may be alright for a while, but the longer it goes on, the harder it will be. Nick won't tell you if he aches for certain things, he's not like that. I'm here to tell you that he does."

I wanted David to just go away and take the pain that was creeping into me. I considered just getting up, leaving the table and running back to Nick. Block it all out. But I knew there was no running from this.

"I don't know what you think I should do. Nick loves me," I mumbled, running my fingers round the rim of the second mug that I would let go cold.

David leaned towards me again. "I know he loves you. He looked at you..." He lowered his eyes and sighed gently before returning his gaze. "The way I used to. I'm fighting hard not to let it show, even now. I've spent nearly my entire Life loving you, so I know it when I see it in someone else. He will be hurt." He gulped and licked his lips. "I am being selfless, Lauren, as any good parent would be. Nick's just starting out in his life, this love will cost him dearly."

David's eyes implored me, and I felt salty water sting my pupils. Outside, the thunder and lightning were working as a team, and day appeared to have turned to night. The weather had changed as quickly as the stroke of the pen on the devil's contract.

"Lauren, you've seen the lengths I've gone to. Please, I'm asking you to end it and be selfless. Nick won't stay where he's not welcome."

My eyes formed cat-like slits as I moved back to distance myself. "I won't do that." I shook my head with tiny movements. "No, I can't. Please, David. I can't. I won't," I snapped defiantly.

His eyes swam as he changed from emotional to angry. "For fucks sake. Have you not listened to a word I've said?... Can you NOT think of your fucking self for once?"

My mobile beeped and I retrieved it from my bag. It was from Nick;

hi gorgeous. hope u r alright. I was worried,weather is shit. miss u and love u :-*

I began to cry. *How could David even ask me to commit such a heinous act?...*

I stood suddenly, knocking the table and wobbling the mugs. Tea cascaded over the edge and onto the floor as I grabbed my jacket.

"I won't do it, David. You can't tell me what to do. I'm not a teenager any more, I'm a grown woman."

He stood quickly. "Then start acting like one."

I started towards the door.

"You can't run away from this, Lauren. This love will destroy him."

I flung the door open and ran out into the storm. I ran as fast as I could with no idea where I was running to, rain stinging my face. I looked behind me every so often in blind panic, to check David wasn't following me. It only took a few moments for the storm to drench me.

Eventually I slowed my pace, and soaked to the bone, I clutched my handbag in front of me and continued on my journey - destination unknown. I began muttering to myself; "Fuck David. How dare he? Who does he think he is?... Break up with Nick? HA!" I shouted.

This love will destroy him... David's words floated into my thoughts. *NO!, NO!... Where am I?...*

I tried to see but the heavy rain was making it difficult, not to mention my tears. I didn't know where I was, my head was scrambled.

Home, go home... called out my heart. *Yes, home...*

I ran to the end of the street I was on and peered at the name. It read; **Henchtree**.

Where the hell is that?...

I turned left, then right.

Shit.... Where am I?...

I took another right and resumed running.

Eventually, I recognised a big grey building.

Shit. Have I gone that far?...

By now I was freezing cold, my sodden wet clothes clung to me, and my shoes began to flop, enlarged from all the water they held. I walked as fast as I could, my shoes flopping like clown's feet.

I stopped and screamed loudly, took my shoes off and threw them, before I ran, sobbing and picking my pace up as I got closer. Finally I got home, and buzzed the doorbell like a maniac.

Nick opened the door. "Oh my God! Lucy..."

My teeth were chattering so much my jaw felt like it was bobbing loose. I fell into him, and he helped me into the flat.

"Fuck, what's happened?"

I couldn't get any words out. Nick sat me on the sofa and ran to get a towel, jumping the coffee table in a leap. He began to undress me, and I felt like a dumb child.

"Lucy, Please. Why are you crying? I'm going mad here. Has someone done something to you?"

Yes..., I thought. *Someone took my dream away...* I raised my hand and touched my cheek. *Yes, it's wet, and it's not raining in here...* "I... I don't feel well. So I came home," I explained, weakly.

Nick took my shirt and bra off and put a towel round me, patting me dry. He made me stand and unbuttoned my skirt.

"So, what?... You thought it would make you feel better if you walked home in a storm?" He peeled the skirt off, followed by my knickers.

"I needed some air," I said.

He helped me sit again and pulled the towel right round me. "Why are you crying then?"

I stuck out my bottom lip. "My tummy hurts." And it really did, I was in torturous pain.

"I'm going to get a blanket." He felt my forehead as he stood. "Just checking you haven't got a temperature."

As I watched him leave the room, I thought; *Kind, loving, caring, Nick... He'd make a fantastic Father...*

I realised I really would be depriving him of all that, and the chance for a child to shine under the glow of his love. I began to cry again, silently.

He came back quickly, in a hurry to be with me, and sat close, cradling my head. "Oh, baby. Can I do anything? Do you need a doctor?" I shook my head. "Okay then, you're here on the sofa. I'm making a hot lemon drink for you - Doctor Nick's on hand."

I drew back and focused on him. He was the most beautiful thing I'd ever known.

"I love you," I whispered.

If you did love him, you'd let him go... Was that a Demon or an Angel talking to me?

He laid me down and tucked the blanket round me.

"Could I have a large whisky please, Nick?"

"Hmm, do you think that will help your stomach?"

If there'd have been heroin in the house, it would have been coursing through my veins as we spoke. I wanted to numb the pain. I pouted my bottom lip and he went off and got me the large whisky, handing it to me before returning to the kitchen. I gulped it until the glass was empty, then laid my head down and closed my eyes to shut out the fear.

In my head, I could see Nick sitting at the big table in his family's kitchen back in Devon. The whole family was there, all grown older. Food was being passed happily amid constant chatter.

A woman in her early twenties sat next to Nick, and they were smiling, happy together.

'Daddy!' a small toddler called, and ran round the table to where his father sat, beaming and holding his arms outstretched.

'What is it, Jason?' Nick asked his son playfully.

'Tabby won't let me play with her toys,' Jason answered.

Nick stood, and picked up the boy. 'Well, if Daddy comes and plays as well, then your sister will have to share.'

The young woman smiled. David and Angela held hands on the table, admiring their family.

Maggie, also a young woman, got up from the table. 'Nick,

wait. I'll come and play with the kids.'

Angela got up and began to clear the table. 'Nick says you're all going to stay with your parents next weekend?'

'Yes,' the woman replied, as she rose to help.

'Lovely people. Must have them down again soon. Maybe Easter. The kids love them,' David said, and then lit a pipe.

The door to the kitchen opened and Nick came back in alone, his face ash-white where he'd been crying. He was much older now and the kitchen was empty and devoid of life, the air acrid with the smell of detergent. Nick was staring with eyes that were deep red from tears at someone seated at the table.

'I... I haven't been back here for so many years,' He stared bleakly around the room. Wearing a black mourning suit, he held out his hand. 'We'd better go then,' A bony old shrivelled hand took his, an old woman with grey hair tried to stand on her frail bones, but was finding it difficult. Nick's kind voice reached her failing ears; 'Come on, Lucy. I'll help you up.'

Then there was screaming, someone was screaming.

"Lucy! Lucy!" someone else shouted.

It was me, *I* was screaming. I sat bolt upright, sweating and breathing hard. My bulging eyes skirted the room rapidly, I was disorientated and didn't know where I was.

"Lucy, it's okay, it's okay. I'm here."

I focused slowly on Nick's real, beautiful young face.

A dream, a nightmare. A nightmare of a dream...

"Nick?"

"Yes?" He sat on the edge of the sofa and gently rubbed my back.

"I... I had a bad dream. I don't remember falling asleep."

"Yep, straight after that whisky. Come on, sit back. You really do look ill."

I sat back without argument. "Is it late?"

"No, it's only seven-thirty. Hungry?"

I pulled a face and shook my head. "I might have a bath though."

Nick smiled. "That's a good idea. Maybe I'll make some soup, in case you're hungry in a bit?"

"Mmm..." I answered, trance-like, as I got up and went to the bathroom.

I filled the bath as full as I could, the temperature almost scalding. The nightmare tormented me.

I've a right to be happy though, don't I?... Me, Me, Me... The Devil scoffed at me. *You've had your fun, you signed the contract, now it's time to pay...*

Nick poked his head round the door. "You okay?"

A thin, weak smile was all I could manage in reply.

"Only you've been in here nearly an hour an a half."

My pupils dilated with surprise. The water was almost cold. Time was becoming a foreign concept. I put on my dressing gown and headed for the sofa, where I stayed all weekend.

Throughout Saturday and Sunday Nick worried constantly. "I've never seen you like this, Lucy. It's hurting me to see you this way."

I was merged into the world in a zombie-like state, and by Sunday I was battling hard with my evil twin inside. Nick was sitting on the sofa with me. The TV was on, but neither of us were really watching it.

"Nick?"

"Yeah?"

"Do you miss your family? I know how close you all are."

He cocked his head slightly and ran his hand through his hair. "A little, but not that much." He smiled.

He's lying... He won't tell you even if you ask... David's words gnawed into me like rats feeding on a carcass.

"Do you want children, Nick?"

"Woah! What's with all the questioning?"

I lowered my eyes. "Sorry. I was... Well, I was just thinking about it."

Mild shock showed on his face. "What?... About having a baby?"

"No, that's just it, I don't want to have one. So... So, do you?"

He crinkled his forehead. "Well, it's not something I've thought about a great deal, but..." His eyelashes fluttered downward and a knife twisted in my stomach. "Well, maybe, but I love you. This is here and now, we can't predict the future."

"But if you stay with me you'd be giving that prospect up."

He shook his head. "How could I be giving something up if I've never had it?... You're not making sense, Lucy."

He scrutinised me, reaching down through the windows of my

soul and transfixing me with his gaze.

"What's happened?... Something's happened."

"Nothings happened," I responded, way too quickly.

"Is it Jenny? Did she do something on Friday morning?"

I stared at the TV screen. "No, she didn't do anything. Just ignore me, I feel really groggy."

Though I knew my answer hadn't satisfied Nick, he didn't press me any further.

This love will destroy him... This love will destroy him... David's words played like a stuck record.

I looked at Nick out of the corner of my eye and saw youth and health radiating from him. I quickly looked back at the TV, where a vision of the frail old woman from my dream had appeared.

'*You will drag his youth and spirit from him for your own selfish gain...*' Her bony finger pointed at me, and I stared back at what I was to become.

Sleep was filled with hideous nightmares. I was running scared, fighting a battle inside of me. I cried while Nick slept, so he wouldn't see what a wreck I was. I sat on the bed hugging my knees and watching Nick sleep as the tears silently fell. I wasn't sure which side had won, Dark or Light, but one of them had.

David was right, I *was* being selfish. The sacrifices Nick would have to make were just too great, it wasn't worth it for my love alone. By letting him love me, I was forcing him to forfeit his choices, to give up everything else. The price seemed way too high.

You're not worth it, give him back... He was only on loan, did you really believe it was forever? Fool... "Shhh." I hushed the Devil out loud.

His voice seemed to have become the same as David's.

He won't stay where he's not wanted...

I spent the rest of the night staring gauntly at Nick, before I quietly packed a few things that I needed to take with me. I kissed his forehead and left a note on my pillow. I held my hand to my mouth to encase the sobs of consuming grief that struggled to escape. As I shut the door, I felt I'd never feel truly alive again.

ULTIMATE SACRIFICE

Using the last of my money, I bought a train ticket. This time it didn't take me to work, but the other way. Numb as Novocaine, I stared out the window at all the houses, shops and streets speeding by.

My tears were constant, as was my internal dialogue; *Maybe I should get off at the next stop?... Go back, hold him and tell him everything is going to be alright...* But it wasn't.

Doing the mature thing hurt, but for Nick's sake, it seemed like the right thing to do. I had already convinced myself of that, since the nightmare I'd had which still haunted me.

If I leave now, some of the pain can be averted. Nick will go home, and Angela need never know who I was, and would just be pleased it has ended... His family will have him back...

I bit my lip as hard as I could, silent tears threatened to turn into bursting hysteria. I wanted to give Nick the unlimited choices he deserved. A buffet trolley rattled past as my eyes continued to glaze out of the window.

I'll never be able to eat again...

Eventually, towns turned into countryside and the familiar looking Broads with their windmills dotting the landscape. I'd entered Norfolk, and I turned my phone off knowing Nick would probably have read my note by then. It had simply said;

I will call you later.
It is all done for love.

I knew it would be impossible to explain to him face to face. My resolve would weaken, my heart couldn't cope if he was in front of me. I knew I was taking the coward's way out, but it seemed like the only way out.

In my tear factory, the ducts were on overdrive and I constantly had to wipe my cheeks.

Stupid old Lauren. You are truly something to laugh at..., The Devil spat at me. *One day he will wake up, look at you, and realise he has wasted his life...*

Bitter with regret, I held my head in my hands until I heard the name of the station I wanted; Wymondham, pronounced Wind-ham. As I stood up, I hoped my Aunt Patty would be in, and willing to take in a stray.

Aunt Patty was at home, fortunately. She opened the door looking surprised and worried as the smell of joss sticks floated out onto the doorstep.

"Lauren. What a lovely surprise..." Then she frowned. "Is everything alright?"

Without waiting for an answer she ushered me through to her conservatory, which looked as if it had been invaded by plants.

"Sorry I didn't phone, Aunt Patty, but..." My lips trembled. "Can I stay here? I'm..." My croaking voice cracked as tears began to pour.

Aunt Patty placed an arm round me, engulfing me with her floral caftan.

"Oh, my poor dear. Of course you can stay. Let me go and make you a chamomile tea for your nerves." She flowed from the room.

I sipped the tea, not wanting to talk, and then asked if I could maybe take a short nap.

Thankfully, Aunt Patty took me to the room I normally stayed in, and let me be. I curled up into a foetal position on the bed, cried myself to the point of exhaustion and fell into a fitful sleep.

When I awoke, I checked the time; *6:30pm*. Normally I'd have been home by now, with Nick. I knew this phone call to him would be the hardest thing I'd ever done. To leave without ever saying anything would be cruel, the injustice of my flight was bad enough.

I went downstairs and found Aunt Patty cross legged on a large pillow holding a joss stick in each hand.

"Oh, Lauren! Just give me a moment. I'm cleaning the negative ions from the air." She beamed her positive energy at me.

I lethargically asked if it would alright to have a small glass of wine. I knew Aunt Patty always kept some home-made plonk in the house. She frowned slightly, but told me where it was. I got a glass of elderberry and took it to my room, drinking nearly all of it in one gulp. Hands trembling and tears forming, I dialled Nick's number.

His cheerful voice answered. "Hey, you. Where are you?... What's with all the mystery?"

I opened my mouth but nothing came out.

"Lucy?"

"Nick..." I heard myself squeak in barely a whisper.

Then his question took on a troubled tone. "Lucy?... What's wrong?"

I gasped for air that didn't seem to be there. "I... I..."

I bit my lip as hard as I could, hoping it would jolt me into finding the words. My stomach churned and bile hung at the back of my throat.

"Lucy, you're scaring me... Please."

IT WILL DESTROY HIM!..., David's voice shouted, in my head.

"Nick... I've made a decision. It's... It's..."

Tiny sobs escaped me as tears dripped from my chin. I pulled my knees into my chest and hugged them with one arm.

"Lucy?" His voice was soft. "Can't you tell me to my face? Won't it wait until you get home?"

I wondered where my home was now.

Home is wherever Nick is... "I'm not coming home, for a while. I've decided that's where you should be, Nick. I think you should go home."

I screwed my eyes tightly together in an attempt to hold back the flood and listened to the silence.

Nick's tone became flat. "I was right. Something's happened. Lucy, tell me what it is?"

I didn't want to cause any more upset, or distance Nick any further from his family by telling him about his father's visit.

"Yes, Nick. Something *has* happened, I've made a decision. My... My love will cost you too much." Every word was trapped within a sob.

"Jesus Christ, Lucy!... You're not making any sense. *Not* having your love will cost me more... This time last week we were at the hotel. How did it go from that, to you thinking like this? Leaving, for fucks sake!" His voice heightened with panic. "Well, I won't go. Not until I've seen you face to face."

I could feel the Devil physically tearing my soul like tissue into infinitesimal pieces.

"Nick, it's done. I'm staying away." My voice seemed hardly audible. "I'm not even in London now. Jonathan is going to live there. I've caused him not to be able to stay with our parents, so I can try to repair one small shred of damage. It's my fault, so... go home, Nick."

"So... You don't love me?" Bitter frostiness coated his enquiry.

I rocked and convulsed in my grief. "Yes. Yes I do. That's why I'm doing this!..." I was shouting. "I don't want you to be a fucking martyr, giving this grand gesture." My voice cracked.

"I only want *you*. Please."

For now you want me, but in the future I wont be enough..., my addled mind told me.

"Jonathan will be there in the morning." My words broke away and were replaced by silence as I clamped my hand over my mouth to hold back the soul-wrenching rasps.

"I was wrong. If that's what you've decided, Lauren, then I'm gone." His voice was replaced by the dialling tone.

Instantaneously the sobbing and tears stopped. My wide, wild eyes stared at the wall, pupil's devoid of life as I clutched my phone.

It began in the pit of my stomach and travelled at high velocity, a demonic howl that metamorphosed into a banshee's high-pitched screaming. At first I was glibly unaware that Aunt Patty was next to me, unable to prise the phone from my grasp or stop the uncontrollable screaming. As she cradled me, the screams turned to sobs.

She stroked my hair. "My poor, dear child. Do you want to share it with me?"

I shook my head and she let me just cry. Eventually she got me off the floor and into the bed, where she finally managed to remove my phone from my hand.

"Lauren, I'm going to quickly make you a Valerian tea. It'll help you sleep, and it will settle your nerves."

She left the room without waiting for the confirmation that wasn't coming from me.

I turned to face the wall and hugged my knees to my chest in that ancient foetal position. The door opened and closed, the tea got left.

At two-thirty in the morning, I called my brother, robotically. It rang and rang, and eventually he answered.

"This'd better be fucking good, big Sis." He was sleepy and irritated.

"You can stay at my flat. Go there in the morning, and get the key off Nick. He's going," I informed him nonchalantly.

"W-what? What's going on?"

"Just go tomorrow morning. You can stay until I get back."

I hung up, turned the phone off and removed the battery, resuming my previous position.

After three days, Aunt Patty's pleading finally drew me out of my room. But during those three days I saw the return of old habits I thought I'd conquered long ago. My whole being rejected the idea of food. I only forced down a piece of bread with Tahini spread on it because my Aunt had refused to leave the room until I had.

Insomnia ravaged and raped me, without sleep I was in a zombie-like state, but at least there were no nightmares or dreams or images of Nick. Even the Devil was slumbering since the moment I'd died spiritually, at the end of that last call to Nick. I was only breathing and walking because I was operating on some primaeval instinct to function. I was fighting sleep using some dark low-level internal mechanism. I don't even recall going to the toilet once.

Patty led me down to the glass conservatory. A small carved wooden table was covered in fresh food; Salad, nuts, vegetables and fruit. I spotted it and swallowed hard as an acidic taste sloshed in my mouth.

I sat in a wicker chair, Patty preferring the cushion on the floor. That day she had teased her hair until it was huge and wild like a Tasmanian Devil.

"Mint tea?"

My Aunt poured it without waiting for a reply and handed it to me. I felt light-headed, and my hands shook so much I had to use both hands to take it.

"Lauren dear, I'm worried about you. All this no eating and hardly sleeping is appallingly bad for your ions. Please." Her voice was gentle and appeasing. "Let me do some Reiki on you? I can help you throw away all that negativity," she beamed.

I put my cup down and nodded dully. *Why not? I don't care about anything...*

Patty went over to the radio and turned it up. "Music's always inspiring."

She floated over and knelt on a cushion in front of me, trying to heal the un-healable.

Halfway through my therapy, a song broke the barrier and filtered through to me as Frankie Bubbles belted out Nick's song. It's bad enough listening to songs on the radio that remind you of lost love, but that feeling is intensified a thousandfold when you're listening to one that's been written just for you.

I pole-vaulted out of my chair, making Aunt Patty start and gasp.

"I can't do this," I cried, and ran back upstairs.

Once inside my room I threw myself on the bed, facing the wall as usual.

Patty came in. "Well, young lady. I think that's quite enough... Have you any idea what damage leaving in the middle of a Reiki session can do?" She reprimanded me curtly as she sat on the bed. "Lauren, please. Tell me what the bottom is going on?"

I turned round coquettishly and saw my Aunt's cheeks flushed with concern. I told her the basic, no-frills version of events, although re-living it unlocked my tears and caused them to flow forcefully once again.

I sobbed wretchedly. "So... so you see, Aunt Patty? I can't ruin everyone's lives... It was just th... The song," I croaked through tears that marched forth.

She stroked my hair again. "You poor, dear, child."

"Please, Aunt Patty. Help me... I can't stand the pain." My lips trembled.

Patty patted my shoulder and stood up. "Selfless acts and deeds are often the most painful, that is the nature of the choices you've made."

She wisped from the room, and I could hear her opening the big cabinet above the basin in the bathroom. The mirrored doors were adorned with self-help incantations, such as; YOU ARE BEAUTIFUL, SHINE FROM WITHIN, etc.

Returning, she handed me one pill. "I keep these for absolute emergencies..."

I grabbed the glass of water from beside the bed and threw it down my throat, greedy for any numbing assistance.

"to help you sleep..." was the last thing I remembered, before I fell into unknowing slumber for the next ten hours.

During the next two weeks my weight plummeted. Every time I stood up, dizziness corkscrewed through me. My only venture was to the toilet and back.

That first week my mother called to find out why Jonathan was living at mine, and to tell me how inconsiderate I'd been, not telling anyone where I was, once again. Aunt Patty fielded the call, and told my mother that I needed to energise emotionally, and she didn't know how long the process would take. I imagine she said a lot more, but good old Patty kept it to herself. My aunt's only question for me, no doubt posited by my mother, was about my job.

"Have you taken a holiday from your job, Lauren?"

I smirked, wryly. "Yes... a very long one."

One night on the second week I found Aunt Patty cross-legged outside my door, chanting.

"Oh, Lauren. Are you alright? Do you need something?"

"Er, yes... A pee?"

"Oh." She carried on chanting.

By the third week Nick's face and voice possessed me, tormenting me, and only allowing me to snatch one or two hours of randomly spaced sleep. I felt so weak most of the time, even when I was still. A skeletal look began to creep over my body, complete with dark bags under the eyes. I asked Aunt Patty for more pills, but she refused, saying that drugs were not the long term answer.

My only achievement was to manage to get to my Aunt's computer where I permanently deleted my Facebook profile. In my deluded sleep-deprived state, I thought it would help, but it only made me feel even more dead.

The beginning of the fourth week, and Aunt Patty threatened to call an ambulance, as apparently hospital is where I was headed.

"I can't just sit here while you slowly dissolve... You need help."

I decided I liked the word - 'dissolve.'

Yes! I'm dissolving... I began to laugh insanely, causing my Aunt to look even more distressed.

Half a bowl of porridge, the odd piece of fruit and one piece of toast had been the only food to pass my lips. I'd drunk a lot of Valerian tea, however.

I swung my wasted legs from the bed and noticed it was dark, and therefore probably night. I needed my hand on the dresser to help me up. My thoughts hadn't been clear for days, I was a sleep-deprived Alice in Wonderland, manifested in my Life as a serial incarnation.

I got to the door and leant on the frame, opening the door stealthily. Aunt Patty wasn't on her cushion. I used my hand to guide me along the wall to the bathroom, where I closed the door behind me, sat on the toilet and waited for nothing to happen. My bladder was hurting, complaining about my non-existent diet. I stood up, went to the basin, and leaning on the edge, cast an eye in the mirror. I was shocked when I saw who was looking back at me.

My eyes seemed to have sunken in, and black circles ringed my eyes. Smoker's yellow, paper-like skin was draped over prominent cheekbones. Looking at that image of myself sent me into despair.

Aunt Patty's basin held a variety of knick-knacks all around; Small pink rose shaped soaps, necklaces, face cream, an old teabag, some loose change and a bald nail-brush. I opened the cabinet and began looking through bottles and lotions and sanitary towels with no conscious idea why I was doing so. Behind a can of hairspray, I spied a small glass prescription bottle. I took it out and squinted at the label, though by then I already knew they were the sleeping pills. I shut the cabinet and clung to them so hard my palms began to sweat, swaying and staring, swaying and staring.

My addled mind began to form thought as I looked back at myself in the mirror.

I'm already spiritually dead... Fate started all this, it only seems fitting to end it on the same note...

I picked up one of the coins on the basin. Two choices were before me, and I decided to flip for the answer.

TAILS - Get the strength up to go to Devon and face the future.
or HEADS - ?... I glanced at the bottle of pills. *To run away forever...*

I flipped the coin and it flew high in the air before falling into the sink, still spinning. Gradually it stopped and I looked back into the mirror.

FATE had made its decision...

Soon to come ...

The next in the *Mis-adventures of a Femme Fatale* series
from Trixie Bloom - ***TWITTER ME PINK***

find out what's happening at
trixiebloom.com

<u>Playlist and credits.</u>

The Communards ~ Don't leave me this way
Abba ~ Dancing Queen
Shakin Stevens ~ This old house
Etta James ~ I just want to make love to you
Adam and the Ants ~ Stand and Deliver
Depeche Mode ~ Just can't get enough
Donna Summer ~ I need Love
Human League ~ Don't you want me, Baby
Thompson Twins ~ Hold me now
Take That ~ Back for good
Frankie Bubbles ~ Desire

Acknowledgements
Ms. Fiona Black for her Photography and body-painting. Cordelia Fellowes for her invaluble support. Bootz for transcripting, and editing. Musical Composition by the talented Roop Murphy. The gorgeous Frankie Bubbles for singing *Desire*.

I would especiallly like to thank my parents for their infinite patience, despite my constant shennanigans over the years.